The De-Conversion of Kit Lamb

The De-Conversion of Kit Lamb

Kate Kasten

ISLET PRESS ❖ IOWA CITY

BY THE SAME AUTHOR

Ten Small Beds
Better Days
Wildwood: Fairy Tales and Fables Re-Imagined

Islet Press, Iowa City
www.katekasten.com
Copyright © 2010 Kate Kasten
ISBN-13: 978-0-615-39085-7

To the Memory of My Parents

Elizabeth & Carl Kasten

❖ One ❖

July 28, 1982

The Rectory, Iglesia Sta. Maria
La Florita
Departamento de Huehuetenango
Guatemala

Dear Mom and Pop and the rest of the clan,

It's 5:00 a.m. and Doña Serafina's and Doña Marta's competitive roosters have commenced their merciless reveille. El Señor Viejo beats out El Señor Gallito for the honor of earliest to rise, while Gallito distinguishes himself by crowing the loudest. Although rivals, they sing in harmony — Gallito in no way apologetic for his outrageous falsetto, nor Viejo for his hopeless attempts at singing baritone. Their cries resound off the Cuchumatane slopes across the valley, making our village sound rather like an Arabian city at the hour of the call to prayer.

This is my time for sitting quietly, looking out at the mountains, and asking the deep questions: What is heresy? Who receives revelation? Why isn't Doña Ana's diarrhea remedy working? (Yes, the scourge is back.)

Well, now I have to tell you some things that can't be sent through the mail, so this letter will go in the ecclesiastical satchel of the visiting Canadian Sister who is leaving for the U.S. this afternoon.

You may have read in the New York Times recently that the White House is pushing Congress to authorize military aid to Guatemala, claiming human rights here have improved. In fact, human rights conditions have worsened. Since General Efraín Ríos Montt came to power, I have seen many wretched victims of his policies and heard countless survivors' stories. I will not sicken you with the specific acts of unspeakable brutality inflicted on these innocent people, but I will tell you that the army is responsible for at least ninety percent of the violence. The insurgency does not have entirely clean hands, of course, but it does not indulge in the insane savagery the army perpetrates on civilians. Any village approached by the guerrillas becomes a target for annihilation.

Don't let anyone tell you these are random acts by a few rogue army officers, as the regime likes to pretend. Slaughtering and branding as "communists" anyone who flees the invading army is an intrinsic part of its military strategy. The first century historian Tacitus wrote of the Roman army that it "creates a desolation and calls it peace." This is an apt description of Ríos Montt's systematic policy of terror, the end of which is total military control of the indigenous population.

The dictator's claim to being a born-again evangelical Christian is not insincere or even opportunistic. He truly believes himself to have been put in power by God, like the Sun King. I also think his born-again evangelical supporters mean well (my disputatious little sister may say the same of me!). And I won't call it bribery—the services and aid U.S. evangelicals rush here to provide (far be it from a Catholic mission priest to cast that first stone). But their starry-eyed support of the dictator's regime seems to me so naïve as to be unconscionable. His army tortures dissidents and massacres whole villages.

Tomorrow I've promised to take four people in the parish truck to the dentist in Huehuetenango. It's not the best of times to be on the open road, but their misery is such that they are willing to take the risk, and I believe that my presence as a foreigner will offer some protection. We'll leave as soon as Hector and his donkey get back from scrounging cans of gasoline and I can finish patching the leak in the oil pan. Of all my years of theological training, the semester I spent at Sterling Automotive School may have been the most profitable.

My passengers tomorrow will never have traveled farther than their family maize and bean plots, three miles up the mountainside (if you don't count their hellish trips in covered trucks to work at cotton plantations on the coast). Despite aching teeth and gums, they are all afire to see the big city. I would be more excited for them if I weren't contemplating the eight-hour round trip (barring breakdowns) with the rhetorical question: Does a padre shit in the woods?

On that cheerful note, I'll sign off. Give my dearest love to everyone at home, and pass on the following message to that Socratic sister of mine (I don't have her newest address): Colleen, I promise a marathon theological debate with you in September when I come home for my next visit.

Your loving son and brother,
Ftr. Tom

❖ Two ❖

March 26, 1983, military outpost, Escuintla Departamento, Guatemala

Neck spasms shook Kit's head with sharp, involuntary "no's." Every part of him was trembling.

The soldiers had left the light on when they went out. He registered for the first time the dark stains on the table and the floor and the walls. A wide, rust-red smear ran down the wall opposite him from head height to the cement floor.

A sentence came to his mind. Who had said it? Daniel Meijia, on the bus after they heard Ríos Montt preach. He had said it proudly: "The Guatemalan army only massacres demons."

What would they do when they came back? How could he ready himself? He couldn't allow them to find him still quivering like a trapped rabbit, his heartbeat pulsing in his throat.

The little dog was dozing on its cushion again. It had barked excitedly. Kit recalled the yapping now, after the fact. The small rib cage rose and fell. He watched it for some seconds and tried to get his own breathing in synch with the dog's. A fly that had been sitting in the dog's bowl flew up and lit in the smear on the wall.

Kit averted his eyes and tried to suppress his trembling. Do they think I'm a demon? In its sleep, the dog wagged its nub of a tail and made soothing, snuffling sounds.

❖ Three ❖

The thrill of takeoff, the steady backward slide of miniaturized fields and towns, white landscapes gradually turning green as the plane moved south, had occupied his attention until he arrived at the New Orleans airport, where he changed planes. There, he emerged from the press of luggage-laden travelers and sat for a few minutes at his gate.

Through the window, he read the words *"Aviateca"* on the side of the small incoming plane. As he sat and watched the converging baggage carts, the signaling of orange-vested men, the moving lips of the pilots inside the cockpit, he had a sudden terrifying sensation of there being no person, no self behind his own eyes registering these things, and he got up unsteadily from his chair and crossed to the window to peer at his dim reflection in the plate glass.

He half expected to see a desolate twelve-year-old reflected back to him, or a sullen, slouching sixteen-year-old. But the window mirrored a tall, grown-up young man with trim hair, trim clothes, nearly erect posture—a nicely dressed mannequin in a store window. He put his hand to his face but there was no more sense of contact between these parts of himself than a mannequin would have felt.

An unthinkable idea darted into his mind before he could censor it: that Ezra and Jeannette and the Light and Life Tabernacle were illusions just as empty as himself. If a mirror could be held up to what he had thought was the truth for the last five years, there would appear a crèche tableau outside a church at Christmas—a doll in a box and people wearing bedsheets—the truth he had been living by, and eating and sleeping and swearing by just a story, like a fairy tale read to a child.

He grew short of breath. His legs felt weak, and he had to sit down. The door leading down to the tarmac had opened and people were coming out, others lining up to board. They stood only a few yards from him, but they might have been standing on the other side of a street. His heart banged against his ribs as if it had come untethered. He passed his hand over his cheeks and chin, dragging his palm against the hint of stubble that had grown since morning.

Then a man in the line spoke impatiently in Spanish to his child and gave her arm a mean little yank. Kit felt an automatic flare of anger. He half rose from his chair, but the man and child passed through the doorway and out of sight. Certainty and relief filled the dark void of doubt. He realized that it had only been the devil trying to suck out his faith, that was all. Only Satan, not ... whatever it was (now it was slipping away). Just old Satan, who could lure you so easily toward the pit. Of course, good old Satan.

Restored by the familiar horror of damnation, Kit picked up his day-pack and rose to follow the people out the door. When he walked off this plane called *Aviateca*, he would be in a foreign country for the first time in his life.

The small plane was crowded with well-to-do Guatemalans returning from the States. Saks and Gucci shopping bags and gift-wrapped packages poked into the aisles. Across from Kit the gestures of two quarreling women sent tiers of gold bracelets sliding up and down their arms. He shut his eyes and tried without success to catch a word of their staccato Spanish. It comforted him to remember that Ezra, too, had never been able to learn a foreign language, but that once the Lord immersed Ezra among the people he had been called to serve—in Kenya and again in Thailand—*His ears were opened and the string of his tongue was loosed.*

The Caribbean waves below flashed a Morse code of sunlight. Kit gazed down at the bright sea and prayed to justify his pastor's confidence in him. His lips were moving, and he pressed them shut, stealing a look at the young woman in the seat next to him. *Be not ashamed to proclaim your faith.*

His seatmate, the one passenger besides himself not engaged in lively conversation, was reading a Spanish language newspaper. She was about his own age he guessed, twentyish. Her straight, light-brown hair was pulled back and fastened by a barrette at the nape of her neck. She wore a short-sleeved peasant blouse and cotton skirt. He wondered if she was some kind of hippie. You couldn't tell, though. Even a few evangelicals dressed that way these days.

They had exchanged hellos when she sat down and, like him, spent some moments figuring out what to do with her long legs in the cramped space. He uncrossed his own legs to give her more room, and she smiled and thanked him. They introduced themselves. Her name was Colleen. Not a Guatemalan, then, despite the newspaper. Her blue eyes were almond-shaped, the lids drooping a little at the corners. He made a discreet survey. No cross hanging on a chain at her throat. No ring on her left hand.

Your body is the temple of the Holy Ghost ... you are not your own.

Below and to the east, the plane's shadow crawled along a stretch of land. The white breakers were just distinguishable from the pale strip of coastline that edged the brilliant green. He pulled out a map from the day pack at his feet and found the Caribbean. The coastline must be Cuba. It was much closer to the U.S. than he had realized. Ezra's sermons on Cuba came to mind—those clusters of people huddled together on small, overloaded boats, exhaustion and fear on their faces, the longing for God in their eyes. Kit reminded himself how blessed he was. Where he was headed, the president himself, with open arms, had invited evangelicals to bring the Savior's light to his country. Efraín Ríos Montt. By God's grace, the first born-again leader of a nation.

Kit leaned his forehead against the window pane and watched Cuba slip from sight. Now there was nothing but whitecaps flashing and dissolving hypnotically on the dark blue water. He could hardly grasp how he had gotten here. One day he had picked up a rock and thrown it through a church window. Five years later he was looking down at a foreign sea from the window of a plane. How could that miserable sixteen-year-old have ended up on such a voyage?

He wondered where he would be now if he had let the rock drop to the ground, if he hadn't been angry enough to throw it, because Dean had never entered his life and his father had never left? Tracing it back and back, you could see the straight path from there to here.

Colleen touched his elbow lightly. "Excuse me," she said. He turned, blushing in spite of himself. It was just an old reflex, Jeannette always reminded him. God had taken away his shyness.

"Do you have the right time?" Colleen held out a slender wrist encircled by a loose, chunky, man's watch.

"I have 4:33," he said. "I've forgotten when we get in."

She set her watch and wound it. Her smile was reserved but friendly. He felt the pull of her sleepy blue eyes.

Would she be open to the discussion? He tried to think of a way to begin. Her newspaper lay folded in her lap. She had taken up a book, but he couldn't see the title without being intrusive.

"This is the first time I've ever flown," he said, after a pause.

She leaned toward him. "Really? How do you like it so far?"

"It's fantastic! I feel so blessed."

At this she sat back in her seat. Her eyes narrowed. He prepared himself to make his little speech: My pastor and his wife are sponsoring me to study Spanish so I can do the Lord's work in Guatemala, and— Her eyes had fastened on the small silver cross at the open neck of his shirt, and, as if at the sight of a deformity, darted away. Out of the corner of his eye he watched her pretend to read her book He knew what she was thinking. Jesus freak. Bible thumper.

He decided to try again anyway and cleared his throat. "Is Guatemala your final destination?" he said.

"Mm hm," she answered, without looking at him.

"I heard it's called the Land of Eternal Spring," he persisted. "Have you been there before?"

"Yes."

"What are you going to do in Guatemala?"

She paused. "Just … brush up on my Spanish."

"I'm going there to study Spanish, too," he said. "Where will you be studying?"

"In Antigua." She flipped a page of her book.

"Really? Me too. At the Spanish school?"

She looked at him sidelong under half-lowered eyelids. "There are dozens of Spanish schools in Antigua. Everybody teaches Spanish there." She shifted a little toward the aisle, making a wall of her shoulder.

Don't take rejection personally. "My school is called—..." He took the brochure from his day pack. "*Instituto de Español Tres Américas.*" He stumbled over the words. "My Spanish is nonexistent," he apologized. "I flunked it twice in high school. My pastor and his wife are paying for the school. I hope I don't wash out."

"I'm not studying at *Tres Américas.*" She turned another page of the book and resumed her reading.

His face heated up and he won a brief battle inside himself not to call her, even in his mind, a sinful name. It was just as well this kind of release was forbidden because if he said what he wanted to, he would expose the hypocrisy of his anger—*turn the other cheek*—and his voice would reveal how vulnerable he was to her judgment. It seemed that no matter how much he prayed, he could never correct this weakness. It had been the source of Dean's power over him.

The day after the wedding, when he was twelve and they moved into Dean's fake Tudor mansion with its leaded windows and cross-timbered front, Claudia had put some of his drawings on the refrigerator door—something to say that Kit lived there, too.

They were good drawings. He had figured out perspective all on his own and drawn detailed pictures of castles with arrows flying off the turrets, battlefields of armored soldiers in the distance. Dean said, "Just what I like to see first thing in the morning—gore and mayhem on my refrigerator door." He pulled the pictures off, pressed the foot pedal on the trash can, and looked back at Kit's flaming face. "Oops!" he said, with that smile. "Are these precious to our little Sir Lancelot?"

He had secretly studied Dean to figure out exactly what about him was so detestable. His features were regular, hairline receding a little, average height and weight. You wouldn't remember him later if you passed him on the street. He didn't drink or chase women. He wasn't physically violent. It was all in the smile, the way he cocked his head back and looked down at you with his mouth half-open as if he was barely suppressing his astonishment and amusement at your stupidity.

That night Kit was in his room singing a song he had been practicing in sixth grade chorus—"I Am a Poor Wayfaring Stranger." Every time he sang it, he saw the Wayfaring Stranger walking along an empty road that stretched on and on through a treeless, peopleless landscape. The road narrowed and narrowed until it disappeared.

"I'm just a-goin' over Jordan, I'm just a-goin' over home ..."

He thought he couldn't be heard with the bedroom door shut—Claudia and Dean downstairs at the other end of the house in the kitchen—and he let the fullness of feeling into his voice, but it must have come through the heating duct because when he came downstairs, his mother said, "Was that you, Kit? It could have been a singer on a tape. You sing like an angel!"

Leaning against the refrigerator, his head cocked in that way he had and the half smile on his face, Dean winked at Claudia, "A *castrato*, you mean. In the Middle Ages they took little boys with voices like Kit's here, and removed their private parts to keep them singing soprano." Kit's face turned so red he thought it must be hot to the touch.

"Now, don't tease him," Claudia chided.

Turning toward his seatmate as well as he could in the cramped seat, pulling his shoulders back to put more space between them, he asked, "Why are you going all the way to Guatemala to brush up on your Spanish?"

She shrugged, her eyes fixed on the page of her book.

"Okay," he said, "I'll stop bothering you, but I have one question." Did the cross on my neck disturb you for some reason? His mouth went dry and he started to sweat. *Don't hide the Light under a bushel basket.* Instead, he asked, "How do we change our money when we get to Guatemala City? I only have dollars."

She stared. "You didn't change some money before you left home?"

"I forgot to. Was that a mistake?"

"Well," she said, "it's Friday afternoon. We're getting in after the banks close for the weekend, and your only option will be to change your money at the airport." Each phrase ended with a little dip in pitch as if she were explaining something to a child.

"So I can change it at the airport?"

"If you want to lose a third of your exchange."

"Oh boy." He had sat with Jeannette at the Tinkers' dining room table and painstakingly put together a budget. His small allowance had to stretch. He was an idiot.

She said, "You'll need money just to get from the airport to the city."

He caught himself biting his upper lip and released it. Childish, stupid-looking habit. "I'm on a pretty tight budget," he said.

She sighed. "Where were you planning to stay tonight?"

"I was going to catch a bus to Antigua. The brochure said the buses go every hour." She shook her head as if to say, Can this guy tie his own shoes?

"The last bus to Antigua leaves at six. You'll never get through customs in time to get to the bus exchange. You're going to have to wait until tomorrow morning."

What would a night in a hotel cost, with food and bus fare? And then a whole weekend to get through before classes started. He shut his eyes. I'm in your hands, Lord.

When he opened his eyes, she was studying him. She sighed again. "Okay," she said, as if giving in to a demand. "I'll lend you some money for the bus into the city. You might be able to stay at the Peace Corps hostel for two or three *quetzales*. That's where I'm staying. You can pay me back in the morning after we find a money changer who gives a decent rate."

"Thanks a lot, that's really generous of you," he said. Thank you Jesus!

"You don't want to change your money on the street. For one thing, you don't want to do it with someone who hasn't paid the police to look the other way."

"It's illegal?" Of course it was illegal. Stupid question.

"In practice it's only illegal for poor people," she said coldly, as though this were his fault. "There's a place where the Peace Corps volunteers change their money when the banks aren't open."

"I'm sorry to put you to so much trouble. Are you a Peace Corps volunteer?"

"No," she said and resumed her reading.

He turned from her to look out the window and found nothing there. They were flying inside a cloud. It made him claustrophobic, and he turned away to lean his head against the head rest. In the crack between the seat backs he could see the crown of an infant's head, a whorl of wispy black hair. He would have liked to touch it, his fingers remembering the two stand-up cowlicks on his sisters' heads when they were babies.

It was funny how disgusted he had felt when he learned Claudia was pregnant, considering how he came to feel later.

They were delivered by cesarean section on December 20, 1976, perfectly formed identical twin girls with dark hair like their father's and faces that could have come off baby food jar labels. Edith and Loretta, named after Dean's two grandmothers. Kit viewed them at the hospital nursery, just small, red-faced, animated trophies of Dean's. But later, when Claudia took the twins from Dean before he had time to object, and placed them in the crooks of Kit's arms, the daintiness of their featherweight bodies touched him. He looked down into their faces, back and forth from one to the other, into the wondering blue wells of their eyes, which seemed to search his. The two sets of tiny fingers were opening and closing in little fists.

Claudia pulled off their stocking caps. The reddened foreheads screwed up into indignant frowns and as quickly unscrewed, the downy eyebrows rising in apparent astonishment. One moment the petal-pink lips pursed disapprovingly, the next they spread into toothless old woman grins. In their selfless gaze—before their bobbling heads brought some other universe into their sightlines—he was their world.

As he held them, he scarcely registered Dean hovering close at his elbow and uttering a stream of sarcastic asides to Claudia—"Watch Two Left Feet here drop them on their heads." He felt a sudden unexpected pang of tenderness, almost like pity, and he had to restrain an impulse to press his lips to the babies' smooth, fat cheeks.

❖ Four ❖

At *La Aurora* airport Kit hurried to keep up with Colleen as she strode, backpack, tote bag and camera case bumping her hips, toward customs. An immigration official separated them, steering Kit to another line. He was asked questions first in Spanish, then, when he looked blank, in thickly accented English. His bags were searched meticulously. A number of soldiers holding automatic rifles stood by watching. Kit stumbled over someone's suitcase as he craned to keep Colleen in sight. What if she changed her mind about helping him? The officer finally stamped his papers with three brisk motions and waved him through.

Colleen was waiting for him at the other end. As she stood looking around—not at him—she unclasped her barrette, shook out and smoothed her long hair, and fastened it again. She was tall, slim, a little boyish. Attractive.

She dug her fingers under the waistband of her skirt and pulled out a homemade money belt. "Here." She put some paper money into his hand—green one-*quetzal* and lavender five-*quetzal* notes bearing the faces of nineteenth-century generals against a background of Mayan pyramids. It looked like board game money. "This should be enough for tonight." From her pocket she drew several coins of different sizes. "This is for bus fare into the city." She replaced the money belt inside her skirt and led the way out the exit. "Let's try to catch that bus."

A bright blue, old-fashioned school bus waited at the curb about a half block away. It was decorated as if tattooed with colorful slogans in quotation marks and pictures of flowers and birds and haloed saints. Colleen took off at a trot toward the bus, and Kit hurried after her. The evening air of Guatemala City was thick with diesel emissions and a sweet, indefinable scent. It was 6:00 on December 31; the sky was dark, yet the temperature was like summertime, just cooling at the end of a day of dry heat. When he had left home, Des Moines was thawing from an ice storm. Here, flowering bushes bloomed in the packed dry dirt at the curbs. Palm trees grew along the street edging the parking lot. Palm trees! He felt as if he were standing outside himself looking on. Kit Lamb, walking on a street in a foreign country.

Ahead, a crowd of people gathered around the bus, some in clothes like those worn at home, but others—a cluster of small, brown-skinned women—in heavy woven blouses with bright patterns of red and yellow, blue and purple. Colorful headdresses embellished their black hair. On their heads they balanced huge round baskets three or four feet across laden with earthen pots, or fresh produce, or live chickens packed together under nets to keep them from escaping. There were brown-skinned men, too, in battered straw hats and worn cotton trousers. They carried bags of grain on their backs. A man on top of the bus was reaching down to hoist their burdens to the roof.

Indians! Kit's hand went automatically to the small sketchpad and drawing pencil protruding from the pocket of his day pack, but there would be no time to capture the shifting, colorful scene on paper, so instead he took out the instamatic camera Jeannette had lent him for the trip. He raised it and snapped the shot. The flash failed, and he guessed the single street light would not be bright enough. As he was putting the camera away, Colleen frowned at him.

After the bus was loaded, the porter climbed down and a fare taker boarded the new passengers, packing them in, three to a double seat. Kit and Colleen stood squeezed together in the aisle, with their bags and backpacks taking up the space of two. The porter slapped the side of the bus and it pulled away from the curb. Swaying as one dense breathing animal, the passengers had no need to hold onto the poles or hand grips; pressed so close together they couldn't have fallen. A wisp of Colleen's hair had come loose from its barrette. Kit quelled the urge to tuck it back in.

He fingered the coins in his hand. "We didn't pay!" he said in her ear.

"He'll collect it."

Somehow the fare taker managed to snake his way down the aisle to take the fares. Squeezing past Kit and Colleen, he handed them their change from a sweat-stained leather pouch at his waist. After working his way back to the front, he stood on the running board and locked one arm around the door handle as the bus took a corner and swung him out over the pavement.

The brown Indian faces with their high cheek bones—Mayan faces, he knew from the literature Jeannette had given him—looked unperturbed. To the Indians, jammed together like the chickens in the baskets overhead, it all must be routine, Kit thought.

Colleen was gazing impassively ahead. Kit said, "It's great, isn't it?"

"What is?" she said.

"Everything. The palm trees, this bus, the Indians—"

In a low voice she said, "It's disrespectful to call them Indians. That's what the *ladinos* call them, *Indios*."

"Who are *ladinos*?"

"Mixed-blood Guatemalans. They don't speak the Mayan languages. They look down on indigenous people."

Her disparaging tone seemed directed at him personally, and he flushed with anger. How was he supposed to know?

"Also," she said, still looking ahead, "Don't take their pictures. You're not at Disneyland."

"Oh," Kit said. "I wasn't thinking."

The people lurched and swayed in silence. He and Colleen rode in silence, too, as the bus passed through dark, dusty neighborhoods of small, one-story stucco houses and shops. He was getting tired of her attitude. Why did she disdain him? Because he was a Christian? Fine. Let her.

Eventually the bus emerged into a brightly lit commercial district where well-dressed women in high heels, men in suits and ties, arm-in-arm girls wearing the white blouses and pleated skirts of school uniforms strolled the streets. The *ladinos* Colleen had mentioned? One by one, the Indians—the indigenous people—got off the bus. Here and there along the sidewalks such people sat on pieces of cardboard or on blankets, their wares spread out in front and their sleeping children curled up beside them.

Inside a glass-fronted department store, people were riding escalators, peering at display cases. At the door of a jewelry shop, a soldier in camouflage leaned on an automatic rifle. A man in a sports coat and a woman in a low-cut dress emerged from the store and passed the soldier without appearing to notice him.

Kit and Colleen pushed their way down the aisle and out of the bus onto the busy street. "It's about a ten-block walk," Colleen said.

They helped each other readjust their packs and other baggage. Kit opened his mouth to ask if he could carry something for her but shut it again; she was tall and strong and would probably resent the offer.

"Thanks for helping me out," he said, but Colleen was already walking ahead of him. Why had he thought she was attractive?

There was no room for him at the hostel. All the Peace Corps volunteers were stopping over after holiday trips to the States. Backpacks and sleeping bags jammed the halls. Colleen had reserved her space in advance. He would have to find a cheap hotel.

"Oh," Kit said. "Thanks anyway."

He turned toward the open street door framing a rectangle of darkness. Two of the young volunteers stepped around him and walked out. The slap of their sandals against the cobbled pavement diminished quickly and died away. *If you have faith as a grain of mustard seed, nothing shall be impossible unto you.*

"There are several hotels within walking distance," Colleen said, "if they have vacancies." The slight rise in her voice on the word "vacancies" instead of "if" sounded almost friendly, and in spite of himself he felt not only relief but a little rush of pleasure.

"Could I ... call to find out?" he said, ducking his head to hide the flush coming again to his face.

"Only the luxury hotels have phones."

"Okay. I'll just go in person." He hesitated. "Would you mind drawing me a map?" She took out her plane ticket envelope and started to draw with a pencil stub.

"I'm sorry for holding you up," he said. "You probably want to relax and hang out with your friends."

She put the pencil down. "I don't really know these people," she murmured. She tightened her lips, then shrugged and pushed her bags behind a door. "You'll need a translator," she said, and motioned him into the street.

They walked at a good clip for five or six blocks, Colleen a little ahead, her camera case still over her shoulder and bumping her hip. The gray stucco of the first hotel's two-story façade was broken off in large sections. A worn stone step led to a wooden door whose blue paint had all but peeled off. In an inner courtyard lacy trees reached airily above the second-story interior balconies. Christmas lights draped the railings. Colleen spoke in rapid Spanish to an elderly woman who poked her head out of a living room taken up almost completely with a crèche scene. The hotel had no vacancies. Outside, they turned down a narrow street where dogs rushed at them before darting ahead and disappearing down an alley.

She took him into progressively darker streets and dingier lobbies until at last they found a hotel with one room left. The man who took their money had a sightless, cloudy eye shot with blood. Kit pulled out the money Colleen had lent him and stood holding it foolishly in his palms as she counted out two *quetzales* and change.

They climbed a narrow open staircase with a loose banister rail. Kit held his bags close to avoid knocking against it. On the landing they turned immediately left into the room. The door stood open. A single bed, covered with a threadbare sheet and thin cotton blanket, and a bed table with no lamp, made up the entire furnishings. The only source of light in the room was a bare bulb with a pull string broken off so high that even Kit — as tall as he was — could only grasp it with the tips of his fingers.

"The toilet is probably at the end of the hall," Colleen said. "When you use toilet paper, don't flush it. Throw it in the wastebasket." She told him she would come by for him at 7:30 in the morning. They would get something to eat and change his money and he could catch the 9:00 bus to Antigua. She moved to the door. Turning, she added, "Don't drink water from the tap or brush your teeth with it. And if you go out, take your valuables with you." She paused. "Do you have any water?" Seeing his embarrassed look, she reached in the pocket of her pack and took out a plastic bottle. "Here," she said. "I have two."

17

He followed her onto the landing, and she descended the rickety stair-case without looking back. An apparently drunk man, passing her on the stairs, stumbled against the railing and Kit thought it would give way, but it held, and the man shouted something violent in Spanish. Colleen continued down the stairs and out into the street.

Kit shut the door quickly. He tried to lock it, but the door had settled so that the bolt no longer lined up with the catch. The floorboards felt sticky under the soles of his shoes, so he set his bags on the bed and sat down next to them. A woman and man were shouting at each other in Spanish somewhere down the hall. A door slammed and the room shook. Kit shut his eyes and took several deep breaths before bowing his head.

"Heavenly Father," he prayed, "I praise Your wisdom in bringing me here to do Your will. Help me to keep up my confidence and spirit—" He heard running steps. The door burst open, smashing into the wall. The drunk man frowned at him, backed into the corridor and slammed the door behind him.

Kit leapt up and grasped the knob in both hands, straining to raise the door and push the bolt into place, but it wouldn't budge. He returned to the bed, trembling, and sat several minutes facing the door, unable to think of what else to do. Only then did he remember his Bible. It was a leatherette King James Version that Ezra and Jeannette had given him on the day that he got saved. Now he took it out from the tote bag and laid it on his lap. He was dismayed to realize he had left it in the bag all the way from home even though there had been plenty of time to read. Those strange moments of panic at the New Orleans airport came back to him. Always, he said aloud, go back to the Book. He passed his fingers over the raised gold lettering.

More than four hours he had spent with Colleen and let her intimi-date him into saying nothing about his faith. Had he even mentioned the word God to her? He had—if he was honest with himself—avoided mentioning God.

It was sinful to shrink from ridicule. He thought he had overcome it once and for all after those weeks preaching on street corners—the long-haired college kids in their bell bottom pants and tunics harassing him like flies at a picnic. "Where's your proof, man?" After the first few times, he stopped blushing. Then the Lord put the perfect words in his mouth. "You know that children's song we all grew up with—'Jesus loves me, this I know, for the Bible tells me so'? That's all I need, I don't need proof."

Kit opened the cover of his Bible and read the words inside: "To Kit, beloved child of God." On the flyleaf there was the familiar color illustration of Simon Peter casting his net into the sea, a golden sun rising behind a horizon of purple mist.

He sat on the bed in the hotel room and held the book up in both hands to fan the pages slowly with his thumb. The light breeze they made puffed delicately against his face as though from a divine breath. Some fifty pages of the Bible were discolored and wavy from his days of preaching in the rain. He ran his fingertips over the undulations, not yet seeking a particular verse to which God in his wisdom would lead him, but just allowing the touch of the Book to soothe him. Then he let his eyes fall on a verse: *Unto Thee, O Lord, do I lift up my soul. Oh my God I trust in Thee; let me not be ashamed ...*

The Twenty-fifth Psalm. *Remember not the sins of my youth, nor my transgressions; according to Thy mercy remember Thou me for thy goodness sake, O Lord ... O keep my soul, and deliver me; let me not be ashamed; for I put my trust in Thee...* He had been ashamed of his faith in front of Colleen. He would not hide it again.

After reading the Twenty-fifth Psalm, he decided to read *Psalms* aloud from beginning to end. Ezra had taught him how to feel its poetry. *Blessed is the man that walketh not in the counsel of the ungodly, nor standeth in the way of sinners, nor sitteth in the seat of the scornful ...* There was a beautiful rhythm to it and when he finished reading he felt elevated. He closed the Bible, set it gently on the bag, and knelt on the sticky floor. "Dear Lord," he prayed, "though I am undeserving, by your grace you have come into my heart tonight and taken away my cowardice and self-centeredness. Today you put Colleen in my path. Tomorrow morning I'll witness to my faith and do my best to open her heart to your message. Amen."

He stood up, refreshed and hungry. He ate a crushed candy bar he had been carrying in his pocket and took a drink from the bottle of water, remembering Colleen's fingers touching his when she handed it to him.

After a while he opened the door and peered out. The landing was empty. He slung his day pack containing his passport and money over his shoulder and stole down to the bathroom. It was the size of a closet, with a small sink, gray with soap scum, and a wastebasket full of soiled toilet paper. The toilet seat was smeared with dried feces. He had wanted to have a bowel movement, but he would have to put it off until morning when he could do it somewhere else. When he finished urinating, he opened the single water tap with his fingertips and ran the cold rusty water over his hands, splashing some of it onto the tap before touching it again to shut it off. He dried his hands on the sides of his khakis and went back to the room, relieved to find that the door was still closed and the big backpack wasn't missing.

Having piled his bags precariously on the small bed table, he lay down, fully clothed, on top of the cotton blanket. Voices and slamming doors kept him awake for some time. Then, just as he was dozing off around midnight, he was wakened by a series of loud pops.

He sat up quickly and listened. Some of the shots were faint, others closer, possibly just out on the street. He strained to hear people running or shouting. Finally, he got up and put his ear to the door before opening it a crack. Nothing. The hall was dark. He didn't venture out, but went back and sat on the bed, his heart pounding.

Were there guerrilla soldiers in the streets? He imagined the door bursting open again, the cold metal of a rifle pressed against his temple, the shot that would send him out of this world. Or some horrendous torture—the binding of his arms and legs, his live body being hauled away. Into his mind came one of the images he had seen last summer. Mangled corpses piled on the ground like animal carcasses, some of them castrated.

"This is not a nice picture to show at lunch," *Señor* Oscar Reina had said. The clink of spoons on dessert plates abruptly ceased. "But you must know what happens to Christians who defy the communist guerrillas in order to practice their faith. Anyone who doesn't join them is their enemy." He removed his glasses, and passed his hand across his liquid brown eyes as if to hold back tears.

Ezra had arranged for *Señor* Reina to bring his presentation—"The Struggle for Guatemala's Soul"—to the Christian Businessmen's Alliance meeting.

Reina explained the dilemma of the ignorant and poverty-stricken Indians, how they were promised a utopian society and threatened with retaliation if they didn't cooperate. "We Christians in Guatemala fight a double enemy—" *Señor* Reina said in his lyrical Spanish accent, "—the poverty of the people and the apostasy of the subversives. But God has given us a president who is a born-again Christian evangelical. Tirelessly, he wages a battle against communist atheism and corruption in government. But he cannot do it alone. Outsiders do not know how our country bleeds."

Señor Reina's presentation showed a picturesque land and people—"Ripe for the picking. Who will harvest this crop? We, followers of the Lord? Or communist rebels?"

All of them in the room, once the talk was over, stayed to write letters to their senators and congressman and to President Reagan. Reina directed them to plead urgently for the lifting of a congressional embargo on military aid to Guatemala, to untie the Guatemalan army's hands in its fight against the subversives. Kit took up a collection for stamps and gathered the letters in a manila envelope.

Sizable donations resulted from that meeting, giving Ezra his idea about the fire truck. For a pittance, the church could purchase from the city an outdated but serviceable fire truck. Would such a vehicle be useful in some poverty stricken area of Guatemala? Certainly! *Señor* Reina was enthusiastic. Indians' cornstalk huts were always vulnerable. Whole villages sometimes burned to the ground. He would personally arrange the details.

Within two Sundays the small congregation of Light and Life Tabernacle had come up with the money to buy and dispatch Pumper No. 5. Two months after the slide presentation, a letter arrived from the people of the village Santiago de Atitlán, expressing their pride in their new fire truck and thanking the merciful Lord Jesus and the good, generous Christians of Light and Life Tabernacle.

The Bible lay atop Kit's pack. It would give him away to the guerrillas.

He reached to put it out of sight, but stopped himself, thinking of the Christian martyrs. *And I saw the souls of them that were beheaded and they lived and reigned with Christ one thousand years.*

He lay on the bed in the dark, listening, feeling cowardly. An hour went by and the gunfire became more sporadic; within another hour it died out altogether. Whatever battle had been fought, it was over. He wondered if Colleen was all right. Would she be able to get back to his hotel in the morning? Would there be corpses in the street?

He woke in a cold sweat. In his dream he was trying to get his little sisters into a boat floating away from the shore of a placid lake. Their feet were stuck in mud. From the boat he reached out to pull them by the arms, but he was afraid of pulling their arms off. Just before he woke, he was trying to decide if they would be better off dead or missing an arm, and he remembered that if they died now, they would die unsaved.

He turned onto his back and lay staring into the darkness. The little girls would be curled in mirror poses on their bunk beds right now, Lorie on her right side in the upper bunk, Edie on her left in the lower—like two little islands, awash in the sea of toys that Dean had inundated them with.

He thought about why he had loved the girls right away, from their first days of life, even though they were Dean's, and even though the care Dean lavished on them showed that his merciless belittling of his stepson could not be chalked up to a complete inability to feel affection.

There was only one way to account for his own love for the twins: the Lord had put it in his heart. Once again it could all be traced back. If he hadn't loved Edie and Lorie, Ezra could never have blackmailed him into coming to church. The Lord's hand was in it as plainly as if He had left big whopping fingerprints.

Kit rose from the bed and pulled the light cord. It was 6:30 a.m. by his watch. He read his Bible for half an hour before the cowardly feeling began to needle him again. He put the Bible away, hefted his backpack onto his shoulders, picked up his daypack and ventured down the rickety stairs. At the outer doorway he hesitated. What signs of the violence in the night would he find?

22

An indigenous woman with an infant on her back pulled a rattling handcart past the door. The front grill of a small shop had been rolled up and the proprietor was sitting by a counter stacked with soft drink bottles and cigarette cartons. He swatted away a passing dog, who stopped to sniff at his shoes. The day was cloudless and the sun was just brightening the sky. It was all as if nothing had happened. No furtive, frightened looks, no bullet-riddled corpses. Kit's anxiety began to dissolve.

He waved to the soft drink vendor and called, "*Hola,*" one of the few Spanish words he remembered from high school. To his surprise and pleasure, the man smiled and returned his greeting. "*Hola, señor.*"

He was tired and hungry and uncertain whether Colleen would keep her promise to come for him, yet his mood lifted. He was chosen to do some good in the world. It wasn't only Ezra telling him so. He felt it himself.

Colleen came at 7:30 exactly. She, too, must have slept in her clothes. She had braided her hair without combing it, and fastened it loosely with rubber bands. He felt suddenly tender toward her, remembering the crackle of electricity and his sisters' two patient, trusting little heads holding still under his fingers as he brushed their hair.

"I thought we'd better get an early start," she said. She squinted toward the sun shooting its rays between buildings.

No greeting. No, 'How was your night?' Nothing about the gunfire.

He wished she would smile, at least. He hadn't been treated so coldly by a girl since high school.

"Do you know what was going on last night?" he asked.

"What do you mean?"

"The gunfire. Did you hear it?"

"No!" she exclaimed, frowning. Then, "Oh … you mean the firecrackers?"

"Firecrackers?"

"Last night was New Year's Eve."

He lowered his head to adjust a strap on his backpack, hoping she wouldn't see the blush rushing to his face. "Oh yeah!" he said. "Happy 1983." But she was striding off.

"Where is all your stuff?" he called, hurrying to keep up with her.

"At the hostel. I'm staying in the city till Monday. I have something to do."

"Oh." He had imagined them on the bus to Antigua together. During the ride he would stand up against her hostility and talk to her openly about his faith. Maybe she would respect him for that and warm to him again once she understood.

"The money changer is up here." She was holding a hand-drawn map. "We may be able to get breakfast there."

The walls of the bar were lined with posters of Germany—castles, alpine villages, cathedral towns. Antique beer steins were displayed behind the counter in front of a long mirror. Hanging from the ceiling, an oversized bird cage held a glass-eyed stuffed monkey, whose long tail hung stiffly through the bars.

"I really don't like the idea of trading with this guy," Colleen said in an undertone. "They said he's an old Nazi."

To the fleshy man with sparse white hair and puffy eyelids who came to their table to serve them, Colleen held up a dollar bill. He beckoned them to a back office, where Kit handed him fifty dollars in travelers checks and received forty-five *quetzales* and change. Colleen watched carefully as the money was counted out.

Kit asked to use the restroom and found with relief that it was clean. When he returned to their table, Colleen took back the amount she had lent him and they both ordered bratwurst sandwiches and bottled water. As Colleen began to eat, Kit closed his eyes and said a brief grace. For some minutes they ate in silence.

"I heard that Guatemala is being overrun by communists," Kit said finally, to make conversation.

Colleen stared. Quietly, she said, "I don't know where you got that idea, but don't talk about politics here."

He lowered his voice, too. "Because of the Nazi?"

She gave a short laugh. "I mean anywhere in this country. Don't talk about politics, not even with someone you trust."

The door opened behind Kit with a tinkling of bells. Colleen's gaze immediately dropped to her plate. He turned to look. "Don't," she said.

Two Guatemalan army soldiers came in, casually toting rifles. They passed the table where Colleen and Kit sat, and out of the corner of his eye, Kit saw the German come from behind the bar and shake hands with them. The three disappeared into the back, but reappeared only seconds later, one of the men tucking an envelope into his breast pocket.

"Christ," Colleen said under her breath. Kit winced. Now, he thought, I'll talk about it. But she stood up abruptly and grabbed her camera bag. "Let's get out of here," she muttered. "I can't eat in this place."

She took him to a street where a line of colorfully painted, exhaust-belching buses was taking on and letting off a stream of early morning workers—indigenous and *ladino*.

"This is where the Antigua bus will come," she told him. "It should be here in a half hour or so."

Kit thanked her again, hoping she would wait to see him off, but she said goodbye and walked away. Once again he had missed his chance.

❖ Five ❖

The bus to Antigua wasn't quite as crowded as the city bus had been, and he was able to sit down, but he rose again and offered his seat to an indigenous woman who got on with a baby swaddled in a shawl tied behind her. The woman accepted with a brilliant gap-toothed smile, and sat down heavily. Kit stood beside her, gripping the pole as the bus lunged forward and began its journey out of the city. He tried to read the billboards and signs that multiplied along the dusty road, but even an advertisement for Coca Cola—*¡Beba Coca Cola!*—baffled him.

After a minute there was a tug on his sleeve. The indigenous woman and another sitting next to her in the window seat were holding out their hands to him.

Begging? he thought. Well, why not? They were very poor.

He wasn't sure what to do. Then the woman on the aisle seat tapped his backpack, and both women made beckoning gestures. The woman unwrapped the baby and shifted it to the other one's shoulder.

"Aquí, aquí," she said, pointing to her lap, and Kit realized she had been holding out her hands to take the heavy backpack from him since he was standing. Quickly, he waved away the offer. "No, *gracias, gracias,"* he said.

How to say, You're so kind, but it's not necessary? He couldn't even think of the right word for *you*. Formal or informal? *Usted* or *tú*?

The two women were nodding vigorously. A man standing behind him suddenly lifted the pack off his shoulders and handed it to the seated woman, who received it with a smile and a nod. The woman by the window, now with the baby supported against her shoulder, reached across and lifted his daypack off his arm, too, and set it on her free knee. The baby gazed up at Kit with brown eyes as round as pennies.

"*Gracias,*" Kit said, helplessly. *Gracias?* Was he a fool? Would they sneak their hands into the bags as soon as his eye wandered? Steal his money and passport and extra travelers checks? His Bible? Or somehow squeeze past him at the next stop and get off with both bags in hand? Or would they ask for money at the end of the trip?

It was wrong to be so suspicious. *Whoso putteth his trust in the Lord shall be safe.* And he saw that the woman with the baby had leaned her head against the window and closed her eyes, while the woman in the aisle seat reached a finger across his day pack for the baby to grasp in its little fist. It struck him then that theirs had been a simple act of charity, and that it must be a customary kindness, a matter of course.

He caught the eye of the baby, who rocked on its feet at him and uttered joyous, incomprehensible syllables. The mother smiled up at Kit.

"Hi, baby!" Kit said. "*¡Hola!*"

The woman said to the baby, "*Saluda al señor,*" and the baby gave an earsplitting screech that woke the other woman and made her laugh. For a while Kit and the baby amused each other until the motion of the bus put the child to sleep.

At intervals Kit bent his head again to look out the windows. They were traveling now through a valley at the foot of a low, cone-shaped mountain covered with rows upon rows of narrow, ribbon-like terraces. Why plant crops on the sheer sides of a mountain? How could anything grow? Here and there in the distance, he made out the small figures of people tending the narrow plots and looking as if they must have to dig their toes in to the earth to keep from tumbling to their deaths.

In an hour, they arrived in Antigua. Noticing him standing alone in the bus lot looking uncertain, the two women who had held his bags pointed in the direction taken by most of the disembarking passengers. He followed the crowd and found himself headed into a bustling market. Scores of vendors sat in the open or under rows of canopies and alongside piles of beans and chiles and flowers in baskets, crude leather sandals, wooden masks and white cotton dresses.

Crowds moved through the aisles: clusters of teenage boys and girls; short, sturdy women followed by stair-step lines of children helping to carry baskets and bags; weathered men in straw hats; a few European-looking tourists in Birkenstocks and sundresses or shorts.

Kit barely felt the weight of his bags as the moving crowd nudged him slowly along. His six-foot height made him conspicuous—children stopped to look up at him—but it enabled him to see over heads and shoulders down into the stalls. The exotic, colorful trinkets lured him to spend recklessly. He was tempted to buy the bright fringed sashes for Claudia and Jeannette, strands of coffee bean necklaces for the twins, maybe one of the straw hats and rough cotton shirts for Ezra. But he thought of his budget and resisted temptation.

When he emerged from the market, it was 10:30 in the morning. The sky was a postcard blue, the air dry and fresh. He breathed in the strange and wonderful foreign scents and seemed to breathe power into his soul. There was a subtle lifting of a weight he didn't know had been sitting there. He grinned extravagantly. *Glory Halleluja! Amen!* An old man leaning on a cane caught his eye and grinned back.

Green mountains rose from the countryside around the town in grand sweeping curves. A wisp of a cloud hovered over one of the peaks, and he saw that this was an active volcano and the cloud was smoke. Directly ahead were the tile- and tin-roofed buildings and domed colonial churches of Antigua. Kit followed laden shoppers heading away from the market through the bus lot and into town.

Across a wide avenue, he entered a cobblestone street where cars were bumping along, the drivers blaring their horns at blind corners. One and two-story stucco shops painted white, pink, blue and rust lined the streets. He had to step down off the high, narrow sidewalk to keep from bumping into other pedestrians, a mix of *ladinos* and indigenous, as in Guatemala City, but also a few young foreigners, conspicuous with their backpacks and cameras—the girls in long skirts and halter tops embellished with bits and pieces of indigenous Guatemalan clothing, some of the boys shirtless with guitars strapped across their backs.

He stopped a young English-speaking couple to ask about a hotel. They removed their sunglasses and studied the list of lodgings that the school had sent him.

"Man, you don't have to pay that much," said the boy.

The girl nodded. They were staying at *Pensión El Arco* for only a dollar a night and the rooms were clean. She showed Kit on his map. "*5ta Avenida Norte* #32. Go in at the gate. The landlady's apartment is on the right."

They were Canadians and had been traveling through Central America for two months. Kit told them of his plans: to study Spanish in Antigua, meet other evangelicals, and visit the village where his church had donated a fire truck.

"Thank you again for your help," Kit said as they parted. "God bless you."

They gave each other a look, and Kit heard the boy say as they walked off, "Did someone sneeze?"

Kit turned abruptly down a side street and headed away from the hotel they had suggested. Halfway down the block, though, his cowardice once again shamed him. *I will speak of thy testimonies also before Kings and will not be ashamed.*

The choice was not his. The Lord, he told himself, had just provided him with a cheap place to stay and an opportunity to witness to those who mocked him. He followed the directions to *5ta Avenida Norte* #32, entered through the gate into an inner courtyard, and knocked at the landlady's apartment.

His room was a concrete cubicle accessed by a padlocked door opening directly onto the courtyard. One small curtainless window was set high in the wall. A single bed held a pallet mattress made up with clean white sheets, a woolen blanket, and a feather pillow. On a low dresser there were two bottles of purified water. An overhead lightbulb operated with a pull chain. The concrete floor was bare and scrubbed.

It was a considerable improvement over the room of the night before. In the courtyard he saw other young travelers coming and going, some in sandals and shorts, some emerging from a communal shower room with towels around them; others hanging up laundry on a clothesline. Trees and flowering bushes grew in the courtyard. Kit felt heartened again.

After settling in, he padlocked his belongings in his room. For the first time unencumbered by luggage, he strolled out and walked the two blocks to the center of town—a block-square plaza bordered on one side

by a cathedral and on the adjacent side by arches fronting a colonial building that housed municipal offices and a bank. The bank was guarded by
an armed soldier. Across the plaza was a similar colonial-style building,
and on the fourth side, shops.

Guatemalans and tourists sat beneath ancient trees near the edge of
a dry fountain in the center of the plaza. Up and down the broad steps of
the cathedral were spread piles of colorful woven blouses, skirts, pants,
and sashes. Indigenous vendors sat among the stacks and bargained with
tourists.

Glancing both ways as he was about to cross the busy street to enter
the plaza, Kit noticed an elderly indigenous man who had fallen down
on the cobblestones on a side street close to the intersection, apparently
having misstepped off the high walk. Cars were driving around him
dangerously close, and the armed soldier at the bank stood within ten
yards of the old man, without seeming to take notice.

Kit ran to the intersection, but at once stopped, confused to discover
that the bent old man had not fallen, but was on his knees in the street,
holding a small rusted trowel, and very slowly digging weeds from the
hard, dry earth between the cobbles. He wore a battered Panama hat to
shade himself from the sun, and rags tied around his knees to protect
them from the stones. Kit watched, appalled. At any moment a driver
might round the corner, miss seeing the man, and run him down, but
the man paid no attention to passing cars. He bent low over his work, his
face obscured by his hat.

Painstakingly inching his way along the street, he dug at the stubborn
weeds and pulled them out one by one, placing them in a basket by his
side. His knuckles were raw and arthritic-looking. Kit cried out as a taxi
veered to avoid a tourist and almost hit the old man. The man edged back
a few inches to let the car pass before resuming his labor.

Kit broke into a sweat. Could the man be doing some kind of voluntary
penance? He had heard of Catholic fanatics scourging themselves or
making their way for miles on bleeding hands and knees to the shrines
of their saints. But this man seemed to be simply working.

How much did he earn risking his life to pull weeds from a busy
street? Couldn't the work at least be done earlier in the morning when

there was no traffic? Couldn't a team of strong young people get the job done more quickly?

He looked up the side street and saw that all the cobblestones on the block were free of weeds. The elderly man must have been steadily at this work since early morning.

What mean ye, that ye grind the faces of the poor?

Kit bit his upper lip. How could he just go his way, cross the street into the town square and continue on as a carefree tourist. Scripture required him—his own compassion required him—to do something. But what?

Reject not the supplication of the afflicted; neither turn away thy face from a poor man ... But the man wasn't supplicating. He was working, according to terms and stipulations Kit didn't know anything about. Still, wasn't his plight itself a supplication?

What if he stepped down into the street, took the trowel and basket from him, helped him to a seat on the curb and gave him the water bottle he carried in his pocket, then turned back and did the work in his place? Isn't this what Jesus would have done?

But would it be presumptuous? Were there considerations he didn't understand? Maybe the man would get in trouble. And how would he communicate with him, ask him how long the work must go on? What if there was no end to it?

Maybe the best way to help him was to give him money. Kit felt in his pocket for the change the landlady had returned to him, and he remembered how little money there was to last until the banks opened on Monday. How much, in any case, could he allocate to ... what would you call it? Alms, charity? It wasn't his own money to give. It had, in a sense, been given as charity to him. And maybe the man would be insulted.

Another car dodged the old man, who took a dirty handkerchief from his pocket, removed his hat and wiped sweat from his furrowed neck and brow. His tousled white hair stuck up, poignantly boyish. Kit closed his eyes. The scene was too painful to watch.

Jesus, guide me.

Snatches of Ezra's homilies were crowding into his mind—*The righteous considereth the cause of the poor; but the wicked regardeth not to know it. ... He that hath pity upon the poor lendeth unto the Lord.*

He prayed. *Lord, help me to understand Your will.*

When he opened his eyes, the man was gone.

Kit looked up and down the street and thought he saw him among other indigenous people on their way to the market. He had apparently finished the job and was going home. Kit felt relief, then almost immediately, guilt. Where and what would be the home of an old man who pulled weeds from a busy street?

He cut through the central plaza and went to stand at the foot of the bustling textile market on the steps of the cathedral. Squatting on their haunches or moving among their wares like living advertisements, the black-haired indigenous vendors were clad in the same multi-colored garments as those arrayed in piles next to them. He wanted to capture it. If only he had paints to do it justice.

Vendors began to press samples on him as he wandered among the stacks of textiles, marveling. "This so beautiful. You like?" "Buy for you wife!"

"No, *gracias*," Kit replied, smiling and shaking his head. But in their pleas he began to hear an undercurrent of desperation. "I'm only looking," he had to keep repeating, moving a little faster until he reached the bottom of the steps and crossed back to the plaza, where he sat down on an empty bench.

A few feet away, an indigenous girl of about seven—barefoot and dressed in a long wrap skirt and colorful blouse—rocked a husky, squalling toddler in her arms while her little brother spread her shawl out for her on the ground. The girl knelt and set the heavy toddler on the shawl and proceeded to feed it with a piece of a tortilla she had pulled from inside her blouse. She fed bite-size pieces to the baby, then broke off some for herself and her brother. While absently stroking the baby's abundant black hair, she sat chewing. Soon the toddler's lids drooped shut, the long lashes lying across the round, tan cheeks, and the girl laid it down on its stomach.

The two children now occupied themselves with a scrap of red balloon on the ground. They began to fill it with stones to see how far it would stretch. While the girl stayed with the baby, the boy scoured the plaza for more stones, carrying them back in the front of his grubby T-shirt and dumping them onto the shawl.

Would it be all right to draw them? Was a sketch different from a photograph? There was no one to tell him. He began to draw the girl.

It was a while before the children noticed Kit squinting back and forth from the girl to the drawing. She came to stand in front of him, the brother following. Kit held up the sketch. Her brother pointed excitedly, "¡Rosita eres tú, eres tú!" His gestures illuminated the foreign words. "Rosita," Kit repeated. He held the drawing out. "Eres tú." The little girl's eyes grew wide. She laughed and clasped her hands together.

She tucked the drawing into her waist sash, then gathered the sleeping toddler up in her shawl and raced across the plaza—the heavy baby bumping aginst her chest—crying, "¡Mira mamá!" The little boy, leaning against Kit's shoulder now, brought his face close and pointed to himself, shyly whispering some words of Spanish.

Kit took the boy gently by his thin shoulders, planted him a few feet in front of him and started work on the portrait. The child stood without fidgeting, chin drawn in and shoulders squared for the entire ten minutes it took to complete the drawing. The rattle of vehicles circling the park, the appeals of the textile vendors on the cathedral steps faded as Kit became lost in the boy's dark, wondering eyes and stiff little torso. Before finishing, Kit stood back to look at the sketch, feeling he had missed something. Then he rubbed out the arms and hands, held so straight at the sides, and re-drew them cradling the handful of stones against the folds of the T-shirt. When at last Kit turned the portrait toward him, a radiant smile drove dimples deep into the little boy's cheeks.

Kit pointed to himself. "Kit," he said. He touched his index finger to the boy's chest. "And you?"

"¡Marco!" the little boy exclaimed.

Kit took the drawing from him, wrote *Marco* on the corner and handed it back. Then the girl returned, her mother in tow, a small young woman—too young, Kit thought, to have three children. The mother, who carried the toddler now, was clothed like her daughter in a striped skirt and red woven blouse embroidered with colorful birds, her braids done up with ribbons that streamed down her back. Carefully, between thumb and forefinger, she held the sketch of Rosita.

Rosita pointed at Kit. "*Mamá, éste es el hombre.*" Marco tugged at her skirt and pressed his portrait into her hand. "*Éste soy YO.*" She studied it in wonder and said, with a smile that melted Kit's heart, "*Este hombre es un artista.*" The toddler stirred. The young mother handed the portrait back to Rosita, deftly tied the shawl across her chest and tucked the baby into it. She lifted her blouse for the baby to nurse.

Kit began to sketch the mother. Her smile never left her face, though it was not posed, and she stood patiently rocking on her feet to lull the nursing baby. Kit longed for the colors that would do justice to the tinge of pink in her high, brown cheekbones, the gorgeous hues of her clothing, the halo of blue sky framing her black hair.

He was so engrossed that he didn't notice, until he finished, the little crowd that had gathered. Four or five other indigenous children, two teenage *ladino* boys, and an old man stood behind him at his elbow, silently watching the woman's face emerge on the page. When the drawing was complete, others stepped up—quietly, courteously, with self-conscious laughter—to be drawn too. The boys, sixteen or seventeen years old, smoothed back their hair before posing and stood unsmiling until Kit was done.

By the time he finished the rest of the portraits—three little sisters in identical puff-sleeve dresses, a young couple who held hands and laughed bashfully, a middle-aged man who tipped his straw hat back to expose his high forehead—Kit's hand was beginning to cramp. His neck ached, and he had worked up a terrific appetite.

"*Adiós,*" he said. The little crowd returned his wave and dispersed, carrying their portraits out ahead of them like holy relics. Though he wasn't sure how to spell it, he now had a new Spanish phrase. It sounded like "deeboohemme" and it meant "draw me."

By God's grace I can draw, he thought to himself. And it occurred to him that this would be his way in. When he had enough language, he would use his gift to bring people to the Lord.

Kit found a pleasant-looking restaurant a block east of the cathedral. He studied the menu and prices on the front window. One dollar was worth one *quetzal* and one *quetzal* was one hundred *centavos*. The restaurant wasn't cheap, but he was too hungry to resist. He went in and was seated at a table in a blossom-filled courtyard under a shady veranda. It was almost 2:00 p.m. and he had the place to himself. A small bird bathed in the dust between flagstones. Another swayed and sang at the end of a flowering branch.

A friendly English-speaking waiter laid down the silverware in a cloth napkin and took his order. Pleasantly drowsy, Kit sat back to enjoy the scent of flowers and the quiet breeze of the empty courtyard.

The lunch—over which he prayed quietly—was the *plato típico*, translated on the menu as chicken, rice, beans, salad and tortillas. He was halfway through his meal when two little boys of about four and six— crept through a gap in the shrubs and came to stand beside him. They were barefoot, their faces and hands dirty, their black hair matted and tangled; the younger boy's nose was running. The older one pointed at the food on Kit's half empty plate and murmured, without expression, "*¿Comida?*"

Kit laid down his fork. He reached out and touched the smaller boy's shoulder. The child drew his shoulders in and stood stock still. Hurriedly, Kit cast around for something to put food into, almost sacrificing the restaurant's cloth napkin before he thought to tear sheets of drawing paper from his sketch pad. He divided the remains of his meal and wrapped them in the paper. These packages he handed to the children, who took them without a word and turned to leave.

"*¡Eh!*" shouted the waiter. He was hurrying across the courtyard, water splashing from his pitcher. Clutching their packages of food, the children scampered past him and disappeared through the gap in the bushes. The waiter returned to Kit's table, shaking his head. "Don't feed them, *señor*, please," he said in English. "They will come back. They come around like dogs. They're all swindlers."

"They just wanted food," protested Kit.

"Yes, food. They look up at you with those big *indio* eyes. You feel sorry for them. I see it every time. Watch them in the Plaza counting their money."

"But really," Kit insisted, "they only asked for food."

"The money will be next. I see it many times."

Kit paid him silently and left. At the end of the street he turned the corner and saw the two boys with a third child—a little girl—squatting on their haunches in the rubble of a demolished building. The older boy broke a tortilla in two and gave a piece to the girl. The three sat in the dust and chewed.

The rest of the day he spent walking around Antigua—venturing into shops, peering into hotel courtyards and the entrances of ruined convents and churches. He glimpsed a large cross erected at the top of a hill overlooking the town. It was a plain cross like the one inside Light and Life Tabernacle at home, not like the Catholic crucifixes all over Antigua that seemed to let Jesus hang there in torment forever, and he liked how it appeared, now and then, at the end of a tunnel of buildings as he crossed an intersection and looked north.

Nowhere in his wanderings did he see the old man who picked weeds from the street, though he saw many like him on roads leading in and out of Antigua. They were always carrying heavy burdens—even the old women and pregnant women and young children—on their backs or their heads, for how far he didn't know. They walked barefoot, bearing their heavy weights uphill and down under the hot sun. They were photogenic, gorgeous, exotic. If Colleen hadn't warned him against it, he would already have used up all his film just on what he had seen so far. But their picturesque poverty disturbed him, the exhausting patience and submission it must require.

He stopped at a small grocery store—a *tienda*—to get more bottled water, and at a stationer's to buy a large drawing pad, but stood for a long time considering a box of colored pencils in eight basic colors alongside a much larger box that showed through its cellophane window an enticingly full range of hues. Could he justify the cost after his expensive lunch? But if he hadn't bought that lunch, three children would have gone hungry. Had the Lord guided him to that restaurant? What might God have in mind right now, putting this choice in front of him? With a pang, he selected the smaller box. Then, almost to the cash register, he went back and got the bigger one instead.

He bought only an orange for his dinner and ate it on a bench in the *parque central*—the central plaza. In the early evening light, fronds of a palm tree cast drowsily swaying shadows across the dry fountain as if water moved there. Soon the sun slipped down behind the mountains ringing the town, and a few street lights came on. He had to keep reminding himself it was January.

The vendors were packing up the piles of textiles on the cathedral steps and bearing them away on backs, on heads, and in carts. In front of the bank, a new soldier had replaced the one Kit had seen earlier. Slouching with boredom, the soldier leaned on his rifle and smoked a cigarette. A young *ladino* couple strolled into the park and stopped to sit on the edge of the fountain. Kit listened to their melodious murmuring, unable to make out a word of it. They talked shyly, without touching, their faces slightly averted from each other. The girl wore high heels and a dress with a lace collar—clothes she might have worn to church—and the boy, too, was dressed formally, in a tie and freshly pressed shirt, his black hair oiled and combed flat.

The couple made him envious. He thought of Laura, the rosy-cheeked, ponytailed girl from church who laughed at his jokes and told him that getting physical wasn't a sin as long as they didn't "go all the way." She had traced a finger down his long nose and declared the flared nostrils, which he thought clownish, to be "regal" and kissed his lips and called his rabbity overbite "sexy."

At church camp they had stood in the middle of the tent between the bunk beds and kissed, her breasts pressed against his chest, her hands hot on his back under his shirt. He sifted her fine silky hair between his fingers as he kissed her. They moved to the edge of his bunk, neither of them leading the way, just moving there naturally and sitting down and then stretching out. He pulled her on top of him, taking her under her arms and sliding her up his body. The weight of her breasts and belly and the small hard mound at the top of her thighs dragged against his erection. He clutched her, found her mouth again, thrust against her through their clothes.

A wave of lust was beginning to crest at the sounds of their lips meeting and parting, her little audible sighs. But then she whispered something in his ear that brought everything to a dead stop: "Oh God, oh God, I love you, Kit," she had said, and the wave sucked back on itself and ebbed out as fast as it had come.

He lay on the narrow mattress with one arm damp and heavy on her sweating back and the other at his side. There was only the sound of their lungs filling and emptying, moving their chests up and down against each other. He felt embarrassed by the sound and by the conspicuous deflating of his erection under her belly. He didn't speak and she didn't either. He didn't want to be the one to say it was sinful—as if it were her sin and not his, too. *All that is in the world, the lust of the flesh, and the lust of the eyes, and the pride of life is not of the Father, but is of the world.* So he didn't say anything. But he felt numb, slightly in shock, like someone who has swerved just in time to avoid being in a car wreck. Oh God, oh God, she'd said.

Later, he forced himself to tell Ezra what had happened. It was just after he moved into the Tinkers' basement and Ezra had come downstairs to bring him an "apartment warming" gift—a tabletop easel. Kit was ashamed to accept it, knowing what he had done. Ezra sat down in the maple rocker that Jeannette had donated and said, "Something wrong, son?" When Kit finished stammering out the story, Ezra stood up and put a hand on his shoulder. "Kit, I'm very proud of you. A month ago you turned eighteen. God has just given you your first tough test of faith as a man, and you passed it with flying colors. Trust the wisdom He's put in your heart." And he knew he was right to have stopped seeing Laura.

The young couple got up and walked past Kit, taking away their romance and sweetness.

❖ Six ❖

He was alone in the *parque central* now. The bank and municipal building were dark, and the soldier had left his post for the night. Kit got up and walked the four blocks to his *pensión*, wondering what he would do with himself tomorrow, Sunday. At home he would have spent most of the day at Light and Life, helping Ezra. He wished Colleen had come with him to Antigua.

He took out a picture postcard of *Cerro de la Cruz*. That was one thing he could do—find his way up to the cross on the hill at sunrise to pray.

When he returned to *Pensión El Arco*, a small party was in progress—six or seven young people roughly his own age gathered in the courtyard. They were dressed in that hippie combination of overalls, hiking boots, bandannas, indigenous clothes. They sat cross-legged on the ground or sprawled on benches, drinking Guatemalan beer. Two played guitars, another blew into a breathy instrument that looked like pan-pipes, and the others were singing along to an old Beatles song, "The Long and Winding Road." Candles flickered on the flagstones. There was a smell of marijuana in the air.

The Canadian couple was a part of this group. Seeing Kit enter the courtyard, the girl palmed a lighted joint and hid it behind her back. Several of the group acknowledged him with disinterested "hi's" as he crossed to his room. They were a tribe, Kit thought, and he was an outsider if only because of his clothes—very straight, he knew, even down to his thick-soled sandals with white socks. He smiled, thinking about his khaki pants, button-down shirt, short hair. The irony of ending up dressed the way Dean wanted him to for so many years.

It was okay. He didn't mind being cold-shouldered by the Canadians

39

and their friends. He wanted to read his Bible for an hour before turning in and then get up at dawn for his visit to the cross on the hill. Still, as he passed the group, he hummed under his breath the bass part of the song and felt an unexpected yearning to stay outside with them in the courtyard. He slowed to search his pockets for his key. Why didn't he just walk over and sit down with them? They stopped singing. He glanced back. They were waiting for him to leave so they could pass the joint. He smiled, said, "Praise God for this beautiful night," unlocked his door and went in.

Despite the seventy- and eighty-degree days, winter nights in the foothills of the Guatemalan Highlands were cold, sometimes as low as thirty-five or forty degrees. He was glad of his wool blanket, and even so, at 6:00 a.m. he got up shivering and had to put on a sweater and a jacket before going out in the early morning darkness to search for the way up the *Cerro de la Cruz*. He walked north, then east on *Calle Ancha*, and north again until he came to a rutted dirt road that led uphill through thick underbrush and stands of tall trees. The dawn lightening the sky over Antigua hardly penetrated the tunnel of trees, and Kit wound his way upward in darkness, the rhythmic chunk of his footsteps amplified in the silence.

He thought of Jesus's sadness as He trudged toward Calvary under the weight of the cross, His loneliness in the midst of the jeering crowds. The dismay at His Father's silence. Kit felt close to tears. He was near the top of the hill, but it was too soon; he should be joyful, yet for some reason there was so much sadness inside him. He knelt in the road and closed his eyes.

"Lord," he prayed. "I know you walk beside me wherever I go. I know you're with me now. I'm not alone." He said this prayer several times until he could imagine a hand helping him to his feet.

The sun was shooting its rays to the heavens when he got to the top. The cross, dark against the sky, was mounted on a large stone sphere atop a pedestal of stone blocks forming steps that led up to it. A soldier sat on the top step smoking a cigarette, a rifle across his knees. Kit stopped, uncertain. Below, Antigua spread out over the valley toward the foot of *Volcán Agua*, which swept upward into a perfect cone, taking up half the horizon to the south. The soldier looked at his watch, got up and stretched. He tossed his cigarette on the ground and gestured Kit forward.

Without speaking, the soldier gave Kit a once-over as they passed, then he ambled away down the road and out of sight. Kit walked to the center of the clearing and climbed the steps to look up at the rough, plain cross towering over him. He wondered how it was that this symbol of torture could be so transformed by the Savior's sacrifice that it could give him now a sense of peace and comfort when minutes before he had been feeling so sad.

He knelt and prayed for God to protect all the people he loved. He asked Him to give Ezra and Jeannette a long life of service and to protect their missionary children in Kenya and Thailand. He prayed for Claudia and Edie and Lorie—that they would come to accept Jesus—and for the meanness to be rooted out of Dean's heart. He thanked God for Ezra's loving guidance. He ended his prayers with this request: "If it's your will, Lord, show me today where to find a community of believers."

The streets and alleys and courtyards in the town below were washed in a pale golden light. Bells rang faintly and small figures moved along the streets toward the colonial churches. By the *parque central* Kit could see people climbing the steps to the arched central doorway of the *Catedral Santiago*.

Within ten minutes after he came down from the hill and wandered back through the outskirts of Antigua, his prayer was answered. On the *Calle Hermano Pedro* was a storefront he had passed several times without noticing. A handwritten sign by the door read, "*La Iglesia Evangélica de Jesús Cristo. Horario de servicios: domingos de 9:00 a 11:00 y miércoles y jueves de 19:00 a 20:00.*" Kit laughed aloud. He consulted his Spanish dictionary. *Domingos* was Sunday. *Seek and ye shall find.*

At 8:45 a.m., after going back to the *pensión* to eat a little breakfast, pick up his Bible and go for another walk, Kit returned to the church. The sounds of clapping and singing poured out of it, and his heart began to race with anticipation as he sped up to join the crowd of people pushing inside. He stooped to pass through the low door and squeezed in at the back of the room.

On a platform at the front a woman strummed a guitar with exuberant energy. A man accompanied her, equally energetic on an accordion. Another woman shook a bright red tambourine. The people clapped, jumped, whistled, and waved their hands in the air, shouting *aleluya*. Kit felt a goofy grin spread across his own face. He was home.

"Thank you, Jesus!" he shouted. A man in front of him turned around, extending his hand. A young man next to him patted him on the back.

Kit sang out in his booming bass voice. He clapped to the rhythm and bounced on the balls of his feet. For the first time since his night in the hotel room in Guatemala City, he felt the Spirit move in him again.

The music went on for a good hour, yet Kit wasn't at all tired when the preacher, a squat, florid man with a black mustache and basset-hound eyes, finally rose to speak. It didn't matter that the sermon was in Spanish or that the preacher's voice through the speakers was shrill and distorted by feedback. Kit was filled with happiness and gratitude. When the collection plate passed, he threw all his pocket change into it without a qualm.

Toward the end of the service the preacher brought onto the platform a young couple who looked to be North Americans. They spoke to the congregation for a few minutes. A sheen of sweat glistened on the man's prematurely balding forehead, and he spoke fluently in Spanish with a radiant smile that never left his face. The woman, small and brown-haired with round, bright eyes like a sparrow's, mostly listened.

After the service, Kit hung around outside the door, waiting for the couple to come out. Those who lingered in the street to chat greeted Kit with handshakes, gestures, nods and smiles.

At last the couple emerged, and Kit introduced himself. They were missionaries from California—JoAnne and Tim Campbell. They would be leaving the country the following morning, having spent five months working among the Ixil Maya of the Western Highlands. Tim's beaming smile seemed to be a permanent fixture. He shook Kit's hand warmly.

"Is there any chance," Kit said, "you'd have just a few minutes to tell me about your mission before you leave? I might begin missionary work here, if God calls me."

Tim's eyes shifted for the barest second to glance at JoAnne. "Sure," he replied, after a moment's hesitation. He suggested Kit join them for brunch at their hotel.

Kit backed off, embarrassed. "No," he said. "I can see you're busy. You probably have a slug of other people to talk to."

JoAnne spoke up for the first time. "We'd be glad to talk with you." But she didn't sound glad.

The three of them walked the two blocks to the Campbells' small hotel, where a modest meal was spread on a buffet table. Kit glanced quickly at a posted menu and noted with relief that the prices were reasonable.

"How did the Mayans relate to you?" he asked after they were seated at a table in a corner. "Most of them are Catholic, aren't they? How do you approach them?"

Tim said the mission worked mostly with internal refugees. There was already an established evangelical presence in the Highlands, partly due to the influence of Guatemala's president, Ríos Montt, who was a born-again Pentecostal Christian. "The president encourages evangelistic work among the Indians," Tim said, "because he's a believer and because he's fighting against the communist subversives." He filled Kit's glass from a bottle of purified water on the table.

"Were there guerrilla soldiers where you worked? Did you see fighting?"

Tim again glanced at his wife. JoAnne was blinking rapidly. To his dismay, Kit saw that she was trying not to cry. He realized, in fact, that the whole time the three of them had been together, possibly even when she was standing on the platform at the church, she had been holding back tears. Abruptly, she got up and excused herself.

When she was gone, Kit said, "Is she okay? I'm sorry if I—"

Tim's smile turned apologetic. "She's feeling pretty emotional. Unpleasant things happened in the Highlands."

"The communists?"

"Well, not so much that. I mean, yes, the communists are the main cause, but—" He stopped speaking for a moment, and when he resumed, still smiling, he lowered his voice. "We worked in one of the model villages—"

"What are model villages?"

"Camps the government sets up for refugees from the war. And after we got there, we began hearing stories from some of our converts about beatings and death threats by the soldiers."

"The guerrillas?"

"No, actually... the army." Tim stopped here and looked rather furtively around the room. He took his voice a notch lower. "The army runs the camps, and they sometimes go overboard. They bring whole villages of Indians in from where they've been hiding in the mountains, and they put the word out that if the Indians surrender, they'll give them food and shelter in the camps—in the model villages. Then they put the Indian men—even boys fifteen, sixteen years old—into civil patrols to guard the area. Only they don't pay them or give them real weapons, and sometimes they mistreat them. We've heard that they put them in uniforms and send them ahead of the soldiers into ambushes to draw fire, things like that." He stopped to clear his throat for a moment before continuing. "And there were a lot of stories of young Indian girls getting raped."

Kit had stopped eating and his foot started to jiggle under the table.

"If people complain," Tim continued, with a dry, meaningless chuckle, "they disappear or get found dead. Sometimes even evangelical converts have been swept up in reprisals by the army. By accident." He folded his arms across his chest. "They can't always take time to figure out who the real enemy is." He was silent for a moment. Then he cleared his throat again and said, "The thing is, a born-again Indian girl that JoAnne was working with was raped and beaten by a group of soldiers."

Kit's jaw tightened. An old, familiar rage swelled up in him. The heat of it filled his face. He had to put a hand down on the top of his thigh to still his jiggling foot.

"JoAnne caught them at it." Tim's lips bunched up and his eyes narrowed so that his smile became tight like a grimace.

Kit wanted to shout at the man. *Stop smiling, goddamn it!* He had to suppress the sudden urge to shout this blasphemy or crude expletives he had abandoned long ago when he was saved, words he shouldn't even allow himself to think. He gripped the half-empty water bottle.

"Yeah." Tim nodded, stirring his rice around his plate. "JoAnne almost got the same treatment. But one of the soldiers recognized her as an *evangélica norteamericana,* and they backed off. The commanders are very sensitive about any behavior that gets the U.S. Embassy down on them. Heads can roll for that," he added, grinning into his plate. Kit set down the bottle. Tim's perpetual smile, he realized, was a nervous tic, like his own agitated foot.

"JoAnne complained to the *comandante.*" Tim smiled down at a thin paper napkin he picked up and began to pull apart. "That's why we left, actually. We were supposed to stay for a year, but he sent us out of the camp that same day. He told the church to send us home or he'd close down the mission."

"What was his excuse? Why—"

"He said the girl and her family were communist sympathizers. He couldn't expect his soldiers to control themselves after seeing their brothers in arms killed by the guerrillas." Tim tossed the napkin on the table. His eyes were narrowed into a fierce squint above the eerie smile. He shook his head vehemently. "They *aren't* communist sympathizers. We worked with them for five months. The girl was our best Bible teacher. Her whole family converted, and not just to avoid being killed by the army—" He stopped, seeming to realize what he had just said. "I mean ... she was a true Bible-believing, born-again Christian."

"I thought the president of Guatemala was a believer. Why would—"

"He's trying!" Tim exclaimed in a tense, semi-whisper. "He only has so much control. The army are fighting a war against communism! They have to be tough on people. How are they supposed to know who the enemy is?" Kit frowned and Tim leaned toward him, tapping on the table for emphasis. "It comes down to a choice between the lesser of two evils. Either a fairly violent counterinsurgency or a communist victory, which would totally destroy the freedom to spread the Gospel. Those are the choices."

"But if even Christian converts are—"

"Not many, though. Only occasionally. By accident." Tim's voice had dropped to a whisper, as if to warn Kit to keep his own voice down. "Look at the alternative," he said. "The whole country turned into a communist prison camp with no one allowed even to mention the word of God. That's what Ríos Montt is up against. So we have to support him even if his presidency isn't perfect. And the missionaries do have some influence." He crumpled what was left of the napkin and dropped it on his plate.

A woman and man who had finished eating walked by their table on the way to the door. Tim was silent until they had passed. Then he leaned again toward Kit and touched his arm.

"Ríos Montt asks our Mission Board for specific recommendations for controlling any army abuses. I think he's doing his best. And he's a whole lot better than the last guy—" Kit nodded, though he knew nothing about Guatemala's politics or history.

"He's had a big effect on reducing corruption in the government," Tim continued. "He holds prayer meetings with his top advisers every week." He glanced at the door to the hotel, where JoAnne had retreated, but he seemed unable to stop talking. "There's no doubt the Indians are suffering. From army abuses, from being caught between the army and the insurgency. And they were already poor and landless. But,—as bad as it is —and I'm not saying that it's good that they're suffering—" He shook his head vigorously. "Not at all! But I think good things can come *out* of it—" His fingers curved around an imaginary good thing and held it up. "—Because when people are really desperate, isn't that when there's the greatest opportunity to bring them to the Lord? When they have nowhere else to turn?"

Kit frowned.

"I'm not saying it's right that innocent people ..." Tim paused, "but ... how do we know that it isn't a case of God pushing people against a wall in order to save them?"

Kit didn't reply. Tim was right. It had been true for him when he had been pushed to the wall. Yet he felt an irrational defiance. His swinging foot was shaking the table. He stopped it. He had to rein in his defiance. It was arrogance. Adam's sin against God. Ezra spoke of it almost weekly. Still ...

"But," Kit said, keeping his voice low, "if the army kills people before they're saved—?"

"I know. I know. We just have to work harder." Tim sat back in his chair. He looked over toward the door again. "I'd better go see how

46

JoAnne's doing. She's worried about that girl. She's in bad shape and there's not much medical care at the camp—the model village—except what the missionaries provide. And now that we're gone, there may be army reprisals against the girl and her family."

Kit stood up. It was impossible to look at Tim's face any longer. Tim rose too. "But they're solid converts," he kept on. "They'll put their trust in God. I think they'll be okay." Kit started toward the front where a woman worked a cash register. "The thing is, she feels guilty about going to the *comandante*. But we had prayed about it beforehand. We didn't think Jesus would have stayed silent."

Kit began to take his billfold out of his pocket, but Tim pushed it back. "The meals are already covered by the mission," he said.

He shook Kit's hand then and produced the radiant smile Kit had seen during the church service. "I hope you don't let any of this discourage you," he said, pumping Kit's hand. "Working in Guatemala is a high calling. It's God's work."

"I'll pray for JoAnne," Kit murmured, turning away. "For both of you, and that girl."

In the center of town, the streets were filling again with late-rising tourists and families returning from eleven o'clock mass. Kit didn't know what to do with himself. He felt unsettled after the encounter with the missionaries, and, unexplainably, guilty.

He found a bench under a tree several blocks from the central plaza in a quiet, enclosed square and took out the small bundle of postcards he had bought the day before.

"*Hi Ezra and Jeannette*," he began. "*Well, I made it to Antigua, praise Jesus, and it's spectacular here, as you can see from this card.*" He turned the card over to the view of Antiqua from *Cerro de la Cruz*, its clustered roofs and pastel walls like candy in a bowl between the perfect cones of *Volcan Agua* and *Volcan Fuego*. It *was* spectacular. From that distance you wouldn't be able to make out an old man kneeling in the cobbles.

"*There's a lot of work to be done for the Lord, though.*" The generality sounded empty and clichéd. He stopped and chewed on the cap of his pen. He wanted to tell them about the Campbells' experience and get their advice. These things weren't to be mentioned in a postcard, though—he remembered Tim's lowered voice and Colleen's warning about politics—but he wasn't in the mood to write breezy clichés.

He had intended to send his sisters cards depicting indigenous women in their headdresses and gorgeous figured blouses—*huipiles,* he'd heard them referred to—their beautiful woven *huipiles.* The little girl from yesterday, hunkered down in the rubble with the two boys sharing his handout of food, had worn a miniature *huipil,* threadbare and dusty but still colorful, tucked into the little cotton wrap skirt that came all the way to her bare feet. Now, sending these postcard pictures seemed heartless.

He put the cards in his daypack, got up and started walking again, aimlessly. He passed the address of the school he would be attending tomorrow. Shuttered windows and a high wall prevented his seeing inside. What would the school be like? The question called up images of all the classrooms he had endured to get where he was now. Sterile rooms with harsh fluorescent lighting and rows of molded plastic chairs all facing front.

The Lord had given him a great opportunity, of course. He should be looking forward to it. And it would be a relief to be around a group of people after these last three days on his own. Soon he would be assigned a host family to live with and could move out of the *pensión.* Maybe the people would be Bible believers—one of those warm, welcoming families who had greeted him after church this morning.

He passed the entrance to the *Convento Santa Clara,* stopped and turned back to read the placard by the door. Antigua tourist brochures advertised the fascinations of these great ruined edifices, which stood on practically every corner. Massive stone churches and convents, many of them reduced to hollow shells by a major earthquake in 1773, they still endured as monuments to the colonial period when Antigua was the capital of Guatemala, and Spain controlled the country.

The thick wooden door opened, and two tourists emerged. Kit caught a glimpse of a sun-bleached grassy courtyard inside, bordered by stone arches. Along the inner walls, crumbling stone staircases led to nowhere. Visiting this Convent of Santa Clara, or any of the other ruins would help him pass the time, but he wasn't sure it was proper to set foot in these monuments erected by people who, Ezra said, worshipped saints and the pope.

He passed the convent by and carried on south for another two blocks before coming to a tourist market near the Church of San Francisco. From here it was possible to see *Cerro de la Cruz* to the north. He sat down on the ground, took out his new sketchbook, and began drawing a picture of the cross rising above the town. In the evening he would write to Ezra and Jeannette and enclose the sketch.

❖ Seven ❖

He slept well in his warm sweater, covered by the wool blanket and a jacket spread over his legs and feet. The sun was angling into the *pensión* courtyard when he emerged from his room. People were stirring, calling back and forth from doorways. From the showers came the hollow patter of water on concrete. Kit ducked in and out of the cold shower quickly, pleased to be offered the use of a communal shampoo bottle by one of the guitar players of the night before. Another showed him a stone basin—a *pila*—where he could wash clothes. Yielding to the unspoken dress code of his fellow travelers, he dispensed with his white socks and slipped bare feet into his cold leather sandals.

He hoisted his large backpack onto his shoulders, picked up his day-pack, and set out to meet the challenges of Spanish verb conjugations and masculine and feminine nouns.

At a hole-in-the-wall *comedor* he gobbled down an egg, some orange slices, and a stack of warm corn tortillas. He could have eaten twice as much but was gratified that the bill was only sixty *centavos*. Tonight he would begin eating with his host family, all meals prepaid, and he could stop thinking about the cost of food.

Through the door of *7ta Avenida Sur, #2* he followed several people also encumbered with backpacks and luggage into a nondescript room furnished with folding chairs and two utilitarian tables holding refreshments and books. After a few minutes of self-conscious milling around while students were arriving, a slender, sallow-faced man in a crested blazer and open-neck shirt asked everyone to be seated.

"I should like to introduce myself," he said, in a pronounced British accent. "I am Phil Bellingham, the director of *Instituto de Español Tres Américas*. I'll be the one behind the scenes, as it were, so you won't see quite as much of me as you will of my co-director—" he nodded at a woman by his side "—my wife, Rita Ortiz Bellingham." Phil took a step back and his wife fluttered her fingers at the group.

"*Buenos días, estudiantes. ¡Bienvenido a las Tres Américas!*" The petite woman, in a Day-Glo orange minidress with nails and lipstick to match, stood high on three-inch heels. "You see?" she said in English, with a lilting laugh. "You learn already a little Spanish, and it is the *español auténtico* because I and all *nuestros maestros*—our teachers—*son Guatemaltecos*—are Guatemalan." It was hard for Kit not to focus on her mobile, painted lips exaggerating the shapes of the Spanish words. Phil, withdrawn to a chair in a corner, sat resting his ankle on his knee and idly manipulated a gold fountain pen back and forth between his fingers.

Rita introduced the dozen or so Guatemalan teachers—soberly dressed men and women of varying ages sitting in a row against the wall. They smiled blandly at their prospective pupils as if they had been through the orientation many times. Each student would work individually with a teacher, who would rotate every few weeks to allow exposure to differences in accent and teaching style.

The teachers were assigned, books distributed, and everyone invited to take coffee and a sampling of *pan dulce*—sweet Guatemalan pastries. Before he could stop himself, Kit had eaten four of them.

Students and teachers emerged onto the street and trooped to the classroom, which was not in the orientation room but a block farther down. Kit's teacher, Carlos, introduced himself and after attempting a brief, unsuccessful exchange in basic Spanish, walked a little ahead. Kit trailed silently after him along with the others to a narrow arched entryway through which they passed into a sunny inner courtyard.

The courtyard was bounded on all sides by a covered corridor, which shaded small tables at intervals, each set with two chairs, a roll of newsprint, and pencils. Palm trees grew in the corners of the courtyard, and a fountain in the center dripped water into a pool, where golden carp swam. Around the fountain grew bushy, scarlet flowers.

The teachers led their students into the shade and sat down with them at the small tables. Carlos moved one of the chairs next to the other and gestured for Kit to take a seat. A yellow, canary-like bird twittered and fluttered out from under the eaves above Kit's head and lit on the edge of the fountain.

This is a classroom? Praise Jesus! Kit leaned back in the wooden chair and crossed one leg over the other. Carlos did the same. They smiled at each other.

"*Me llamo Carlos,*" the teacher said for the second time, pointing to himself. "*¿Y tú?*"

"*Me ... llamo ... Kit.*"

"*¡Bien!*" said Carlos.

A pleasant brush of gooseflesh traveled across his back in the cool shade. He slipped off a sandal and stuck one bare foot onto the sun-warmed flagstone. *Bien.* Yes! *Bien.*

Carlos nudged the textbook toward him. A breeze caught the pages. Kit stared down at the print. Even the English was incomprehensible: present indicative, definitive endings, stem changes, subject pronouns.

"*Página seis,*" Carlos said, holding up six fingers. Kit leaned his elbows on the table. He turned the pages one at a time, watching Carlos's face. "*Bien,*" said the teacher when Kit came to page six.

Carlos pointed to a word: *cantar.* "*Por ejemplo*"—he said. "—For example," he added, in heavily accented English, and broke loudly into the first bar of "Yellow Submarine." "'Een a town where I wahss born leev a man who sail to sea ...' To sing." he said. "*Cantar.*"

Kit smiled. "To sing. *Cantar.*"

Carlos pointed to himself and sang the next two bars: "'Ahn' he tol' us ahf hees life een the lahn' of soobmahreens...' <u>Yo</u> *canto,*" he said. "I sing." Then he tapped Kit's chest with a finger and cocked his head slyly. Kit sang the next line, "'So we sailed up to the sun ...'" "*Tú cantas,*" Carlos said, and raised an eyebrow at Kit.

"*You* sing?"

"*¡Bien!*"

So it went, Carlos enlisting the teacher and student at the next table to demonstrate *he* or *she* sings, putting an arm around Kit's shoulder and eliciting a duet for *we* sing, pointing at the people bent over their books on the other side of the courtyard to illustrate his sighing lamentation, "*Ellos no cantan.*" They finished the song just for good measure, several joining in from other tables: 'We all live in a yellow submarine, yellow submarine, yellow submarine,' and Kit felt something let go in his shoulders and chest. He pulled himself up straight to study the list in the middle of page six. "*Yo canto,*" he read aloud. "*Tú cantas. Usted, Él, Ella canta. Nosotros cantamos. Ustedes, ellos, ellas cantan.*" Words from those weary days in high school Spanish were trickling back.

"*¡Hola!*" Rita returned just before the lunch break waving home-stay assignments.

She told Kit, "*Señor y Señora* Martinez have ten children—so many!" According to the information on the card, the youngest was seven years old, the oldest twenty-four, all living at home. "As well, there is the great aunt of *Señora* Beatriz Martinez. She has one hundred and three years old, can you imagine?" Kit would have his own room. There was no hot water. "But," —Rita tapped the card with an orange-painted fingernail— "has a shower."

The father, Lorenzo Martinez, was a high school principal who took the bus to Guatemala City every day very early and returned late. The oldest children had jobs and the younger ones were in school. *Señora* Martinez was to cook breakfast and lunch for Kit. The evening meal he would eat with the whole family, and he was to tell *la señora* in advance if he planned to eat a meal outside. "Okay?" Rita breezed on to the next table.

Before she left the courtyard, she returned to Kit with an envelope. "I forget to give you this."

Kit tore open the envelope. First, a note from Jeannette fell out, containing motherly advice on a number of practical matters—*Don't try to save money by doing your laundry yourself. You can send it out at very low cost and give a needy woman an honest addition to her income*—and a short poem clipped from a mission newsletter, warning about parasites abroad. It ended with the lines,

These are the plagues that do beset us
Who drink from taps and eat the lettuce.

The note was dated three weeks earlier. Tears pricked Kit's eyes. Ezra and Jeannette had made sure there would be mail waiting for him when he arrived.

Then he read the letter from Ezra, written on the blank side of an old church bulletin—waste not, want not, typical Ezra. Kit ran a finger over the familiar handwriting, like the penmanship of a diligent third grader.

> *Greetings Kit, beloved brother in Christ,*
>
> *You haven't left yet and Jeannette and I and your good friends at Light and Life already miss you, but we praise God for sending you out into the world to spread His good news. I've sent this letter well ahead of time because I know from our own tours of duty in underdeveloped countries that mail service can be highly unreliable.*
>
> *Son, by God's grace you have been blessed with personal skills and talents—your art, your music, your deep under-standing of children—and your faithfulness to His word, which will aid you in your endeavors. But God will also hand you challenges that may seem overwhelming. Remember that Jeannette and I are always here for you, and that no burden is so great that it can't be eased by prayer.*
>
> *I'll write again soon. Bless you, Kit.*
> *With love in Christ,*
> *Ezra*
>
> *P.S. Every day I praise the Lord for putting that rock in your hand.*

That's where it had started. With the rock.

He hadn't even noticed it was a church at first. It was just a nondescript prefab steel building. He was riding his bike past when he caught sight of the sign in front, "Our Heavenly Father Calls Us To Witness!" He pulled to a stop. "Jesus freaks," he muttered.

From the curb, he picked up the rock, took aim and launched it, shattering the front window. Immediately, they had come running around the side of the building. Kit lurched toward his bike, stumbled and regained his balance, but the man had planted himself in front of the bike and the woman took hold of the handlebars to pull it upright.

"What happened here?" the man said. Kit thought how ridiculous the guy looked—a shrimp, maybe five feet three or four, with a bulbous nose in a skinny face. Middle-aged. He wore a white, short-sleeved shirt tucked into stiff new jeans with the cuffs turned way up. The woman was taller, by an inch or two. Perspiration shone on her forehead. She was wearing gardening gloves.

They all glanced at the broken window. The man frowned. "You'll want to pay for the window, won't you, son? Because a lot of hard-earned nickels and dimes and quarters went into buying it, and they were offered up willingly for the love of the Lord."

"Pay for your own goddamned window." He wrenched the bike out of the woman's grasp, looking around for the quickest way to escape. Neither of them put out a hand to stop him, but as he straddled the bike and stepped down on the pedals, the woman, in a matter-of-fact tone, recited his bicycle license number. This gave him pause. She smiled mildly. She was plump and freckled with reddish hair fluffed out in a frizzy halo around her head. Her calmness made him want to drive the bike into her stomach and knock her down.

"We wouldn't want to call the police on you," the little man said. "Everyone who loves you would be disappointed and hurt. But how else can we see that the Lord is repaid for His window?"

He was on the verge of riding off anyway—Fuck the little Bible-thumping freak—but he stood gripping the handlebars. What would his stepfather do to him if he were arrested for vandalism? This time Dean would do more than sneer at him or ground him or remind Claudia what a worthless son she had raised. This time he would separate Kit from his sisters as a bad influence, and Claudia would go along with it.

Kit stared at the ground.

"Tell you what," the little man said. "We'll strike you a deal. You come to services here this Sunday and the Sunday after that, and we'll consider your debt paid." He held out his hand.

55

Mealy-mouthed blackmailers. No way I'm going to set foot in that holy roller nuthouse. Let him turn me in. Who cares! Kit wheeled his bike around the couple, slowly, to throw his who-gives-a-shit attitude in their faces—he was so much taller than this shrimp. Watch me ride casually out of here. But he couldn't keep it up. The creepy little jerk had him in the palm of his hand.

Smiling, Kit folded his letters back into the envelope and put them in his pocket. At noon, when Carlos left to go home for lunch, he stayed a few minutes longer to take the letters out and read them again.

There was a two-hour break for lunch. Kit donned his backpack and walked the ten blocks to the neighborhood called *La Colonia Candelaria*, where his host family lived. It was a dusty, one-block-square compound of single-story cement block houses surrounding a vacant lot where dogs and children played.

Was it impolite to come empty-handed? He felt an attack of nervousness and went back down the street to a little bakery, where he spent fifty *centavos* for a sack of *pan dulce*.

Señora Martinez, a short, thick-waisted woman in her early forties with red cheeks and soft brown eyes, came to the door in an apron. She greeted Kit cheerfully in Spanish and accepted his gift with nods and smiles, taking him by the arm into the kitchen, where she put the pastries into a wooden bowl in the center of a long, cloth-covered table that took up most of the room.

There was no sink in the kitchen but a counter holding two wash basins. Pots and pans hung from nails on the wall. An apartment-size refrigerator was tucked underneath a counter next to a small electric range with two burners. Kit counted the chairs around the table—all different styles and heights—ten for a household of fourteen including himself.

The front room was dark and small and formal. On one wall hung a color picture of a blue-eyed Jesus Christ with long, light-brown hair, a softly curling beard and mustache, and a glowing red heart in the middle of his chest. On the opposite wall hung a large wooden crucifix. The family was Catholic.

Señora Martinez showed him his room. There was a single bed, a dresser, and a lamp. He dropped his bags on the floor and followed her for a tour of the rest of the house, which—like every other building he had been inside so far—consisted of rooms built around a courtyard. The Martinez courtyard was crisscrossed with clotheslines. In the center a *pila* with a single faucet was piled high with buckets and baskets of dirty clothes.

Señora Martinez opened the door to the one tiny bathroom equipped with a narrow, leaking shower, a small sink and a toilet. Matter-of-factly, she pointed to a plastic wastebasket under the sink filled with soiled toilet paper, then led the way to the other rooms. The bedroom of *Señor* and *Señora* Martinez had space only for a double bed and dresser. There was one bedroom for the girls and one for the boys, each room containing tiers of bunk beds and baskets of folded clothes.

In the last room, stretched out on a narrow single bed, lay an ancient little woman with paper-thin skin and a few strands of white hair covering her skull. She was on her back asleep, rosary beads loose in the hand that rested on her chest. On the floor next to the bed was a small palette mattress on which were set a Bible and a child's nightgown, folded neatly. *Señora* Martinez whispered, *"Angélica, la tía de mi mamá."*

She took him back to his room, and, holding up fingers to show that lunch would be ready in fifteen minutes, left him to put away his things. He took out his Bible and his Spanish-English dictionary and set them on the dresser before unpacking Ezra's hand-me-down cracked leather shaving kit and the clothes Jeannette had washed and set out before the trip. He sat down on the bed for a moment. In a few hours thirteen strangers would fill the rooms surrounding his. In a few minutes he would go into the kitchen and try to make conversation with a woman whose language he didn't speak. He prayed for courage.

"Cómo se llama?" Señora Martinez asked him, once he was seated at the table, his dictionary close by his elbow.

He told her his name.

She made a face as if she found it impossible for anyone to be called by such a name. "Keet Lahm?" she repeated.

He wrote on his tablet: Kit = Christopher.

"Ah!" she said. *"Cristóbal!"*

"*Sí,*" Kit replied, and quickly consulting his dictionary, wrote: "Lamb = *Cordero.*"

"*Cristóbal Cordero!*" she exclaimed approvingly. "*Es un buen nombre. Se parece al nombre de Nuestro Salvador Jesús Cristo.*"—A name like that of our Savior—He got that part.

Cristóbal was how *Señora* Martinez introduced Kit to the rest of the family after he returned from his afternoon class and the others came home one by one, eventually sitting down to dinner at seven o'clock.

Tía Angélica was wheeled up to the table in a rickety wheelchair by one of the little girls, who then stood by her side to help her eat. That accounted for two of the missing seats. *Señora* Martinez never sat down, but was constantly moving back and forth, serving and taking plates away, and eating from a plate at the counter. That was three. The youngest child sat on the oldest's lap.

Señor Martinez nodded but failed to shake Kit's hand upon meeting him, and Kit wondered if he was irritated at having a guest who took up a whole room just for himself. But then, the family probably needed the boarding fee.

Señor Martinez said grace before the start of the meal: "*Bendícenos Señor por esta comida y abundancia que nos da Cristo Nuestro Señor, Amén.*"

From the head of the table, *Señor* Martinez looked steadily at Kit and asked him, "*¿Cristóbal, que aprendiste hoy?*"

Aprendiste. Kit smiled nervously and riffled quickly through the pages of his dictionary—*aprehender, aprehension, aprender*—'to learn'. *What are you learning?* "Uh ...Yo ... apren ... dido ..." but that was the wrong ending.

Señor Martinez picked up his knife and began to cut through his chicken. He asked for the pepper sauce. Before Kit could form his answer, *Señor* Martinez had turned to one of the little girls and asked her the same question. She fired back a long and complicated reply in her piping, child's voice. Kit felt the sweat breaking out on his forehead. His leg started to swing. *Idling,* Dean used to call it. "*Shut the kid down before his motor shakes apart.*" Kit pressed down on the jumpy leg.

The youngest child, sitting on her sister's lap by his elbow, held out a serving plate and said shyly, "*¿Aguacate, Cristóbal?*"

Kit took a piece of avocado. "*Muchas gracias, señorita.*"

The little girl giggled, covering her mouth with her hand.

How would he remember all their names? He asked her, "*¿Cómo se llama?*"

"*Me llamo SARA,*" she replied emphatically. He gestured toward one of her brothers across the table, and she said, "*Se llama Alfredo—Fredi. Repite, Cristóbal!*"

"Fredi," Kit repeated.

She slid off her sister's lap and stood up then, to point at each family member in succession, saying the name and making Kit repeat it. When they finished, he went once more around the table and said the names slowly from memory: *Sara, Manuel, Tomás, Ana Luisa, Fredi, Concepción, Tía Angélica, María Teresa, Jorge, Pepe, Clara.*

Señora Martinez and the children applauded.

"*Cristóbal tiene una buena memoria,*" commented *Señora* Martinez. Her smile wrinkled the corners of her warm brown eyes. *Señor* Martinez smiled distantly and cut another piece of chicken.

Kit awoke at 5:45 a.m. shivering under his one cotton blanket. From the courtyard came the sound of water being drawn at the *pila*, then, a minute later, the faint clattering of pots and pans and the soft voices of *Señor* and *Señora* Martinez in the kitchen. Soon the aroma of coffee floated in.

Suffering from a full bladder and rumbling bowels, Kit lay in bed listening as the household, one by one, made use of the bathroom.

Two hours later, quiet settled over the rooms, and Kit crossed the courtyard, pushing through the damp towels hanging from the clothesline. In the bathroom he relieved himself with painful control, aware all the while of *Señora* Martinez on the other side of the thin wall. Then he turned on the shower and thrust portions of himself under the icy spray, gasping and withdrawing at every shock.

In the kitchen, a breakfast of scrambled eggs, avocado, *pan dulce* and coffee were laid out for him on the long table. *Señora* Martinez was carrying a washbasin full of dirty dishes and a kettle of boiling water out to the *pila*.

"*¡Buenos días, Cristóbal!*" she greeted him. He tried to take the heavy basin from her, but she brushed him off. "You eat!" she said in English, and, gesturing at his watch, added, "*No llegues tarde al instituto.*"

As Kit was rounding a corner on his way to school, his heart took an extra beat. A tall, slender woman wearing a peasant skirt and carrying a camera case on a shoulder strap was walking purposefully a block ahead. Colleen? He felt a tingling of anticipation and hurried to catch up with her. When he reached the corner, she was halfway up the steps to the cathedral and by the time he got there, she was already inside.

He hesitated. He had never entered a Catholic church before. From the doorway, he peered in at its shadowy heights, illuminated by the flickering light of hundreds of candles. Two old women brushed against him on their way in, and he stepped quickly aside. He had been blocking a stone basin into which they dipped their fingers before crossing themselves. They made their way down to a pew in front, where they knelt and bowed their lace-covered heads.

She was sitting in the back row, not kneeling or bowing her head but just sitting, with a straight back. The candlelight caught the sheen of her long brown uncovered hair pulled into a barrette. It was Colleen, no question about it. He wanted to go down to the pew and slide in next to her, but his nerve failed him in this alien place. He waited instead in the doorway for some time, hoping she would come out soon, but she kept sitting there, almost without moving, and at last he turned away because he was already late for his class and didn't want to keep Carlos waiting. Still, at least she was in Antigua now. He would run into her again, and he wouldn't be helpless or clueless as he had been the last time they were together.

He thought about her on his walk to school. She had been cold toward him, even rude, but he had to admit to himself he was attracted to her— her voice, so low and ... and her eyes—the way they slanted down at the corners sleepily.

But, no, it wasn't only that. He guessed she was one of those people who insisted on rational argument and dismissed any knowing that came from faith alone. He wanted to discuss this with her because he had felt that way too, once. He was maybe the best person to witness to her. He could show her how much more reliable was knowledge revealed by faith.

During the morning break, Kit met some of the other students, who were sitting around the fountain. There was a Mennonite missionary couple—the Bontragers. Marlena Bontrager wore a white, lace-trimmed net cap bobby-pinned over a tight bun at the back of her head. Her husband Rudy wore a beard.

There were two women, Sunshine and Myrna, in their thirties or early forties, Sunshine quite a few pounds overweight and Myrna getting there. Sisters, Kit guessed, they looked so much alike. To tell them apart he noted that Sunshine was the one who wore dangling earrings and Myrna was the one who dimpled when she grinned. Sunshine showed Kit a picture of a four-year-old who looked two—a little, hollow-eyed, stick figure of a boy with a lopsided stance due to congenital hip dysplasia. They had been waiting three months to adopt the boy from an orphanage for children who had lost their parents in the war. Rolando, his name was. They called the boy "Roli" and spoke of him as if he had been their child for years.

"How did you choose Roli?" Kit asked.

"We didn't," said Sunshine. "He was available and we said, This is the child God wants us to have. He's a gift."

A barrel-chested man sitting at a table in the shade caught his eye with a casual salute.

"Hey, *amigo*. Your name's Kit?" he called, extending a hand so that, to shake it, Kit had to leave the group at the fountain and cross the courtyard. "Chuck Nystrom," the man said. "Most people call me 'Rub'."

Rub?

He was probably in his late forties, short, with muscular arms. Severe acne must have made his high school years a misery. The raw, pocked face was the color of bazooka bubble gum, as if someone had tried unsuccessfully to smooth his skin with sandpaper. He wore a crewcut so short it was hard to tell the color of his hair.

"You're from Iowa," he said.

Kit blinked. Someone from home? "How did you know?"

Rub threw an arm across the back of the empty chair next to him. He was wearing a tight, white T-shirt—presumably to display his pectorals and biceps. There were no tattoos on his arms, though he seemed the type to have them. "I must have heard it somewhere from someone."

"Oh." Kit felt a little let down.

"You a farmboy?"

"No. I'm from Des Moines."

"In college?"

"I just finished junior college. In graphic design."

"You need Spanish to do graphic design?"

"No. My pastor sponsored me to come here. I—"

"Oh," said Rub, cocking an eyebrow at him. "Your pastor."

The teachers, who had been out smoking, came back then and Rub said, "Back to the grindstone."

On the sheet of blank newsprint that served as a blackboard and was spread over the table every morning, Carlos wrote the verb *saber*, "to know" and handed Kit the pen. They had conjugated it the day before. For homework, Kit had memorized the conjugation. *Tú sabes* he remembered: "you know" and *Él, Ella sabe*: "he, she knows." He could do "we know" and "they know," but he couldn't for the life of him remember "*I* know." Carlos sat back and waited.

Yo ... yo ... sabo? No. It was an irregular verb. First person was something unexpected. *Sabeo? Sabi?* Kit felt stupid and sluggish—summer school all over again.

Suddenly he wanted to be out of there, free from the whole idea of school. He didn't want to be at the Martinezes' house either, fumbling through his dictionary and searching for the simplest words. He wanted to be in Ezra's and Jeannette's living room, Jeannette thumping out an old-fashioned hymn on their upright piano. Or in his one-room nest of an apartment in their basement, sketching a design for the Sunday bulletin.

He slumped back in his chair and stared at the blank piece of paper. He shook his head. "*No sé*," he said.

"*No sé?*" Carlos repeated. His mouth was working as if he were trying not to laugh.

Was Carlos making fun of him? Kit tossed his pencil on the table. *"No sé. No sé."*

Carlos eyed him for a moment. *"¡Correcto!"* he said.

Kit stared back at him.

Then, *"Sé!"* he exclaimed. *"Yo sé!"*

"Sí, es sé. ¿No entiendes sé?"

They broke into laughter, Kit laughing so hard he overturned his chair. People at other tables turned to look at them. Myrna called over, "Somebody's having too much fun. What are you guys up to?"

Kit called back, *"No sé!"*

It was happening! Thank you, blessed Lord! Just as Ezra said it would. He had just used a Spanish word without thinking.

The moment Kit stepped out on the sidewalk at noon, he surveyed the street in both directions. It wouldn't be much of a coincidence to run into her now, Antigua was so small. He set out in the direction of the Cathedral.

He felt a hand on his arm.

Chuck Nystrom—Rub—said, "Which direction you headed?" and without waiting for an answer fell in beside him. "I'll walk with you a ways."

They walked toward the *parque central*. Kit wanted to hurry to the Cathedral on the chance that—but it was absurd to think she would have been sitting there for three hours. He adjusted his long stride to Rub's shorter one.

"So your pastor sent you down here, did he?" Rub tilted his head upward, giving Kit a sidelong glance.

"He's sponsoring my Spanish study for a few months," Kit said.

"You born again, are you? Filled with the holy spirit?"

God is not mocked, for whatsoever a man soweth, that shall he also reap.

"I came to the Lord when I was sixteen." Kit walked a little faster, but Rub slowed to a saunter and Kit had to fall back again.

"You gonna work with the Indians? Teach 'em scripture, that kind of thing?"

Kit shrugged. "I'm not sure yet."

"Government's pretty harsh on the Indians, don't you think?"

"I don't know much about it," said Kit. He paused. "I've heard … you shouldn't talk about politics here."

Rub stopped walking. "Who'd you hear that from?"

Kit glanced toward the Cathedral. "It's just … an impression I've been getting."

At the *parque central* they parted ways. Kit thought he should have been more forthcoming about his faith since Rub had given him the opportunity, but Rub's vaguely mocking tone and intrusive questioning had caught him off balance. It was probably better to wait, he decided. He couldn't say why, but the man struck him as untrustworthy.

Kit thought of climbing the Cathedral steps and looking in again but resisted the temptation.

That afternoon, Carlos took Kit for a *'viaje del vocabulario'* around the town. Kit filled a notebook page with new words. He hadn't realized that the elegant colonial building near the park housed a military headquarters—*cuartel militar*. The word for 'army' made him laugh—*ejército*—it sounded lightweight and airy like a woman's sneeze. 'The *ejército* will make a man out of you!' 'The *ejército* wants YOU!' He smiled as they passed the soldier leaning on his *macho* submachine gun in front of the bank.

Back at school, Carlos asked Kit to form questions with the word *gustar*—"to like."

"*Te gusta tu trabajo?*" Kit asked Carlos. *Do you like your work?*

Carlos shrugged. "*Mediano,*" he said, with a 'so-so' pivot of his hand.

"*¿Otra trabajo? Qué quiere?*" Kit didn't know the grammar for '*If you could, what else would you do?*' but Carlos got the gist.

"*Enseñaría a los niños en una escuela,*" he replied and wrote it on the paper for Kit to translate.

"Teach children in a regular school?" Carlos nodded. Kit had learned that his teacher understood quite a bit of English, but wasn't supposed to speak it during the lessons. "*¿Por qué… no …?*" Kit began.

Carlos shrugged again. Quietly, he said, "*No tengo amigos en posi-*

ciones importantes." He repeated it slowly for Kit to translate: 'I don't have friends in high places'—*"Además no tengo dinero para..."* '—or money for...' Carlos didn't finish the sentence but, shaking his head, held his hand just below the level of the table and rubbed his thumb and forefinger together.

Kit nodded slowly, paging through his dictionary. On the newsprint paper that covered the table, he wrote: *Soborno,* bribe. "You don't have enough money for a *soborno?"* Carlos gave a barely perceptible nod.

Phil, the director, appeared at the end of the day, dressed in a suit and tie and carrying a wrapped parcel under one arm. "I just dropped by," he said, "to mention that if you arrive at the point where you crave a bit of English conversation, I recommend Café Aurelia. Foreigners like to gather there. The food's tolerable and you can get beer from anywhere in the world. There's a marimba band on the weekends as well."

Kit put his dictionary in his backpack and reached for his notebook. Carlos was scribbling something in it. Then he closed it and handed it back to Kit. As Kit turned to say good-bye, he saw Carlos methodically black out the word *soborno* and the sentence he had written about it on the newsprint. Then Carlos took up the paper, tore it into strips and placed them in the bottom of the wastebasket. He looked up and met Kit's glance. His face was expressionless.

Guiltily, Kit turned left instead of right out the door to evade Rub. Maybe the guy was lonely. And he was at least willing to bring up the subject of faith. But Kit was tired. This day, though full of small successes, had left him exhausted.

The exhaustion vanished in a moment when nearing the *parque central* he turned a corner and saw Colleen again. She was halfway down the block standing back from the pavement and adjusting her camera lens. Across the street was a wall eight or nine feet high, embedded along the top with broken bottle shards. This particular wall enclosed an entire square block, but otherwise it seemed like any other wall in Antigua. He wondered why she was taking its picture.

When he was close enough, he called out, more casually than he felt, "¡Hola, señorita! ¿Cómo estás?" She whirled, and there was a flash of fear in her eyes before it faded and she said, "Oh. You."

He ignored her tone. "What's interesting about this wall?"

"Nothing particular," she said, putting her camera back in its case. There was a pause. She began to walk up the street and he walked alongside her. He thought of Rub and his twenty questions and kept his mouth shut.

After a short silence, she said, "How is your class?"

"Great! I feel so blessed. God's given me a very cool teacher, extremely patient."

She turned a look of annoyance on him. "Don't you ever give that a rest?"

Why pretend not to know what she was talking about? "Well," he said, smiling, "the thing is, I feel the Lord's blessing twenty-four hours a day."

She stopped and put her hands on her hips. "Is there a reason why the Lord blesses you twenty-four hours a day and leaves orphaned children to pick food out of garbage dumps seven days a week, even Sunday?"

He swallowed back the words he had been going to say: Jesus lifted me up when I was as low as a kid can get.

Then, for the second time since they met, he saw her soften at the sight of his discomfort. "How is your Spanish coming along?" she asked.

"Good," he said. They walked on in silence again.

At the end of the block, he said, "I know what you're saying, about the *real* suffering in the world. It's something we can't always understand—why God allows it."

"Why people *inflict* it."

"Yeah. Well, *that* I understand."

"You do?"

"They're filled with evil—"

"—you got *that* right—"

"—because Satan has blinded them to the sacrifice and love of the Savior."

Colleen sighed irritably. "I've had too many conversations like this in my own family. I'm fed up with it."

Kit was surprised. "Are they believers?"

She snorted. "Oh yes."

"But you're not?"

"Not anymore."

"It must be hard for them."

"Yeah, you could say that. One of my brothers is a priest and two of my sisters are nuns."

"Oh," Kit said. "You're Catholic."

"*Raised* Catholic."

"Colleen, did you ever think about becoming a Christian?" He couldn't seem to hold back the tenaciousness in his voice.

"I just told you. I was raised Catholic. I got *out* of it."

"I don't mean Catholic. I mean Christian."

"Excuse me?" she said, staring.

"Christians worship one God."

"Who do you think Catholics worship? Zeus and Athena?"

"Well, you worship saints and Mary and the Pope—"

She grabbed a tourist brochure that was protruding from his daypack, turned it over to the photos of Antigua's ruins and shoved it in his face, stabbing with a finger at the cross on the façade of the Convent of Santa Clara. "What do you think this cross represents? The Pope's hat rack?" She thrust the brochure into his hand, turned on her heel, and headed back in the direction they had come.

In his fantasies, he had assumed there would be a battle, but that he would win it through the simple persuasiveness of God's word. Now he saw how completely unprepared he was in spite of all his street preaching, in spite of praying and studying the Bible, in spite of everything he had learned from Ezra. What would it take for him to stand up to her before the Lord?

❖ Eight ❖

That night, not in the mood after all to study, he decided to follow Phil's advice and take a rest from Spanish. If the café Phil had recommended attracted English speakers, he might run into Colleen there. He left the house and strolled back through town.

A crowd of foreign backpackers was seated outside Café Aurelia. Two tables had been pushed together and were occupied by half a dozen young people who laughed and chatted over bottles of beer and the remains of a meal.

As he approached, he recognized in corner chairs at one end the Canadian couple. The girl's lift of her eyebrows gave no hint of welcome. When she leaned forward to pour beer into her glass, a young woman partly hidden on her other side, was revealed to be Colleen. He felt the blood rush to his face.

The Canadian girl turned to her boyfriend and said something under her breath. Colleen looked up, her long hair swinging off her shoulder. Her expression offered no encouragement. Across the table from them a tall, broad-shouldered boy with a slight German accent held up a bottle of beer and exclaimed in very good English, "Hey there, join us!"

Kit's height was in his favor, he thought. It made him look like someone significant, not—as he felt just then—an insecure outsider. "Thank you," he said, taking a seat on an empty chair to the left of the German, who started to pour beer into a clean glass for him. "No beer, thanks" said Kit, "but I could use some water."

The German flagged a waitress. "*Por favor, ¿me da un agua mineral?*"

Kit counted out the money and gave it to the server. The mineral water cost twice in the restaurant what it would have cost at a *tienda*.

He darted a glance at Colleen. He could count out change now. But she wasn't looking.

The boy to her left leaned in Kit's direction. "Where are you from, mate? Canada?" Kit wasn't sure about the accent—English or Australian? He had the lean, sandy-haired look of Australian characters in a movie he had once seen.

"No. U.S."

"Oh," said the boy. "A Yank." He sat back and took a swallow of his beer.

The German said, "What are you doing in Antigua?"

"I'm studying Spanish."

"Who isn't?" There was general laughter.

Next to the Australian, a French girl, whose jet-black, blunt-cut bangs hung down into her eyes, protruded her full lips to pronounce her question in English: "At which school do you study?"

"*Instituto de Español Tres Américas,*" he said, a little self-consciously, remembering his poor pronunciation when he spoke of it on the plane to Colleen.

An outburst of snorts and snickers erupted around the table, but it wasn't because of his Spanish.

"So," said the German, "you pay twice the fee of any other Spanish school in Antigua for the privilege of attending only with other Yankees?" He leaned back in his chair so far it looked as if it might tip over.

The Australian boy—his Australian movie star drawl accentuating his disdain—said, "*Tres Américas* caters to rich U.S. fundies and the CIA."

Was this what Colleen had objected to about the school? Across the table she appeared disinterested.

"*Speaking* of which," said the Canadian girl under her breath and nodded significantly toward the street. Everyone turned to watch Rub saunter up the sidewalk. Passing their table, he gave the group his languid salute and entered the cafe under the awning, stopping at a table inside where three young women were finishing a meal.

"Someone should warn them about Mr. Intelligence," said the German.

"Oh, they will soon enough find out," said the French girl. The others sniggered. Except for Colleen. Her expression was blank.

They watched Rub sit down with the women, apparently without being invited from the looks of surprise they gave each other.

"You'd think he wouldn't be so obvious about it," said the Canadian girl.

"He can't help himself," said the German. "He has no other pickup line."

"I don't think he is a CIA," said the French girl. "Maybe once, but they—how do you say it?—'booted' him out."

"Yah," said the German. "He's too much of a drunk."

"What are you talking about? The CIA is full of drunks," said the Canadian girl.

"He told me the government was hard on the Indians," Kit said, feeling an impulse to defend Rub.

The French girl and the Australian and German laughed. In a clear imitation of Rub's gravelly voice, they barked out in unison, " 'The government is pretty harsh on the Indians, don't you think—*amigo?'* "

"But why would he ask everyone that question if he wasn't in the CIA anymore?" said the Canadian girl.

"Because he is like a dog who is taken on a long walk. He must piss on every lamp post even when he is out of his territory," said the French girl.

"What else is he going to do with himself except play the role of Mr. Interrogator?" added the German.

Rub rose from where he was sitting with the three women.

"Oh dear," the French girl laughed. "He has been shot down so quickly."

As Rub sauntered by their table, the German, with a wink at the rest of them, hailed him over. "Come sit with us," he said. Rub paused, then took the chair on the other side of the German's and looked around for a waiter.

"So," said the German, leaning back in his chair with a mocking smile. "I have heard that you are a G-man. Is this true?"

Rub turned an appraising gaze on him. " 'G-man'," he said blandly, also leaning back in his chair so that the two of them looked like belligerent, precarious bookends. "G-man!" Rub repeated. "Christ, I haven't heard that expression since I was a kid. Where'd you pick it up? Maybe an old American comic book some GI gave your mother when we pulled out of her hometown?"

All eyes turned on the German now, who took only the slightest beat before hooking his elbow over the back of his chair and stretching his long legs out in front of him. "So tell me, Rub. If you are a *Gee*-man—" he emphasized the syllable "—aren't *Gee*-men supposed to be inconspicuous? Don't you have to fade into the crowd?" He drew his fingers up and down his cheeks in a scrubbing motion, and Kit realized he was making fun of Rub's acne-pitted skin. "It would be a handicap, I suppose. *If* you are a *Gee*-man. Perhaps this explains your nickname."

Kit looked away. The French girl's pouting lips were partly open, caught halfway to a smile. Colleen was sitting very straight. Kit turned back to Rub again.

His expression hadn't changed, but he tilted his chin up slightly and cocked his head to one side. Kit knew the posture was meant to convey indifference and disdain, but now that he could see it from the outside, he was shocked to realize how much else it revealed. Suddenly, he cut in.

"Your Spanish is like a native speaker's," he said to Rub. "You must be good at languages."

Without changing the angle of his head, still gazing blandly at the German from under half closed eyelids, he said, "Learning a language is like learning to screw." The Australian boy slapped a hand appreciatively on the table. His hand lay close to Colleen's elbow. "Almost anyone can do it," Rub continued. "The finesse comes in giving satisfaction." Over his shoulder he said to Kit, "For example, you wouldn't say 'G-man' because you'd heard it in some old black and white movie from the `fifties and wanted to sound like a tough American. The right word for the right time in the right place—" Here he looked directly at the German. "Beyond simple screwing, it's the delicate touch that brings the lady off." Kit felt a blush rise to his face.

Rub stood up then and slid the chair back into the table, grazing the German's outstretched legs. The three women at the table inside glanced up, then bent their heads over their bill. "Well," Rub said. "I got things to do." Turning to leave, he nodded at Kit and saluted.

Before Rub was quite out of earshot, the German laughed and slapped his knee. "The man is a fucking cartoon!" he said.

Kit glanced at Colleen. Her eyes looked very blue and her skin tan against the pale turquoise of her gauzy shirt. She hadn't said anything during this conversation but had sat back, close-mouthed.

The Australian was stealing a tortilla from the French girl's plate, and she slapped his hand. The Canadian boy said to the German, "You know, if he really *is* CIA, you probably ought to be more careful."

The German took a swig of his beer. "What is he going to do, have me disappeared? The German embassy isn't like the American Embassy. It would actually *do* something." Turning to Kit he said, "So which kind of American are you? Born-again or CIA goon?"

Kit put down his glass. He had to be dignified, not defiant, not fanatical. He took a breath. "I've been given new life through the sacrifice of our Savior."

Around the table there was a collective grimace, except from Colleen. She opened her mouth and seemed about to say something.

The German said, "So if we have not been saved like you, we are all to burn in hell? Is that the idea?"

<u>You</u> *will*, thought Kit. He immediately banished the sentiment to the mental trash can where he shoved all his unworthy, sinful thoughts, and tried to bring his restless leg under control.

Before he could gather his wits for a reply, the German said, "If I believed in such a being as your Satan, I would say he had got hold of you born-agains and cleverly tricked you into making Christianity a weapon against the poor." Kit looked around at the others. The Canadians, the Australian, the French girl were watching him carefully, like a pack of dogs waiting for the snarl of the leader, the signal that they could all join in the attack. Kit hoped they couldn't see the subtle trembling that had taken possession of him.

I only came here for some company.

He felt his eyes start to well up. Horrified, he prayed, Jesus, please no, don't let me lose it in front of …

"What are *you* doing in Guatemala?" From the end of the table, Colleen spoke for the first time. She was staring at the German.

He and the others turned to her. Kit blinked and wiped away the impending tears. The German's pale blue eyes fastened on Colleen with a flirtatious glint. He said, "I am meeting interesting people like you. I am trekking for six months before I go back to university. Experiencing the beauty of Mayan ruins, the mountains, sea. I enjoy the freedom of carrying everything I need on my back—"

"In other words—" interrupted Colleen, "you're taking advantage of the low cost of living in this land of extreme poverty?"

He narrowed his eyes. Then he smiled as if amused. "You are a Yank, too? But I suppose you're not CIA. Does that make you a born-again?"

"You're a German," she replied. "I suppose you're not a Nazi?"

The French girl laughed.

He threw up his hands in mock surrender. "Okay, I get it. But, you know, I would not have taken you for an American."

This, Kit realized, was meant as a compliment.

"You mean," said Colleen, "you wouldn't have taken me for a Canadian or a Brazilian or a Mexican?"

"Yes, yes. They are all Americans, of course we know that, but it's you from the States who claim the word as your own."

"Did you hear me use it?"

This shut the German up. He poured beer into his glass and everyone was quiet while he drank. Then he said to Colleen, "So what are *you* doing here?"

She pulled the strap of her camera case over her shoulder and got up. "Exactly the same as the rest of you," she said. She lay some coins on the table and left.

Kit sat immobile, watching her.

She was halfway down the street already when he pushed back his chair and rose to go. "See you," he mumbled over his shoulder to the group and hurried after her. He heard the Australian drawl loudly, "That's the Yanks for you."

He overtook her as she turned onto the dark, quiet street behind the cathedral.

"Hey, wait up," he said, trying to sound casual. When she saw who it was, she shook her head and kept on walking.

73

"You are not going to save my soul, Kit."

Kit. It was the first time she had called him by name. It felt as if she had put out a hand and touched him.

"I'm not," he said. "I was just wondering if what they were saying about my school was true. It only admits Americans?"

Well," she stopped walking, "have you met any other students there who weren't from the U.S.?"

He hadn't. "I guess not. But why would they only admit *us*?"

She shrugged. "I suppose they prefer fees in dollars. Doesn't it always come down to money? And of course these rich mission churches are gold mines that never give out."

"My church isn't rich at all," he said.

"Really? And yet your pastor paid you to come down here to proselytize. The money came from somewhere. Did he fleece the congregation or is he one of those televangelists—nine tenths of the donations socked into personal investments in the Cayman Islands?"

He felt a tremendous sense of relief. She wasn't right about everything.

"My pastor isn't paid by the church. He's a furniture salesman. He and his wife took money out of their personal savings to send me here."

"So they say."

"No," Kit said firmly. He knew he was on solid ground. He reached for her arm. "Colleen," he said, thrilling a little to the sound of her name in his mouth and the sensation of her slender forearm under the gauzy fabric of her shirt. "I know my pastor. I've seen absolute, one hundred percent proof of his integrity. I started out more skeptical than you. I *spied* on him. Ezra—" the name sounded sacred as he said it "—he is on the inside exactly what he looks like on the outside."

He waited for her to shake off his hand, but she didn't, and after a moment when they just looked at each other—her expression obscured by the darkness—he took it away of his own accord.

"Another thing," he said, "is I wanted to tell you ... It was nice of you to stand up for me back there. I don't know why you did it."

"I hate bullying," she said. "Also ... you're so ... transparent."

"What does that mean?"

"Just ..." she shrugged and started walking again.

It was cold now, and she undid a sweater that was tied around her waist and put it on. He thought of putting his arm around her shoulders but didn't. They walked together in silence and soon emerged from behind the cathedral to cross the street that faced the *parque central*. Barely illuminated by the few dim streetlights, all along the sidewalk lay dark oddly-shaped bundles.

"What—?" he asked, but almost as soon as the word was out of his mouth, he got his answer. Indigenous people—children, men, women, young and old—were curled up together like sleeping animals, the whole length of the sidewalk. Some were covered with thin scraps of blankets, most only by their clothing. They lay on the bare stone or on pieces of newspaper or cardboard. Kit thought of the cotton blanket on his bed at Martinez's—how he had to lay a sweater and jacket over it at night and still wasn't warm enough.

"Oh man," he whispered.

"Yeah," Colleen said.

"Where do they wash? Where do they go to the bathroom?"

"Good question."

At the corner, Colleen paused, unzipped her camera case and reached in, but then pulled her hand out. She stood looking away from him for a moment as if undecided about something.

"Well," she said in a subdued voice, "this is where I turn off."

They were standing in front of the bank, where the soldier usually stood guard. He was not on duty now.

"Where are you staying?" Kit said. "I'll walk you."

"Not necessary." She hiked her camera case around to her back. "I'll see you around."

In the darkness he watched her walk a block and a half up *5ta Avenida Norte*, then turn in at a gate a few yards before the Santa Catalina arch. *Pensión El Arco*. It was where he had stayed the first two nights, probably the cheapest *pensión* in Antigua.

He stood for some moments listening, as if for the echo of her sandals on the stone courtyard. He imagined the metallic click of her key in the padlock, the creak of the door. What room would she have? Maybe she would lie down on the same bed where he had lain reading his Bible.

Whosoever looketh on a woman to lust after her …

He hummed "His Eyes Are on the Sparrow" and kicked a loose stone along the sidewalk until it fell into the street.

It was only 9:30. There was still another hour before the Martinezes' front door would be locked for the night. He crossed the street to the *parque central*. It was getting colder now and he zipped up his jacket before sitting down on a bench. Here and there along the sidewalk across the street, the sleeping people stirred. He closed his eyes and shut out the sight.

Still lingering was the sensation of her arm under his fingertips. That moment when he stood with her in silence after he told her about Ezra. He imagined himself taking her hands and drawing her to him in the silence, enfolding her in his arms, kissing her lips, her neck, her shoulders.

The flesh lusteth against the Spirit, and the Spirit against the flesh: and these are contrary the one to the other: so that ye cannot do the things that ye would. Ezra had praised him once for passing this same kind of test.

Kit raised his face in the darkness toward the place where the cross on the hill overlooked Antigua. *Keep thyself pure,* he thought, then realized he had said it aloud. But as he felt his head tip up, he imagined her face tilting, her eyes closed, to receive his kiss. Her long hair skimming the backs of his hands as his arms went around her.

There was a faint, distant click in the darkness. Kit's eyes fluttered open and caught the flash of a bright light across the street, momentarily illuminating the huddled, sleeping people. A slender figure was slipping away toward the end of the block and around the corner out of sight. His heart beat fast. He wanted to run after her, but he controlled himself. Why had she waited until he was gone to snap the picture? Maybe she didn't want him to think of her as a hypocrite. Maybe she wanted his good opinion.

Walking slowly back to the Candelaria, he thought about what Ezra would have to say about his lust. He remembered the scene he had come on two years before—arriving at the church unexpectedly and entering at the back.

A single light illuminated Ezra kneeling and praying silently at the wooden cross. He looked almost like a little boy, half drowning in his oversized clothes and completely oblivious to his appearance.

Not wanting to disturb Ezra at prayer, Kit stood in the shadows at the back. The side door opened. Karen, the pretty, petite church pianist, stood there. She was gazing at Ezra with fervor in her eyes. Kit held very still, afraid.

"Pastor," Karen said in a choked voice. Ezra turned, with that unfocussed look of someone coming out of a deep, dream-filled sleep. "I'm sorry to interrupt you, you're praying."

Ezra got up stiffly as if he had been on his knees for a long time. Karen began to sob into her hands. Ezra took a step toward her. "What is it, Karen? Shall we pray about it together?" he said. He put a hand on her shoulder, and at his touch, she closed her eyes and wrapped her arms around his neck, drawing him to her and pressing her cheek to his. "I love you," she cried, through her sobs.

Under the dim light of the overhead lamp, they looked young and dramatic like star-crossed lovers in a movie. Kit felt a thrill in his groin, and, at the same time, dread.

Without speaking, Ezra stepped away and gently led Karen, still crying, to a chair in the front row before the cross and sat down next to her. From his pocket, he took out an old-fashioned white handkerchief and put it in her hands.

"I don't know why someone as sweet and pretty as you would do me the honor of loving me as a woman loves a man, Karen." She raised her head and looked into his eyes. "You're maybe a little blinded by the role I play as your pastor." She shook her head. "But I understand that your feelings are deep and sincere and that you're crying because you know that to act on such feelings is a sin. You know that I'm joined with Jeannette for all of our life. Our union is sacred and beautiful in the eyes of the Lord. And in my eyes too, Karen. Nothing can ever break it."

Nothing can ever break it.

Tears were spilling down her cheeks. She mopped at them with the handkerchief and nodded.

"But when our Lord chooses to bring you together with a godly Christian man who is free to return your love, that man will be a very fortunate fellow because you are a good and devout woman." She shook her head vehemently. "Yes," he said. "You are."

Then he closed his eyes and put his hands together. Slowly, she bent her head.

"Dear Lord," he prayed, "we thank you for the gift of romantic passion which you have given to humans, that we may unite in worldly love with the one who will be our partner through life. And we pray that when loneliness leads one of your children to bestow that worldly love upon a person other than the one you command, you will help her to transform that affection into an abiding and more fervent love for You. Father, lead your daughter Karen toward the peace that comes from embracing with a whole heart your Holy Commandments. Amen."

He stood up. Karen stayed seated in her chair, her head bowed. Kit's heart was racing. He felt like a thief, rifling through Ezra's private drawer of temptation.

Karen rose finally, and, still clutching the handkerchief, allowed Ezra to guide her by the elbow to the door. Ezra held the door for her and waited in the doorway. Kit heard the sound of her car engine and the crunch of the wheels on the gravel. He slipped out the back.

That night in his small room at Martinezes' he asked God to show him how to bring Colleen to Christ, and he prayed to resist the temptation of lust. To that end, he picked up his vocabulary notebook and turned to the words he had learned on his *viaje del vocabulario* that day. He paused for a moment, puzzled. In the middle of the page was a thick oblong of black ink. Then he realized what it was. Carlos had blotted out the words *cuartel militar*. Was it political just to write the words?

❖ Nine ❖

His Spanish was progressing. On Wednesday he spent an hour in the park after lunch drawing the indigenous children and found he could communicate with them in phrases and simple sentences. The children ran around the plaza excitedly waving their portraits at each other. "*Mira! Mira!*" they cried. —Look! Look!

Whatever Kit pointed to they shouted the name in unison: paper —*papel*! pencil —*lápiz*! sidewalk —*acera*! But when he pointed toward the city hall and the bank across the street to learn the word for "building," the children went silent, and their eager round eyes grew solemn. It was the soldier, Kit realized. The soldier, whose presence he had begun to take for granted, stood guard as usual in front of the bank, the submachine gun propped against his thigh, one of his hands wrapped casually around the barrel. Kit turned and pointed to the block of buildings across the plaza from the cathedral. It took the children a moment to recover before they shouted, "*¡Edificios!*"

His brain was tired after a day of lessons and *Señor* Martinez's drilling at dinner. He had to drag himself out to prayer service, but he was glad he did, for as soon as he rounded the corner and saw the stream of worshippers heading into the open door of the little storefront *iglesia*, as soon as he heard the guitar chords and the lively percussion of the tambourine he hurried inside.

There were several faces in the congregation that he recognized now from his earlier visit, almost like being at home. A warmth of affection and nostalgia rose in him for Light and Life Tabernacle and the people there who knew and loved him. When the prayer leader instructed the congregation to greet their neighbors, Kit enthusiastically shook out-stretched hands and bent to return offered embraces.

Blessed Savior, thank you for bringing me to Guatemala, to this life-changing experience, he prayed. Please keep guiding me in the right path, Lord, and help me overcome my ignorance. Open Colleen's heart to your word and lead the Martinez family away from idolatry. Bless Ezra and Jeannette, Lorie and Edie and Claudia ...

He couldn't bring himself to include Dean's name, though Ezra would have wanted him to. A tug of guilt yanked him out of his serenity, but only for a moment. The soaring praise, the clapping and shouting, though all in Spanish, drew him back. "*Gloria, Gloria a Dios, Aleluya, Amén.*"

Students finished their terms and were replaced by new ones, but the Mennonite Bontragers, the sisters Myrna and Sunshine—still waiting for their boy Roli to be released—and Chuck Nystrom—Rub—continued to come every day. Kit didn't see much of them outside of class, but as the weeks passed, he felt a certain satisfaction in being one of the "old timers." Rub seemed distant since the incident at Aurelia's. There was no more bantering call of *"amigo"* from across the courtyard. He usually took himself off at lunch time and after school, like a man with things to do.

The hours in class went by so fast that Kit was startled sometimes when Carlos, with a *"Bien!"* pushed back from the table and stood up. Kit would think a new *ejemplo* was about to be demonstrated before he realized that his teacher was ready for his lunch.

After three weeks of silence, a pile of postcards and letters arrived at the same time. There was a chatty one from his mother, enclosing school pictures of Lorie and Edie. It shocked him to see how grown up they looked. Being away from them so long, he had begun to remember them as the toddlers they had been when he was still living at Dean's house. There were also letters from Jeannette and Ezra and a stack of postcards from members of the congregation. Nothing, of course, from Dean.

Following lunch alone at *Señora* Martinez's long kitchen table each day, he walked around town for half an hour, stopping to sketch a carved doorway or a grilled window. He was always a little on the lookout for Colleen. After school he sat in the *parque central* and sketched people.

Children and teenagers continued to flock for their pencil portraits, and now, at the bottom of each drawing he wrote in Spanish, "Come to the Lord Jesus Christ for life everlasting." The *ladino* children in their school uniforms would read the inscription and ask if he was a priest. "Just an ordinary follower of Jesus," he replied. The indigenous children— standing with skinny hips cocked to accommodate a sleeping toddler or a bundle of belongings, seldom asked the question, and he realized that few of them could read what he had written.

In the Martinez household the adult and teenage children treated him with polite indifference. He wondered if they shared their father's resentment at the necessity of having him there. But probably they were just busy with their lives and their friends. They had seen *Tres Américas* boarders come and go. The younger children he won over by treating them as experts in their language. He didn't mind their teasing him for his mistakes in pronunciation. "*No es uste̲d̲d̲, Cristóbal. Es uste̲d̲,*" Sara, the youngest, liked to chide him. With the children's earnest tutoring, he was beginning to lose some of his lazy-sounding *gringo* accent.

He attended Sunday services and Wednesday evening prayer meetings at the *iglesia*. He had begun to introduce himself as Cristóbal. It was, he thought, a righteous name. Members of the *iglesia* invited him to dinners at their homes. They were kind and patient with his struggle to express himself, but when the evening ended he was glad to escape.

He was beginning to understand words and phrases in the Guatemalan newspaper *Prensa Libre*, but there were days when he was so tired of coping with Spanish that he picked up *The New York Times*, which Rita delivered to school every day. It was a relief, almost fun, to read *The New York Times* in English. One week he read a long article about the lifting of a ban on military sales to Guatemala because violence had declined since Ríos Montt took power. He tore it out to show Colleen if he saw her again.

At church on the second Sunday in February, Kit was pleased when the prayer leader handed out a flyer which he could translate: On Sunday, February 27 at 8:30 a special bus would take members of the congregation to a church service at *Iglesia del Verbo*—Church of the Word—in

Guatemala City, where the Chief of State, the evangelical General Efraín Ríos Montt himself, would be preaching. For this, Kit decided, he could justify the expense of the bus fare. He wrote that day to tell Ezra and Jeannette the news.

That afternoon he spent a pleasant few hours helping the Martinez children make *cascarones* for their *carnaval* parties at school. *Cascarones*, Kit found out the hard way, were decorated eggshells, hollowed out and filled with confetti, to be cracked over the heads of unsuspecting victims. All over town peoples' hair and shoulders glittered with confetti, and he soon knew from suppressed giggling behind him, to brace himself for the crack and the laughter that would follow. *Carnaval* came just before Lent. On February 16 the foreheads of everyone in Antigua were smeared with ashes. It was the beginning of the largest celebration of Lent and Holy Week in all of North and South America. This he learned from Rita, who had come to school that Monday and handed out a mimeographed schedule of processions, vigils—called *velaciónes*— and funeral march band concerts over the next six weeks.

From Wednesday on, it seemed that every time he turned a corner he was met with a solemn procession of thirty or forty men dressed in purple robes and white head coverings held on by braid. The men, all of the same height, carried on their shoulders enormous flower-draped floats—*andas*—weighing two or three tons and bearing intricately carved and brilliantly painted life-size wooden effigies of the disciples, or grieving Virgin Marys crying tears of real diamonds, or bleeding Christs bent under the weight of a gilded cross twined with relief carvings of grape vines. *Graven images* was the phrase that came to Kit's mind.

Then, on the first Friday of Lent, the statue of the *Jesús Nazareno*, which resided at La Merced Church, was paraded to the cathedral and back along streets covered by *alfombras*—carpets of flowers and colored sawdust.

If you overlooked the strain on the bearers' faces, the massive hardwood *anda* and its larger than life sculpture appeared to float like a ship on a gently rocking sea of purple waves. On all sides, as the float swayed along, onlookers crossed themselves. Tears streamed down peoples' faces. The bearers, under the tremendous weight of the *anda*, moved forward with extreme slowness as if they were carrying the Savior Himself, and Kit found he had to turn away. It was a statue, and they were worshipping it like a god.

But he couldn't resist turning back for another glimpse and then could not tear his eyes from it. The figure's shining brown eyes seemed to gaze both inward and upward, conveying in a single expression intense love, wonder, hope, terror, and joy. Its parted lips seemed on the point of speaking: *Now what I've told you is coming to pass.*

On Monday morning all the teachers rotated. Wistfully and with a twinge of jealousy, Kit waved at Carlos, who was now at a table across the courtyard, laughing and chatting in Spanish with the bearded Mennonite, Bontrager.

"*Lo siento, Señor Lamb,*" Kit's new teacher, Berto, apologized each day as he ambled in late, throwing up his hands in a gesture of resignation. "*Tuve que solucionar un problema personal.*" Always some personal problem.

Kit missed Carlos's helpful *ejemplos*. Whatever Kit didn't understand, Carlos explained with an example. Which *be* verb describes people: *ser* or *estar*? "*Depende si es una condición o una característic. Por ejemplo: Kit está listo*"—Kit is ready—" *pero Kit es listo*"—Kit is clever—."

"*Lo siento, Señor Lamb.*" On Thursday, Berto begged off two hours early for some vaguely described appointment in Guatemala City. Tomorrow they would study two extra hours, he promised.

Left with a free afternoon, Kit wandered down the cobbled street with no destination in mind, but with the habitual, half-suppressed hope of running into Colleen.

He had not, so far, overcome his reluctance to visit the massive ruins of colonial churches, convents and monasteries. But today the glimpses of quiet, colonnaded courtyards through great arched porticos tugged hard at the artist in him. It was probably all right to have a look. God might even want him to see how the temples of idolaters had been reduced to rubble. ... *God's destruction cometh as a whirlwind...*

At the corner of *2da Avenida Norte y 2da Calle Oriente*, he came to the entrance of the *Convento de Las Capuchinas*. He walked in behind a middle-aged tourist in a blouse embroidered at the cuffs and neckline with *quetzal* birds and a Mayan sash for a camera strap. He wandered behind her down a dark stone passageway to an inner patio surrounded by a circular gallery of tiny, austere rooms. The woman took several snapshots of a bush heavy with pink flowers and then sat down on the edge of a dry fountain.

"Bougainvillea," she said, with a Minnesota accent. "I sure wish I could grow it, but we're too far north."

Kit smiled politely. "You see flowers like that and you just want to thank God for such a gift," he said. He wasn't really in the mood to evangelize, but it would be negligent to waste the opportunity. Apparently taking no notice of his comment, however, she said, "Have you been to the cellar room?" She jumped up and exclaimed, "Oh, you've got to experience it! I'll show you."

She led him back into the passageway and down a flight of wide stone stairs. At first there was no sound except the echo of their footsteps. Then, from somewhere below came a voice—a pure, sweet alto, rippling like water.

"Oh," said the woman. "Someone else has found it, too." She took his arm and hurried him along.

The stairs led to a low-ceilinged underground room. A small embrasure high up on the wall provided the only light. In the center of the room, a squat, hour-glass-shaped pillar fluted outward where it supported the ceiling.

Some wild, fluttering bird beat its wings inside Kit's ribcage, for just under the curve of the pillar stood Colleen, singing. She stood slim and tall. Her arms hung at her sides and her chin was lifted only slightly, but she looked as if she could have raised the ceiling with just her voice. It filled the chamber with a stream of pure, soaring notes that resonated off every surface and sent a shock of desire through his body.

His companion scurried down the last few stairs and danced over to Colleen. "I see you've found it, too!"

To Kit's astonishment she began to accompany Colleen, at first in a thin, quavery soprano; then, drawing confidence from the acoustics, in perfect, resonating harmony.

Colleen stopped singing. She smiled at him. "It's a round," she said. "It needs a third part. Can you sing?" He nodded. "It goes like this," she said, and the two women sang the simple melody through together:

> *Dona nobis*
> *Pacem, pacem*
> *Dona nobis*
> *Pacem.*

Kit picked it up on the first try.

Colleen began again. Her voice spiraled up the pillar and cascaded down from the ceiling. The woman joined in, pealing out like an answering bell. When Kit opened his mouth, his profound *basso* poured out, lifting the other voices and melting into them with a resonance that filled his whole body. Kit fixed his gaze on Colleen's face, and she—who had never done more than glance his way—gazed back.

The singing went on and on. Each time the soaring melody seemed to draw to a close, Kit was ready with another breath to go again. From far away there came the sound of footsteps on the stairs, and Kit became vaguely aware of other faces peering in, but his eyes stayed fastened on Colleen's and they kept on singing.

Abruptly the soprano voice stopped. The woman had abandoned her turn and the whole thing was over. Kit and Colleen stood in silence, looking at each other.

There was a scattering of applause from the stairs, and then a few tourists came forward to try singing themselves. Two children ran up, hooting and listening for their voices to be thrown back at them. Finally, Colleen looked away. From his face to his knees, Kit felt drenched with heat.

"Wasn't that amazing?" exclaimed the woman. "They say they don't know what this room was for, but golly, what *else* could it have been used for? Well—" She opened her guidebook again and drifted toward the stairs. "I thank you for the musical experience!"

Colleen stooped to pick up her camera case. "Have you been to the roof?" she said.

She led the way up the two flights. With each step her shining brown hair swung across her back. One of her shoulders was raised slightly to keep the camera strap from sliding off. If he had dared, Kit would have slipped the strap from her shoulder, slung it over his own, and taken her hand.

Sunlight slanted across the stone stairwell from the second floor, which the ancient earthquake had opened to the sky. Colleen walked to the edge and stood a few feet away from it, looking out. To the south and west the slopes of *Agua, Fuego* and *Acatenango* joined the more distant mountains that made up the horizon. Below were the lanes, inner courtyards, and roofs of Antigua.

"I love this view," she said. He followed her to the edge.

"What were we singing?"

"The *Dona nobis*."

"Is it—Spanish?"

She laughed. "Haven't you ever heard Latin?"

"Oh." He reddened. "Yeah." But there had been no ridicule in her voice. "What do the words mean?"

"They mean, 'Give us peace, peace. Give us peace, peace.' It's sung a lot in Catholic masses." Kit lifted his eyebrows. She nodded. "Yup. You just sang in the language of the Catholic mass."

Kit shook his head. "Oh, boy."

"Sorry about that," she said. Kit took her hand. For just a moment her fingers curled lightly around his before she slipped them away.

She looked intently over the town.

"Are you going to take a picture of it?" Kit said, nodding at her camera.

She paused for just a moment before replying, airily, "No, I've got plenty of volcano pictures."

"Well, I think *I* will." He took Jeannette's instamatic from his day pack and backed up a few steps. "Stay there, and I'll get you in the foreground."

Quickly she moved out of range. "No, no, don't take my picture."

"Why not? You're not *Maya*, are you?" He lowered the camera. "See? I remembered what you told me."

She smiled, distracted, and continued to side step around him. "Yeah, well …"

He aimed his camera at her again and she darted away.

"Come on!" he said. "Are you one of those pretty girls who thinks she looks bad in pictures? My Mom is like that."

"Yeah, sort of—" She walked across the rooftop, keeping her back to him.

"Okay. I won't," he called. He put his camera away and followed her to the other side. "But you're wrong. I hope you know that God blessed you with amazing beauty—" Instantly, he wished he could take it back. Idiot! The timing was completely wrong, to say nothing of his sounding stiff and artificial. "Oh, man!" he blurted, before she could reply. "You're going to think I never have anything on my mind but religion."

She had turned and was looking at him with a chilly expression. "No," she said. "I just think it's bizarre how some men seem to have nothing on their minds but conquest."

"*Conquest*!" His heart sank. "I'm not thinking of conquest."

"You aren't? This isn't a case of sweet talking a soul for Jesus? A snow job for the Savior? That's what I call killing two birds with one stone. And you know what?" Her voice was becoming shrill. "This whole country is getting the same goddamn treatment. Sweet talk the poor with Bible platitudes, then round them up and screw them over."

Kit flushed. "What are you *talking* about? You think *I've* got a one track mind. Listen to *yourself*. Every conversation, you turn into a political thing."

She drew back sharply. With a strained smile she said, "I probably do. I just read too many books. Sorry." She touched his arm. It wasn't at all a friendly gesture but a fake-friendly one, and it hurt him more than the accusations she had just made.

"Well," she said, affecting a light, jokey tone, "it was nice praying for peace with you." She crossed the roof and disappeared down the stairs. Kit hit the side of his head with his fist.

"*God!*" he exclaimed then drew an anxious breath through his teeth. Forgive, me Lord. Forgive me.

On his way back to school after lunch the following Friday, as he walked down *3era Avenida Oriente*, he saw two indigenous women squatted in a recessed doorway and pressed up against the door as if to make themselves inconspicuous. One held a baby in her lap. As Kit approached, the other woman silently held up a *huipil*. There was no stack of textiles beside them; this was the only garment they were selling.

It was different from any *huipil* he had seen at the market—a deep, true red embroidered with a procession of whimsical multicolored figures across the center: strange birds and cats, a tiny man standing on a cat's back. Zigzags and diamonds formed another line across the shoulders, and at the neck a pattern of thin white threads that reminded him of sputtering sparklers.

The women themselves wore plain white cotton blouses, stained and dirty. He knelt on the pavement and let the woman put the garment into his hands. It was of heavy handwoven cotton, soft, like well-worn jeans. He thought of Jeannette's crowded beds of zinnias, bachelor buttons, and marigolds. How she would love this.

"It's very pretty," he said in Spanish. "Your work is very good."

They gave no response, no gap-toothed grins or encouraging nods as there would have been in the market. Perhaps they only spoke a Mayan language and didn't understand Spanish, or at least his Spanish.

"*¿Cuánto cuesta?*" he asked.

"*Veinte quetzales,*" said the woman with the baby. Twenty dollars. The cheapest *huipiles* at the market cost thirty to thirty-five dollars. He considered it. But even twenty dollars was too much. Ezra's and Jeannette's money had to last.

"I'm sorry," he said, shaking his head. "I don't have much money." He rose to his feet, handing the *huipil* back to her, but she wouldn't take it.

"*¿Cuánto?*" she said, tonelessly.

He shook his head. That week he had sat down with himself and decided on ten dollars for all gifts put together, no more, if that. He laid the *huipil* in her lap and backed away. "I'm sorry. It's very beautiful, your *huipil*, but—"

"*¿Cuánto?*" the woman called, rising a little. The baby's head lolled on her lap, and its half closed eyes moved listlessly.

"I only have *diez quetzales.*" He held out his empty palms.

The first woman picked up the *huipil* again and waved it at him. "*Diez quetzales,*" she said. "*Está bien.*"

He hesitated, would have said, "I'm not trying to bargain with you. I just can't spend more than that." But he wasn't sure how to say it in Spanish, and now she had risen and brought the *huipil* back to him. She was gazing at him with dull black eyes.

At last he took out two five-*quetzal* bills from his pocket and handed them to her. She hung the *huipil* over his arm and stuffed the bills under the sash of her skirt. The other woman stood up then, slipping the baby into a shawl slung across her chest. The two moved slowly down the sidewalk without looking back.

"*Gracias,*" Kit said.

Phil and Rita were in the courtyard when he came back to school. The *huipil* still hung over his arm.

"Ohh, Kit! Let us see what you have!" said Rita.

"You got sucked into the market, I see. Let's have a look," said Phil, pulling out a pair of glasses.

Kit didn't want to show the garment, but it was too late, Rita had snatched it from his arm.

"Ohh, pret-ty, pret-ty!" she exclaimed.

"Very nice indeed," said Phil, fingering the embroidery. He turned it over and touched a stain on the back. "Authentic stuff. From the *Ixil* region. You didn't get this at the market."

"No," Kit said, reluctantly. "It was from two women on the street, in a doorway."

"Oh *ho*!" exclaimed Phil. "That was a lucky break. They were selling illegally. They're supposed to buy a permit to sell from the market. What did you pay?"

"Ten dollars," Kit said, embarrassed.

"Not bad at all." Phil sniffed at the fabric. "Smell that." The cotton folds gave off a smell of wood smoke and something faintly like sweat. "That's straight off someone's back." He arched an eyebrow. "Someone who won't need it anymore, I should think. Hand-dyed, one hundred percent cotton. A lot of them weave their own clothes with polyester now—can't afford the cotton thread. Yes, you did very nicely indeed. A pity you couldn't get the whole *traje*, though—skirt, head wrap, waist sash—the whole kit." A bit reluctantly, it seemed, he relinquished the *huipil*.

"He could have get that one for less," Rita chimed in. "They will sell for what you say."

"I wasn't trying to bargain," Kit said. He folded the *huipil* and put it out of sight in his day pack.

During the break, which Berto usually drew out to half an hour, Kit read through the school's copy of *The New York Times*. Scanning the front section, his eye caught the word Guatemala in an article captioned "U.S. Rights Reports on 12 Nations Criticized." He had to read the article twice to understand it. Human rights groups— Who? Americas Watch, Helsinki Watch, Lawyers for International Human Rights—were saying that the Reagan administration's report on human rights had let some countries off the hook on their abuses because they were friends of the U.S. Guatemala was one. Kit frowned. He wanted to ask Phil or Rita about the article, but remembered Colleen's warning.

That night he took the red *huipil* out of his day pack. He found he couldn't look at it. The baby came to mind, its lolling head. The women's insistence, *¿Cuánto?* He slid the *huipil* under his t-shirts in the bottom drawer of his dresser. *Diez quetzales. Está bien.* He could have gotten it for even less.

On Sunday morning, Kit was the first to arrive at *La Polvera*, the empty lot—once the site of a gunpowder factory, hence the name—where the buses came and went. It was the day that members of his *iglesia* were going to Guatemala City to hear Ríos Montt preach.

On the bus a small, red-cheeked *ladino* man in his thirties took the seat next to him and introduced himself as Daniel Meijia. He shook Kit's hand and told him in heavily accented English that he managed the *Hotel Los Conquistadores*. Kit knew the hotel. Through its half open carved wood doors, he had several times glimpsed the aquamarine water of a swimming pool in an inner courtyard and tables spread with snowy white tablecloths and arrangements of tropical flowers.

Being in hotel management, said Daniel, it was necessary to become fluent in English, and although he admitted his speaking "no is good," he welcomed opportunities to practice with English-speaking foreigners.

Daniel talked for much of the trip about *Hermano Efraín*—Brother *Efraín*—the president of Guatemala, *El General José Efraín Ríos Montt*, whom he spoke of with almost the same reverence he used in speaking of *Nuestro Señor y Rey*, our Lord and King.

"*Hermano Efraín*, God send him for save Guatemala from the evil one. Our leaders before *Efraín* did not care about the *corrupción* and killing the innocent people. They are themselves doing these things. *El General* no permit these. He is not weak. Those without morality he punish."

A woman across the aisle held out orange slices on a napkin for them. Daniel was quiet for a few minutes while he ate. They were traveling through the mountains now. The tiny terraced plots clinging to the steep slopes struck Kit as before. Who did they belong to?

"Yes," said Daniel as if the monologue had been continuing in his head. "Ríos Montt is *dictador*. But is good *dictador*, like strong father. *Autoritario*. Your *presidente* Ronald Reagan speak that *Ríos Montt* is a man high of *integridad, rectitud*." Daniel had watched *Ríos Montt's* long Sunday sermons on television many times, but this would be his first chance to hear him preach in person. Next week, Daniel informed Kit, the Pope was coming to Guatemala, but he, Daniel, would not go to Guatemala City to hear him speak, not take even one minute to see it on television. "No! General Ríos Montt a thousand times is more than the Pope a *cristiano auténtico*!"

By the time the bus pulled up in front of Ríos Montt's *Iglesia Cristiana del Verbo* Kit was beginning to catch some of Daniel's excitement. The church the president of the country belonged to turned out to be a large green and yellow striped circus tent erected next to a hotel. Inside, the seating consisted of rows and rows of ordinary folding chairs much like the ones at Light and Life Tabernacle. Sunlight filtered through the striped canvas of the tent roof. People of all ages, mostly prosperous-looking, middle-class *ladinos*—six or seven hundred of them, maybe even a thousand—had almost filled the tent. More were still pouring in.

Voices shrill with excitement resounded off the metal chairs and mingled with the amplified music. Friends and relatives lavished kisses and hugs and broad smiles on each other. Keyed up children—little girls in Sunday frills and little boys in miniature suits and ties—chased each other in and out among the rows, evading parents' restraining arms. The atmosphere was electric, more so than Kit had ever experienced at Light and Life. On a good day, the congregation of Light and Life amounted to only sixty or seventy.

But now, Kit's excitement was replaced by an unaccountable jangling of his nerves. Like some ineffective mantra doggedly repeated, the thought looped through his mind, Let's get this over with. It reminded him of the fear he had felt so many years ago on the Sunday after he had thrown the rock. Exactly like that.

He had come downstairs early, that morning. They were taking the girls to Dean's parents. Claudia said, "Get dressed quick and come with us." Kit didn't move from the kitchen table. Would Dean make him come? Sometimes he did, sometimes he didn't.

"We don't have time for this character to get his act together," Dean said. He unlatched the high chair trays and lifted the girls out. "Go to Grandma's now, girlies? Grandma's and Grandpa's? Go bye-bye?"

Kit stood at the door watching as Dean and Claudia made their way to the car, encumbered with twins, diaper bags, and strollers. As they moved down the walk, Edie, over Dean's shoulder, turned to Kit and waved.

"Bye-bye," she said distinctly.

Dean laughed. "Bad boy?!" he exclaimed. "Hear that?" he said to Claudia. "Edie said, 'Bad boy'!"

"Oh, she did not," said Claudia. "She said 'Bye bye'."

"No, she said 'Bad boy'!" Dean laughed again and jostled the baby affectionately. Edie looked back over Dean's shoulder and waved again at Kit.

"Ba' boy," she said. "Ba' boy."

When they had driven off, Kit stared at the retreating car. "You fucking asshole!" he shouted. His voice broke on the obscenity, ending foolishly on a falsetto note. He blushed and savagely kicked away a folded circular that lay on the stoop.

He arrived at Light and Life Tabernacle with three minutes to spare. His stomach felt constricted and a little sick. He hadn't been able to get down any breakfast. Before entering, he killed time in the doorway of an auto supply shop and watched to see what kinds of people were going into the church. Today the sign in front read, "By Faith Shall You Be Saved."

The parking lot was almost full. A pretty, petite woman, hurrying two children before her across the lot, carried a Bible in one hand like a pocketbook. Two elderly men in suits stood at the doorway and patted the children's heads as they passed in. Kit wheeled his bike across the street and locked it to a post behind the church. The broken window had been boarded over. It made the plain metal building look shabby and disreputable. His heart was fluttering as if he had stagefright.

"Good morning, young fella." One of the old men at the front door put out a hand. Kit had no choice—the man's hand closed around his and held it for several seconds. He gazed into Kit's eyes and smiled with a pushing friendliness that made Kit take a step back. The other man put a church bulletin in his hand.

There were fifty or sixty people seated in rows of old-fashioned wooden folding chairs padded with lawn chair cushions. Only a scattered few of the seats, near the front, remained unoccupied. Ceiling fans hummed overhead. A window air conditioner rattled.

The chairs looked toward a low, carpeted platform furnished with a cloth-covered table. On the table vases of flowers flanked a big gilt-edged Bible spread open at the middle. Behind the table, to the left, were a free-standing movie screen, a piano, a flute lying on top of a stool with a guitar propped against it, and a drum set, where a teenage boy in suit and tie stroked the cymbal idly with his brushes. The brushes made an ominous hiss.

On the other side of the platform stood a tall wooden cross constructed of two rough-hewn six-by-six pieces of lumber. Below the cross was a wide carpeted step holding several boxes of Kleenex. The Kleenex boxes disturbed Kit even more than the cross.

Suddenly, the man with the bulletin was taking Kit by the elbow and guiding him to a seat in the third row, second from the aisle. Several people looked up and smiled as he passed. Kit's face heated up. They were probably thinking *there's that kid who broke the Lord's window. That's him.* The aisle seat was occupied by a tall, hulking man in khaki pants and a putty-colored nylon shirt that stretched too tightly across his huge chest, revealing sagging breasts. On the other side was a small elderly woman in a black curly wig. After squeezing past the Hulk, Kit had to pick up a hymnal on his seat before he could sit down. He held it in his lap with some embarrassment as if it were a smutty book. His knee shook so nervously that the book slid off, landing with a loud bang like a gunshot on the concrete floor.

He bent to retrieve it, feeling the congregation's stares, but when he sat upright again, no one was looking at him. Then the little man who had caught him breaking the window was leaning into his row, reaching across the Hulk. Before Kit could tuck his hands into his armpits, the man had grabbed his hand and was shaking it.

"Nice to have you here, young fella. I didn't get your name last time we met." He winked.

"Kit," Kit muttered and pulled his hand away. The man's large ears stuck out almost at right angles to his bald head, and a prominent Adam's apple bobbed in his scrawny neck.

"Welcome to Light and Life, Kit. I'm Pastor Tinker." He said it as if he didn't know it sounded funny. "We're blessed to have you with us today." He patted Kit's arm and withdrew, greeting the Hulk, "Hello, Bill," and gripping his hand, too, in passing, before trotting down the aisle. Kit sneaked a look at the program. The preacher's first name was Ezra. Ezra Tinker. That figured.

The flute and guitar players stepped onto the platform and took up their instruments. The drummer's foot hit the cymbal pedal several times and two high school age girls stepped up to share a microphone. On the floor next to the platform a table had been placed with an overhead projector on it. A little boy sitting alongside fumbled with a transparency, first placing it upside down before sliding it into proper position. As the music started, the movie screen lit up with the words to a song. The congregation jumped to its feet.

Kit slouched in his chair, hemmed in by people in front and behind and the hulking man and old woman on either side. Eye level to their midsections, he felt like a sulking child among towering grown-ups. Grudgingly, he slid the hymnal under his chair and stood up. He wouldn't sing, though, or even pretend to.

The singing went on for a good forty minutes, starting with a series of rousers, familiar, apparently, to everybody else, and accompanied by enthusiastic hand clapping. The lyrics seemed parodies of themselves. Then a slow, dreamy, harmonious song began. People swayed to the rhythm, their heads lolled back, eyes closed and hands raised in the air.

> Deliver me, deliver me,
> Oh righteous King, deliver me
> From all temptation, sin and doubt,
> From Satan's grip.
> God, cast him out.
> Heavenly Warrior, mighty Lord,
> Strike sin from me with righteous sword.
> Deliver me, oh gracious Lord
> Deliver me, oh gracious Lord

The chorus was repeated six, eight, a dozen times until Kit wanted to shout *Deliver me from being bored!* He fought the urge to laugh and ducked to hide his face behind his long hair.

The lyrics of the final song seemed embarrassingly sexual.

> Jesus, you are the only one.
> Jesus, Thy will be done.
> All day, all night
> Fill me with Your blessed light.
> Jesus, I love you so.
> Take Thou my heart and soul.
> All of me is Thine.
> All of me is Thine.

Next, he thought, they'll throw their clothes off and fling themselves at the foot of those two scraps of lumber—*Take me Lord, take me!* He took a breath and blew it out.

He stole a look at the Hulk, who was mouthing the words to the song and glancing at his watch. In his big paws he had rolled his program into a tight cylinder as narrow as a cigarette. That guy wants to be home in front of the tube, drinking beer and having a smoke, Kit thought. What the hell is he doing here?

New lyrics came on the screen—words to a traditional hymn that Kit knew from grade school chorus, *Blessed be the tie that binds* ... The lyrics had never meant anything to him, but the old tune filled him with an unexpected nostalgia. In spite of himself, he hummed the harmony under his breath on the final verse. He felt embarrassed, yet when the song was over, he wished there had been more verses.

At last the singing ended. The music faded into quiet, continuous background accompaniment, but people remained standing. Kit's lower back was tight and beginning to ache.

The little preacher hopped up, gnome-like, onto the platform, holding a cordless microphone practically as long as his arm. He wore baggy cuffed trousers that broke over his instep and dragged at his heels, and a shiny gray suitcoat with outsize shoulder pads. As he topped the platform, Kit got a glimpse of bony ankles and lime-green argyle socks.

The preacher began to speak in a clipped, nasal voice as the people settled into their chairs.

"If there are any here today," he said, "in need of divine healing, come down to the cross now and receive God's grace and blessing. I'll ask our elders to come forward at this time and pray with any of our sisters or brothers who are besieged and beset by pain, grief, hopelessness, or doubt." The elders—two middle-aged women who had been sitting in the front row, rose and stationed themselves beside the altar beneath the two crossed timbers.

Oh, man, thought Kit, Here it comes! He was sweating but didn't want to call attention to himself by taking off his jacket. He stared down at the floor and slouched low, folding his arms across his chest. Try to force me up there, you freak!

There was a pause. The dreamy music continued to play in the background. Kit felt a rustling next to him and turned. The Hulk rose to his feet, set his hymn book on his chair, and stepped into the aisle.

Yeah, get your ass out of here. I wish *I* could.

But the man walked to the front, not to the back. His huge sloping shoulders overshadowed the bowed head, and he walked with a slow, massive bounce as if his bulk were so great the floor beneath compressed and recoiled under him. When he arrived at the cross, he lowered himself heavily to his knees. One of the elders came over to stand beside him. She murmured something to the man, but the preacher's amplified voice and the low, dreamy music drowned out whatever she was saying. To Kit's relief, the preacher said, "Let us close our eyes now to avoid being distracted by the sights and sounds around us and let us pray together." The congregation closed their eyes.

"Father, we pray that you come amongst us this morning to help heal the pain and sorrows afflicting some in this room today, and to heal the pains and ills of our city and of our country—"

Several people behind Kit called out, "Amen!" and "Praise Jesus!" In the front row more hands came up.

"—Oh Lord, these are times of great division. Children divided from parents, wives and husbands at odds with one another, generations divided by disapproval and distrust—" Several more in the crowd shouted words of praise.

Kit watched the Hulk uneasily. The elder had stooped to say something in his ear and he fell forward on his elbows and knees, his backside raised, the khaki stretched across his buttocks. *Jesus!* thought Kit, *the guy is nuts.* The woman placed her hand on the man's great bowed shoulder, and he let out a deep wrenching sob. Kit jumped in his seat. He looked around to see how others were reacting, but their eyes remained closed.

"—Bring us together in Your name, Heavenly Father, for You are the source of all unity. In Your name we pray to be shown the way of forgiveness."

The Hulk was sobbing continuously now, his shoulders heaving. The elder continued to whisper in his ear. The man groaned. Shaking his head back and forth, and with shrill, womanish cries, he wailed over and over in a watery voice, "I'm lost! I'm lost!" The woman put a tissue into his hand.

Kit was sweating through his jacket. The swaying, the murmuring, the unremitting drone of the preacher's words and the hypnotic music were closing in on him. He slid into the chair by the aisle. Everyone's eyes were still closed. He looked up the aisle toward the exit. The two elderly greeters sat at the back, one on either side of the door like security guards. Their eyes were closed, heads nodding, lips shaping amens.

Fucking Tweedledum and Tweedledee! Kit wanted to laugh. He looked around at the bowed heads, the swaying bodies and waving hands. If Dean knew he was in on a weird stunt like this, he'd never let him hear the end of it. Praise the Lord! Kit's getting saved! God spoke last night: Kit! Stop impersonating The Savior and get a haircut!

The man's wailing escalated, almost to a scream. Kit looked away. Christ, quit blubbering, you moron! He watched to see if people were giving each other looks, Not *that* guy again! But there were no looks.

Suddenly the Hulk fell into a crouch and pounded his forehead on the carpeted step. The thuds were audible. The woman who seemed to be praying over him knelt by his side, simultaneously looking toward the preacher with a question on her face. Two or three people in the congregation opened their eyes.

The preacher clicked off the microphone, set it on the table, and stepped from the platform. He walked over to the weeping man and sat with him on the step. The woman on the other side stood up and withdrew. The music subsided.

The Hulk had thrown his arms and hands over his head like someone expecting the roof to collapse. The little preacher gently removed the big man's hands from around his head, and put his own hand on his shoulder. At his touch, the man raised his head and turned toward the preacher in what seemed like slow motion then eased himself down again until his cheek lay on the preacher's knees.

Kit couldn't look away. The little minister with his Dumbo ears and scrawny neck and bobbing Adam's apple, sat on the step with his legs drawn up, and cradled the giant's head.

The Hulk threw an arm around the preacher's argyle-clad ankles and pressed his cheek into the gray trousers covering the little bony knees. His florid face was crumpled with anguish, his dark eye swimming, the expression focused inward on some incomprehensible pain.

The preacher began to speak, without amplification.

"Sometimes we feel so worthless, so sinful that we think there is absolutely no way out." He touched his fingers to the man's brow. His voice sounded less nasal, deeper and more powerful than it did through the microphone. "We feel even God cannot forgive us or help us because we're so low we can't look to His light. We grope in the dark alone, thinking that no one, nothing, can lift us up."

The hulking man held onto the preacher's trouser cuff and sobbed. The preacher began to rock him slowly. Kit blinked tears back. The man wailed, clutching tighter.

The preacher raised his voice above the wails. "In our loneliness and hopelessness, Bill, we deny the Lord. But our Father never denies us the opportunity to come to Him, no matter how impossible it seems, no matter how long it takes. The day you wake up knowing He has washed away your sins, He'll be there waiting for you. He's looking on right now at the beautiful lamb that you are. He knows your suffering because He was a Lamb, too. He felt lost too, didn't He?"

Hallelujah! someone shouted from the back.

"Remember our Lord's cry on the cross, 'Father, why hast thou forsaken me?' Even Jesus was struck with that bitter loneliness and despair that you're feeling. He must have questioned Himself. 'Oh Father, is it because I'm unworthy?' That was part of the human suffering that the Lamb had to feel for all of us in order to wash away our sins—"

"Amen," someone cried, and "Praise Him!"

"—The same doubts and fears and unworthy feelings torment you now, don't they?" The big head nodded into the preacher's knees. "Oh, He knows just exactly how you feel. He sees into your heart and knows everything about you—all the good and all the bad. And what He sees, Bill, is a lonely, scared little lamb, trotting this way and that, just trying to find safety. The little lamb is wandering into cold crevices and dark valleys, but his nose is to the ground, you see. As soon as he looks up, that little lamb is going to realize that the Shepherd has been right there beside him all along, waiting to bring him back to the fold."

"Walk with Him!" "Amen!"

"Brother, this pain that you're feeling is a gift from God to help you grope toward His light and safety. You are a blessed child of God, Bill, and Jesus loves you."

The big man drew his head back for a moment. His brows were drawn together in pain. His chin thrust out and his lower lip trembled just as if he were a little broken-hearted child.

The tears in Kit's eyes welled up close to the point of spilling over. If he blinked again, they would splash out and roll down his cheeks. He took deep breaths and brought a hand up, pretending to scratch the corners of his eyes. His nose was running, but he didn't dare sniffle. It's not because of this blubbering Hulk or this phony, Bible-thumping shrimp. It's nothing to do with that!

Against his will, he looked up again at the two men. The preacher's fingers were still touching the forehead, like a mother's hand testing for fever and soothing at the same time. Kit felt a fleeting sense of himself in the big man's place, the soft gabardine against his cheek, the thumb stroking, stroking his forehead.

A muffled "Hnh!" forced its way out of Kit's mouth, and at that, he bolted up the aisle, past the two guardians of the door, and out onto the sidewalk.

He ran around to the back, fumbled with his bicycle lock, threw himself onto the bike and sped away. Tears so blurred his vision he could barely see to ride. A woman standing at a stoplight looked at him as he passed. He felt like the Emperor who had no clothes.

He rode to his old hideout by the tracks under the overpass where he had always come when Dean drove him into a rage. At the top of the railroad cut, he threw his bike down and scrambled to the bottom, sobbing. Under the overpass he ran up the slope to the concrete wall and pounded on it with his bare fists until they bled. He screamed and sobbed obscenities. After a while, he collapsed onto the moss and curled up, his back against the hard concrete, his hands covering his face. The tears kept coming. There was no stopping them. His blood pounded and rushed in his head. His sobs echoed back at him. He pressed his cheek into the soft, furred earth. Licking at the salt streaming from his eyes and nose, he tasted mossy dirt on his lips.

Eventually the sobs subsided, and he lay exhausted, still curled into himself. He felt lightheaded and strangely cleaned out as if some earth-moving machine had dredged a load of sludge out of him. He turned onto his back, threw his arms above his head, and lay spread eagled and limp, looking up into the vaulted ceiling.

It was easier to breathe now. In fact there seemed to be no limit to the air he could take in. His chest and belly filled and emptied, filled and emptied. He seemed to be floating just above the ground. He might almost be able to float up to the arch of the overpass where swallows swooped in and out on air currents, their long curved wings boomeranging them out and back. It struck Kit how self-sacrificing the birds were, by some powerful nurturing instinct ceaselessly bringing food to their young. They never stopped to rest. How long did they keep it up?

He lay there for a long time. The muscles in his face let go and his mouth relaxed into a slack-jawed, ecstatic smile. Every part of his body was at rest. He couldn't have gotten up if he wanted to. Aloud, he laughed at himself. I'm jelly.

And now he was laughing uncontrollably. What is this? The laughter rolled and rolled out of him until his eyes were streaming. He had to sit up to get his breath, and still the laughter kept bubbling up. "Jesus! I'm a maniac!" he exclaimed when it began to subside at last. "What the hell *is* this?"

He stood and began to notice the details of his surroundings—the glint of sunlight angling off the iron railroad tracks, a dark trickle of water worming its way down the blackened wall face, the imprint of his body where he had lain in the moss. There was an herby, weedy smell in the air, which brought a fleeting sensation of being a little boy again walking somewhere outdoors, his hand held in a larger one. The breeze that brought the smell lifted and combed through his hair and did the same for the waving seed heads of the grass beyond the hideout.

At last the church elders took their places on the platform and faced the *Iglesia del Verbo* congregation, now crowded in to capacity. The music had begun and a forest of hands was already raised in the air, swaying and clapping. Daniel drew Kit forward to take seats at the end of an aisle for a better view.

"Now," Daniel said, "you will see with your eyes, you will hear with your ears what a great man is he."

At first the great man didn't appear. Kit had seen Ríos Montt's picture in the newspaper and didn't recognize him among the men on the platform. If he was somewhere up front, Kit couldn't see him through the crowd. At all the entrances, men in suits stood looking around impassively. It occurred to Kit that even though they didn't carry visible weapons, they must be bodyguards.

Except for a few elderly people, the congregation remained standing, and for almost an hour the church elders led them in songs and prayer. Everyone sat down during the offering, and while Kit waited to put his *quetzal* in the collection plate, his restless leg started up. He concentrated hard on restraining it.

Where was the great man? Was he a rock star, that he gave himself the right to keep everyone in suspense? Ezra, at the beginning of a service, was always right there, jumping down to unfold chairs for latecomers, greeting people at the door. But then Ezra was only a furniture salesman.

Then, suddenly, the music swelled and a thickset man in a dark business suit rose from the front row, climbed the steps and stood with the two elders who had led the prayer service. He had been sitting in the front row all the while. Kit recognized him at once, though he had only seen pictures of him in military uniform. Now *Jefe de Estado, Brigadier General José Efraín Ríos Montt,* stood facing the congregation, his head tilted upward so that the diffuse sunlight illuminated his strong cheek bones and the deep curve of his brow. He was shorter than Kit had imagined, but imposing nonetheless.

The people rose, and hundreds of pairs of hands lifted into the air as the General raised his, holding a microphone. Even from a dozen rows back, it was possible for Kit to see the light emanating from the president's deepset black eyes, a light that radiated not at the congregation of believers, but upwards, as if he were eye to eye with God.

The General looked like a different type of person in business suit, vest and tie than the one photographed in military camouflage, but the bass voice that boomed from the speakers, invoking *"Jesús Cristo, mi Señor, mi Salvador, mi Rey, Hijo de Dios en el cielo"* could well have been issuing orders. Kit thought the General's posture—head tilted back defining the dense muscles of his neck, his arms upraised, exposing wrists and forearms from the cuffs of his white shirt—was the posture of a worshipped, not worshipful, man. But at that moment the General went down on his knees. With a vast rustle of movement, the crowd knelt with him. He bowed his head and started to pray.

"*Te rezamos, Señor, por la liberación de nuestros pecados y nuestra inmoralidad que debilitan y destruyen a las familias y esos oficiales y hombres de negocios quienes persisten en corrupción y de los traidores quienes buscan destruir el gobierno con el uso de las armas.*"

Daniel was at Kit's ear, translating in a fierce undertone: "He prays for free our country from immorality that makes weak our families, and from businessmans and officials who stay in corruption. And from traitors who fight with arms the government."

Kit didn't try to keep up with the General's Spanish but attended instead to the staccato t's and rolled r's, the fulminating, commanding tones that boomed over the crowd, drowning out their fervent *améns* and *aleluya*s. Ríos Montt may have been on his knees with head bowed, but the voice, the *voice*, demanded *submission*. It sounded to Kit like the clang of iron on iron, and he felt himself resisting it.

Ríos Montt prayed aloud on his knees for a long time. When he finally rose and again stood upright on the platform, he began his sermon in a clear and deliberate voice. Between Kit's own recognition of phrases and words and the broken translation Daniel murmured in his ear, Kit was able to catch much of it.

"*Satan,*" intoned the General, "*uses some Christians who join forces against the government to make the Gospel an instrument of external revolution rather than a true revolution inside the hearts of each in-dividual. Change for Guatemala depends not on arms, not on the false promises of subversives, but on the moral changes that you, sir, or you, ma'am,*" he pointed an index finger at people sitting below, "*you choose to make. It is in your heart. Demonic forces tear Guatemalan families apart, tempting husbands to drunkenness and cheating on their wives. In the past, evil men in positions of public trust have served their own selfish interests. But corruption is no longer tolerated.*"

The General thrust his right hand in the air and the crowd leapt to its feet. He extended his thumb, and a thousand other thumbs shot up.

"*¡NO ROBO!*" shouted the congregation, punctuating each syllable. He raised his second finger, and a mass of forefingers and thumbs, like pantomimed guns, pointed to the ceiling. "*¡NO MIENTO!*" the people shouted. Ríos Montt extended his third finger, and with the crowd shouted "*¡NO ABUSO!*" Excited children pranced in the aisle, waving their three fingers in the air.

"'I do not steal! I do not lie! I do not abuse!'" Daniel said in Kit's ear, ticking the phrases off on his fingers. "It is famous pledge. Every official of government—high or low—must promise, including he himself."

The General lowered his hand and the crowd rustled back into their seats.

"*The problem of our country,*" Ríos Montt continued, "*is disorder. I do not propose an economic program but rather an ethical and moral one. We need law, order and discipline. Hunger, misery, ignorance and subversion,*" he declaimed, "*are the four horsemen of Revelation, the consequences of worshipping the beast ...*"

Colleen would despise this guy, of course, Kit thought. She would mock the TV preacher voice, the finger stabbing at the audience as if they were teenagers who had come home past curfew. But what the General was saying, how could she argue with that? *Don't drink. Don't cheat on your wife. Don't steal, don't lie, don't abuse.*

"*Through our prayer campaign— 'Jesus is Lord of Guatemala'—you must wage spiritual warfare, prayer warfare to bind Satan's power of corruption, violence and poverty.*" The president's dark glowering eyes under the heavy brows seemed to contradict the smile on his face. Was he sincere or putting on a show?

It couldn't be a show. Satan must be sneaking this idea into his own mind. Ezra would have no problem with what the guy had to say. Kit pictured his pastor beaming out at the Light and Life believers, his protruding ears practically flapping as he rose up and down on his toes with the thrill of conveying the Good News.

But this General—a warrior for sure, no mistake about that—spiritual warrior, prayer warrior—he almost wished the guy *was* wearing the camouflage uniform and tinted glasses from the newspaper photos. It would be … more clear? Somehow the business suit, the glasses case in the pocket, the wedding ring glinting on his finger, seemed like a disguise. Kit felt a pang at the thought of the shiny pants cuffs lapping the toes of Ezra's old scuffed shoes.

Kit looked at his watch. The General had been speaking for more than an hour. The incessant hammering of his emphatic Spanish was beginning to numb Kit's brain. His chest, on the other hand, felt tight and uneasy.

The General's sermon on morality would be an easy mark for Colleen's ridicule. But Ezra, *Ezra* would reach her. Give Ezra ten minutes with her. Kit closed his eyes then and shut out the General's scolding harangue and Daniel's urgent, whispered translation.

"Dear Lord," Kit prayed silently, "let me meet Colleen again and this time find the power to soften her heart toward your message of salvation. Give me the wisdom to find words that will open her to the truth." In the *parque*, in the darkness, Colleen beside him, not talking, the thrill of her arm under his hand.

Kit opened his eyes. The General was directing his stern gaze down the aisle and pointing his index finger right at him.

It was another forty-five minutes before the General ended with a rumbling exhortation: "*Subversives, terrorists, hear me well. You bent your knee to the powers of Satan, and now you are seeing how God strikes evil down. We, children of our merciful Father, have called on the Almighty with prayer to weaken you and wipe our Fatherland clean of you and your destructive violence. Our Savior and King has listened and driven you back, sent you shivering into the wilderness.*" He took a step forward. "*¡No lo duden por un momento, comunistas!*" he thundered, shaking his finger at the imagined enemies. "*¡No lo duden por un momento!*"—Don't have a moment's doubt, communists. "*Every one of you will be delivered unto the Lord's judgment!*"

"*And to you, oh children of God, I tell you that you must pray and pray and never cease to pray so that our Lord will open up the skies and rain down his blessings, casting the demon out of our country forever. Aleluya. Amén.*"

"He is *militar recto*—soldier of justice," exclaimed Daniel on the trip back. "Those people who talks against him, they are *demonios*. They tried to say he give orders to kill *indios*. But what does he command to the soldiers in the *campos*—in the rural areas?" Daniel shook his finger in imitation of the General's vehement gesture: 'You do not take even a pin from the population! You do not take liberty with the women! You pay fair price whatever you are buying! You respect the costumbres Mayas— traditions! You do not abuse the peasant hospitality, *nunca*—never!'"

The three-hour service had left Kit's brain exhausted. He leaned his head against the bus window and let Daniel's eccentric English flow in and out of his consciousness. He felt some uneasiness, some vague anxiety, which he wanted to push away as being sinful. To come away from a church service with an agitated heart instead of a peaceful one was like starting down from the peak of a steep hill and finding only loose stones under foot and nothing to grab onto.

He remembered how he had wanted to hold onto the cleaned out, ecstatic sensation he felt under the overpass after that first church service at Light and Life. But it slipped away as soon as he returned home and found Dean and Claudia and the twins in the kitchen. He remembered what Dean had taught Edie to say—*Ba' boy*—and the sludge started to fill him up again. He bounded up the stairs to his room, grabbed his headphones and pressed the play button on his boombox, cranking up the volume on *The Clash*. Who cared if it messed up his eardrums? "White Riot" blocked out his ability to think.

All week every time the phone rang, he thought it would be the police about the broken window. He hadn't stayed at the church for the whole service on Sunday, so he had only gotten a taste of the preacher's phony sentiment and fanatical music. If he went back, would he be ordered to come a third Sunday to make up for leaving early the first time? Would the blackmailing little creep ever let him off the hook?

In spite of the peace he had finally felt in his hideaway, he was some-how sinking even lower than before. He started to watch for more signs that his sisters were being taught to despise him. And something else kept looping through his mind and bothering him. No matter how hard he tried, he couldn't get out of his mind that freaking little preacher's hand stroking the Hulk's forehead—how it must have felt to the big guy—and how that fabric must have felt between the guy's cheek and the preacher's skinny little knees. He couldn't banish the image: the preacher holding the hulking man in that half embrace in a halo of light as if the big man were the preacher's child. If he returned to the service on Sunday, he had better come early to get a seat at the back. Then when the service was over, he would be out the door before anyone could get their hooks into him and that would be the end of it. He'd have kept his part of the bargain, and Dean wouldn't find out about the broken window.

That week, on an afternooon of ninety degree temperatures and an un-relenting sun singeing the lawn, Claudia asked him to watch the twins while they splashed in their plastic wading pool and she made dinner.

As soon as Lorie and Edie saw where they were headed, they squealed with happiness. The pool was set up under the larch tree, whose branches drooped to make a great inverted umbrella of shade. Kit plopped the girls, gloriously naked except for ruffled plastic pants over fat diapers, into the pool. He lay next to them on a lawn chair recliner, soothed by their intermittent squeals and shrieks. Whenever they smacked the water with their chubby palms, they would close their eyes and screw up their noses in a grimace that revealed two identical little nubs of front teeth. He reached over and smacked the water with his big hand, and they screamed and laughed.

This was all he wanted. He could do it over and over without tiring. Smack the water and make his sisters happy. No worries. No fears. He could almost feel again that peaceful, jelly-like inertia he had felt in his hideout by the tracks.

Eventually, Lorie, trying to stand up on the slippery plastic, toppled forward and fell face down in the water. Her look of shock, when he pulled her up, crumpled into fury and misery. Kit hoisted her out just before the wails began. "Got a snootful, did you? Poor Lo Lo!" Edie looked up at them from the pool, her eyebrows tilted empathetically. Why, Kit wondered, did anything ever have to interrupt the purity of their pleasure? He sat back on the lawn chair, Lorie's dripping body cool against his warm chest.

At dinner, Claudia passed the corn on the cob and said to Kit, "You guys were having quite the time out there. You're a regular splash machine. You've got the patience of a saint!" Kit gave a dismissive half smile. Dean waved an ear of corn at Claudia.

"You don't see anything odd—" he winked at her "—about a sixteen-year-old boy who has no objection to staying home and playing with little girls?" Claudia turned to look at him and frowned slightly, without replying.

Jesus! thought Kit. He likes playing with them, too. Does that make him less of a man? Asshole. He took his knife and viciously stripped the corn off his corncob.

"Why don't you use the cob holders and eat it normally?" Dean remarked, dipping his corncob in a boat of butter.

It wasn't until late that night that the more sinister implication of Dean's comment struck him. *A sixteen-year-old boy who has no objection to staying home and playing with little girls.* He sat up in bed, sick at the stomach, remembering Claudia's frown. Was it possible she took the comment seriously? But if Dean really believed it, he would have booted Kit out of the house. So what was the frown about?

He got out of bed and stood looking out the window at the shadowy circle of the wading pool on the lawn. It was inconceivable to think of the twins in that way. He felt for them not even like a brother, but almost as if he were their true father.

Kit picked up his T-shirt from his chair with an urge to get dressed and leave the house, ride away and disappear. Otherwise what would it mean for him now that this suggestion had been casually planted in his mother's mind? Could he not kiss the girls anymore or hug them? Not pick them up and comfort them when they cried? Cuddle them only in secret? And if so, how would he begin to see himself? He put on his headset and punched play on *ACDC* to drown out the images, but the beat was too sexy, and he punched the power off. He paced the room, feeling so caged in the close, air-conditioned space that he wanted to pick up his boombox and hurl it through the window.

On Friday evening at dusk, he left the house without saying where he was going, rode out to the overpass and climbed down in the darkness. He stood balancing on a steel rail and thought about how he could get Dean to come close to the tracks, because he would need to lay the body across them to make it look like suicide. What if he got blood on his clothes, though? And how would he clean the crowbar? As he pictured it, he knew that killing Dean was an idea some loser who watched too much TV would dream up. Nobody would believe Dean would commit suicide. He had everything he wanted. The stepson would be the first person suspected.

He stared into the darkness at the fireflies lighting up and extinguishing. The toneless static of cicadas pulsed in his ears. His head felt packed with a lifetime of stupid ideas and old, bad thoughts. He wished he could take off his overstuffed head and lay it down somewhere, just walk away without it.

The moonlight reflected off the iron rails. He lowered himself onto the tracks and curled on his side with his temple on a rail, his shoulder between the wooden ties. The hard steel against his skull felt good. He was tempted to lift his head and let gravity drop it back down, bash against the rail and rattle all the crap inside. He felt exhausted, and after a while, the whine of cicadas lulled him to sleep.

He was startled awake to the earth shaking and a wide beam of light shining in his face, the roar of an oncoming engine. Crab-like, he got to his knees, flailing his arms and legs, and flung himself off the track. He rolled down the gravel incline as the train thundered over the spot where he had just been lying.

"The communists tell lies in the international newspapers, say that Ríos Montt massacres the *indios*. No! It is the *comunistas* themselves that massacre, and blame the army. The majority of *indios* are happy in their life. It is the *subversivos* that make them flee and take up arms. Brother Efraín protects the ones who accept his protection and the protection of *Jesús Cristo*.

"No, when the army massacres, it massacres demons—those *indios* who are demon possessed. They are communists or they are *idolatros* who worship gods and saints, the images of *Satán*. Is difficult for the army because the demons are inside those *indios*. So of course they must be killed. The army only massacres demons."

Kit lifted his head from the window. Did he just dream the words? "The army only massacres who?" he asked.

"*Demonios*," replied Daniel.

❖ Ten ❖

Just before noon on Tuesday, Rita clicked across the paving stones on high-heeled sandals, clapped for attention, and announced a Friday evening party at *Casa Fuego*, the house she and Phil had recently bought.

"That's nice of them," someone commented.

Rub, whose coldness had slowly thawed over the last week, leaned toward Kit and said in an undertone, "Nice, *hell*. How else are they gonna show off the plunder? You spend a quarter of a million bucks, you gotta show *some*body."

Kit chose not to pursue the meaning of this line of gossip, and on Friday night was quite unprepared for the opulence inside Phil and Rita's one-storey corner house on the *Calle Oriente*. From the outside it looked like all the houses that abutted the sidewalk in Antigua—plain, white stucco walls, terra cotta tile roof—nothing to distinguish it except the large carved wooden door and lacy grille work at the shuttered windows.

Kit arrived exactly on time and used the brass knocker lightly. An indigenous maid appeared and ushered him into a vaulted entryway lit by a low-hanging chandelier.

The wall to his right was covered floor to ceiling with slabs of stone incised with exotic figures. Kit was examining these when Phil came forward, drink in hand. He patted the wall.

"They're called *stelae*, these slabs. The characters are *glyphs*. I've got the translations written down somewhere."

"It's Mayan writing?" The stone was blotched with white, the glyphs worn and smoothed out in places.

"Early Classic period—probably 300–400 A.D.," Phil replied, gesturing at the wall with his drink as if toasting it.

Kit remembered what the crowd at Aurelia's had said about Phil's school. Could U.S. dollars buy all this?

From niches in the other wall, a series of large green stone masks stared down. "Jade," Phil said. "The details are obsidian with shell. Probably 600 to 700 A.D. From southern Mexico." He turned toward the sound of splashing water coming from the interior. "Come in. Join us."

They entered a large inner courtyard lit by candles in sconces along a pillared corridor. The corridor was open to the courtyard and ran the length and breadth of it. In the center was a stone fountain that spilled water into its scalloped basin.

"Eh, *amigo!*" Rub called to Kit, raising his glass. Making no concession to formality, he was wearing a muscle shirt and cut-off shorts. He leaned back in his chair, his legs splayed out and a drink in his hand.

"A refill on that?" Phil took Rub's nearly empty glass and passed it to Rita, who took it to a sideboard bristling with bottles.

"*¡Hola!* Kit," she sang out. Tonight she was wearing a sarong-style wrap dress, huaraches, and looping crystal earrings that twinkled as she moved. Passing the glass to Rub, she said to Kit, "And for you?"

Kit asked for any kind of soda, and she wagged a finger at him, calling to Phil over her shoulder, "You see? I tol' you. These boy, he's a good *evangélico*—no alcohol!" She poured him a lemon Fanta and put it in his hand. "*I'm* not tempt you," she said, tapping his cheek with her long fingernails. She led him to a bench and sat down next to him.

Kit looked around at the lush bougainvillea and clipped lawn of the courtyard, the large banana palm in one corner, two other trees forming canopies with their thick, dark leaves. Guests were sitting in Spanish-style carved wooden chairs. "From the street," he said, "you'd never know all this was here."

"Yes, they're quite private, these villas," said Phil. "Actually this one is rather modest. There's a general from the capitol whose Antigua house takes up a whole block. All you can see from the outside is blank walls."

"Oh, Kit, is too bad is winter!" exclaimed Rita. "Two months later you can see so much flowers on these trees, like blue umbrella and red umbrella. So pretty. This one is *jacaranda* and this one is *árbol de fuego*. Felipe, what is that in English?"

"Flame tree. That's what the house is named for. That and the volcano. Here," said Phil. "I'll give you the tour. Bring your drink."

Rita rolled her eyes. "Are we a *museo*? Come *on*! Let the boy relax." But Kit was on his feet. He was already out of small talk.

Phil took him across the courtyard, pointing out a Moorish-style archway of gray stone, through which they walked into the *sala*—the dining room. The room was dominated by a long, seventeenth-century Spanish colonial table and chairs of carved mahogany, the chairs upholstered in red brocade. On the walls were paintings of armored conquistadors and of soulful madonnas with round, flat halos behind their heads like gilded dinner plates.

The wood-paneled ceiling was crossed with heavy beams. "Cypress," Phil pointed out. "From the great Cypress forests in the Chicoy Mountains, sadly diminished, alas. Took me two years to get the lumber here. Everything takes ten times as long in this country."

Everywhere, in niches and on tables and pedestals, Mayan artifacts were displayed—burial relics and household articles of jade, stone and terra cotta.

"Where did you get all these things?" Kit asked. "It must have taken a long time."

"Oh," said Phil, vaguely. "I've been at it for a number of years. I don't keep everything I collect. People come to me, of course." He laid a finger by his nose and winked. "It can be lucrative. Rather a give and take process."

"There you are!" cried Rita when they finally returned. "You are *not* lost!"

More students had arrived—new students whom Kit hadn't met. Rub was sitting apart.

"Duly impressed?" he called out to Kit. He had sunk lower in his seat, resting the crease of his thick neck against the upper edge of the chair.

Kit sat down next to him.

"Yeah." he nodded. "It's amazing, all this stuff."

"Ninety percent illegal, of course." His eyes were glassy.

"What do you mean?"

113

"National treasures. Not kosher to hack 'em out of tombs. Or in Phil's case to *buy* 'em from people who bought 'em from people who hacked 'em out of tombs."

"Really? But he's not hiding anything."

"He's as discreet as you need to be when you got contacts in the right places. It wouldn't be *my* game. But he does live high for a schoolmaster." He had emptied his glass again and he shifted as if to stand up, lost his grip on the arm of the chair, and sank back down. Rita glanced at him from the other side of the patio and came over. He held up his glass and tapped it. "No," he said, turning to Kit, "I wouldn't want to be encumbered with all this crap. You gotta stay mobile."

Rita sat down on the edge of Rub's chair. "You," she said, poking Rub in the chest, "will not able to walk home."

"You got that right, darlin'. Maybe you can extend your hospitality for a few more hours."

"Of course." She hailed the maid, who was passing canapés on a tray, and spoke to her curtly in Spanish. To Rub she cocked her head and smiled. "Don' worry. We will fix up for you a room." She hopped off the chair then and joined her husband at the fountain, bending close to him and speaking a few words.

Rub said, "Yep, it pays to have the right contacts. Remember that, *mi amigo*. Oh, wait a minute, what am I thinking? *You* got a straight line to *Jesus*. You don't *need* contacts. Am I right?"

Kit looked into Rub's bleary face. He paused. Help me say it right, Lord. "You could have a straight line to Jesus, too," he said. "All you have to do is let him into your heart."

Rub slapped the arm of the chair. "That's what I like about you, *amigo*. It saddens you to see my ass hanging out over the brimstone. Believe me, I'd oblige you if I could, 'cause I know it'd be a real feather in your cap— whatever the fuck that means— to save an ass as corrupted as mine." He picked up his empty glass, looked at it and set it down again.

"That's not why I—" began Kit.

"But you can't make a person believe nonsense just because it's reassuring nonsense."

Kit drew away a little, chilled. The temperature of the night air seemed to have dropped several degrees, but he also felt as if the house and all its stone relics were contaminated with the bad air of a tomb. He felt an acute longing for Light and Life Tabernacle. Its rickety folding chairs, homemade curtains on the windows, the simple rustic cross made from six-by-six pieces of raw pine lumber. He wished he were walking down the aisle before a service between Ezra and Jeannette, Ezra's hand on his shoulder and Jeannette's arm around his waist. The choir telling him to hurry up, they had one little part to practice before the service started. The drummer, Robert, restlessly skimming his brushes over his cymbals. And the feeling, somehow transmitted from Ezra's hand to Kit's shoulder, that Ezra was filling up with the Spirit, almost floating down the aisle to the altar, soaring on the glory of God's grace.

Kit prayed, Lord, according to your desire and your will, I will do whatever I can to serve you here, but please hold a place for me back home.

Santiago de Atitlán, the village that had received Light and Life's donation of a fire truck, was located in the Highlands, only about forty-five miles from Antigua, but the trip would involve a bus ride of three hours through the mountains, and a boat ride across Lake Atitlán.

Overhearing Kit ask Phil how to arrange the trip, Rub offered to drive him. "I'm heading up to *Pana* on Saturday anyway."

"*Pana?*"

"Panajachel. It's a *gringo* tourist town. Santiago's the other side of the lake. You can hop a motor launch and be across in an hour."

"I thought I'd just take the bus," said Kit.

"You want to stand up all the way on some damn chicken bus? It'll be crammed to the rafters with *indios* losing their lunch all over you on the switchbacks." Rub shook his head. "Forget that. I'll get you there in under an hour, with all your ribs in place. It won't cost you a single *quetzal.*"

"I wouldn't want to—"

"No trouble. I've got a little old Peugeot coupe chomping at the bit in her stall. The mare needs an airing."

The week before the trip, all anyone talked about was the Pope's visit. The Martinez family went to the house of a relative to hear about him on television. Kit read in *The New York Times* that Pope John II had asked Ríos Montt to spare the lives of six men who had been found guilty of subversion and sentenced to execution in a secret military trial. Despite the Pope's request, the men were executed anyway. In Guatemala City, speaking to hundreds of thousands, the Pope criticized torture, kidnappings and other injustices. In the Highlands, he told an indigenous crowd: "The Church is aware of the discrimination you suffer and the injustices you put up with; the serious difficulties you have in defending your lands and your rights; the frequent lack of respect for your customs and traditions."

Kit wondered what *Prensa Libre* would have to say about the Pope's speech. He scanned the Guatemalan newspaper and found the article he was looking for: "*Mensaje de Ríos Montt.*" It was a small article on page fifteen, continued on page sixty-eight. Ríos Montt's response was to ignore the Pope's criticism.

He met Rub on the next Saturday morning outside Rub's *pensión* near the school. The Peugeot was parked in the enclosed courtyard. It appeared to have been seriously vandalized; one fender and all the hubcaps were missing, a makeshift sideview mirror was duct taped to the driver's window and a long scar was scratched into a fender.

"I keep her this way," Rub said, patting the car's flank tenderly. "People think she's a piece of crap, they don't try to steal her. Not that anybody wants a small car in Guate anyway. It's the minivans and station wagons with polarized windows they mostly rip off." He threw Kit's day pack and his own small duffel into the trunk.

Out on the street, Rub blasted through intersections and squealed around corners without regard for the narrow, cobbled roadways or pedestrians. Kit held his breath and clenched the door handle until Rub entered the relatively empty highway leading northwest, where he slowed down to a leisurely pace, taking his sunglasses from the dash and putting them on, then resting an elbow out the window.

"So," he said, taking his eyes off the road to look at Kit. "Why are you headed for Santiago? Most people have *Pana* in mind when they go to Atitlán. You going to save souls?"

They were already ascending into the mountains on a blind curve. Kit kept his eyes on the road, hoping Rub would take the hint. In a few words, he told Rub about his church's gift of Pumper # 5 and his commission to visit the village where it was sent, to take snapshots of the fire truck and its recipients and give them a photo of the Light and Life congregation standing in front of their church. He had some mini-New Testaments in Spanish to give out, too.

Rub pulled a cigarette pack and lighter from the glove compartment and lit up. "So, you found Jesus, did you? You kneel at the altar of J.C. My Lord and Savior is J.D.—Jack Daniels." He blew cigarette smoke out the window. "I respect the work you *evangélicos* do up there in the Highlands, though. Catholic Church doesn't do squat to rein in these radical nuns and priests. They're all over the villages preaching revolution."

You just sang in the language of the Catholic Mass. Kit recalled the light, teasing way she had said it, the sensation of her hand curving momentarily in his, his stupidity at such a moment. *Every conversation you turn into a political thing.* Why did he say it?

"These ignorant *indios*," Rub said, "they'll follow whoever waves a cross in their face. Give 'em anything like superstition, they eat it up. The *evangélicos* have gained a shitload of influence in the last ten, fifteen years. Country used to be ninety-nine point nine percent Catholic. Today, twenty, twenty-five percent are born-agains and they're growing. As far as the government's concerned, the born-agains can do no wrong." Rub darted his glance periodically back to the road throughout this speech, keeping his eyes on Kit in the intervals. Kit faced rigidly forward, expecting to go over the mountainside at any moment. "Ríos Montt's a holy roller himself. Down on his knees every Sunday preaching on TV—'Praise Jesus and pass the ammunition.'"

Kit took his eyes off the road then. "I heard him speak in person," he said.

"Oh yeah?" Rub raised an eyebrow. "All fired up about the communists was he?" Kit didn't answer. Don't talk about politics in this country.

"Everyone's screaming 'Human rights! Human rights!' " Rub said. "But you don't get rid of subversives by playing patty-cake with them.

You've got to put the screws on. If you only get rid of a few of 'em, a hundred more'll creep out like cockroaches.

"You've got to take blanket measures. That's why Ríos Montt burns down the villages. Smoke 'em out and smash 'em while they run." Rub threw the cigarette butt out the window. "It's the only way. I saw it in 'Nam. 'To catch the fish, drain the sea.' Only we didn't have someone like Ríos Montt or Reagan to do the job. That pansy Nixon, sucking up to the Chinese, pulling out … He should have drafted the whole damn country—get the women into combat, they're so hot to be like men—overrun the fucking gooks. But they never listen. They call us in, then ignore our advice—" Rub went silent and brought his concentration back to the road. They were rounding a sharp curve. Three white wooden crosses decorated with plastic flowers were planted at the cliff edge.

"You were in the war?" asked Kit.

Rub shrugged. "Let's just say the army needed a bit of off-the-record advice. I was what you'd call a hands-on Ann Landers."

Around a bend a vista of distant mountains opened up. The peaks appeared to skewer the layers of flat, low clouds.

Kit turned to Rub and said, with some trepidation, "You haven't even thought about letting Jesus into your life, Rub?"

Rub tapped his fingers on the steering wheel. "Do you know that every religion in the world—Jesus, Buddha, Mohammed, whatever—they have the same message somewhere in their teaching: *Don't do to others what you wouldn't want them to do to you.*" Golden Rule. Confucius preached it five hundred years before Jesus Christ ever walked the earth. But do any of their so-called followers practice it? The opposite. People are naturally cruel to each other, especially in the name of religion. It's human nature."

"I felt that way too, before I opened myself to the Lord." Kit tried to see Rub's eyes behind his sunglasses. "Then I realized God's infinite love and forgiveness. It completely turned me around."

"To each his own."

They were coming up on a military jeep and covered truck parked on the side of the road. Several soldiers stood around, one of whom stepped onto the pavement and gestured at them to pull over.

"Army checkpoint," said Rub. He took papers from an envelope in his pants pocket and passed them through the window. The soldier glanced at them, said a few words to Rub in Spanish, and waved them on.

Kit looked back. "Some of those guys look like kids. It's weird to see them carrying rifles."

"Yeah, the army snatches these *indio* kids, seventeen, sixteen, even fifteen years old and younger. They take them out of the villages, stick them in the barracks, apply certain ... coercive techniques on them. It takes— what, three or four months to break them down to where they're willing to off other *indios*—people from the next mountain over, who speak a whole different language, so it's not like killing their own grandma. Gets to be as natural a use for their *Uzi* as chopping cane was for their machetes." Rub chuckled. "Oh yeah. What boy could resist putting an *Uzi* to good use? Especially knowing if he does resist, it'll be used on him."

"It's legal to take them that young?"

"Hell, no, it's not legal. Kidnapping little boys for the army? But where else you gonna get the rank and file to fight your war for you? You gotta get 'em from somewhere. You fudge a little on their age, call it volunteering, it makes it okay."

"Does the President know about it?"

"Ah. Ríos Montt." Rub turned to grin at Kit. "*El General*. They call him 'The Brassière.' Know why?"

Kit shrugged.

"They call him 'The Brassière' 'cause he covers up the things that people most want to get a look at." Rub started to laugh then stopped. "No, wait, that's not right. That's *my* punchline. How *does* it go?" He thought for a moment. "Oh yeah, I got it! 'A brassière is that which suppresses those within in order to impress those without.'" He slapped the steering wheel appreciatively.

"I thought ... you liked him."

"I *admire* him. The guy's got Reagan believing he's been given a 'bum rap' on human rights 'cause he stopped the *archivos* from murdering people in the city. Sounds good, don't it? No more stepping over dead bodies for the city folks. The Brassière just ratchets it up in the countryside where the middle class don't have to look at it."

Kit didn't know what to say. Was Rub trying to draw him out? *The government is pretty harsh on the Indians, don't you think, amigo?*

Rub slowed down as they approached a blackened crater taking up most of the road and encircled by rubble. Soldiers, who were throwing the rubble into the hole, waved them on, and the Peugeot squeezed past the spot on the inside, adding another scrape to its fender.

"See? Now if you'd taken the chicken bus, you would have had to sit here sweating for two hours while they fixed the damage, *chapín*-style— one chunk at a time."

"What's *chapín*-style?"

"That's what Guatemalans call themselves. '*Chapines*.' "

"Is it a put-down?"

"Nah. But don't you use it. It'd be like some white guy calling some black guy 'bro.'"

"What happened to the road back there? A rock slide?"

"Dynamite. The *guerrilleros* were busy little beavers last night."

"Is it dangerous to travel up here with the war going on?"

"If you're a Yankee *gringo*, you've got nothing to worry about just so long as you make it clear what side of the religious war you're on. You go up there in the sticks with your protestant Bible, you'll be fine."

"But the guerrillas are against the evangelicals aren't they?"

"I'm not talking about guerrillas. The *guerrilleros* don't attack foreigners. Mostly they just go after military bases and infrastructure. I'm talking about the army. The army should leave you alone if your papers are in order. But if you do get in a pinch," Rub hooked a finger under the chain and cross that hung out of Kit's collar, "just flash your little piece of jewelry at them and drop the name of *Hermano Efraín*."

They were silent for a while, taking curves that sprang sudden vistas on them: deep, converging valleys—patchworks of greens and browns scattered with clusters of cornstalk huts, the sunlight glancing off the corrugated tin roofs—volcanic peaks rising above the valleys. Rub lit another cigarette. "You don't smoke, I'd guess." Kit shook his head.

They passed through the town of Chimaltenango and a village called Zaragosa without stopping. Then, descending into a valley, they saw a man and two young boys walking toward them up the slope on the side of the road. They trudged steadily upward, one foot in front of the other, each leaning into the steep grade under the weight of something heavy. As the car passed them, Kit saw that all three were carrying huge loads of firewood on their backs. Leather straps across their foreheads were attached to ropes that ran under the loads. It seemed as if at any moment the weight of their burdens would bring them to their knees.

"How can they carry loads like that, up mountains?" Kit said, looking back at the figures diminishing in the distance like illusions. He had once helped Dean unload a cord of firewood. He remembered the weight.

Rub threw his cigarette out the window. "They were brought up to it. It's all they know."

"Where are they taking the wood?"

"Probably to the Antigua market to sell."

"That's ten miles back, all mountain roads."

"*Fifteen* miles. They'll sell the wood, buy cooking oil, rice, other shit— probably a hundred pounds worth—strap the *mecapal* on and carry it all home, twenty miles back."

"I'd never be able to do it." Kit looked behind again but the three were out of sight.

"You would," Rub said, "to survive." He started to pull another ciga- rette from the pack, thought better of it and put it away. "*We* wouldn't stand for it. But peasants are *burros*. You put a load on a *campesino's* back, he carries it. It's just these Reds that are stirring them up. Indians have been hauling firewood up and down these mountains for centuries. Why complain now?"

Kit sat silent for some minutes. Then he turned to Rub, and in a voice that came out louder than he meant, he said, "Why *not* complain?"

Rub put both hands on the wheel. He fixed Kit with a long look. Then he rested his elbow out the window again and turned his attention to the road.

"You're a total innocent," he said. "I'll bet you've never even been laid." Kit flushed. "You think about it all the time, though, don't you." He nudged Kit in the side. "Huh? Isn't that right?" Kit shoved Rub's elbow away. Rub gave a triumphant snort. "You're a babe in the woods, *chico*. You don't know *nada*." He drove on silently. After a while he said,

"Listen. Don't go around saying things like, 'Why *not* complain?' It ain't healthy around here." He nudged Kit again. "*¿Sabes?*"

Panajachel was disappointing after the crumbling colonial grandeur of Antigua. It consisted of two main commercial streets and five or six cross streets lined with concrete block and stucco fronted houses, *tiendas* and *comedores,* the facades rising directly from the sidewalks. It seemed to be populated primarily by a smattering of European backpackers and U.S. long-haired hippies of both sexes who strolled the main streets or lounged outside the cafes bargaining amiably with the persistent, doe-eyed child vendors who dogged them.

Rub drove to the shore of the lake and parked near a rickety dock. *Lago Atitlán* lay in the basin of a collapsed volcano. The lake was sixteen miles at its widest point, Rub said, and fed by many rivers. Towering cumulus clouds were reflected in the black water, which appeared bottomless. The mountains that surrounded it were checkered with tiny cultivated plots. Just now the sun hung high above the southeastern range of peaks.

"You'd better catch this next launch," Rub advised. "It's almost eleven o'clock. "By noon or so, the *Xocomil* starts. You'll have a rough ride back, but at least you'll only have it one way."

"The *Xocomil*"?

"Major wind in the afternoon. It whips up the water. The bottom of this lake's gotta be hip-deep in tourist upchuck."

A motor launch was approaching with a loudening, irregular chug.

"When you get back to *Pana,* just do the rounds—you'll probably run into me somewhere. I might have something going on with a lady friend here, though. If you don't find me, it means I got lucky and I'll probably stick around for a few days. You can catch a bus back to Antigua. There's one at about 5:30."

Kit waited with a handful of tourists to board the wooden six-seater launch that was now idling alongside the dock. In a few minutes it was full and the boatman, a lean, deeply tanned *ladino* wearing a dirty straw hat pulled to his eyebrows, took their twenty-five *centavos* and turned the boat out into the lake.

Kit sat at the front, where the breeze and a light spray cooled his face. All at once he felt elated. This—more than the dozens of other new things he had experienced since coming to Guatemala—seemed to mark the real beginning of his adventure here: lighting out across the lake in the shadows of these ancient mountains that God had raised at the beginning of the world.

He felt ten years older—an ambassador of the Lord about to bring the people of two worlds together. There rose in his heart an upsurge of compassion for the unknown people of Santiago. Not *burros*, as Rub had characterized them, but children of God, and being tested by God to the limit. His sisters and brothers in Christ. And who could tell—this might be where he was destined to begin his mission. He felt an upsurge of compassion for himself, too, for the younger self inside him that he was sometimes still ashamed of—that insecure, wounded boy who had slipped into Light and Life on that second Sunday, passing the elderly greeters before either of them could fold a program into his hand or guide him by the elbow to a seat.

Keeping his head lowered, he had skirted behind the back row to the far end and taken the aisle seat. As he sat down, one leg of the chair dropped into a rough place in the concrete floor, and for an instant seemed to be collapsing under him. He clutched at the seat in front until the rickety chair righted itself. He lowered his face to hide the blush rising to his scalp.

Suddenly he heard a voice close to his ear and felt a hand rest lightly on his shoulder. "Praise God for bringing you back to us today, Kit." The voice was quiet—not secretive, but as if he and the preacher were simply alone. Out of the corner of his eye Kit glimpsed the preacher's baggy pant leg—the same shiny gray fabric as the week before, the cuffs hanging over the tops of the small, dusty shoes. Kit held his gaze on the shoes and said nothing.

"I praise Jesus for blessing us with your presence on this beautiful, beautiful morning," said the preacher, giving Kit's shoulder a little shake. Each of the five spots on which the preacher's fingers rested on Kit's damp T-shirt pressed a small button under his skin, releasing a sudden stream of emotion that rushed into his chest, filled his throat and rose behind his eyes.

"I didn't have any choice," he said. His neck tensed with the effort of keeping his head from leaning into the sleeve.

"Kit,"said the preacher in the same quiet tone—and the meager syllable of his name seemed to swell—"you've kept your side of the bargain. We won't say anything to your folks about the window. You're free to go if you want to." Kit turned, then, to look at him directly—at the oversized ears protruding from the sides of the balding, cartoonish head, too big for its skinny neck.

For a moment he had the urge to laugh in the preacher's comic book face. But for the first time he noticed the deep lines in his forehead and around his mouth and eyes. It was as if in the days that had passed since Kit first saw the man, he had become real and had grown old.

"The Lord called you in, Kit." The preacher looked down into Kit's eyes. "The door will always be open."

Then he lifted his hand, leaving Kit's shoulder tingling under the damp T-shirt. The preacher moved down the aisle. The singers and musicians were taking their places on the platform, but Kit made no move to leave. He sat as if attached to the seat. If I get up, he told himself, the chair might fall over and everyone will turn and look.

The boy at the drum set bashed the cymbal and began whomping out a jumping-and-shouting beat. Those in the congregation who were still seated leaped up. Kit rose with reluctance and stood rigidly, not allowing a single part of his body to move, not an inch. Up front, above the field of waving hands, Kit thought he recognized in the great rounded shoulders the man who had lost it the week before—the Hulk. His hairy-backed paws were extended high in the air and bobbed with the rest of him, like a boisterous, overgrown dog who keeps popping up behind a fence in a steady attempt to leap over it.

Kit stared at his back, willing him to turn around. Was the man just going along with the crowd or had he gotten saved last week? Then the man did turn around. He *twirled*, like a lumbering ballerina, and twirled again as he jumped. Kit caught sight, in that instant, of the Hulk's face, the mouth hung open and cheeks lifted in wonder and delight like the face of a toddler seeing snow for the first time, alight with raw, unselfconscious joy.

Somehow it wrenched Kit's heart to see the big man behaving as if he had no idea his gestures looked ridiculous. Sunlight streaming in the east windows bathed the front rows and reflected off the perfectly round bald spot at the back of the Hulk's head. *Bill's* head, his name was *Bill*. What was going on in Bill's head? What was it like to be so filled up with joy that you didn't care what anyone else thought of you?

Bill was clapping double-time to the music now, and all at once, with a shout, he plunged into the aisle and took off running—down front, around the first row, up the side aisle, around to the back and down again—galloping in a circle around the congregation. Then others started to peel out of their chairs and join him, running in time to the music and shouting hallelujas.

Kit kept his eye on Bill, who was no longer lumbering but light on his feet. For a moment, Bill looked his way and seemed to see him. The eyes were clear and bright, with no trace of the pain that had glazed them the week before. He was smiling with his whole face, as if all his suffering had been a brilliant, hilarious joke and he had just now understood the punchline, which was: happiness.

Behind Bill, the glow of the sunlight through the windows seemed to fill the tabernacle, turning golden the waving hands and arms of those people still standing by their chairs, like a field of wheat bending to a strong wind. Those who were running in the aisles seemed hardly to touch the ground, like birds skimming across a pasture. Of their own accord Kit's arms floated into the air and stretched full-length. His body swayed to the music. Tears slid down his cheeks and dripped off his chin.

All his resentment, defiance, and tension dissolved without a struggle. For just a moment, as he realized this, he felt a small wave of panic at an image of himself hollowed out and empty, but as quickly as the panic appeared, it was gone, and the space left inside filled up with a feeling of peace, strength, and vitality he had never known, his limbs energized as if he had the body of the best athlete in the world. With no forethought he slipped out of his seat into the aisle as the runners came around the back again. He knew what had happened. He had just accepted Jesus into his heart.

...

And the spirit of God moved upon the face of the waters and God said, let there be Light, and there was Light. He glanced at the others in the boat—some with cameras hanging from their necks, a woman in a halter dress, holding out a tube of sun screen for another woman to apply to her naked shoulders. He wanted to shout, You see it? It's here all around you! The goodness of the Lord Almighty! Look!

❖ Eleven ❖

The boat ploughed steadily around a curve of land and then they were through the inlet and there was the village—its humble shops and houses climbed away from the dock a little way up the hillside. A ribbon of street divided them and led to the white colonial church at the top. Kit could make out figures near the shore standing knee deep in the water, others squatting on the grass, and as the boat drew closer, he saw they were women and girls washing clothes in the lake, slapping them clean against the rocks and draping them on the shrubs and grass to dry in the sun—long red ribbons, red and white striped pants and skirts, pale blue *huipiles*.

A crowd of children met the boat. As the passengers disembarked, they surged up, outstretched arms hung with bright trinkets.

"*Regalos para tu cariño. Cinturones, cinquenta centavos.*"—Gifts for your sweetheart. Belts, fifty cents—"Pret-ty, pret-ty neck-lace! *Veinticinco centavos por los dos.*"

They were selling dainty handwoven belts, and necklaces of dyed beans. Kit was drawn to the colors, which half disappeared against the vivid patterned clothing of the children themselves. Should he succumb? For two dollars and fifty cents he could bring back a necklace and a belt each for Lorie and Edie, Claudia and Jeannette.

Seeing him eye the merchandise as if to make a choice, the children pressed in on him from all sides. Here were not the shy smiles and twinkling round eyes of the children he sketched in the park. These children's eyes were hard and grim. He stood amidst their clamor, unsure what to do. As the other tourists began to open their purses and finger the goods, some of the children swarmed away like a flock of birds settling

127

on a new tree. There were ten or twelve of the little vendors. Could he buy from some and not from all? It would end with his spending much more than he had intended—five or six dollars, just to buy trinkets, and more than he needed. He had already spent his allotted gift money on the red *huipil*. He couldn't make up his mind what to do, and it seemed shameful to stand surrounded by such desperation while debating over the expenditure of five dollars versus two dollars and fifty cents.

Having edged away, shaking his head and murmuring in Spanish, "No thank you. Maybe later," he escaped the dock and walked up the hill of the main street. A small Saturday market was in progress in front of the church. *Ladinos*, indigenous, soldiers, and a few tourists proceeded uphill and down, past shops and tiny hole-in-the-wall eating places. Down the narrow side streets Kit could see tunneled perspectives of the lake and within a very few blocks the dwindling of the village into mountain slopes. There were hardly any cars. Those there were, squeezed past each other or waited to take their turn at the intersections of the cobbled cross streets.

There was a considerable presence of armed soldiers in the town. Some ambled through the market. A few sat in the open air cantinas, smoking cigarettes and drinking beer. He became aware of the sensation of being closed in, stranded between the lake and the mountainside.

For a while he searched the main thoroughfare for a town office or town center, then turned down a side street. Here the narrow way intensified his claustrophobic feeling. One- and two-story buildings pressed close against each other and sagged into the street. The few people he encountered did not return his smiles or greetings. They watched him blankly or averted their gaze and slipped back into doorways out of sight.

At the end of the lane, he found himself above the inlet where the women were washing clothes. He looked for some sort of communal festivity in their work, but the women labored silently. A little girl walked backward across the rocks, stooping to unroll a length—maybe twenty or thirty feet—of woven ribbon. Across her back, a baby was swaddled in a shawl, and the girl stopped at intervals to hoist the infant back into position. Two of the women wore no *huipiles*, but were clad in brassières. A third, bare-breasted, was using a bar of soap to wash her hair in the lake.

He wished he had oil paints to capture the colors—the blue sky, the pink-tinged clouds, the women's brown skin and black hair, and the extravagant colors of their clothes spread out to dry.

With pencil and pad he drew a sketch of the woman up to her knees in water as she bent to rinse the soap out of her long hair. It was only a quick sketch with lines enough to suggest her curves and the unconscious grace of her bent posture. He looked back and forth between the drawing and the woman, who remained unaware of his scrutiny. For a few moments he viewed the sketch with satisfaction, even pride, until the real woman, who had straightened and was squeezing the water out of her hair, gazed up toward the village. He shrank back into the shade of the lane. Had she seen him? Probably not, but his motives shamed him. Would he have drawn her if she hadn't been half naked? The woman may not have owned more than one *huipil*, her only one drying on the rocks. It was a sketch he would never be able to show Ezra. Or Colleen.

He made his way back to the partially ruined church—another victim of earthquake—and saw a *ladino* man leaning against the doorway.

He introduced himself and asked if the man knew where the fire station was.

"*¿Eh?*" the man said, frowning.

Kit had looked up the word for fire station and prepared the question ahead of time. He repeated the phrase, which sounded very little like 'fire station' to him: "*¿Dónde está la estación de bomberos?*"

The man gave a shrug. Kit blamed his flat North American pronunciation and said it once more.

There wasn't any, the man said.

"*¿Dónde está el camión de bomberos?*" Kit tried again. —Where is the fire truck?

The man pursed his lips doubtfully and shook his head. "*No sé nada del camión de bomberos.*"

No fire truck? How could that be?

A nun came out of the church. The man turned to her and repeated Kit's questions. The nun also shook her head.

"*No hay una estación de bomberos ni camión de bomberos,*" she confirmed. Why was he asking?

Because … How could he explain why he was asking? He reached into his pocket for the letter from *Señor* Reina, on behalf of the villagers. Clipped to it was the photo of the Light and Life congregation standing in front of Pumper No. 5.

The nun looked at the photo and studied the letter, her lips moving as she read. She appeared to be translating, perhaps without much ability, but relying on the words in Spanish and English that were alike. When she finished, she said she was sorry but they hadn't received any fire truck. It wasn't there.

"*¿Conoces al Señor Reina? Señor Oscar Reina?*" Kit asked.

The two shook their heads. "*No, no lo conozco,*" said the nun.

Kit thanked them and left. In the distance, the volcanic peaks sweeping down to the shores of the black lake loomed like an illustration to a dark fairy tale. The wind was whipping up white caps, and the launch, tied up at the dock, thrashed at its tether, making it difficult for passengers to climb aboard. Several young men grabbed at its sides to hold it against the pier.

What could it mean that the fire truck wasn't here? Kit looked again at the letter:

> *I write on behalf of the people of Santiago de Atitlán to convey their gratitude. Here are their very words which they have asked me to repeat to you:*
>
> *We citizens of Santiago de Atitlán thank you and pray for God's blessings on you, our brothers and sisters of Light and Life Tabernacle, U.S.A., for your generous gift of fire engine Pumper No. 5. Your blessed modern technology gift is given us by the grace of God to prevent terrible disasters in our town when sparks excite into fire by the blowing wind of Xocomil in dry seasons. We are proud that the Almighty God has led you, kind people of Light and Life Tabernacle to bestow this gift on our poor pueblo. May the Lord Jesus Christ bless you all your lives.*

It was dated four months ago. There seemed no question which village the truck had been sent to and that it had arrived. Kit himself had been at the fire station on the day in June when Light and Life's congregation watched an off-duty firefighter—a born-again Christian—drive it away to the railway yard. It was to be conveyed on a flatbed car to Louisiana, where— *Señor* Reina had written to say—he had arranged for it to go by boat along with a shipment of building supplies donated by U.S. evangelicals.

So, where was Pumper No. 5?

Kit walked down the hill to a small *comedor* open to the street. It was 1:30 p.m. He felt dizzy with hunger. He went in and ordered a plate of *tamales* and rice. As he waited for his food to arrive, four soldiers came in. They pushed two tables together, hung their rifles over the backs of their chairs, and sat down with a creaking of boot leather and ammunition belts. A weatherbeaten old man who had been drinking a beer at the only other table put some coins down and left quietly, his beer half finished.

The owner of the *comedor* came quickly over to take the soldiers' orders, then disappeared into the back, where Kit could hear him speaking in clipped, harsh undertones. Leaning back in their chairs, the soldiers spoke jokingly with each other in a rapid Spanish laced with slang.

After the owner had brought the soldiers their food and four bottles of *Gallo*, one of them turned to Kit and called: "*¿Eres gringo?*"

Kit nodded. "*Soy gringo. Soy de* United States—*los Estados Unidos.*"

The other held his hand out palm upward to the soldier sitting next to him, who slapped a *quetzal* into it. He had won the bet, apparently. He turned back to Kit and said good-naturedly, "Hel-lo. How are ju?" The others laughed and parroted his attempts at English.

"Do you speak English?" Kit asked, moving his chair closer.

"A leetle, leetle," said the soldier. The foreign syllables sent the others into fits of laughter. "*Leetle leetle leetle,*" they mocked him, but he ignored them. "Ju like beisbol?" he asked Kit. "New York Yahnkeess? Bruleen Dozhairss?"

"Brooklyn Dodgers," said Kit. He had no interest in baseball and knew nothing about either team. "*Y usted?*"

"*Yahnkeess,*" the soldier replied and added amiably in Spanish, "So we are enemies, eh?"

The soldiers went back to their meal and Kit's food came. He finished it quickly, paid the bill and was starting to leave when he decided to ask the question.

Had a fire truck … —he didn't know the grammar for the passive form, *been delivered*— … arrived in Santiago recently?

The soldiers looked at him. "Why would a fire truck arrive here?" said the Yankees fan.

"It was a gift to the village," Kit said.

The soldier snorted and gulped down the last of his beer. Smirking at his comrades, he said, "*Es mucho mejor quemar un pueblo que salvarlo del fuego.*" The others snickered and raised their bottles.

"*Por favor, ¿repite?*" Kit said. He wasn't sure of the word *quemar*. The soldier repeated it, slowly and deliberately, performing a pantomime of lighting a match and tossing it toward the kitchen. There was a half-bold, half-furtive leer on his face. *It's much better to burn the village down than to save it from fire.*

The small motor launch heaved and dropped into the troughs of the waves as it chugged back across the lake. Shutting his eyes and turning his face to the wind, Kit took deep breaths. Under his closed lids pictures came and went—Ezra hugging *Señor* Reina in that encompassing embrace of spiritual enthusiasm, disregarding the usual difference in size between himself and the person he was hugging. The two men praying together, their heads bent, *Señor* Reina's hand resting on Ezra's shoulder.

With the lurching of the boat, clammy sweat broke out on Kit's forehead and uneasiness needled the pit of his stomach. For a moment he thought he might have to retch out his lunch over the side. But he breathed back the impulse and tried not to think about the image sickening him—his pastor as a deceived, therefore deceivable, man.

Kit wandered up and down the streets of Panajachel, poking his head into a dozen bars, cafes and shops, on the verge of giving up the search for Rub and returning on the 5:30 bus. He had stopped in front of a cantina when he heard a piercing whistle and his name called from overhead. Rub was sitting on the balcony of the corner bar with his feet on the rail, a bottle of beer in one hand and two fingers at his lips readied for another whistle. Rub dropped his feet to lean over the rail.

"Find your fire truck?"

Kit shook his head.

"Come on up." He waved his bottle at Kit with a little flourish, causing it to slip between his fingers, roll on the balcony floor and wedge between the rails. Rub, watching the beer make a foamy waterfall to the ground below, said indifferently, "Damn."

To the waiter who had followed Kit up the stairs, Rub said, "Ginger ale *para mi amigo. Él tiene un estómago Xocomil.*" Gesturing to Kit to sit down, he said, "Queasy?"

"Yeah," Kit said. "The ride back was rough."

"And no dice on the fire truck."

"No." Kit looked away.

"No surprise there. What good would a fire truck be in a minuscule little ville like Santiago? You can barely get a car down those so-called streets."

"This guy, *Señor* Reina, said it was there. Maybe he changed his mind where to send it." Kit frowned. "But in his letter he says it got there."

He had taken out the folded letter again, not intending for Rub to read it—the possibility of Ezra's having been duped was a notion he wanted to keep to himself —but Rub plucked the paper from him. When he finished reading, he slapped it down on the table. One edge of the letter darkened where it lay in a pool of spilled beer.

"Yeah, that truck never got there."

"But why did *Señor* Reina specify that particular village if—"

"You kidding? Picturesque little burg on the shores of a lake? Colorful, barefoot *indios*? It'd get Scrooge to dig into his pockets, that's my guess. I'll lay a hundred bucks your *Señor* Reina handed Pumper No. 5 over to a government crony back in GC. Swapped it for a business favor."

Kit picked up the letter, blotted the corner with the dry edge of an otherwise sodden napkin, and replaced it in his pack.

Rub leaned back in his chair with his hands behind his head. "Yeah, ten to one your truck's sittin' in a nice plush station in *Zona 12* where all the government honchos and foreign ambassadors have their villas."

"*Señor* Reina is a Christian businessman—" Kit said.

"—Christian or any other kind, that's how business gets done here. Here? Hell, *every*where."

"But he's a Ríos Montt supporter. Ríos Montt doesn't allow corruption in government. I've heard him preach."

"Oh, you mean—" Rub pulled himself upright, puffed out his chest, and thrust his thumb and two fingers in the air. Kit nodded. Rub chuckled. "You'd like to think, wouldn't you?" He smiled blearily. "Oh Christ, don't look so goddamn mournful. Think of it this way, it's better than the alternative."

"What alternative?"

"Communism. That's why we're in this country. That's why we deal with these thugs. They keep the country safe for Coca-Cola and Del Monte. You want your cheap supply of Coke and bananas cut off? To say nothing of coffee." The man in the apron brought Kit his ginger ale and left. Rub whistled him back. "*Un café*," he ordered, "*sin crema*." Turning back to Kit, he said, "That's the bottom line, sonny. Your right to cheap Coke, bananas, and coffee. And sugar. And cotton. The bottom line."

Rub closed his eyes and heaved a deep sigh. Kit wondered if he was about to drop off to sleep, and asked, "What happened to your plans with the lady?"

Rub raised his eyelids. "The lady." He shook his head. "The lady had another thing going." He stared gloomily at the heads of the passing tourists on the street below and ran a hand over his face. "This place is depressing."

They both sat without talking for a few minutes, Kit thinking about his walk through the village, the closed faces of people on the street, the hurry of the *comedor* owner to bring the soldiers their plates, the claustrophobic feeling he had experienced.

"The people over there in that village seemed kind of unfriendly," he said. "Even the little kids, the vendors."

"Oh yeah." Rub stirred himself and spoke with more animation. "Now that I think of it, they came in for some punishment a while ago in that burg. Army was in there mopping up subversives. They probably haven't bounced back yet. Takes a while before the mercenary spirit overrides fear—" What kind of punishment, Kit thought, but stopped himself from asking. He didn't want to know. "—And before that, the village priest got himself killed. Guerrilla sympathizer."

"Killed by the army, you mean."

"Another fuck up. He was an American. Every time they off an American, Congress squeezes its ass tighter on military aid."

Kit frowned. "I don't understand why Catholics would be on the side of the communists. I know Catholics aren't exactly true Christians, but they are religious, and communists don't allow any religion, do they?"

"Well, what the hell is a communist? It's a label. It's a generic term. These Chinks, Indios, Cubans, they're different breeds, different cultures, know what I mean? Half the communists I had the pleasure of ... entertaining ... in Vietnam, were fucking Buddhists. There were Buddhist priests that sloshed gasoline on their heads and set themselves on fire just to protest Uncle Sam's presence. And *indios,* most of 'em are all some version of Catholic. You can't keep 'em from lighting candles for their dead grandmas. It's a one-size-fits-all kind of term, communism. You need it to simplify the dialogue."

"What dialogue?"

"*Us* vs. *them.* In Vietnam, communism was pretty much just nationalism—Vietnam for the Vietnamese. In Guatemala, its land rights, Indian rights, workers' rights. But the end result is the same."

The coffee came. Rub tasted it and shoved it aside. "Christ! Nescafe!" He curled his lip. "Guatemalan coffee's the best in the world, but you can only get it in the USA." He hoisted himself out of his chair, swaying as he got to his feet.

"Maybe we should stay over tonight," Kit suggested. "You look ... tired."

"Wasted, you mean?" Rub gave a short, barking laugh. "Looks can be deceiving, my son." Then as if deliberately to make Kit nervous, he said, "I think I'll have one for the road. You got any change on you? I only got big bills left." Kit delved into his pockets and pretended to come up empty. Before he could protest, Rub was rummaging through the flap pocket of Kit's daypack, and the sketchpad fell open onto the floor.

"What have we here?" Rub grabbed it up and began to flip through it, stopping at a picture of the Antigua textile sellers on the cathedral steps. "Whoa, *amigo*," he said. "Who knew you were a fucking artist?" Kit tried to snatch the pad back, but Rub held it out of reach, riffling through the pages until he came to the sketch of the woman at the lake. He whistled. Kit flushed. Tapping a finger on the woman's breast, Rub said, "If that picture wasn't giving me a mild boner, I'd say it was art." He shook his head. "Hidden talents, man. Hidden talents," and handed the sketchpad back to Kit. "Where the hell is that waiter? ¡*Mesero*! *Garçon!*" he called.

To distract him, Kit said, "How about I draw a sketch of *you*?" He took out his pencil and opened the pad to a blank page and laid it on the table. "You'll have to hold still, though."

"Christ, no." He turned away. "I pride myself on having the mug of a *diablo*," he said. "You don't want to look at it too long or you turn to stone."

"You have an interesting face to draw," Kit said, sketching a few lines. Rub took the pencil out of his hand.

"It's interesting all right. Useful, too." He tossed the pencil onto the table. "Saves me a shitload of time and bruised knuckles when someone needs to be intimidated." He shook his head. "No, I'm going to get one more drink and then, *vamanos!*"

"Really," Kit said, taking the pencil up again. "I'd like to draw you."

"*Amigo*, I'm not in the mood."

Rub's back was to the waiter, who had come to the top of the stairs and was raising an inquiring eyebrow. Kit shook his head discreetly and the waiter retreated. Rub leaned forward and shouted over the balcony, "Hey someone send that goddamned *mozo* up here." He slumped back in his chair with a grunt and gazed at Kit, who was unconsciously tapping the pencil on the table. "Oh fuck it," he said. "I don't give a shit. *Draw* my goddamned 'interesting' face. Then we're getting out of here."

He bent over and fished the bottle from between the balcony rails. There were still a few drops at the bottom. He tilted his head back and shook them onto his tongue. Then he settled into a side-leaning, half upright position with one arm on the table and squinted over Kit's shoulder at the *cantina* across the street and the mountain beyond the town.

With a few spare strokes, Kit drew the face, adding the severe crew cut, the knit band at the neck of the T-shirt, the trace of Adam's apple buried in the muscled neck. Then he stopped and scrutinized the sketch. If he had been drawing it in color, the shot capillaries in Rub's eyes and the pink rims of the lids would have brought out a sense of blurry dissipation in a habitually drunk man. But the blacks and whites and half tones of his pencil, catching a glint of the watery pools behind Rub's slack underlids gave the effect, surprisingly, of a contained sadness.

Sketching in the fan of small wrinkles around the eyes and the deeper ones between the eyebrows, he began to see someone other than the man he thought he had been looking at across the table. Rub's lips had parted, his mouth having fallen slightly open so that the jaw no longer retained its bulldog thrust. The unconvincingly defiant cock of the head was gone, too.

Kit paused before the final task of representing the ravaged skin. The more Kit studied the face, the more responsibility he felt not to flatter Rub or condescend to him by ignoring the scars altogether. You could almost look past the rough surface and into the core, as you could through the transparent lamina of the human body in biology texts. With a few subtle shadings, he suggested here and there on the cheek, on the throat, on the forehead, the texture of Rub's face, the layers, laid bare and sealed up again.

Kit laid the sketch on the table for Rub to see. Before looking down at it, Rub drew back a little, thrusting his jaw again into its bulldog pose and cocking his head.

When he allowed his eyes to fall on the sketch, his head gave a little involuntary jerk. "Jesus," he muttered.

The waiter came up the stairs then, but Rub didn't seem to notice. "¡Qué bien!" the waiter said, looking from the portrait to Rub and back again. "¡Se parece a él!"—It's just like him!

Rub shook his head. All he said was, again, "Jesus."

He didn't order another drink. Instead he rolled the sketch up carefully and slipped it into his pants pocket, then rose and threw some bills on the table.

"Okay," he said quietly to Kit. "Party's over."

As they went down the stairs, he lay a hand on Kit's shoulder, a comradely gesture, but also, apparently, to steady himself. Rub's hand on his shoulder gave Kit the impression of a man staggering under a heavy weight.

They made their way to where the Peugeot was parked. Kit knew there was no way Rub would let him take the wheel. He thought about giving an excuse to stay on and return by bus in the morning, but even more than he wanted to avoid Rub's ridicule and perhaps wrath at such a suggestion, he didn't want to be left in the dismal town to sit in some dingy room with his thoughts as his only company.

Rub took the drive back with suicidal obliviousness to the sheer drop-offs. Kit turned at one point and noticed that Rub's eyelids were drooping. "Hey," he said, nudging his arm. "Are you awake?"

Rub's eyes fluttered open. "Just giving the old peepers a break." He put on his sunglasses, which made it harder for Kit to notice if he was dozing off.

"How come you're studying at *Tres Américas*?" Kit asked, to keep Rub talking. "Your Spanish already seems perfect."

"Naw, it isn't. But it needs to be. Sometimes you can't afford to make even a small mistake. I knew a guy once—a gook spy overheard him make one miniscule grammar error. But it was an error no native speaker would make. That was the last anyone saw him. Whole operation had to be shut down. For all I know he's still in a Vietnamese prison somewhere. Chinese-American. Looked the part but couldn't talk it."

Kit remembered how scornfully the Europeans at Aurelia's had spoken about Rub, as if he was passing himself off as something more than he was. How could he make up a story like this?

"So are you doing the same kind of work here as you did in Vietnam?"

Rub swerved around a *campesino* family leading a donkey. This seemed to wake him up. "Let's say I'm doing Continuing Education right now," he said. "Brushing up. For me it's a vacation. I dig languages. I speak five languages fluently, not counting Spanish—Chinese, Persian, Russian, Vietnamese, Tagalog," he said, ticking them off on his fingers. He didn't seem to be bragging, but only stating a matter of fact. "And I can get by in Arabic, Khmer, Indonesian, and Hmong. Right now I'm also studying with an *Ixil* instructor at *Tres Américas*. There's twenty-two different Mayan languages, did you know that? *Ixil* reminds me of South African *Xhosa*. Makes you sound like you got a ping-pong match going on in your mouth." He demonstrated the exotic consonants. Then he began to switch from one language to another, ending the performance with a recitation of formal and slang expressions for the verb '*to get laid*' in all ten languages.

"I learn by hearing, man. Imitation. Like a baby does. After that, I go back and study it in a book."

That's how I'm learning, Kit thought. It was another way to look at it. Not that God wasn't ultimately responsible, maybe just not as directly as he had thought.

"In high school it was all books," Kit said. "I couldn't figure Spanish out. But I'm actually not all that bad at it."

When Rub dropped him off outside the *Candelaria* neighborhood, he stopped the car and lit a cigarette. "You stood up for me over at Aurelia's when that Nazi kraut asshole was making his bogus attempt to put me down." He wasn't looking at Kit—he watched the smoke he was blowing out the window. "Not that I needed defending, but I appreciated the thought, nonetheless."

He was astonished that Rub would have taken note of something like that. He himself couldn't even remember exactly how he had defended him.

Rub said, "This guy doesn't forget a favor, *amigo*. Especially one without ulterior motives."

❖ Twelve ❖

Early Wednesday morning, hurricane winds swept across Guatemala, knocking over trees and power lines. In the Martinez house, Kit woke to the wind screaming through chinks in the concrete and ripping tiles off the roof. No one went to work or school that day. Kit helped the family patch the roof and in the afternoon joined members of his *iglesia* to clear tree limbs from the roads.

In the *parque central,* three ancient trees, in whose shade he had sat drawing portraits of children, had toppled over. The stone bench, upended when the massive tree roots were ripped from the ground, was being used by a group of children as a slide. He felt disoriented. Only a few weeks ago the *parque central* had been an unfamiliar, exotic place, and now, just when it had become a kind of haven, it was a foreign landscape again. As he picked his way through the debris, he thought this must be how it had felt after each earthquake Antigua had suffered.

He turned toward the sidewalk in front of the municipal building. What had happened to the homeless people when the hurricane came through? Had they been swept away in their sleep and scattered like leaves? "Lord," he muttered, "what was the purpose?" He instantly regretted the criticism implied. Forgive me, Lord. If you choose to reveal your purposes, I rejoice. If you don't, I accept that, too. I know that everything happens according to your plan.

After lunch on Saturday *Señora* Martinez and the younger children went to the bus to see the *señora's* elderly cousin off on a trip to *El Progreso*. Kit went along to carry cousin Pilar's suitcases and to help afterwards with the week's shopping at the *mercado*.

As they were waiting for Pilar's bus to leave, another bus pulled in and let off passengers. Indigenous vendors waited for their bundles to be tossed down while the tourists streamed away toward the market. Standing at the edge of the crowd about to board, Kit felt his heart leap.

She stood in the doorway of the bus in a blue, sleeveless dress. Her hair had come loose on one side, and there was a red spot on her tanned cheek as if she had been sleeping with her head propped in her hand. As he took a step toward her through the crowd, she turned to the driver.

"I want to go to Puerto San José next Saturday," she shouted in Spanish over the noise of the idling engine. Kit moved in closer. "When does the bus to *Escuintla* leave?" she called. From inside the bus, the driver mumbled an answer. "And how long in *Escuintla* between buses? ... One hour? *Muchas gracias.*" She headed toward town without noticing Kit. He wanted to apologize for his stupidity at the *Convento de Las Capuchinas*, but before he could think of what to say, she had crossed the *Alameda Santa Lucía* and disappeared into the Saturday crowds coming from town.

Where had she arrived from? Returning from out-of-town at this hour, she must have skipped yesterday's class, if she *had* one on Friday. She hadn't mentioned anything more about her Spanish study or which school she was attending. Was she actually taking Spanish? She seemed fluent enough.

The Martinez girls were now at his side pulling on his sleeve, "*Vamos Cristóbal, vamos al mercado.*"

"*Un momentito,*" he said. He stepped up to the bus and asked the driver where the bus had come from. The driver jerked his finger in a northwesterly direction. "*Del norte,*" he said, "*Chichicastenango ... Huehuetenango.*"

Chichicastenango was a tourist destination about four hours away. He had almost gone there himself on Phil's recommendation but decided against spending the money. But why would she come back on a Saturday morning? The famous Chichicastenango *mercado* was a Sunday, not a Saturday, market.

Yet she wouldn't have gone as far as Huehuetenango. It was a lot farther north, and it was dangerous. Phil had told him that the branch of their school in Huehuetenango had shut down for the duration of the war. People didn't travel there unless they had to.

He wondered at her fearlessness, traveling alone in a country at war, but he couldn't help being glad she hadn't had a male companion. And next Saturday she was going … where did she say? Puerto … Puerto San José.

"*¡Vamos Cristóbal!*" Sara and Ana Luisa grabbed him by the arms and marched him away.

At church Kit asked Daniel about Puerto San José. It was a small beach resort, he said, on the Pacific Coast. Guatemalan families, and some foreign tourists, too, went there to swim. It was very cheap because of the war. Not as many people were traveling there now as before. "But *no es* dangerous. There have army base and navy base."

At *Tres Américas*, Kit asked Phil about going to the coast.

"Yes, you should see a bit of the countryside—the lowlands," he said. "Big plantations, quite flat. It's the land of cotton and sugar. Hot and humid, so the beach is quite nice—black volcanic sand. I think you'd fancy it."

He warned Kit not to forget his passport. There would be army checkpoints.

"But you should not leave your passport in your room," put in Rita. She appraised Kit's white freckled skin and warned him also of the Pacific rays. "Be sure to cover yourself or put on *crema!*"

The next day she brought him a waist pouch—a cloth pocket with a string attached that he could tie under his clothes—and some zip-closing plastic sandwich bags. "You keep money and passport on your body when you swimming," she cautioned, then touching his belly with the tips of her fingers, she winked. "You keep *all* your valuables close together!"

Kit hung onto Phil's *You should see a bit of the countryside*. If he was going to become a missionary in Guatemala he should know the country better.

His teacher, Berto, left early as usual, but before Kit had the chance to put away his book, Rub slid into his chair. "So you're going to *el Pacífico*."

"I'm still just thinking about it." He was afraid Rub would offer to drive him.

"I wouldn't mind a trip to the beach. Too bad I got business in GC this weekend. You'll have to take the Sardine Can Express this time, *amigo*. Trade sweat with the *campesinos*. It's hotter'n Hades when you get down to the plains."

"Heat doesn't bother me too much."

Rub shook Kit's shoulder amiably. "Tough guy, right?"

Kit shrugged.

"I've put up with a shitload of physical discomfort in my career. Too old for it now, though. Show me the air conditioning."

"Your career is in the army?"

"I joined the army exactly five minutes after I turned eighteen. Sign me up, boys, no questions asked. I would have done it at fourteen if I could have, to get as far away as possible from fucking school and all the rest of the crap." He curled a lip.

"Me, too," Kit blurted impulsively, "I was a hundred-pound weakling. A total blockhead. I flunked Spanish twice. Took three years to get through junior college. That was more school than I ever wanted to see again." He stopped and smiled, gesturing at the courtyard and the tables. "And yet—"

"Huh." Rub nodded at Kit's long, lean frame. "I would have thought you'd have passed through school like a greased rubber. Basketball hero, babe magnet. That kind of shit."

Kit smiled. "Yeah, right."

"Ah, but you found the Lord, didn't you, *amigo*? Praise Jesus! So now you have a reason to keep on keepin' on?"

"Yes, I do. What's *your* reason?"

Rub tilted a pantomimed glass to his mouth.

"Really?"

"Really."

"Not your ... work?" Rub gave a dismissive snort. Kit glanced at a bird in the bougainvillea bush. "Or ... someone you love?"

"And who might that be?"

"A wife somewhere? Kids?"

"One person. One person only." Rub held up his index finger and pointed to his own chest. "*Número uno.*"

"Isn't it hard to look out for number one in the army?"

"You'd think. But it's different when *everyone* has to put up with the crap. Not just you." He leaned back. "No, the only thing that almost made me back out of enlisting was all those shots they give you." He winced. "God, I hate needles. It's why you won't find a tattoo anywhere on my body." He turned up the sleeve of his T-shirt to reveal a bicep decorated only with a trace of old acne bumps. "Last time before I had to go up to the jungle in *El Petén*, they tried to snag me for a yellow fever shot. I says, screw that. I don't do needles. I'll take my chances with the mosquitos. I got skin like leather. No, I can't even watch someone else take a needle." He sat up and leaned across the table.

"You ever see acupuncture needles? Big, long motherfuckers," he said, holding his fingers several inches apart. "They're very fine. A well placed acupuncture needle can get someone to be mighty communicative, without leaving noticeable marks. And if you limit visual access to what's going on, the informant can't even say what it was that made him sing. All the evidence is inside."

The hair rose on Kit's arms.

"Army figured out that trick in Vietnam and passed it on to our friends the *Policía Nacional de Guatemala*—kind of a cultural sharing—hands across the waters kind of thing." He gave an exaggerated shudder. "Jesus, never mind. Just talking about it gives me the creeps. Change of subject." He leaned back again.

"Did you like the army?"

"Shit, nobody likes the army. It's just easier than other things you could do. When I went in I was a latrine-swabbing grunt, like every other high school dropout that got suckered into it. But then, on my first tour—to the Philippines—some officer noticed how fast I picked up languages. In six months I was speaking *Tagalog* like a native." He smiled. "People in the Army are in awe of shit like that, but to me it's as easy as pissing at a target. I just hang out with the locals. After that they could not promote me fast enough. I could name my country."

He chuckled. "Sometimes I think about all the snotty, arrogant assholes I left behind me in school—kids, teachers—sweating it out back in that go-nowhere town now, at some bank or rathole insurance company with a thousand other jerkoffs sticking their heads over the sides of their cubicles to get relief from the smell of their own farts—" He had been staring off into the middle distance of the fountain, but slowly he brought his attention back to Kit.

"*Amigo*, I'll tell you, the military saved my ass. Not like the army's perfect. But what's the point of being finicky? Sometimes you gotta stick your head in the latrine to fish out the $100,000 Rolex someone dropped in when they were shaking off their dick. That, *amigo*, is life. Anyway, I'm not in the army anymore. I got traded, you might say."

He stood up and stretched. "Well, son, I got a man to see. These *chapín hombres* could care less if they keep you waiting, but they get very fucking huffy if you return the favor. Don't study those verbs too hard. Get it from the street, that's my advice."

Myrna and Sunshine didn't show up for class on Friday morning. They had finally broken through the last of the red tape, had gone to the orphanage in Guatemala City, and were bringing home the little boy. Just after lunch as lessons were resuming, a jubilant voice rang out across the patio.

"Here he *is*! Here's our Roli!" Myrna entered pushing a stroller piled with bags and parcels. Behind her, Sunshine held the hand of a tiny, brown-skinned stick figure of a boy with great hollow eyes and sunken cheeks.

Little Roli hobbled all over the patio on his thin legs, the one leg shorter than the other because of his hip dysplasia. "Roliii," crooned Myrna, coming Kit's way with her arms outstretched. "Roli Poli!" She knelt beside them. "*Dále un abrazo grande a tu mamá?*" she said. Give Mama a big hug?

She pressed him to her substantial bosom and planted several smacking kisses on his gaunt cheeks. "Roli. Roli Poli!" She gave him a gentle shake and he chuckled.

Roly poly. With all that mothering, Kit thought, he'll grow into that nickname fast.

Sunshine joined them then and handed Kit a neatly folded wool blanket. "We thought you could use this," she said. "We're taking Roli back to Seattle tomorrow. We've got no room to pack it. You said you got chilly at night," she added almost apologetically, "with just the cotton blanket."

Kit was touched. "Thanks a lot. That's nice of you to think of me, with all the stuff you've got to do. But let me pay you someth—"

"No, no, of course not." She frowned the idea away.

"Well, thanks a lot," he said again. "God has really blessed that kid."

"He's blessed *us*!"

The two women gathered up Roli and the stroller and left amidst goodbyes and good wishes. Sitting at a table next to where Kit stood watching the departure, Rub crossed an ankle over one knee, leaned back in his chair, and said, "See, *there's* an up side to the war. It cranks out a perpetual source of foreign orphans for childless dykes."

Kit turned and stared at him. "What?"

"They can't adopt in the U.S."

"What do you mean?"

"Lesbos."

"They aren't ... lesbos."

"Oh yes."

"How do you know that?"

"Trust me. I know."

"You're wrong," Kit said. "Why would you think that? They're sisters, or ... friends."

Rub snorted. "Yeah, they're sisters alright. *In* the sisterhood."

"They're Christians."

"*Gay* Christians. Ain't that the devil!" He winked. "Live and let live, though, huh?"

Rub's teacher came then, and Kit walked slowly across the patio to his table, where Berto sat reading a newspaper. Throughout what was left of the afternoon, Kit's mind was only half on the lesson. He kept looking over at the fountain, where he had watched Sunshine kneeling next to Roli with one plump, motherly arm around his little shoulders and giggling as he splashed water over the two of them. She had been looking at the boy like he was a treasure she had just stumbled on. Covetously. Myrna, too. They looked like the young couples at Light and Life, when they brought their newborn to church for the first time. He remembered the exhausted, happy faces watching proudly and anxiously as people passed the baby around, relaxing again only when the infant was safely back in their arms.

He couldn't stop thinking about it. Lesbians. Not Sunshine and Myrna but lesbians. The women's relationship was an abomination in the sight of the Lord. How could God allow a child to be delivered to them? A boy, too. Lesbians hated men.

On his way home, he thought of the children he had seen among the people who were again sleeping on the sidewalk next to the municipal building—the same ones as before the hurricane or new ones, he couldn't tell. That might be how Roli would have ended up when the orphanage got too crowded. Or maybe it's how he had been found in the first place—on some sidewalk huddled against the cold among strangers. And now … *Unnatural lusts. Unclean things. Abomination.*

They *were* lesbians, of course they were. He was an idiot not to have figured it out. Probably everyone else at the school knew. "You're a babe in the woods," Rub had said. Dean had been sneering at him for years about his ignorance. "Crack a book, for Christ sake. Read a newspaper. Take those absurd headphones out of your ears."

He wandered into the *parque central*, holding the wool blanket the women had given him. The downed trees from the storm had left the park bare and unshaded. He sat down on a stump and gazed at the naked Sirens carved in stone around the dry fountain. There were holes where water had once flowed from their nipples.

Unaccountably desolate, he hung his head and hunched over on the bench, resting his hands limply on the folded blanket in his lap. That kid—he thought. He might not have had a chance to even survive, and now he's going to be cherished and coddled and probably spoiled—by two women who reject men.

He twisted a corner of the rough wool blanket.

What is it about me?

The sun was sinking behind the volcano *Fuego*. The wisp of smoke rising from its cone had turned blue against the yellowing sunset. He shivered and pulled the blanket to his chest.

Maybe Ezra loved him, or thought he loved him, but Ezra deluded himself about certain things.

He decided that when he went back up to the *Colonia Candelaria*, he would tell *Señora* Martinez he would be eating out that night.

Kit left the house in a hurry, but once he found himself standing on the dark street, he didn't know where to go. There was no prayer service at the church on Friday nights. He couldn't imagine going back to Aurelia's café.

He ended up at the steps of the *Catedral Santiago*. It was just before six o'clock mass. Elderly, white-shawled women climbed heavily to the entrance. Families with infants in arms approached from across the *parque*. Very young children, skipping ahead of their older brothers and sisters, took giant steps up the broad stone stairs.

Kit stopped just inside. The vaulted arches and ornately carved columns disappeared into the shadows overhead. A forest of candles burned at the altar and at intervals along the stone floor.

On the far wall above the altar hung a statue of the crucified Christ illuminated from below. The taut skin and straining muscles of the tormented body had been sculpted to reveal each rib and sinew. In reds, blues and magentas, a tableau of robed worshippers was painted on the wall behind the Christ, the figures crowding at His feet to adore Him.

Kit took a few steps farther in. Voices echoed off the walls as the priest at the altar intoned a prayer and the congregation, scattered here and there in wooden pews, replied in unison. Their words were swallowed up in the cavernous space so that it was impossible to tell if they were Latin or Spanish. The muted drip of water and the rustle of swallows' wings came back to him from years ago. The lofty echo of his own voice. The smell of earth mold. The slam of his fist against concrete.

A nun in a short, gray veil passed, dipping her fingers in a font of holy water before crossing herself and making a curtsy toward the front of the church. She walked silently on rubber-soled shoes down the center aisle and took a place at the front, where she slid onto her knees and bent her head in prayer. Kit crept forward along the north side of the cathedral, keeping close to the wall. Lifelike statues were set into recessed niches at intervals, the folds of their stone robes appeared almost to sway in the flickering candlelight. Graven images.

He took a seat at the end of the pew closest to the back. His eyes closed and again he felt himself in his sanctuary under the overpass, at fourteen or fifteen, drawing pornographic cartoons that featured himself, Kit Lamb, as an irresistible seducer.

Oh Lord. He shivered with embarrassment, imagining God looking down at him as if through a magnifying glass.

Now he was shaking hands with *Señor* Reina after his speech at the Christian Businessmen's Alliance meeting. That firm, masterful handshake—the other hand clamped onto Kit's upper arm. Ezra nodding, nodding like one of those head-bobbing gadgets that sits in the back window of a car.

Reina had never replied to Ezra's letter saying Kit would be coming to Guatemala.

That fire truck is sitting at a plush fire station in Zona 12.

Zona 12. Wasn't that where Ríos Montt's circus tent was, next to that big hotel? No, that was *Zona 4,* Daniel had said.

Ríos Montt. 'The Brassière.'

At Santiago, the women, half naked, washing their only *huipiles* in the lake.

The red *huipil* he'd bought for Jeannette, hidden beneath his underwear in the dresser at the Martinezes'. Some night he could steal up to one of the old women asleep on the sidewalk, lay it across her shoulders and slip away in the dark.

The great hollow echoing space around him with its indistinct murmur of chanting voices did nothing to still his mind. Why isn't there *music* at this mass?

What was this doubt he was feeling? Was it Satan messing around in the places he was most insecure? The thing to do when that happened,

Ezra always said, was to pray. Whether or not the words sounded phony in your own ears, *pray anyway*.

Kit bent his head.

Lord Jesus, drive out my doubt and fear and anxiety. Fill me with the consolation of your presence.

No other words came to him. He opened his eyes and looked around guiltily.

Please, Father, forgive me for praying in this place full of idols. Please understand.

General Efraín Ríos Montt's broad, square, larger-than-life features came to him. The eerie, self-satisfied smile. The heavy, dark eyebrows and wide, flaring nostrils like a bull's. His deep set eyes, glinting. The same triumphant look Kit had seen in childhood on the faces of playground bullies when they pulled off a coup against a weaker boy—stole his coat, knocked him to his feet with a dodgeball, drove him from the playground.

None of those hundreds of people, hands waving in the air, saw the General as I did. What does that say about me?

Back at the Martinezes' he lay down on the bed beneath the wool blanket from Myrna and Sunshine. He had already packed what he would need for his trip to the coast the next day—swimming trunks, a small sketchbook and a pencil, a few toilet articles, a change of shirt and underwear. For a long time he listened to the dying sounds that told him the thirteen members of the household, one by one, were retiring: the splash of the dishpan emptying in the *pila* and the clank of a battered aluminum saucepan being nested inside the others; treble murmurs from the girls' room; the front door opening and closing to let in Pepe and Fredi after an evening of courting their *novias*; a sonorous *'buenas noches'* from *Señor* Martinez and their return *'buenas noches'* as they passed their parents' room; a last flush of the toilet.

He felt the Martinez family and their house partitioning him off. In the room adjacent to his, one of the children would be curled up on the pallet next to *Tía Angélica's* bed—who was it tonight? Sara? What if a sudden earthquake came in the night and dropped the house on everyone's head? What would happen to them all? *Señora* Martinez had a Protestant aunt, an *evangélica*, who had spoken to her about her faith, exposing her to the truth. Still, she, with her lace shawl covering her head, went each Sunday with all her family to the *catedral* and took communion from a priest, who she believed spoke for God. She prayed to the virgin and to the stone saints that decorated the walls of the very church where he had prayed tonight.

Little Sara and the other younger children would go to the gates of heaven and be taken in on the day of judgment. But would Clara be spared at thirteen? What about Tomás? He was sixteen. Manuel was old enough to vote. Jorge was eighteen, old enough to be a soldier.

In the darkness Kit could picture his own absurd body—as if from above—two-dimensional like a child's cartoon drawing. There seemed to be no soul inside him. No *inside* for a soul to inhabit. His body was a grotesque, empty shell, like the cast-off skin of a snake.

Ezra, Jeannette, the congregation—he had no connection with any of them.

He threw off the blanket and swung his legs over the side of the bed. He was disappearing. No one knew him, or cared where he was. He himself didn't know. If he turned on the light, would he recognize the room? He stood up shakily and pulled the light cord. It was the same, yet it looked as it had the day he arrived. A stranger's room.

I don't belong here. It's just a space with random things in it. I don't belong to any place, any thing.

"Christ," he muttered, "get hold of yourself," and went cold at how easily a blasphemy had again slipped from his mouth. He urged himself to go down on his knees but he couldn't get his legs and arms to move.

Say anything, but just pray.

He covered his face with his hands and spoke aloud. "Lord ... Heavenly Father ..." The words sounded meaningless, like words repeated too often.

"Jesus, I'm lost. Help me." He was whimpering into his hands and yet a separate part of him was hovering outside above, disgusted at the sight of him. Shame began to flood in. It started at his head, heating up his scalp and his face and neck, ballooning into his chest cavity, down his arms and stomach and into his groin.

"Dear Jesus," he prayed. "My soul is filthy. Please, take away my sin." He knelt and rested his forehead on the cold floor. "I don't want to live without your light, Lord. Don't leave me." His hands curled around the back of his head, and he rocked, pleading.

For an hour, two hours, he stayed on his knees, shivering, lost. But at least he knew his soul had returned because he could feel it filled with sin.

Eventually he crawled back into bed and drifted into a sleep crowded with dreams: his thug friend from high school, crossing the *Alameda Santa Lucía* on his bike. Not looking where he was going, turning to wave at Kit and crashing into a bus. Ezra preaching to Lorie and Edie under Light and Life's big wooden cross, telling them, "Your brother has a weakness, but it's only a weakness." Colleen stroking Kit's chest. Under her hand is the glowing heart of the Jesus in Martinezes' front room. "Feel this," she says. "Put your hands here. It's warm. It feels good." When he laid his hands on the heart, he felt a surge of sexual heat he couldn't control. He woke, panting and ashamed.

After breakfast Kit went back to his room and stared dully at the day pack sitting on the dresser where he had left it the night before. The time was now 8:15. The bus for Escuintla had been scheduled to leave at 8:00. So that was it. He wouldn't be going now.

He couldn't fool himself: he wasn't Ezra. He wasn't trying to save anyone's soul. He was just chasing after a woman. Like a dog with its pecker hanging out.

The only thing that would have made her consider liking him was if he denied his faith. So was he ready to throw himself right into the temptress's arms?

But she had never tried to lure him. It was always by accident they ran across each other, and she ended up escaping him every time. Even an unbeliever could see his hypocrisy, his lame professions of faith, his lecherous fantasies. Why wouldn't she want to get away?

Outside his door he heard the squeak of *Tía* Angélica's wheelchair being pushed into her room and the piping voice of little Sara "*¿Tía, quieres* *que te lea de la Biblia?"* Then the weak, tremulous reply, *"Sí corazón, sí,"* and the shuffling of the old woman's slippers as she took baby steps from the wheel chair to the bed. *"¡Tía, ten cuidado!* —the little girl helping her. Sara would hop up to sit cross-legged on the foot of the bed and sound out the difficult words of the Bible passage. After fifteen minutes or so, the old woman would say, *"Gracias, corazon lees bien."*—Thank you sweetheart, you read very well. "Now I'm going to sleep a little." Sara would lay the Bible down, hop off, and run to play with her brothers and sisters and the shouting neighborhood kids of the *Candelaria.*

But God has a reason for everything. In her emphatic little voice Sara was struggling earnestly with the language of *Proverbs.* *"Mira, Cristóbal!"* Yesterday she had shown it to him, pushed it right under his nose. Why had she done that?

And why, every time he ran into Colleen, did something significant happen between them? The question leaped into his mind with a sudden prickling of his skin. Can it all be only coincidence? How was it that on that flight full of Guatemalans he and Colleen—the only North Americans—had just happened to end up in seats next to each other? And why did she keep turning up to draw him in and then push him away? Their singing at the *Convento de Las Capuchinas*—was there a message in it somewhere?

There had to be a reason for her being in his life. God might be testing his resistance to temptation, yes, but maybe it was more than that. A larger kind of test, or some kind of opportunity. Why else would He keep putting this one person in his path? It wasn't accidental. There was something to be learned and God wanted him to learn it.

He threw his toothbrush, toothpaste, soap and a roll of toilet paper into the day pack and grabbed his jacket. He stopped at the door, his hand on the latch. What was he forgetting? His Bible. It hit him that yesterday he hadn't planned to take his Bible. He had actually told himself it would add too much weight. *Too much weight!* And now he thought about the long night of doubt and hopelessness he had just come through and he knew without question that it had been a gift. God had stopped him up short, made him think. He took up his Bible and folded it gently into the extra shirt.

He took less than fifteen minutes to get from *Colonia Candelaria* to *La Polvera*. All the way he prayed, "Lord, I know you're going to make that bus late, and I know you've put Colleen on it."

❖ Thirteen ❖

Sure enough, when he ran up, panting and searching the destination signs on the fronts of the three buses idling next to each other, there was the bus to Escuintla—forty-five minutes late. And when he swung onto the top step just as the driver was revving the engine to start, he saw her over the heads of the passengers. Colleen, wearing the same blue dress as before. She sat in one of the back seats staring out the window. Standing in the aisle, holding lightly to the pole, and swaying as the bus bumped onto the highway, Kit felt a surge of elation. Thank you, Jesus! Hallelujah!

All the way to Escuintla they made no eye contact. At some point she must have noticed his head and shoulders above those of the other passengers, but whenever he took a casual glance behind him, she was always looking intently out the window.

The bus was sweltering by the time they descended onto the coastal plains and pulled into Escuintla an hour and a half later. Kit's shirt stuck to his back where his daypack pressed against it. Disembarking, he blinked grit from the wind out of his eyes and stretched muscles tight from bracing him against the sway and pitch of the bus. As the other passengers got off, he stood a little apart from the door, trying to think of how to approach her without self-consciousness.

Hey, Colleen! I noticed you back there. Are you headed for the beach? But she might think he was following her.

The bus driver got out and lit a cigarette. Wasn't she going to get off? If she was on her way to Puerto San José, she would have to change buses. He stood back to search for her through the dusty windows.

Then she was standing in the door, looking straight at him.

"We keep meeting," she said, stepping down and shifting her camera strap. Her dress was damp at the armpits and the fabric clung to her breasts.

"Yeah," Kit said. "It's a small country. Where you headed?" His voice cracked a little on the lie.

"To the beach," she said. Her tone had the same quality as her gesture at the *Capuchinas* when she touched his arm. Fake friendly.

He shoved his hands in his pockets. "Me too," he said and fixed his gaze on a boarded up *tienda* across the street. "When does the bus come?"

She glanced at her chunky man's watch, which hung loose like a bracelet around her slim wrist. "In about an hour."

"I need to move around," Kit said. "You want to take a walk?"

"No thanks," she said, backing away. "I have a couple of errands to run." She turned and walked off down the street. He wished he had said, "Want company?" But he watched her go.

After two short blocks she turned a corner. The neighborhood, if you could call it a neighborhood, was the last place a lone female should be running an errand. It consisted of low, dilapidated concrete block buildings interspersed with empty lots strewn with litter as if a great tide had swept across the area and then receded.

Kit walked in the opposite direction. By the end of the block he was up to his ankles in food wrappers, plastic bags, tin cans, scraps of soiled toilet paper. He smelled the stench of something dead. There were no people around, unless they were inside the crumbling concrete houses which seemed randomly to have survived whatever event had turned the rest of the neighborhood to rubble. Into the middle of it all, a mangy dog with chewed ears and a corrugated rib cage was being challenged by black, yellow-beaked vultures as it nosed in among what looked like garbage and cast-off clothing. Kit retreated back up the block toward the bus area.

He waited for half an hour while passengers began to accumulate: a few weary, blank-faced indigenous peasants with parcels and baskets to be stowed up top, some *ladino* families, and one group of foreign tourists—boisterous males, eighteen or nineteen years old, speaking what sounded like Australian English. They were kicking a can around the bus lot. The can rolled near Kit and he tried to kick it back, but it skittered sideways under the bus and one of the boys had to fish it out. After that, Kit kept himself apart with the other passengers by the curb.

Colleen returned looking flushed and preoccupied, glancing several times back toward the way she had come. She didn't even notice Kit at first and stood close to the shouting, laughing boys. Kit felt momentarily jealous. But no, they didn't speak to her and she seemed indifferent to them.

Eventually, Kit caught Colleen's eye and waved, receiving a nod and a neutral smile. It doesn't matter. There's a reason why we're here together. He took a breath and went over to her.

"Have you been to Puerto San José before?" he said.

"Yes, once."

"Man, it's hot! I'll be glad to get in the water. I can't believe when we woke up this morning it was only like forty or fifty degrees out—" He felt himself blushing suddenly. When *we* woke up ...

"Mm hm," she said. She didn't notice his blush. He took courage and tried again.

"This is where the sugar and cotton and bananas are grown," he said. Stupid. As if she didn't know.

She eyed him then appraisingly. "You've been doing some reading?" she said. "You'll see plantations from here to the coast."

Then she caught sight of the bus and made a quick move toward it, hugging her camera case to her chest. As soon as the bus pulled up, she took a stand near the door, impatient, it seemed, to be among the first to board. She edged her way in front of an indigenous woman and a *ladino* couple with a baby, got on the bus, and made her way to the back. Only one thing could have made her act so disrespectfully, Kit thought. Avoiding me. But he wouldn't take it personally. He would stick around and see what the Lord had in mind.

An old man lowered himself into the seat next to Kit's and gave him a shy, deferential smile. His front teeth were missing. The Australian boys, standing in the aisle, were rehashing a night of barhopping and sexual exploits. Kit sat in his window seat trying not to listen. The scenery from Escuintla to the coast was dull compared to the magnificent green mountains and valleys around Antigua. Kit watched mile after mile of flat cropland, planted in long symmetrical rows, interrupted here and there by concrete or adobe shanties.

After a while the Australians lapsed into silence, evidently subdued by the heat and humidity. Kit felt Colleen's presence in the back and willed himself not to turn around. He rested his head against the window and closed his eyes.

He woke, an exhausting dream slipping away, as the bus was coming to a stop.

Outside, several armed soldiers in combat fatigues and red berets stood by two jeeps and a covered military truck. Their hands rested on the grips of their rifles. One of the soldiers, a stocky, moon-faced man, climbed onto the bus and stood beside the driver, his submachine gun aimed at the passengers. A paralyzed silence settled over the bus. Kit stopped breathing.

The soldier cast his eyes up and down the rows of seats, leaning a little to look around the Australians at the passengers toward the back. Then he made a summoning gesture with his rifle. He did this four separate times and Kit heard a rustling of clothes and parcels as four *campesinos* in straw hats squeezed past the Australians to the front of the bus.

Then the soldier nodded at the old man sitting next to Kit. The man stumbled as he got up, gripping the back of the seat in front of him, his knuckles big with arthritis. Another man and a woman, the only woman, got the nod—all indigenous, or so they looked to Kit. As each one descended the steps, the soldier prodded them slightly with the side of his rifle. The gesture reminded Kit of turning over a dead animal with a stick.

Finally the soldier stepped off the bus. Out the window, the seven passengers were lined up before five or six soldiers who stood behind them, rifles held loosely but pointed at their backs. The moon-faced soldier passed along the line. With eyes averted, the passengers each produced papers from under hats and from inside shirts and pants pockets. The woman, quite young, her hair in a long thick braid down her back—drew her papers from under the wide sash above her waist. Kit noticed that she was very pregnant.

The soldier glanced at each passenger's papers, then stuffed them into his own breast pocket. After examining the old man's papers, he pushed him out of the line, handed the papers back and jerked his chin toward the bus. The old man took a step away but stopped and looked back. As he opened his mouth to speak, the soldier pushed him hard from behind and he stumbled and fell onto his knees. His hat fell in the dirt and rolled away. He didn't try to retrieve it but got to his feet and walked slowly to the bus. When he was back in his seat beside Kit, his breath coming in short gasps, he immediately turned to look fixedly through the window at the catastrophe he had just escaped.

Two of the soldiers, holding lengths of rope looped over their shoulders, moved along the line of people, searching then knocking parcels out of their hands and tying their arms behind their backs with rough, efficient motions—the pregnant woman just the same as the others. No one in the line protested or spoke. All six stared at the ground.

Kit's heart was racing. Some of the other passengers were watching the scene, some looking away. The *ladino* couple across the aisle were pressed close to each other and clutching their child. The Australian boys were bending to peer out the windows, gawking openly but somberly without comment to each other.

What was Colleen thinking? Kit twisted to get a glimpse of her, but the view was blocked. A ripple of terror passed through his arms as, for an instant, he imagined she had stood up and was forcing her way forward to confront the soldiers.

The stocky lieutenant issued a command then, and another soldier pressed the barrel of his rifle into the back of the man first in line and jabbed hard. The man lurched forward, stumbling to catch his balance without free hands, and all six were herded toward the covered truck. Two soldiers jumped into the truck, lifted the first man from behind by his bound arms and dragged him inside and out of sight. The old man beside Kit flinched and emitted a thin whimper. Kit touched him gently. The man's arm trembled inside the thin cotton of his threadbare shirt.

The lieutenant sauntered back to the bus and slapped it with a metallic bang. It took the driver several tries to get the loud, grumbling motor to catch. Then he shifted gears, and began to pull onto the road.

It was at that moment that Kit saw the two soldiers pluck the woman out of line and push her from behind so that with hands tied behind her she fell on her face. Then a soldier turned her over with his foot, took hold of her long braid and dragged her by it to the truck. They hoisted her up and dragged her inside the vehicle, the heavy mound of her belly and her dangling legs sliding out of sight. The roar of the bus engine had covered the screams that distorted her mouth. He swiveled and caught sight of Colleen now. Through gaps between passengers, he could see her tucked in the last seat by the window and turned so that she was partly obscured by her backpack.

She was holding her camera lens just over the lower edge of the window, clicking one shot after another.

In the remaining time it took to get to the coast, no one spoke, no one slept. Kit's heart was racing, but he felt a kind of shocked disbelief as if what he had just seen could not really have happened, yet whenever the bus rounded a curve and the old man's shoulder touched his, he could feel the tremor still shaking the man's body.

They passed one plantation field after another, with ragged straw-hatted *campesinos* plodding along the roadsides. Kit's mind kept tossing up a picture of the pregnant woman being dragged by her hair through the dirt. He squeezed his eyes shut, but it only made the image more vivid. Her contorted face. The unheard scream. The others helplessly waiting for their turn. A whole bus full of people looking on and still no hope. And the soldiers' quick, casual twists and tugs on the ropes, like assembly line motions.

He shook his head almost involuntarily. Couldn't someone have stood up and denounced them in the name of Ríos Montt? Why hadn't *he* done it? Jesus wouldn't have sat on his hands gawking from behind a window.

It seemed impossible that the bus was proceeding down the highway just as if the delay had been caused by road construction or a minor accident, nobody saying or doing anything. Except for Colleen. She knew the danger she was putting herself in by taking those pictures. What she risked was right in front of her eyes.

At Puerto San José, Kit waited for her. When she stepped off, she glanced at him briefly. Her lips were compressed and her heavy-lidded eyes were dull. She passed without acknowledging him and strode away. Kit stood in the street alone. A flutter of panic sickened his stomach. Already the Australians had moved off toward the town center, as had the *ladino* families. The old indigenous man was shuffling in the opposite direction, having been met by a gray-haired, barefoot woman in *traje*, who—at the man's first mumbled words—threw her hands up to her face.

The town of Puerto San José consisted of a few blocks of mostly unpaved streets lined with straggly palm trees, run down bars, concrete block *comedores*, and adobe *pensiones* with handwritten signs on the doors advertising rooms. Kit paid one *quetzal* for a hot, close cubicle whose door opened directly onto the street. There was a second door to a filthy shared toilet. In the unscreened window hung a fly strip, black with insect carcasses.

It was almost noon and muggy. He changed his khakis for bathing trunks and slung his long-sleeved shirt around his shoulders for a towel. Before leaving, he folded a few pieces of sketchbook paper and a drawing pencil into the plastic zip-close bag holding his passport and money in the body pouch Rita had given him. He tied it around his waist inside his trunks then emerged onto the street, locked the door, and slipped the key into the pouch. In a few minutes he crossed over a road that bridged a canal to the swimming area.

The vast Pacific stretched before him to the horizon. Lines of white surf were rolling in, breaking, and hissing up the black sand. *Black sand!* Kit crouched and took up a handful. It gleamed with the ebony sheen of a black cat's coat and was flecked with sparkling bits of red.

Off to his left, a railroad pier raised high on wooden pilings jutted a long way into the water and ended in a wharf where a small boat was docked. Farther out, a steamer sat at anchor. Black smoke rose from its stack. The sky was such a deep cerulean blue, it looked painted.

Just at the foot of the pier were the gates to a naval base. A sailor was standing talking to an armed soldier, who watched the beach as he listened. Kit turned his back to shut out the sight and scanned the water.

Here and there, the heads of swimmers bobbed, but from a distance he couldn't recognize any of them. He kicked off his sandals and stripped his T-shirt over his head, then ran to the shore, dropped his long-sleeved shirt on the sand and plunged head first into the breaking waves. For an instant, the cold took his breath away, but he staggered up, shaking saltwater from his eyes and tasting sea salt on his lips.

He had never encountered the power of ocean surf. He shrieked and howled and plunged into the cresting waves, holding his ground as one after another bashed against his chest, broke over his head and flowed around him. He ducked under the next wave that surged over him and swam a little farther out.

When he came up for air and tried to regain his footing, his legs were dragged out from under him by the sucking undertow and he felt himself being rushed into deeper water. He struggled to stand, but the sandy bottom was gone. He wondered, with a prick of fear, if he was about to be swept out to sea. A great swell was gathering momentum, and his arms and legs seemed to lose strength as he watched it come, but he took a deep breath and paddled furiously as the wave overtook him and the next thing he knew it was carrying him in on its back. Then his toes were pushing against sand and he was able to wade and stumble through the breaking surf back onto shore just as the next fingers of cold water coiled around his ankles and tried to trip him up. He dropped onto the wet sand and sat panting. The spent waves swirled and dug a trough around him before withdrawing harmlessly into the foam.

He crawled out of reach of the surf and collapsed on his back. The sun and sand warmed him, and he took long, deep breaths. The squeals and shouts of children playing on the beach and the rhythmic roar of the surf grew distant.

"Don't get sunburned."

He opened his eyes slowly, a dream receding. Colleen was standing over him, casting her shadow on his face.

He sat up with a sharp thrill. Drops of water dripped onto his thigh from her hair, which hung in wet strands around her face. He blinked at her in the sunlight. She was wearing an old-fashioned one-piece bathing suit, yellow with a little skirt, which gave her slim-hipped, long-legged body the look of a ballerina. Her tan cheeks were flushed.

"Sit down," he said. She dropped to the sand next to him and began squeezing water out of her hair. The V-neck of her bathing suit revealed a slight cleft between her small breasts. There was a pale fuzz of downy hair on the tops and insides of her thighs. He looked away.

"You've been in the water," he said, foolishly.

"Have you been in yet?"

"I almost got carried out."

"Me, too. The undertow is really strong."

She was combing her fingers through her hair. There were drops of water and goosebumps up and down her arms. She uttered a little sigh.

Oh man, how I want to touch her. He was dizzy with it.

For a piercing moment what had happened outside the bus window flashed in his mind. What's being done to them now? Screams. Bound arms straining. No. He shook his head and smoothed a ridge of sand beside him. Fine black and red grains stuck to his palm. Colleen closed her eyes and tilted her face to the sun. Just let me have this, now, he thought, and pushed the dreadful memory away.

He got to his knees, plucked his shirt from the sand and draped it over her shoulders. "Don't *you* get sunburned," he said, and blushed.

She opened her eyes and gazed at him with that downward slant of the eyelids that made her look as if she had either just wakened or was sinking into sleep. She smiled and pulled the shirt around her, hugged it to her chest. Kit stretched out on his stomach with his chin on his hands. He couldn't sit beside her any longer without his state of arousal becoming obvious.

But if she had noticed, she gave no sign of it. She sat silent, raking her fingers back and forth through the black sand. The incident on the bus was crouching there, unspoken between them, and Kit wondered if she shared his feelings of guilt and was also trying to push it out of her mind. But after witnessing a thing like that, what else could you talk about?

He lay on his belly and imagined she saw him as a coward.

After a few more minutes of silence, Colleen said, "Really. You're going to get sunburned," and she jumped up and threw off his shirt. Kit sat up and shaded his eyes to see her tramp purposefully off through the sand. He felt a stab of guilt and panic. She *had* wanted to talk about it and probably blamed him for his callousness, his crass sexual desire.

She stopped some yards away, rifled through her belongings and returned with a tube of sunscreen.

"Here." She tumbled down beside him again, the tips of her fingers touching his as she passed the tube to him. He raised his knees and planted his feet in the sand to hide the rise inside his trunks. How could he be feeling this way after what he had just been thinking? But she didn't notice. She was gazing off at the ocean. He spread the sunscreen on himself and set it in the sand.

The children of the *ladino* families were playing with buckets at the edge of the shore—mothers and fathers sitting in churning white surf up to their waists. The Australian boys had shown up. Two of them were kicking a soccer ball around in the sand; the others, strong swimmers apparently, appeared as heads bobbing in the surf.

He searched for something to talk about.

"Are you still studying Spanish in Antigua?" he said at last.

Colleen picked up the tube of sunscreen. "Do you want me to do your back?" she said. He took a breath and blew it out silently. Oh Lord, it *is* a test.

"Thanks."

She snatched up his shirt to dust the sand off his back. Then she sat up on her knees behind him. With long, cool fingers, she massaged the lotion into his shoulders and down his back in slow, circular motions that made him drop his head onto his arms, feeling as if he might actually faint if he didn't explode first.

"Want to go in again?" she said. "It's probably safer using the buddy system."

"Sure."

Kit had started to put a hand out to help her up, but she had already jumped to her feet. She ran ahead of him and stopped at the water's edge.

When he caught up with her and they waded into the surf together—shrieking at the icy shock of it—she reached out her hand and he closed his around it. They plunged.

"There's a spot," she said into his ear over the roar of the surf, "where the current isn't so bad." She led him through the breakers farther down the beach, away from where the others were swimming. In the troughs between waves they could touch bottom, and by holding hands they could just keep their legs from being tugged out from under them.

With no warning, a wave broke over their heads and Colleen let go of Kit's hand to clutch his shoulder. Suddenly, his arms were around her, pulling her close. He bobbed with her on a surge of water and when it passed they stayed pressed together, the sand digging holes from under their feet.

A corner of his lips touched hers and he felt his face flame up and *now oh yes* he turned and kissed her and she clasped her slender arms around his neck. Her breasts flattened against him. Oh Christ! She flung her head back and he pressed his lips to her neck, her throat. She let out a small cry as her back arched under his hands. He held her tighter, kissing her wet lips again and again.

Another swell took away their footing, and they floated on it, their legs half entwined, treading water. The skirt of her bathing suit billowed and curled around the back of his arm at her waist. She seemed so light, his arms so powerful, holding her up.

A great wave crashed over their heads, wrenching them apart. Kit felt himself tumbled and sucked away from her. Icy water filled his nose as he struggled to the surface. Coughing and choking, he searched for her, his vision blurred by saltwater. She was yards away, only an indistinct face above the waves. Another breaker slammed into him, pushing him momentarily forward before the tug of the current sucked him back and pulled him farther out. He didn't know how to keep himself from being flung and rolled head over heels. He couldn't find his way up.

Still another wave shoved him backward. He was panicking, drowning. He couldn't save Colleen; he couldn't even save himself. Pitiful.

Then Colleen was there with a hand on his arm, dragging him to the surface. "Swim *that* way!" He was blinded by the salt water, and she pushed him diagonally toward the beach. He chopped at the waves. "You can do it!" she said. At these words his shame turned to grim determination, and he plunged into an unsteady crawl, she swimming along beside him, until they made it to the shore together, only a little distance—they hadn't been out nearly as far as he thought. They tumbled, gasping, onto the sand.

"Oh man," Kit said, after he had caught his breath. He lay with an arm across his eyes. He couldn't look at her. "That was ... " He didn't want to say it was humiliating.

"I'm sorry," she murmured. "It was stupid of me to take you out so far."

"No," he said.

"I've been swimming at ocean beaches forever, but maybe you haven't."

He shook his head. Pitiful.

"It was just panic," she said. "It's happened to me, too."

"It's a good thing one of us could swim."

"You swam out of it by yourself."

She was quiet then, and finally he took his arm away and looked at her. She was staring out at the waves with the dull, troubled expression on her face that he had seen when she got off the bus. He rolled toward her in the sand and reached out. She rested a hand on his chest and he pulled her to him. She lay her cheek on his shoulder, and he almost wept with wanting her.

"Colleen," he said. He wasn't supposed to want her and he couldn't say he loved her. He didn't know her.

Almost timidly she reached up and touched his face—just that—but it pierced him and when her fingers brushed his mouth, he grasped her hand and held it to his lips. Her eyes were half closed. Her lashes glittered with tiny grains of sand.

Oh God. Colleen.

Her soft bare instep slid along his ankle. He shut his eyes for a moment, but it was too much. In one swift motion, he rolled her on top of him. One of her long legs came to rest between his. The whole length of their bodies pressed together, only the thin layers of their wet bathing suits separating them. His hands roved up and down her body, and everywhere he touched she stirred and uttered little urgent sounds—for him. For *him*.

He slid the straps off her shoulders and traced the rounded sides of her breasts with his thumbs. She arched upward and seemed to stop breathing as he moved his hands under the fabric of her suit and caressed the bare skin. A remote part of him watched, amazed. This is her body. I'm doing this. A paler, fainter voice told him he was sinning, but that voice quickly died away.

Colleen bent her face to his and kissed him insistently and hard, and suddenly he was bursting with spasms, clutching her, suppressing the impulse to cry out, hoping, in some misty corner of his brain not to hold her too tight. She clung to him silently then, until, with a single shudder, she groaned and lay still.

They lay with their hearts pumping wildly. Kit pressed his lips against her hair and gripped her as if she might run away. The shouts of playing children and swimmers down the beach came distantly to his ears. He didn't want to move or look up, only to lie there with her.

After a long silence, she gave a wondering little shake of her head and murmured into his shoulder, "I don't know what it is about you, Kit."

Her words blasted through his body like the triumphal crash of a symphony finale. He felt proud and elated and full of gratitude. He slid his fingers into her wet, tangled hair and gently drew back her head so he could look into her eyes. "Colleen," he said, "I don't know what it is about *you*. I know I don't love you. But I love you."

She smiled. "Yeah," she said. "Me, too."

They lay in the sand, entwined. He was barely aware of her as a separate person, her body was so much his, even through the fabric of their bathing suits. He grazed his lips up and down her arms, tasting her salty skin. There was a fine grittiness on their mouths from the black, sparkling sand.

He told her everything: how much he had wanted her the night that they stood so close in the dark after she had defended him at Aurelia's. How all the way home he had remembered the feel of her arm through her blouse. How, when they sang together at *Capuchinas*, and held each other's gaze, he so wanted to kiss her.

"I about went nuts," he said, "when we argued and you stormed away again."

It was glorious to pour it out. He didn't think about whether she might have similar confessions or not. Her caresses as he spoke, her stopping the flow of his words now and then to kiss him, were good enough. He said nothing about the incident on the bus, though it surfaced in his mind, maybe in hers, too, and he deliberately, guiltily pushed it away again.

As they lay embracing, he registered for the first time the outline of a square pouch under the skirt of her bathing suit, just inside the hollow of her hip bone—a body pouch like his. He touched it, teasing. "All your valuables, madame?" he said. She pulled away slightly and he took her hand and brought it against the pouch inside his trunks. "Me, too." But he touched hers again. There was something sharp and cylindrical in it. "That's a very strange passport you've got in there," he said. "Lipstick?"

She laughed lightly and took his hand away. "Medicine," she said.

"Oh, sorry. Are you okay?"

"Fine," she said. "But we're going to burn to a crisp."

He felt her withdrawal as if some part of his own body were being torn from him.

"I don't want to let you go." He curled his fingers around her ankle as she stood up.

"Come on." She reached for his hand and he got to his feet reluctantly. They waded into the shallows to splash sand off each other then walked back up the beach, his arm around her shoulders, hers around his waist, and headed for the shade of an open-air palapa.

It was long after lunchtime and they were ravenous. In the shade of the palapa's thatched roof, they sat on a bench at a crude wooden table and ordered tortillas and coconut drinks for a few *centavos* apiece from a thin, tired-looking woman in a stained sleeveless dress and plastic sandals. She patted tortillas into shape and flattened them on a piece of sheet metal set on rocks over a fire. Then she brought two coconuts to their table. With a hammer, she pounded thick penny nails into the coconuts, withdrew the nails and inserted straws into the holes.

They sipped the sweet juice. "Man!" he said. "That's great!"

"You can't get it like this at home, fresh from a ripe coconut right off a tree."

"I've never tasted anything like it."

Colleen shivered a little in her wet bathing suit and Kit slipped his shirt around her shoulders again.

"Aren't *you* chilly?" she said.

"I *was*. But being chivalrous has suddenly made me hot." He ran his hand along her thigh under the table and she slapped it playfully.

The woman brought over the hot tortillas piled high on a cracked plate. Without sauce or oil or salt, the tortillas still tasted delicious.

When they had sucked all the milk out, the woman took the coconuts to the other end of the table and whacked them open with a rusty machete she had taken from a hook inside the door of a small shed standing under the palapa. She returned the halves to them, along with two bent kitchen knives, and Colleen carved a chunk of meat out of Kit's coconut and fed it to him. He closed his lips over the tips of her fingers. "Mm," he said. The coconut was sweet and rich, and they ate until they were almost sick.

For some time they sat gazing across the beach at the water, their sunburned thighs and shoulders touching. Kit's skin had already started to feel tight. There was no way this sunburn could have been avoided. It seemed fitting.

A small child appeared—about two or three years old. He had been sleeping under the table on a blanket in the sand. Now he toddled around the table to stand beside the wooden pole that supported the roof. He wore only a soiled, drooping diaper. His cheeks were smudged black from the sand. Around his waist a clothesline rope was tied, the other end fastened to the pole.

Colleen held out her arms to him. "*Hola cariño, ven aquí,*" she called. The little boy gaped at them for a moment, his eyes dull. Then he let out a scream and fell backward into the sand. The woman swooped down on him and yanked him to his feet. With one hand, she unlooped the rope from his waist and threw it to the ground. Then she picked him up still screaming, thrust him into the shed, and dropped a wooden bar into the slots. The child's muffled screams inside the shed rose to a pitch of terror. Kit gasped.

"Hey!" he shouted at the woman, and leaped to his feet.

She paid no attention, but traipsed back to her position by the smoking grill. Colleen's hand clamped down on Kit's wrist. "No," she said forcefully, jerking him down onto the bench. The screams from the shed were escalating.

"She can't *do* that!"

They heard a weak pounding on the shed door, and the bar jiggled. Kit started to get up again, but Colleen's hand stayed clamped to his arm.

"There's nothing you can do," she said.

"Tell her it doesn't matter if the kid cries at us. Tell her to let him out!"

Colleen hesitated. Then she turned and called to the woman: "*Señora, no hay problema si el niño llora, no nos molesta, lo puede dejar salir.*" The woman shook her head, stone-faced, and muttered something unintelligible before turning away. The child's screams had become hysterical. Kit felt cold all over.

"We should report her!" he said.

"Report her?" Colleen looked straight at him. "To who?" Her voice was low and furious. There were tears in her eyes. The scene on the bus was waiting there between them.

The sound from the shed was becoming unbearable. Kit shook off Colleen's hand. "I'm going to let him out."

"You don't know what's going on," she said.

"The kid is freaked!"

"Yeah, so is she. Look at her." The woman stood stone-faced next to the sheet-metal grill. "What do you think she's earning—two or three *quetzales* a day? And half of that probably going to rent the space." Kit opened his mouth to speak, but Colleen continued fiercely. "She has no help. What do you think's happened to her?" Kit stared at the shed door, his hands clenched. Colleen was spitting the words out now. "What's she supposed to do? What if he cries and she loses fifty *centavos* because someone doesn't like it—" She mimicked an imaginary tourist: " 'Oh let's go up the street for lunch where there's more peace and quiet'—"

The boy's screams had turned to wails now, less terrified, more heartbroken. Kit's leg was jiggling. If he didn't go over there and open that door— But would it comfort the child or terrify him? "It's sinful to just sit here and do nothing!" he said.

"*Sinful.*" Colleen threw down his shirt and left the table for the beach. Kit watched, unmoving, as she stalked away from him once again.

No sound came from the shed now. He imagined the little boy curled up against the door in the dark. Tears welled in Kit's eyes. In three steps he could go and pull off the bar. Let the kid out. Pick him up. Hold him. Then swing the damn bar at someone. Why did she always shove him away like he had no feelings, his opinions were worthless?

He left the palapa and made a straight line across the sand to where she was bending over her pile of things. He didn't care what he said to her now.

The skirt of her bathing suit fluttered in the breeze, revealing two black sand smudges underneath. Like a child who had hunkered down on its bottom to scoop sand into a bucket. It stopped him in his tracks. In spite of himself he felt a little ache of tenderness.

He touched her elbow. She jerked. There was fear in her eyes, and she flashed a glance past him at the soldier, who was now sitting alone on a table at a different palapa, his boots and rifle resting on the bench. Colleen crouched down on her heels to finish stuffing her things into a small cotton totebag.

He would have liked to kick it aside. "Why are you so ticked off at me for wanting to help a little kid?" he demanded.

"I'm not ticked off at you for wanting to help a little kid." He walked around her, trying to force her to look at him, but she kept her eyes on her task. "I'm ticked off at you for reducing everything to that bogus religion of yours."

"Where do you get off telling someone their religion is bogus?"

She pulled a pair of sunglasses from her bag. "Because it *is* bogus," she said. "And destructive. And you're too ignorant to see it."

He shook his head at her, with an effort keeping his arms at his sides, though he wanted to pull her up and force her to stand eye to eye with him. "Don't call me ignorant!" he said.

She rose then and glared at him. "You don't like being called names? I don't either. I don't like any of the names you call me."

171

"What names? I never—"

"'Unbeliever,' 'unsaved,' 'sinner.' That's how you think of me, isn't it?" she accused, brandishing the sunglasses at him. Her feet were planted apart as if she expected an attempt to push her over. She put the sunglasses on, hiding her blazing eyes. What could he say? He *had* thought of her that way sometimes.

"But it doesn't matter what you call *me*." She lowered her voice. "It's what you call all these innocent people. Sinners, communists, heathens, subversives. And that justifies killing them and burning their villages—"

"*I* do that?"

"—and then getting the survivors to come crawling into the fold to save themselves from being murdered. Some victory for Jesus!"

"That's *not* why people come to Jesus!"

"Keep your voice down." She glanced again at the soldier, though he was at too great a distance to hear them, especially with the pounding surf drowning them out.

Kit lowered his voice and took a stance like hers—feet apart. "My faith saved me, and it's saved a lot of people. That's all I'm saying. Hopeless drunks, or wife beaters, or whatever—they completely turn around because of letting Jesus into their hearts. I—" *I was going to bash my stepfather's head in with a crowbar. I was going to lay my head down and die under the wheels of a train.* "—I found out I was loved by God. That's all it took."

"Fine." She shook her head. "Let Jesus into your heart. But don't collaborate in the destruction of innocent people just to protect yourself from doubt."

"Doubt?"

"Were we on the same bus? You didn't see with your own eyes what your born-again dictator, who you evangelicals love so much, allows to happen here?"

"I never said I loved him. But he's trying to get the army under control—"

"Oh *yes*." She tore her sunglasses off. "That's what your friends Billy Graham, and Jimmy Swaggart, and Pat Robertson—all those hypocrites—say about him, right?"

"Because he's trying to bring morality to this country."

"Oh really? Do you know that since Ríos Montt took power, his army has massacred thousands of peasants? Not guerrillas. Just ordinary people. Women, children, old people. Burned their villages to the ground. He calls it 'Plan Victory '82.' And now he's rounded up the survivors into concentration camps—excuse me, 'model villages.' That's called 'Firmness '83.' Is that what you mean by morality?"

"How do you know? Some people say the communists kill a lot of people."

"Are you so gullible you'll swallow any propaganda someone feeds you as long as they stick the word Jesus in it?" Her eyes darted back up the beach. "You know nothing about what's going on here."

"I know." Kit followed her glance. The soldier was scratching his leg with the point of his rifle.

Colleen turned so that her back was partially to the soldier but she could still see him out of the corner of her eye.

"For thirty years, people here have been trying to organize peacefully for basic human rights—schools, hospitals, fair wages, cooperatives to share costs for seeds and farm tools—" she counted the list off on her fingers "—legal fees to get titles to the little plots their ancestors have farmed for *five hundred years*. Is that what you mean by communism?"

Don't go around saying 'Why not complain?' It ain't healthy around here. Rub had said it.

"You know what those efforts cost them," she said. "You were on the bus."

The woman screaming, the soldiers' smirks. They didn't even wait for the bus to leave. They didn't care who saw.

They both went silent. From down the beach children cried out for a white ball that was floating beyond reach. One of the Australians leaped into the surf to rescue it.

"And that was the tip of the iceberg," Colleen pressed on. "Murder, torture, disappearances. By one vicious dictator after another." She seemed to know everything. He knew nothing.

She pulled on a long-sleeved wrapper over her bathing suit. Then she took a light cotton blanket from her bag and put it over his shoulders. "You're getting *burned*."

"Thank you."

She stared down at her feet. The black sand glinted in the sun.

"But why," he said, trying to sound conciliatory and reasonable, "why would the government treat the people like that?"

"Why?!" She was off again, outraged. She took a quick step toward the water as if, in sheer fury, she would plunge in and rid herself of him. "Have you had your eyes closed? Because terrorized and destitute people will work for practically nothing just to stay alive. And if you kill the ones who protest, the others will shut up."

As humiliating as this hammering was, this time he wouldn't back down. He crossed his arms over his chest. "I can't believe a Christian like Ríos Montt would order that kind of killing," he said. "I think he just wants to end the war quickly and show people that they can have a good life if they follow Jesus. And the communists are against that."

"What do you think it means when people have to sleep on sidewalks and huddle in doorways selling the clothes off their backs to buy food for their children?"

"Exactly. That's what I'm—"

"You think this kind of injustice will end when everybody's forced to believe Jesus Christ died for their sins? The Guatemalan elite already believe he died for their sins and they just look the other way while people get massacred and disappeared." She tilted her head and folded her arms across her chest as if he were an obstinate child. "What could you possibly have against changing a system that—"

"The communist system is worse—"

They were at the shore now. The cool water rushed up onto the sand and played over their feet. One part of his mind was remembering the feel of her wet skin against his, the curve of her waist under his hand.

"So let's see," she sneered. "What is it you think these so-called communists are trying to accomplish? They're trying to overthrow the government because the government is so just and fair and protects the liberty and happiness of all the people? And the guerrillas want to turn it into a heartless dictatorship without religious freedom? Oh, I'm so confused! Isn't that what we already *have* here?"

Her sarcasm shut down his ability to think. He wanted to take her by the arms and shake her. *Shut up.*

"Ríos Montt was put in power by a coup. He dissolved Congress," she went on, ignoring, or maybe spurred on by, the anger in his face. "He rules by *decree*. Since he became president, dozens of Catholic priests and nuns have had to flee to Mexico or be murdered by government death squads. Hundreds of indigenous church workers have disappeared—" She broke off.

"Don't sneer at me, like I'm stupid!"

"N-no." The single, wobbling syllable brought him up short. Her jaw, a moment ago pushed forward aggressively, went slack and her bottom lip drew up as if to control her quivering chin. She lowered her head. "No," she said again. "*I'm* stupid—" The words were stopped by a terrible sob.

He reached for her. "What? *Colleen* ..." He tried to pull her into his arms, but she wrenched away, hunching her shoulders and covering her face. He put his arms around her again and she shuddered against him before she slid out of his arms and dropped to her knees in the sand. He knelt down beside her. The blanket was still draped around his shoulders and he wrapped it around hers, too. They sat back swaddled together, shaded from the relentless sun, her bowed back curved against his chest.

❖ Fourteen ❖

For several minutes she cried uncontrollably while he stroked and kissed her hair, hanging in tangles around her shoulders.

"Sweetie. Sweetheart. Baby—" the words poured out—endearments he once used to comfort his sisters.

Finally she spoke, in gasped, broken sentences.

"*I'm* so stupid," she said, "I think I can *do* something about it. But I can't."

"Do you mean … what happened to the people on the bus?"

"Yes … But …" She heaved a shuddering sigh. "My brother …" She swallowed. As she regained her composure, Kit held his breath, afraid she might change her mind and shut him out again. "He was a parish priest in the Highlands."

"He was?" The revelation that dawned on him at the word 'was' filled him with pity and—he couldn't help it—selfish relief. *This* is what it's about. Not me at all.

"For eight years he helped build schools and clinics and … so many things. I visited him two years ago. In '81."

"What happened?"

"The army was burning whole villages, killing village leaders, just anyone. If the guerrillas even passed near a village, the army would show up the next day and murder people randomly to punish them for supposedly collaborating." She leaned into Kit the way Edie and Lorie used to, when they sat on his lap and poured out some disappointment or hurt as he rocked them. Gently, he rocked her now.

"Tom told me not to come," she said, "but I came anyway. The people *loved* him. He helped them keep going."

A wave broke on the shore, and the water slid around their feet, soaking the hem of the blanket that was protecting them from the sun. Colleen clutched at the sodden fabric.

"At one village in Tom's parish the army dragged off two catechists and the mayor. Their tortured bodies were dumped in a ravine."

"Oh Colleen," said Kit. "Were you there then?"

"No. It was after I left. Tom told us about it in a letter he sent back with a priest who had to leave the country. You couldn't say things like that in anything that went through the mail. The death squads—the *archivos*—would come after you. His letters were always being opened."

"So, those people who got killed—?"

"He and their village priest went to the commander of the post to try to get them released. He wrote us, '*el capitán* was less than intimidated.'" She gave a tearful laugh. She pushed the blanket off her shoulders and looked up at Kit. The blue of her tear-filled eyes was as blue as the Pacific sky behind her.

"You wouldn't believe what a great sense of humor Tom had. And his imagination. Most people didn't even realize it, he was so quiet and shy. He made up this game when I was little, called B.C. He'd lift me up on his shoulders and be a pterodactyl and fly me all over the prehistoric world. So sweet."

"Colleen," Kit said gently. "Is that when you lost your faith? When he died?"

The blue eyes narrowed and she pulled away, shrugging off the blanket. "Tom didn't die," she said icily. "And I lost my faith when I was seventeen years old and began to think for myself."

"Oh." He touched her hand, but she withdrew it.

She paused and shook her head as if concluding it wasn't worth the energy to explain it to him. But she continued in a dry, caustic voice. "The priests and nuns working in the Highlands believe it's a Christian's duty to bring down structures of injustice, not just to bring people one person at a time to Christ—" She drew a circle in the sand with one finger and traced it around and around. He was afraid to touch her again.

"—But they also built churches, and they got people to participate in the Catholic rituals. I argued with him about it. I kept asking him, 'Why

do you foist Catholicism on these people? They already *have* a religion.'"
She seemed to be speaking more to herself than to Kit. With the side of
her hand, she erased the circle she was tracing.

"They have the old Mayan beliefs, the old *costumbres*. Their communities have their own religious leaders. The earth is their mother. They
give thanks to corn for growing. Why isn't that good enough?" Kit felt
he should have an answer.

"Tom told me—very sweetly, like always, very gently—that he saw
my point, but 'Christ is the truth and the way, and faith in him will bring
everlasting salvation.'

"The thing is—" She was still working out the argument with herself.
"The thing is, Catholicism divided the people into two camps. Tom even
agreed that it did.

"And you evangelicals,"—She turned on Kit, shaking her finger at
him— "you've split them a *third* way. They used to have communities
and traditions. Now the people who haven't gotten massacred are all
dragged off and thrown together into concentration camps where the
government brings the *evangélicos* in to feed them."

She got to her feet and looked down on him from her long-legged
height. He blinked up at her into the sun.

"And when someone gets picked up at random off a bus and they
can't hold out under torture—" He fought a sudden feeling of nausea.
"—who are they going to accuse of being a guerrilla?—Because you
have to name *somebody*. If you don't, your own family will get the same
treatment. If you're a Catholic you'll accuse someone who follows the old
costumbres. If you're a *costumbrist*, you'll accuse a Catholic. If you're an
evangélico, you have a chance of not being grabbed at all, but if you do,
you can accuse the Catholics *and* the *costumbristas* can't you? Because
aren't they all heathens?"

Impatiently, she wiped a remaining tear off her cheek.

Kit stood, took the blanket from his shoulders and gave it back to her.
She knelt and shoved it in the bag, then retrieved a barrette and snapped
her hair messily into a pony tail.

"In the Highlands," she said, "the *campesinos* all have to carry an
identity card with their religion printed on it. If you're Protestant you

can travel freely. The Catholics can't leave their village without permission from the army."

Kit didn't know how to respond. He had no idea if what she said was fact or exaggeration. Ezra had always said you couldn't entirely trust the viewpoint of someone who wasn't saved.

"Ríos Montt calls any human rights movement 'communist-inspired,' and that puts *you* right on board, doesn't it, because murdering, torturing, disappearing people in this world is less evil than if you don't get the chance to save their souls. Right? This world's suffering is only a blink of the eye compared to eternal hellfire?"

"That *is* true!"

"You're pawns," she said. "You believe everything they say without question, just like you believe all the mythology these preachers spew at you." She shook her head. "It would be harmless if it didn't confuse you and your preacher into propping up bloody dictatorships."

"You're simplifying it."

"Listen, I grew up with that crap. You don't think so, but Catholics worship the same God you do—a jealous, power-obsessed, vengeful, self absorbed, genocidal tyrant who acts exactly like your so-called born-again Ríos Montt, or the last goon, Lucas Garcia, or the goon before that, or Hitler, or any of them—"

"You don't know what you're talking about. God is totally forgiving."

"How can you possibly believe that? Have you actually *read* your Bible?"

"Yes, I've read my Bible—"

"So when you came to the part where God says, 'Hey, Moses, you slew all those bad Midianites for me, but you didn't kill the male children, what's wrong with you?! And, oh, by the way, will you slaughter all the women, too, while you're at it? But, hey, save those thirty-two thousand little girls—those virgins—and hand out ... let's see, what does that add up to ... thirty-two of them apiece, as booty,' when you read that, it didn't make you wonder about your God?"

"Christ's message is merciful. The New Testament—"

"Oh. Yes. The *New* Testament. In the *Old* Testament God was generally satisfied with just stoning a guy to death for gathering sticks on the Sabbath. In those days, it was just *death* to the infidel. It was *Jesus* who picked up on the idea of torturing people forever."

"You're wrong!" Kit protested. But his mind had become paralyzed.

"'*If a man abide not in me,*' she intoned in the voice of a fire and brimstone preacher, '*he is cast forth as a branch and is withered; and men gather them and cast them into the fire and they are burned.*'"

Kit drew a breath. He knew the quotation. It was from John. Or maybe Mark.

Why was he incapable of standing up for Christ?

"You don't know the real Jesus. I felt him. I've met him." He sounded to himself like a whiny child.

"When I was twelve," she scoffed, "I saw a halo of light around the statue of the Virgin in our church. She smiled at me. And when I was sixteen, I saw God while I was on an acid trip. The first vision was hormones. The second was chemicals. They both seemed completely real."

She had no respect for him at all. She had probably perfected her arguments over a long time, with many opponents. But so had he. Why couldn't he shut her up?

Cruelly, he said, "What *happened* to Tom then?"

She pressed her lips together to hold back another fit of crying. She took several steps down the beach.

"I'm sorry," he said, catching up with her. He touched her cheek. "I'm sorry."

"They picked him up," she choked it out. "He was driving some people from the village to a clinic. They took them all to the base. They said, '*Padre*, which ones of these are guerrillas?' They knew none of them were. They just wanted to see if he'd betray someone to save himself so they could tell the whole parish, 'Your *Padre* sold you out.'"

She was hugging herself. Kit enclosed her arms in his.

"They kept him ... for two days." Furiously, she released an arm and punched her fist against her thigh. "It took that long for the fucking bishop to get the fucking U.S. embassy to act. *Two days.*" She shook him off and faced him. "That's how much the United States cares. *Everyone* knows if someone doesn't get you out in the first hours, you'll probably be dead. The National Palace had a direct phone line to that torture chamber. One phone call and they let him go." A grimace of pain distorted her face.

"If you survive the first day... you don't *want* to live anymore." She wept into her hands. "They did things to him that we'll never know about. The doctors who operated on him when he got home told my mom and dad what they knew."

She was silent for a moment. "And I made my mother tell me."

"Oh Colleen ..." he said, helplessly.

"The worst part ... was ... they made him watch what they were doing to the others. They said if he didn't accuse them, they'd go on torturing them while he watched. But ... he knew they'd torture them anyway, so he didn't say anything. Nobody ever saw those people again."

She gazed at the sea. "I *knew* them. *Doña* Ana showed me how to embroider a *servilleta* with birds and flowers and turtles—"

Distantly came the Australian boys' whoops of joy. They were body surfing on the long, breaking waves.

"Tommy's gone," she said. "He's just an empty, blank person. He tried to jump out the window in the hospital. He's a Catholic. He's a Christian. He still believes it's a mortal sin to kill yourself. You know what that means? It means he thought he deserved to be tortured *forever*." Her last words were almost lost as she became incoherent with weeping once more: "And *I*... probably... put that idea in his head." She sobbed and sobbed.

A question came to him in Ezra's voice: How can you minister to her? Kit said, quietly, "Colleen, your brother must know that God would forgive him—"

She stiffened. "'*Forgive*' him?" She threw his arm off and jerked away. He thought she might slap him. "Forgive him for *what*?"

She spit the next words out. "When you saw that woman on the bus being dragged off by her hair to *hell*, I'll bet you were saying, Oh god, I should be *doing* something. But you *didn't* did you?" He felt again the trembling of the old man's body. His own immobilizing, shameful fear.

"Because, as ignorant as you are about what's really happening here, it was obvious even to you that those soldiers had absolute power, complete

181

impunity. They can do whatever the hell they want, and your little, 'Hey I'm an American, I've been saved, and God-will-strike-you-down-for-this' would have been laughable! Tommy knew that, too, but he *tried* to do something in spite of it."

"And so did you."

She blinked and said nothing.

"I saw what you did," Kit said.

"Yeah, sure. My little paltry attempt."

"It was brave."

She shrugged. "I've shot ten rolls of film and today was the only time I shot anything that might— *If* the film even comes out."

"What will you do with it?"

"Give it to a human rights group. They're trying to stop the fucking Congress from handing over *more* military aid to these vicious goons. Reagan has them convinced that Ríos Montt has *improved* human rights." She gave a brittle laugh.

"Listen, I think you're courageous to be taking these pictures."

"Courageous. Right. I was so relieved when I got off that bus and didn't get caught, that now I'm scared to take any more. All I want to do is forget about all of it. I just wish I *could* forget about it."

It struck him then. "It's *film* you've got there?" He nodded toward the hollow next to her hip bone. "Why didn't you tell me?"

"Oh yeah, Mr. Born Again. Like you wouldn't turn me in, in your anti-communist zeal?"

He flinched. "If you thought you couldn't trust me, why did you—"

"I don't *know* why. *God!*" She shook her head violently. "I can't *believe* myself!"

For a moment he held his breath, resisting the impulse to grip her by the shoulders. Then he released the breath and stepped back. "You say something like that to me after—?"

I don't know what it is about you, Kit. Her hand going up to his cheek.

"Colleen, I don't even know your last name."

She cast her eyes sideways as if watching her feelings for him sidle off. He waited. His scalp and ears were on fire with sunburn. He was beginning to feel sick, almost feverish. She walked over to her bundle on the sand and picked it up. "I *still* don't know if I should have trusted you," she said as she turned to leave.

"Wait," Kit said. "Where are you going?"

She stopped and looked back. "I want to be by myself."

He watched her trudge back up the beach, take a wide detour around the soldier, then cross the bridge over the canal, walking with that straight-backed, dogged stride, her tangled hair in its barrette swinging with every step.

He had to get into the shade. The black sand away from the water's edge scorched the bottoms of his feet, and he pranced ridiculously to the place where he had dropped his sandals. There, he put the sandals on and retrieved his T-shirt.

He bypassed the palapa where he and Colleen had eaten their lunch. The woman was sitting on her haunches in the sand. The toddler stood against her, sucking on a bared breast. The woman's mouth was drawn down at the corners, and her eyes stared vacantly at the shore.

Putting on his T-shirt, Kit plodded on up to the sidewalk to a shabby *tienda*, where he bought water—warm and tasting of the plastic bottle it came in. He stood shivering under the tattered canopy while he drank, feeling feverish and nauseated. *Mr. Born Again. Like you wouldn't turn me in.*

But why, if she hadn't trusted him, why then—? *I don't know what it is about you, Kit.*

Then he knew why. She had wanted to take her mind off her brother, off the people on the bus, the canister of film she was hiding. She had only been looking for forgetfulness, that was all, and he was it.

But ... her bare sole sliding along his ankle, the pressure of that tight, slim thigh between his legs. In the water, her back arching under his hands.

He opened his eyes and gazed across at the Australians at the shore. They were flinging the soccer ball into the waves and racing each other to retrieve it. She could have had any one of those guys.

But she chose me.

183

And hadn't he wanted relief, too? From loneliness and doubt? *Not* doubt. Confusion. Still, he had said he loved her and he meant it.

Yeah, me, too, she said.

He finished drinking the tepid water and studied the streets across the canal. Which one had she turned down after she crossed the bridge? When he had first arrived, he hadn't seen her anywhere on the main drag. Maybe if she had been to San José before, she had known of a *pensión* that was off the beaten path.

He hurried over the bridge and took the first side lane he came to, now determined to find her before she hid herself away in a room some-where. He peered down each cross street, but the streets seemed virtually deserted. There were no vendors or hawkers in sight. Only a couple of sailors lounging at a table outside a cantina. She could have turned into any one of the dingy one-story *pensiones*.

At the last intersection before the lane curved back around to the main street, a covered army truck sat idling in the middle of the block. He froze. Where was she? Had she seen it? Were there soldiers waiting in the truck or had they— A violent blow to his back knocked him to his knees. Dazed, struggling in the dirt to get up, he looked over his shoulder. The soldier from the beach stood over Kit, pointing a rifle at his head. The soldier jerked a thumb for Kit to rise. Two others jumped from the truck and ran up, weapons clattering. Doubled over and gasping at the pain in his ribs, Kit tried to get to his feet, but the two soldiers grabbed him under each arm, forced his head down, and dragged him up the street. He could feel the point of the rifle in his back.

They dragged him around the corner, shoved him through the open door of a *pensión*, and pushed him to his knees again. Another soldier—a short, stocky round-faced *ladino* in his twenties, with a gleaming gold upper incisor—sat on a cot, from which the blanket and pillow had been tossed to the floor alongside several beer bottles and cigarette butts.

The *ladino* was the same officer—lieutenant or sergeant—who had called the people off the bus.

There was an excited exchange between the officer and the soldier from the beach, but the Spanish went too fast for Kit. Although the officer was short, he had the bulked-up chest and shoulders of a weightlifter. Kit felt gangly and puny in comparison—an overgrown boy, in his drooping swim trunks, thin T-shirt, and sandals. And all four soldiers were armed with automatic rifles. He wouldn't be able to take any of them on. His ability to think was paralyzed by a clash of two ideas: one, that none of this was real; and the other, that this was God's punishment for his lusting after Colleen.

Then he noticed in a heap on the floor the blue dress she had worn on the bus, her day pack unzipped and empty thrown next to it along with her open camera case. The expensive camera lay in a corner, flung there with its back off.

This is her room.

He started to get to his feet, but he was kicked from behind and sent sprawling. The hard round mouth of a rifle barrel pressed against his skull. He lay with one cheek in the folds of Colleen's dress. It smelled of her salty sweat. They have her. He thought of her long hair, gathered carelessly in the barrette and swinging back and forth as she stalked away from him. God, don't punish her ... I was the one. She resisted. I kept going after her and broke her down.

The officer in charge got up, barked another incomprehensible word, and Kit was hauled to his feet and thrown on the cot. Protect her, Lord, he prayed silently. Be with her, be with me. The prayer mocked him. Be with you *now*, Kit? *Here?* Not on the beach, when her thigh pressed against your dick and you would have stripped her naked and stuck it in her right then and there if she'd let you?

Through the husk of his scorched skin, evil had wormed its way and curled up in the spaces where his faith had been. He had abandoned God and now he was judged and brought to punishment. Goose flesh broke out up and down his body. He felt faint. He thought he might throw up.

"*¿Dónde está la muchacha?*" the officer shouted. The words, though familiar, fell on Kit's ears without meaning. The officer leaned into him, exhaling the smell of stale beer and nicotine, and repeated himself with menacing slowness: "*¿Dónde .. está .. la .. muchacha?*" Where, Kit translated, willing himself to concentrate, *Where .. is .. the .. girl*. They didn't know where she was. They didn't have her.

185

He shook his head, forcing himself not to look away. "*No sé*," he said.

The soldier struck him hard across the face, jerking his neck back. "*Fuck!*" Kit cried. The blow reverberated in his skull. He put his hand to his cheekbone. The other soldiers laughed, mimicking and feminizing his gesture. "*¡Oh pobre chiquillo!*"—Poor little guy!

The officer ignored them. "*¿Cuál es el nombre de la muchacha? ¿Dónde está ella? ¿De dónde es ella?*" Kit's brain was still reeling from the blow to his face, but these simple words translated themselves. What is the girl's name? Where is she? Where is she from?

He had to get his wits together. What should he say? He couldn't think. His Spanish seemed to have abandoned him.

But suddenly the obviousness of it struck him. "*No .. hablo .. español*," he said.

The officer sneered in disbelief. Kit's heart stopped. He had already blurted out the words *No sé*.

He tried again, exaggerating his *gringo* accent. "*Un poco de español*." A *little* Spanish, only.

In Spanish the soldier who had followed him from the beach jeered, "He doesn't speak Spanish. He only speaks the language of love." He thrust out his tongue, drawing it suggestively across his lips. "*Habla la lengua de la lengua*."—He speaks the language of the tongue. He laughed at his own joke.

The soldier was handsome—a square-jawed, athletic type of guy, who bounced nervously on the balls of his feet like a prize fighter before the bell. The other two—they looked so young, maybe as young as fifteen or even fourteen. They grinned with avid, shifty-eyed cruelty. They were short, brown-skinned Mayan-looking boys, one with a long white scar across the bridge of his nose, the other missing a front tooth. Their camouflage uniforms were too big for them. The shirts bagged over their belts, the pants ballooned from scuffed, worn-looking boots. With the hyper-alertness of dogs in the presence of unpredictable masters, they darted glances at the two *ladinos*.

The officer turned on the joker and blasted the *ladino* private with a stream of accusations in Spanish, pointing beyond the walls of the room toward the beach. "Why didn't you follow the woman?" he shouted. The soldier mumbled a reply—something about "staying with the *gringo*."

"¡*Estupido!*" the man in charge yelled at him. "Find her. Now."

The *ladino* private hurried from the room while the officer snatched up the camera, shoved it into the case and slung it across his shoulders. His shirtcuff slid up his wrist to reveal that he was wearing two watches. One was Colleen's.

At the officer's nod, the other two yanked Kit off the bed and prodded him outside at gunpoint. The street was still deserted. Everyone seemed to have disappeared.

The truck was now drawn up to the door. The officer shouted something at the driver, who jumped out. Then the officer sent one of the boy soldiers back in the room—presumably to wait in case Colleen showed up—and held the gun to Kit's head while the driver produced a length of rope, wrenched Kit's arms behind him and tied them tightly behind his back. The knot dug into the underside of Kit's wrist.

At the truck, they bent him over the tailgate, took hold of his ankles and slid him in on his stomach, his raw sunburned skin scraping against the rusty ridges. The tailgate slammed shut, doors opened and closed, and the truck swerved at high speed out of the sandy lane.

An outhouse smell filled Kit's nostrils. The truck floor was slick with feces, urine and blood. As he tried to turn onto his side, a stabbing pain left him breathless. A cracked rib, he guessed. He rolled onto his stomach, breathing shallowly and tensing his neck to keep his face out of the excrement.

They would be taking him to a police station or an army base. Once again a sense of unreality disoriented him. The thudding of his heart, his cheekbone jarring against the ridged metal at every seam in the road seemed to be happening to someone else. It occurred to him that he should have been paying attention to the turns taken by the truck. Too late. All he could make out was that the vehicle was staying on pavement. No dirt roads.

Two hours ago he had been kissing Colleen, too turned on to think about consequences or judgments. Colleen. He saw again the switch of hair swinging back and forth as she walked away from him. They've caught her by now. He wondered why they hadn't grabbed her on the bridge as soon as she left the beach. They must have felt sure of catching her away from the public eye when she returned to her room. But maybe she had unexpectedly taken a back lane, as he had, and seen the truck. Where would she have run to? Where could she find a hiding place in those few dismal, exposed streets?

He thought of the camera with its back hanging open. All this had happened because of the photographs. Somebody had reported her. Somebody on the bus. Now they would ask him about the pictures.

The truck took a corner on squealing tires and Kit drew up his knees to keep from rolling into the muck, but the pain in his ribs tore through him and he had to straighten again. He twisted and turned his bound wrists. Somewhere he had read you could loosen any knot this way, but his attempts just seemed to tighten it. Panic began to overcome him.

He lay still. What should he say when they asked about her? He could tell them he didn't know her, he had just met her on the beach. What if they saw us together on the bus? But she had sat separately from him, barely even looking at him. Had they spoken during the stopover in Escuintla? A few words, but that was before the San José bus arrived. After that, they were like strangers.

The truck slowed, made an abrupt turn and bumped heavily over a ridge in the road before it came to a stop. He heard the sounds of voices— the driver and someone outside the truck. The ride had taken only ten or fifteen minutes. Here it comes. Jesus, I know I'm unworthy, I know I've sinned, but please, please stay by me.

❖ Fifteen ❖

They pulled him out of the truck. When he was on his feet, he saw that they were inside an army base, enclosed by a high, razor-wire fence guarded by soldiers. In the distance two helicopters sat on a landing strip. The truck had pulled up to a low concrete building in the middle of bare, dusty grounds unrelieved by trees or shrubs.

His survey of the surroundings was cut short as the officer and another soldier pushed him, stumbling, into the building. He found himself at one end of a dark, hot corridor broken at intervals by closed doors. Toward the middle of the hallway was a bench, from which an old man half rose as they entered. A stoop-shouldered guard leaning on his gun at the far end of the hall came to attention. The officer shouted something at the guard, and he saluted, clasped his hands tightly around his rifle and drew himself as rigidly erect as his rounded back allowed.

With Colleen's camera case still slung across his shoulders, the officer strode down the hall past the guard. Before he disappeared around the corner, he took off Colleen's watch and slipped it into his pocket. The other soldier pushed Kit down onto the bench next to the old man, who was standing now, his whole demeanor avid and intent.

"*Por favor, señor*—" he began, but the soldier grabbed the man by his shirt and flung him back onto the bench without a word. The soldier commanded Kit to stay where he was and then took up a position near the door.

Close up, Kit saw that the man on the bench was the old toothless peasant who had sat next to him on the bus from Escuintla. The man's bowed back, the furrow between his eyebrows so deep it could have been carved into his forehead with a knife, the knotted fingers curling and twisting on each other—these distracted Kit from his own terror. It was intolerable that the defenseless old man should be made to suffer such anguish.

Kit turned to him and spoke. "*Señor,*" he said quietly, aware of the two guards watching from both ends of the corridor, "*Rézale a Dios. Él te cuidará.*" Pray to God. He will take care of you.

The old man glanced into Kit's eyes, then made a surreptitious survey of the rest of him—this tall, sunburned *gringo* in beach clothes. With a look of uncertainty and hope—maybe in his agitation failing to notice Kit's own trembling or that his hands were bound behind him—he pleaded with Kit to tell him where his son was. The man's son, Kit realized, was one of those who had been taken off the bus.

"*¡Mi hijo es buen hombre! Él no es un comunista,*" the old man whispered fiercely. From his trouser pocket, he produced a dog-eared photo of a young indigenous man standing stiffly in a white shirt buttoned up to his chin. A boy of about three was holding his father's hat with one hand and clinging to the father's pant leg with the other. Next to them, on a straight-backed wooden chair—a little out of focus as if she had moved at the instant the picture was taken—a young woman in *traje* held a sleeping infant.

"*¡Él tiene una familia! … tiene una esposa e hijos,*" pleaded the old man under his breath. "*¡Mi hijo no es guerrillero!*"

"*¡Eh!*" shouted the soldier who had brought Kit in. Kit jerked. He had momentarily forgotten him. "*¡No hablen!*"

Before turning away, the old man glanced at Kit again, seeming to realize his misjudgment. The eagerness left the man's face and he slumped back against the wall, pulling his solitary anguish around him.

The officer returned then, flanked by two new soldiers, both *ladinos.* Lower ranking, but taller than their lieutenant, they had fallen into step with him. The rhythmic strike of their boots was amplified by the concrete floor. Kit's mouth went dry. He straightened as best he could, pain tearing through his ribs. As soon as they neared the bench, the old man was on his feet again, holding up his son's photo.

"*!Por favor Capitán, mi hijo!*"

The two soldiers moved to push or strike him, but the officer waved them back.

Smiling at the old man, a gold incisor flashing, he told him his son was a fucking communist.

"*No, no—*" cried the old man.

The officer cut him off.

"*Su hijo es un guerrillero cabrón.*"

"*¡No! Él es…*" began the man, still holding the photo aloft like some magic entry ticket.

The officer snatched the photo and shoved it under the man's nose. "Like father like son?" he shouted at him in Spanish. He turned and called an order to the guard standing at the far end of the hall. The guard, stiff necked, chin drawn in, took one step to the side, revealing a small window.

The window framed a patch of dusty parade ground behind the building, stark and empty in the harsh sunlight except for one object, which Kit at first—until his eyes adjusted to the glare—took to be some kind of combat exercise dummy.

At the old man's shriek, Kit gasped, instantly realizing what he was seeing. A man was hanging by his wrists—bound behind him—from a six- or seven-foot tall post. His feet dangled several inches off the ground. He was naked, his body covered with large patches of discolored skin. His head bent forward at a cruel angle from his dislocated shoulders. Under the glaring white sun, he jerked and twitched.

The old man flung out his arms and lunged forward as if to push his way past the three soldiers. But before he could take another step, the officer raised his rifle butt and brought it down on the old man's skull with a crack like an axe splitting wood.

The man toppled, senseless, with another crack of his skull as he hit the concrete. The guard near the window came running. Without acknowledging the other soldiers, as if performing the most routine duty, he rolled the old man over and grasped his ankles like the handles of a wheelbarrow. A thin red line was left down the middle of the hallway as the man was dragged past the window and out of sight. The officer turned back and nodded at the soldiers, who shoved Kit down the hall through the next doorway.

Kit found himself in a windowless room with no furniture except for a wooden table. In one corner a brown and tan terrier mongrel was curled up on a cushion.

The terrier lifted its head and cocked an ear, letting out a mild yap. Then it scrambled to its feet with a tongue-lolling smile on its face. The three soldiers ignored the dog, and Kit wondered if it was real. It seemed too strange to be true—an envoy from everyday life that had somehow found its way into his nightmare.

The officer leaned against the closed door and aimed his rifle at Kit's face as the other two soldiers backed Kit up to the table. The taller one had a long, beakish nose and bright darting black eyes. His mouth hung slightly open like a bird waiting for someone to pop something in it. The other one had light brown hair and blue eyes. He could have been from Iowa or Minnesota. He said something jeering that Kit didn't understand, and it seemed strange to hear Spanish coming out of his mouth. The beak-nosed soldier pulled Kit's T-shirt up to his nipples while the other jerked his swim trunks down around his ankles.

They yanked the money pouch from Kit's waist, opened it and dumped the contents on the table. The money and passport they handed to the officer. The pieces of drawing paper they unfolded and examined. Finding them blank, they threw them on the floor, but the blue-eyed soldier took up the pencil and brandished it in the air.

"¡*Mira!*" he exclaimed, grinning. Holding it daintily between thumb and forefinger, he placed it alongside Kit's penis. "*Dos lápices,*" he said, chortling. —*Two* pencils!— and with a snap of the wrist rapped the pencil sharply against Kit's retracted organ. Kit gasped involuntarily. "¡*Oohh-hhh!*" cried the soldier joyfully.

The officer put his head out the door and whistled. The guard from the window came and took away the passport and money. Then the officer muttered an order which made the two soldiers hold each other's gaze for a moment, a look of distaste passing between them. The blue-eyed soldier took a *centavo* from his pocket. "*Cara,*" he said, and flipped the coin. He caught it as it landed on the back of his hand and bent to look. "¡*Cara!*" he exclaimed, triumphantly, uncovering the coin.

The other protested, "¡*Eh!*" and stepped closer to check for himself. But the officer cut short the dispute with a curt command. The loser of the toss swore under his breath—"¡*Mierda!*"—and took something from his pocket. With a snap, he pulled on a latex glove.

Before Kit knew what was happening, they had forced him face-down onto the table and pressed down so hard on his injured ribs he had trouble breathing. His buttocks hung over the edge. He tried to strike out with one leg, but his swim trunks were yanked off him, his feet kicked apart and tied by the ankles to the table legs. He yelled as his buttocks were pried apart and a finger was jammed into his anus.

Kit heaved backward, cursing, but the soldier shoved an elbow straight into his spine, pulled him up by his hair, and slammed his head down again. Kit's already swollen cheekbone hit the table as the finger continued to jab deeply and brutally.

Kit felt cold all over in spite of his sunburn. His body felt brittle. Some part of him was whirling out into space, away from the life he had known, into a vacuum he wouldn't return from because what was being done to him could never be undone.

Finally the probing finger was withdrawn, his ankles were untied, and he was turned over onto his back. They forced his jaws open, and the same gloved finger made a thorough and efficient search of his mouth.

"*Nada*," the soldier reported. The officer shrugged and they let him up. The soldier rolled the glove off his hand and tossed it on the floor. The terrier trotted over and sniffed at it.

The short man stood for a moment studying Kit.

"*Gringos*," he observed to the others with a smile and gestured at Kit's groin—white against his flaming legs and torso. "*Cuando están calientes se les olvida que el sol calienta más.*"—When they're turned on, they forget the sun is even hotter.

There was a knock on the door. The officer opened it and exchanged a few words with the guard, then shut the door and nodded at the blue-eyed soldier, who shoved a knife between Kit's wrists, and sawed through the ropes. Kit's arms came slowly apart and made their way in spasms down to his sides. His hands twitched uncontrollably. Spasms shook his shoulders and ribs. The three men walked out then, leaving him alone. A key turned in the lock.

The soldiers' boots on the concrete receded. The only sounds were his own ragged breaths and the pulse in his ears. He was quivering like someone palsied. Each time he took a breath or swallowed, the taste and smell of shit and latex gagged him. He looked around at the room, at the dog and the table and his things scattered about the floor. On every surface there were stains of other people's blood, and nothing that suggested any possibility of self defense or escape.

With pain shooting through his ribs, Kit bent down and picked up the swim trunks. They were still slightly damp at the hem from his swim—how long ago? He bunched the fabric, brought one damp section of the hem to his mouth and rubbed it over his foul tongue. The faint saltiness brought back Colleen's skin under his lips, and he shuddered at the profane blending of sensations.

Slowly he rolled his T-shirt back down over his chest, stepped into the trunks, and pulled them up. There was a bright red mark on his penis where the pencil had struck it. When he tried to tie the money pouch around his waist, the strings kept slipping out of his fingers and the pouch kept dropping to the floor as if he had mittens on.

Even with no one to observe his uncontrolled shaking, he felt humiliated by it. It seemed for the moment the most appalling part of his situation—that they might return to find him in this state, quivering from what they had done to him and what they might do next. He tried to will it to stop, especially the trembling of his hands, but he kept shaking, like a dog in a thunderstorm. The terrier, by contrast, had curled up on its cushion again and was sleeping peacefully except for the occasional twitch of its tail or eyebrows.

The thought of praying flashed into Kit's mind and flashed out again just as quickly. He could not bring himself to pray with the taste of his own shit in his mouth and the burning in his anus. Why had the loving, forgiving God of Ezra, and Jeannette, and the Light and Life Tabernacle done something like this to him? Was his sin with Colleen so great? Had God set him up for this? The vengeful God that murdered the Midianite boys and gave away the virgins? He shuddered away the image of the man hanging from the post. The father's shriek.

Beside the dog was a plastic bowl filled with water, some of which had slopped out in a pool on the concrete. A second bowl held remnants of the dog's dinner. Kit leaned against the table and stared at the animal, whose small rib cage rose and fell in a steady rhythm. After a while, his own breaths had steadied somewhat, his tremor eased a little. There was a ripple of black fur across the terrier's neck and shoulders like a ruff. Kit had the urge to comb his fingers through it to calm his trembling, but he was afraid of waking the dog and making it bark.

He remembered the pencil and drawing paper and retrieved them from under the table where they had been dumped. On the table, he smoothed out a sheet of paper and took up the pencil. The spasms in his arms made it hard to hold the pencil steady. He tried to breathe deeply for several minutes and laid the pencil down to shake out his arms and hands. Then he tried again.

At first the lines came out jagged and shaky, but as he began to settle to the task —moving his eyes back and forth from the dog to the drawing— the lines came little by little under his control. He drew the curved back, the cropped tail with its droop of brown fur hanging over the stub, the small black nose resting on a front paw, one ear lapped across a closed eye. He sketched the contours of the cushion on which the dog nestled.

It took him about fifteen minutes to complete the drawing. When it was finished, he felt more in control. The quiver was there underneath, but his hands had stopped visibly shaking. He folded the drawing and put it into the money pouch along with the pencil stub, then stood up. Now, with a somewhat clearer mind, he had to figure out what to say when they came back.

But there was no time to figure out anything. There were steps in the hallway, a curt voice, a muttered reply. A key turned in the lock. Straightening to his full six feet, his heart pounding, Kit faced the door.

The stoop-shouldered guard who had dragged the old man away entered carrying two molded-plastic chairs, which he set down by the table. He was followed in by a young *ladino* lieutenant in his twenties—thin and trim with slender wrists and a baby face. His field uniform was crisp, the pants pressed and tucked tightly into polished boots. In one hand he held a spiral notebook. At the sound of footsteps behind him, he stood at attention.

The man who came in behind him was an officer of higher rank—a captain, Kit guessed, from the stripes on his epaulets—a broad shouldered, middle-aged *ladino*, with red, puffy eyes, as if he drank too much or hadn't had enough sleep. He wore no T-shirt under his open-necked field jacket. A small gold cross on a chain nestled in his black, curly chest hairs. He was eating a thick sandwich partially wrapped in waxed paper.

As soon as the captain crossed the threshold, the terrier scrambled to its feet. Standing on its hind legs, it raked its forepaws excitedly down the captain's knees. The officer bent down and scooped it up in an embrace, inclining his head to allow the dog's pink tongue to dart over his ear.

"*¡Eh, Eh, Paquito! ¡Muchos besos para papá!*" the captain crooned. He set Paquito on his cushion and broke off a corner of his sandwich for the dog. Then, at a nod from the captain, the guard left and the lieutenant sat. The captain glanced for the first time at Kit, then sat beside the lieutenant across from him.

He took another bite of his sandwich and gestured for the lieutenant to begin. The lieutenant unclipped a pen from his breast pocket, snapped open his notebook and said to Kit in mildly accented English, "You're from the U.S. You're studying Spanish at *Instituto de Español Tres Américas* in Antigua."

For a moment, Kit was filled with gratitude at hearing his own language spoken in such matter-of-fact tones. He nodded. Then, with sickening clarity, it hit him that they must have caught Colleen and extracted the information from her.

"Why did you arrest me?" he said, taking a step forward.

With his free hand, the captain drew a revolver from a holster that rode across his chest. He laid the gun on the table, keeping his finger on the trigger. He took another bite of his sandwich and mumbled in Spanish to the lieutenant.

"Who is the *gringa* you were fucking on the beach?" the lieutenant translated, with a slight hesitation on *fucking*.

196

Shame and anger rose in him. "I didn't ... We were just fooling around."

"What's her name?"

"I don't know."

The lieutenant translated for the captain, who raised his eyebrows blandly as he spoke with his mouth full. The lieutenant said, "You were 'fooling around' and you don't know her name? Is she a whore?"

"No!" Kit exclaimed before he could stop himself. The captain raised his eyebrows again. "She's just ... a tourist I met on the beach."

Kit studied the translator. The lieutenant was about his own age but without his self-consciousness. He seemed confident of the impression he made, confident that even his superior officer was impressed by him. He could do the job in his sleep. Every English sentence he uttered was spoken with a sense of superiority.

"How do you speak such perfect English?" Kit said. The flattery felt oily in his mouth. The lieutenant's half-mast eyelids dropped a degree lower, while a slight contraction in one side of his face betrayed his gratification. Kit said, "I could study Spanish for a hundred years and never get as good as you are in English."

"I was given interrogation training at the U.S. Army School of the Americas in Panama," the lieutenant said neutrally. Then, apparently unable to resist, he added, "Because I already excelled in English."

The captain stopped eating and muttered a few words, to which the lieutenant told him, blandly, that they were just talking about Kit's bad Spanish. Silently, the captain finished the sandwich, balled the waxed paper and threw it across the room for Paquito to fetch. The dog leapt off his cushion and trotted over with the paper in its mouth.

"Why does your girlfriend take pictures of soldiers doing their work?" said the Captain, teasing the waxed paper from the terrier's teeth. The lieutenant translated.

"What do you mean?" Kit said, deliberately looking the captain in the eye.

"Your girlfriend took pictures of soldiers processing rebels at a checkpoint. Why?"

"I don't know. I didn't see anyone taking pictures. She's a tourist."

"She has a very expensive camera and she removes the film when she leaves her room to go to the beach. Why does she take her film with her?"

Kit shrugged. "I didn't know she had a camera. Maybe taking artistic pictures is her hobby."

"Are pictures of soldiers artistic?"

"To some people they might be."

"Is she a communist?"

"No—" The translator and the captain exchanged glances. Don't sound too sure. "I don't think she's a communist. She just seemed to me like a regular tourist."

"Where is she?"

Where is she? Hope rose in him again.

"I don't know. We had an argument and she left."

"What did you argue about?"

What, what, what. What could they have been arguing about that wouldn't damn her if they found her. He stared at the cross glinting in the captain's chest hairs. He said, "I started to talk about the Lord Jesus Christ, and she thought I came on to her just to convert her."

"You are an evangelical, and she is an atheist? She's a communist?"

"No, she said she was already a Bible-believing Christian and she didn't need to be convinced." The translator's eyebrows arched skeptically. "I saw Ríos Montt preach recently and I might have come on kind of strong." Was he laying it on too thick now?

"Where did you see him preach?" the captain asked.

"At the Church of the Word in Guatemala City. I went with my congregation."

The Captain leaned back in his chair and tossed the waxed paper for Paquito again. "And what did you think of *El General*?"

Kit forced himself to say it without hesitation. "Brother Efraín is a great Christian leader."

The captain sat suddenly bolt upright in his chair and thrust his thumb and first two fingers in the air dramatically. "*Qué dice el General?*" he asked. Kit almost forgot to wait for the translation before answering.

"He says, 'Don't lie, don't cheat, and don't abuse people'."

The translator's eyes were narrowed. He seemed to be making up his own mind if Kit was sincere.

"That's right!" The captain lifted Paquito onto his lap and held the terrier's forepaw in the air. " '*No mientes, no robas, no abusas', ¿eh, perrito?*" he said to the dog. —You don't lie or rob or abuse, do you, doggy? — The dog dropped the waxed paper on the captain's lap and panted happily.

"I don't either," pledged the captain. He laughed the congested laugh of a smoker. "Why," he said then, relaxing back into the chair and flinging the ball into the corner, "does a good Christian evangelical fuck a stranger on the beach?"

"I didn't—" Kit began.

"Yes yes, you didn't fuck her, you just fooled around with her. Still—" He spread his palms and brought his shoulders up in an attitude of mock consternation. "I, too, am an evangelical," he said. He straightened and raised his hand in the air again. "I do not fuck anyone except my wife!" he pledged, and gave another rattling guffaw.

The captain was still laughing when the lieutenant finished translating. Kit waited for his laughter to subside. "It was wrong," he said. "I sinned because I was lonely."

"*¡Oh ho!*" exclaimed the captain. "You sinned because you are a Christian second and a man first." Then he spoke rapidly to the lieutenant who saluted him, snapped his notebook shut, and left the room. The captain stood up, setting the dog on its feet, and returned the gun to its holster.

Winking at Kit, he said to the dog in a high-pitched voice, "*¿Cantas, Paquito, cantas para el gringo?*" The dog stood up on its hind legs, pedaling the air with its forepaws and 'sang' with a tortured, rasping whine that made Kit shiver. The captain let the dog go on for a minute or so before tossing him a treat from his pocket and patting him between the ears. "*¿Muy inteligente eh? Más inteligente que la mayoría de la gente.*" —More intelligent than most people, isn't he?—Kit pretended not to understand.

The lieutenant returned with Kit's passport and money, which he handed to him, saying, "They'll drive you back to San José." In his astonishment and relief, Kit's knees almost buckled under him.

The three of them came out into the corridor again, where the same stoop-shouldered guard still stood in front of the window, a late afternoon sun casting his shadow on the floor.

The horror of the scene beyond that window gripped Kit again, and he stopped in shame at his hypocrisy and cowardice. He could not walk out without some attempt, no matter how useless, to protest. He turned to the captain and gestured toward the window, using the three-fingered salute. "'I don't abuse'?" he quoted, questioningly. The lieutenant seemed to hesitate before translating.

"No," replied the captain, looking steadily into Kit's eyes. "*No abuso.*"

"Then—"

"*Efraín Ríos Montt es un soldado como yo.*" Efraín Ríos Montt is a soldier, like me. "*Él entiende lo que los soldados tienen que hacer.*" He understands what soldiers have to do.

Kit said, his voice cracking, "But what crime did that man commit?"

The captain shrugged. "*No sé. A lo mejor nada.*" The lieutenant darted a look at the captain, hesitating before he translated. "I don't know. Maybe nothing." The captain gazed at the window for a moment and shrugged again. "*A veces nosotros necesitamos ejemplos,*" he said. "Sometimes we need examples."

"*Ejemplos?*"

"*Sí.*"

Kit was driven back in the same covered vehicle. This time his wrists were free and he sat upright on a bench. He took shallow breaths high up in his chest to keep the pain from stabbing him in the ribs. During the short ride back, he stared at the ribbon of dusty highway unfurling behind the truck and prayed that he wouldn't vomit.

They left him at the door to his room. An armed soldier—the Mayan boy with the scar across his nose—peered from a recessed doorway on the other side of the street.

The room had been ransacked—bedclothes tossed aside, the contents of his backpack strewn about. For a few moments it seemed as if his legs could not carry him over the threshold into the stifling, violated room.

Then, because his reaction might be giving pleasure to the soldier, he stepped in and shut the door, quietly bolting it.

His Bible was lying open face-down on the floor, the pages bent. Just the thought of stooping to pick it up made him wince with pain. He was glad for an excuse not to touch the book, but guilt followed at once. Holding his ribs with one hand and breathing shallowly, he bent over and set the Bible on the foot of the bed.

As he straightened, the room spun and a clammy sweat broke out on his forehead. He thought he might finally throw up. His bowels cramped. After all he had been through, was he going to mess himself now? He got to the filthy bathroom just in time, shitting a stream of diarrhea into the toilet as, clutching his ribcage, he leaned sideways over the shower stall and vomited undigested tortilla and coconut into the drain.

He staggered back to the bed and lay down, crying out at the jolts of pain that shot through his back. The foul taste in his mouth disgusted him, and he was parched with thirst, but he felt too weak to go out and buy water. It was so hot in the room that a fly sat inches from his face without moving a wing.

He lay shivering and trembling and tried not to think about where he had just been and how he had conducted himself—his fear and silence and failure to act with courage, and now, his hiding like a beaten dog. The heat of the room and of his own fiery skin, the shooting pains in his ribs—all the afflictions of his body—seemed deserved.

❖ Sixteen ❖

She must be hiding somewhere. But if he found her, he would lead them straight to her. That had to be why they had let him go so quickly.

She would be trying to get out of San José, back to Antigua and out of the country. But there was only one bus a day and it wouldn't leave again until noon tomorrow. Anyway, the army would be watching the bus terminus and the road out of town. She wouldn't dare hitchhike, there would be checkpoints—

Oh Lord, please—

But he couldn't commingle a prayer with the taste of vomit and shit in his mouth. He sat up for a few minutes with his head bowed to keep the dizziness away. He shouldn't stay holed up here. He must go into the town, get something to drink, show himself, show that he wasn't afraid and he was innocent.

Despite the heat and the chafing of the stiff khaki against his skin he changed into long pants. In the bathroom, he threw the swim trunks into the wastebasket with the soiled toilet paper.

Halfway down the street, he glanced back, but the soldier hadn't left his post to follow. Probably he had instructions to stay put and watch for the woman to show up.

On the other side of the bridge there was a little more life on the street than earlier. Dusk was coming on. On the black sand scraggly palms threw blacker shadows. Kit was shocked to realize that only a little over two hours had gone by since he had been taken to the base, detained, and brought back. It seemed as if a whole day and night must have passed.

Across the peach-colored horizon stretched a long lavender smudge of smoke from the steamer's smokestack. The sun, a glowing ember, was slowly dousing itself in the sea. A few tourists and sailors had come out again. Kit bought two bottles of water from a vendor, took sips, sloshing the water around in his mouth and spitting it onto the sand until the first bottle was used up. Then, from the other, he drank deeply.

He stood as casually as possible, trying not to look as if he were scanning the beach for her. The Australians were still there, or maybe they had left and come back again. They were lounging in the sand drinking beer and passing around a joint. A different soldier was patrolling the beach while another stood surveying the scene from the naval station gate. At the sight of them, Kit's heart pounded. He suppressed the urge to flee. The soldiers paid no attention to the Australians, but seemed to throw regular, sidelong glances at Kit.

The palapa was abandoned now, the tortilla seller and her child gone. Kit sat down at the table. The last of the sunset was fading to purple.

Where *was* she, and how had she been able to slip away?

Supposing, after she'd left him, she took the side street back to her room and saw the army truck and headed back toward the beach. But where would she have hidden?

Watching the surf roll in, curl on itself and break in the waning light, it occurred to him that the only place a person *could* hide in this whole place might be in the water.

He stood up in nervous excitement. Is that what she had done? Run to the water and plunged in among the other swimmers? Was she there now? She might have swum to the pier and hidden underneath, even while the disgraced soldier was being dispatched to find her. The soldier would have gone directly to the beach to keep watch. She might have been in the water for the last two hours, clinging to a slippery piling as the cold waves surged around her. It was almost dark, but Kit didn't dare look toward the pier. Where else could she have gone?

The Australians were shadowy, capering figures around a fire they had built from bits of driftwood. It looked as if they were going to make a night of it. Two of them were singing drunkenly. Then, as the horizon turned black, only the ghostly glide of white breakers and the orange glow of the bonfire were visible in the dark. There was no moon. The soldiers switched on high-powered flashlights and swept the long beams rhythmically up and down the beach.

If she was out there, she would have to come in before exhaustion and cold overcame her. He felt again her reassuring touch as she had guided him to shore through the surf. *It was just panic. You swam your way out of it.*

What was she enduring alone now, while he sat here in the darkness powerless to help her?

He was caught briefly in the cross beams of the two flashlights, and it suddenly struck him what he could do. If she was in the water, she needed a chance to get out and slip off somewhere else.

He turned to look over his shoulder toward the town, and despite the pain in his ribs, held this position. A few seconds went by before a flashlight beam hit him again. When it did, he waited a moment, then rose and walked purposely toward the bridge. He moved just fast enough to arouse suspicion.

The flashlight beams found him again and began to bounce along as the soldiers hurried after him. As he got to the sidewalk, he heard the gritty chunk of their boots in the sand some distance behind. Still intermittently caught in their lights, he crossed the canal and turned onto the main street. In the colored lamps of the cantinas he was completely visible now.

He turned in at a two-table cantina and sat down. Out of the corner of his eye he saw a soldier, gun in hand, stop and lean against a wall. In the back of the cantina, the proprietor extricated himself from a string hammock slung from the roof rafters. He glanced at the soldier and eyed Kit before approaching the table.

Kit ordered a Fanta, but when it arrived, the syrupy orange smell made him nauseated and he couldn't drink it. He paid for the bottle and asked if there was *un baño.* Any tourist could be expected to know this word without being proficient in Spanish. The man glanced past Kit, then shook his head. "*No, no baño,*" though Kit could see plainly a door in the back with a handwritten sign: "*Damas y Hombres.*" He wondered if his very presence in the cantina would get the man into trouble.

All at once Kit was overcome with panic. He couldn't get a breath and his heart started racing again. There was no way out of this nightmarish trap. No authorities to turn to except the ones who jammed a finger up your ass.

Two drunk sailors came sauntering along the street, and he hunched over his soda bottle till they had passed. He got up, holding his ribs, and limped the half block to his room. Across the street the Mayan private was still watching the door. As stifling as the room was, it was a relief to be inside. Kit bolted the door and collapsed onto the bed in the dark.

After a while, he closed his eyes and tried to open his heart to the Holy Spirit. Instead, behind his eyelids flashed the intolerable image of the hanging man. He blinked it away, but it kept coming back, a photonegative in harsh sunlight. Then came the old peasant man holding up his dog-eared photo—holding it up and holding it up with the naïve hope of finding someone, in that outpost of horrors, with ordinary human compassion. The man had to know he wouldn't find any, yet without hesitation he had made straight for the torturers' den and offered himself up. He loved his boy that much.

Kit's ears filled with the old man's shriek when he saw through the window the tortured body of his son.

Kit jumped to his feet in fury. "What the fuck is this about?" he shouted, pain assaulting his ribs. "What the fuck are you thinking?" He was yelling at Jesus, but the face of the Savior that loomed in the dark had the mocking smile of the captain holding his dog's paw in that three-finger pledge.

You don't rob, you don't lie, you don't abuse.

The pain grew worse, doubling him over. There was a thick knot on his back where the soldier had slammed the rifle into his ribs. But he couldn't lie down. At every noise outside the door, he tensed. He was just as helpless as before—they could break in and the whole thing could start over again.

He was suddenly filled with hatred for Colleen. She had known she was doing something dangerous and had let him get sucked into it. Took the choice right out of his hands—stupid lovesick jerkoff that he was. She was always sneering at him for being ignorant. But all he had come down here to do was to spread the Gospel, not to become some political martyr. That was *her* thing. Fine. Let her be a goddamn martyr for her goddamn sainted brother. And what was she doing fucking a stranger on a beach?

They *weren't* fucking. Oh God, what *were* they doing … against his shoulder, her cheek rising in a smile. Could such happiness bring down so much punishment?

He shook his head. What arrogance to think that all of it—that tortured man, the murdered father, Colleen's disappearance—was part of a plan to punish *him*. Punish him … for what? For *touching* her. It was absurd.

His mind careened back to Colleen on the beach, kneeling in the sand, stroking sun lotion into his shoulder with those silky, circular motions. Even now, after everything that had just happened, he felt himself grow hard. Then he felt the terrible twinge and ache where the jeering soldier had snapped the pencil against him. Shame burned in him again, as if Colleen herself had been standing there watching what they did to him. *Jesus!* Would he ever be able to feel good about those brief moments they had had together?

He *wanted* the memory, the whole thing, intact. Her slim body in that dainty skirted bathing suit. Her surprisingly shy voice. *I don't know what it is about you, Kit.* Somehow it seemed to raise him above all the other things—his oily flattery of the translator, the lies, the captain's amusement. *Does a good Christian evangelical fuck a stranger on a beach?*

She had always tried to keep him at a distance, had never even told him where she was staying in Antigua. The night she had defended him at the café, she hadn't let him walk her to her door. In Escuintla, she had hurried away and not spoken to him or even looked at him when she got back on the bus. Why?

It came to him then, accompanied by a pang of longing for her. She had known that being with her was dangerous, and that if she ever got caught, he could get dragged away, too.

But then why did she seek him out on the beach when she was most nervous about the danger?

A spasm of pain made him grunt. He cursed himself for his absurd preoccupation. 'She likes me, she doesn't like me.' You stupid, stupid fuck! How could he wallow in it? People with only a tortilla and a few beans in their stomachs hauled hundred pound stacks of wood up and down mountain roads just to survive. Others were locked away in secret, bloody rooms, dying slow deaths.

He opened his door. The miserable paeon of a private was still hunkered down across the street. They were still looking for her.

The moon was up, the air less sultry. Mariachi music came from a radio somewhere. He thought he could hear the surf rolling in on the beach, unless it was just the swish of overhead fans in the cantinas along the street where sailors were drinking. Where was she now? Maybe she had not been hiding in the water at all. Could she somehow have gotten out of town? If only he knew, then at noon tomorrow he could get on that bus and be out of here.

No tourists were on the streets, probably for good reason. The sailors eyed him steadily as he passed. Every man in a uniform seemed to be watching him.

His pants legs chafed his flaming skin like sand paper. He came to the canal and stood by the bridge rail for some minutes, his anxiety and helplessness seeming intolerable.

Then a new thought struck him. She had said, after all her standoffishness, *I can't believe myself!* She had let herself turn to him even at the risk that he might be on the side of the enemy. He had been her weakness. *Her weakness.* The prick of satisfaction at the thought disgusted him.

He stared through the dark at the point of light that was the Australians' expiring bonfire, and yearned to go down and join them even though they weren't saved—not if they smoked pot and got drunk. Most of the people in the world weren't saved. They would all writhe and twitch and their agony would never end, because although they had heard the story of the merciful and loving God, who sacrificed his Son for their sins, they had had the arrogance not to believe it.

Then all those bouncing thoughts came at last to rest on the hanging man. How long, oh Lord, had he been left to hang there? How long would they make use of their *ejemplo*? Would they just let him hang there until he died? How long?

207

"Jesus," Kit prayed. "Cut him down. Please. Or if you can't—" But He could do anything— "If he has to hang there until he dies, let him die *now*. Don't let him keep on suffering. Please, Lord." It was wrong to wish someone dead, even to end suffering.

"If it's Your will—" he started again, but left the phrase unfinished. Something seemed to drain the blood out of his heart. He stood, his mouth open in horror. He was helpless to prevent the idea from possessing his whole body, weakening him so that he had to put a hand on the bridge rail to hold himself up: If the hanging man died an unrepentant communist, his torment wouldn't end with his death. Dangling from a post in the burning sun was just a gentle reproof compared to the eternal torture God had in store for him.

Dread seemed to fall down around Kit like a great collapsing tent, trapping and smothering him. His breath came fast and his heart tripped, the way it had when he woke as a child in the empty apartment, those nights his mother had to leave him alone to go to work. Terrified, squeezing his eyes shut. It was like this now. A sense of abandonment and mortal danger.

A piece of ground that he had been standing on seemed to break off, and carry him away into an empty sea. He looked out into the darkness at the pinpoint embers of the boys' dying fire. Until now, damnation had been an abstract catastrophe. The thousands, *millions*, who would be cast into hell on judgment day had seemed like victims of an earthquake or flood that you heard about on the news, and shook your head over and said, how terrible.

But now he could see with his own eyes the lost ones in torment—like the hanging man, the woman on the bus—only a few feet away, and he couldn't do anything for them, only watch in horror. God's *ejemplos*. Where had he read that punishment was supposed to fit a crime? 'Cruel and unusual punishment.' How could a simple failure of belief earn you eternal torture?

Disoriented, in a panic, he stumbled down the beach toward the Australian boys, who rested by their glowing fire in the sand. In his mind he was calling out: I'm in trouble. Help me. He ran headlong toward them.

But then he stopped midstep beyond their small circle of light, suddenly remembering that he was contaminated by his association with Colleen. The idea that these carefree young guys—oblivious, unsuspecting—might be picked up and subjected to the ineradicable horrors of that military base made him turn around and stagger back up the beach. But, Oh Jesus, there was nowhere to go.

And then, just like that, his belief in damnation left him. It was utterly gone. He wanted it back, but it was too late.

The Bible Ezra had given him was where he had left it in his violated room. Just a book, printed on a printing press along with thousands of others, its leatherette cover glued on, gilt applied by machine to its edge. And the words—the black ink stories and psalms and red ink quotations of Jesus—the meaning of the words inside seemed to drain out from the pages. He sank down on the sand. He was afloat on a sea of meaninglessness.

The sand was damp and cold now that the sun was gone. But he sat for a long time shivering in his burned skin before he found the will to make his way back to the room. He pulled the light cord and stood immobilized for some time before picking up his Bible. In the harsh light of the single overhead bulb he scanned the Gospels for the passage about hell that Colleen had quoted. *John 15:6*. The quote was accurate. He spent an hour scanning for other references in the Gospels to the fire and eternal torment of judgment. One by one, he found them in *Matthew 5*—the Sermon on the Mount—*Matthew 13 and 18, Mark 9, Luke 16*, at the end of *Revelation*.

The unbelieving shall have their part in the lake which burneth with fire and brimstone … that never shall be quenched where their worm dieth not … wailing and gnashing of teeth … the smoke of their torment ascendeth up forever and ever and they have no rest day or night.

He read the passages aloud, over and over, but he could see no other way to interpret the heartless, savage words.

Dread gave way to a hollow dullness. He lay down and waited out the rest of the night. When dawn came at last, he got up and used the toilet. His T-shirt clung to his back, reeking from the sweat of his fear and anxiety, but he had nothing else to wear, and it didn't matter. The soldier was not at his post.

Three emaciated dogs sidled past Kit in a pack and disappeared down the street. A few vendors and *tienda* owners were setting out their wares. A *ladino* family was sitting at the cantina where he had ordered the soda he couldn't drink. He was going to have to do what the old man had done. Go straight back into the lion's den. He would head toward the beach, where he would be most likely to find a soldier.

At the cantina, at the table in the back, sat a thickset *ladino* man in Hawaiian shirt and sunglasses. The man set down a coffee cup and leaned back in his chair as Kit walked by. When Kit came to the canal, he looked back to see the man in sunglasses in the street. Just to be sure, he took the turning before the bridge and doubled back to the main thoroughfare again. The man slid into a doorway and lit a cigarette. Kit felt lightheaded. They didn't have her. He was still being followed.

But what now? The relentless sun made it hard for him to think. He bought another bottle of water and, though it was more necessary than ever to hold onto his dwindling *quetzales*, bought a straw hat pressed on him by an insistent vendor. The brim scratched his tender forehead, but the covering gave some relief.

Under the palapa, the tortilla seller had again tethered her child to the table leg and was feeding sticks into the fire under her grill. The rusty machete lay atop the table next to a basket of bananas. He knew he ought to eat something. He might be able to hold down a banana if he ate slowly.

The woman took his money with no indication that she remembered him or the scene of the day before. He thought of Colleen throwing off his shirt, and looked for it now to protect him from the sun. It wasn't there. Someone had probably made off with it. He wished he had had the presence of mind to look for it last night.

The banana and the water eased his nausea, and he walked—hunched against the pains shooting across his back—to the shore and along the beach. Now and then he caught glimpses of the man in the sunglasses— once by the palapa, then by the pier. Soon the sun drove Kit back into town, where he prowled the streets just to keep in motion.

He decided to go to the bus at noon, and then what? He could return to Antigua, if he wasn't prevented from leaving, and get help from Phil and Rita, or stay and wait to see what would happen, but— if he stayed, what would he do when his money ran out? Always before, prayers had soothed him, just saying the name of the Savior aloud brought comfort. Now it made his stomach clench.

He wondered if he had been wrong last night about hell and damnation. Maybe when he finally had his head together, he would see something that would allow him to believe again. The straw hat was irritating his raw, sunburned forehead. He took it off and rested it on his knees.

He got to the bus twenty minutes early, still without a plan, and sat crosslegged in the only shade he could find, under the few spindly fronds of a stunted palm tree. Across the street, two soldiers sat smoking inside a covered truck with the doors hanging open. One of the soldiers was the stocky lieutenant who had struck him in the face in Colleen's room. The other was the square-jawed private who had followed him from the beach and slammed a rifle into his ribs. A little beyond the truck idled a Cherokee Chief station wagon with tinted windows. It had no license plate.

The bus pulled up miraculously on time, announcing itself with a misfiring of pistons and the shriek of unlined brakes. Kit was instantly filled with longing to be on the garishly painted vehicle, traveling away from this place. But he got to his feet slowly, still uncertain what he should do.

The driver and fare collector were not the same men who had brought the bus there the day before, but as they got out, they eyed the army vehicle somberly. The private came over and spoke to them. They got back on the bus, and the soldier stood just outside the open door. The waiting passengers became quiet then and made no move to enter the bus until the soldier jerked a thumb at them to move forward.

Half a block away, the Australian boys came trotting. Sunburned and grubby, encumbered with water bottles, straw hats, and soccer balls, they came, and Kit's heart stopped as he saw, camouflaged and flanked by them on all sides, Colleen.

He recognized her at once despite her drastic transformation. Her hair was hacked into a ragged crew cut. She wore a long-sleeved shirt—

his own—flopping loose and untucked—and a pair of oily, torn men's trousers, baggy in the hips and legs, but too short, and baring her unmistakable ankles. Her shoulders were hunched to conceal her breasts. She wore no backpack but clutched a string bag full of coconuts she must have taken over from the boys.

The soldier, too, had noticed the approaching group and was pushing back the visor of his cap. Kit felt paralyzed with fear. There was no way her disguise would hold up under close inspection. This soldier had spent a day watching those boys on the beach; all he would have to do is count. Yet, how many would Kit himself have guessed? He saw now that there were five. With Colleen, six.

For a split second as the group drew up alongside the bus, her eyes met his, and the terror he saw there shot adrenalin through his limbs. She was about to pass within inches of the soldier. Kit's heart raced. What, what could he do? How could he draw the private into a conversation when he wasn't supposed to know Spanish?

He turned to the soldier, with no plan. The man was restlessly shifting his weight from one foot to the other. Ask him anything. The cost of the bus fare. Every tourist knows how to open a palm full of money and say, '*¿Cuánto cuesta?*'

He reached under his waistband for his money pouch, and felt inside it for coins. Encountering the folded piece of drawing paper, his fingers, as if having a presence of mind that his brain hadn't achieved, drew out the paper and unfolded it. He stepped a little aside and held the paper aloft.

"*Señor,*" he said. "*Señor,* excuse me." The soldier gripped his rifle and shot a glance over his shoulder at the truck. The stocky lieutenant got out as Kit pushed the paper under the private's nose. "For the *Capitán!*" he shouted. "For the *Capitán.* It's *Paquito.*" The soldier looked at the drawing and frowned.

Colleen and the Australians were behind Kit now. He felt them hesitate. Out of the corner of his eye he saw Colleen's bare ankle and sandaled foot on the bus step. In the next moment she and the others were crowding on, while the private and the lieutenant scrutinized the portrait of the sleeping terrier. Kit turned to the lieutenant and held the drawing up for him. "*Gracias* to the *Capitán,*" he said. "*Muchas gracias.*" Then he held up the thumb and two fingers of his right hand and, forcing a sickly grin, winked at the men. The private eyed the lieutenant and said uncertainly in Spanish, "It's the Captain's dog."

"*Yo sé.*" said the lieutenant impatiently.

He snatched the drawing away. "*I'll* give it to him." He gave Kit a long, mocking once-over. "*El capitán y tú,*" he said, derisively, "*Ustedes si quieren a los perros.*"—You and the captain, you're both in love with dogs.

Kit was the last to board. The lieutenant slapped the side of the bus and it pulled away.

All the way to Escuintla, Kit watched for army vehicles stopped along the road. He watched the fare collector to see if he seemed interested in the Australians, who were sitting toward the middle of the bus. He listened for snatches of conversation behind him and the sound of Colleen's voice, but the motor noise was too loud. It wasn't until they were entering Escuintla that he realized they had passed no checkpoint. He stepped off the bus, weak with relief that here, too, there was no military presence.

In Escuintla, Colleen and the Australians crouched in the dust, taking swigs from their water bottles and sharing pieces of coconut. They didn't speak much, Colleen not at all. There was no way of knowing who or what the boys thought Colleen was.

On the Antigua bus Kit sat by a window, squeezed onto the same seat with two brown-skinned teenage brothers with identical Mayan noses. The younger boy sitting next to Kit struggled to stay awake, but his head kept flopping onto Kit's shoulder until the other boy, with a gesture both matter-of-fact and infinitely tender, eased the younger one's head and torso down onto his lap, where the boy lay asleep for the rest of the trip, his brother's hand resting on his arm. Kit's eyes filled with tears.

They were ascending into the Highlands now. At a crossroad the bus stopped to let on a smiling, toothless *campesino* in colorful, tattered vest and trousers. Through the door came a breath of cool mountain air. Kit leaned his cheek against the window and at last fell asleep.

He woke when the bus jounced over a curb and squealed to a stop at *La Polvera*. For a moment he had no idea where he was. He shambled off the bus in a daze and stood blinking in the sunlight.

Immediately, he caught the brash drawl of the Australian boys behind him. She was there still camouflaged among them as they made for the center of town. He followed slowly at some distance, hunched against the needles of pain again shooting through his ribs. His swollen cheek throbbed and his skin in the cool mountain air felt tight as if about to split.

At the square he expected Colleen to detach herself from the Australians and head for her room at *Pensión El Arco,* but she carried on past her street, sticking close to them. They passed the *parque central* and turned a corner two streets beyond the cathedral. Kit tried to keep up without being too obvious, but when he reached the corner, they had disappeared, the whole group of them. Gone.

Apart from a woman sweeping her sidewalk, the narrow street of houses and *pensiones* was deserted at the moment. A car appeared at the other end of the street. The driver seemed to be watching him.

Kit turned to go back the way he had come, but he saw that the driver had only been waiting for two other cars to pass, the street being too narrow to accommodate more than a single lane of traffic. Then he noticed that the second of the two cars was a dark blue Cherokee Chief station wagon with smoked windows. The one in San José, was it dark blue or dark green?

The vehicle bumped past him along the cobbles. There was no license plate. If he had gone blundering down the street looking into doorways, he might have led them right to Colleen.

He trudged toward the *Colonia Candelaria,* almost feeling the station wagon creeping along, leaving the distance of a block between them. But when he turned up *1era Avenida Norte* the vehicle was gone.

❖ Seventeen ❖

Now he had only one thought—to strip off his filthy clothes and lay his exhausted body on a clean bed. Eventually there would be a cold shower, too, and food and time to think what to do next.

He pushed on the Martinezes' front door. It jarred loudly against the chain.

"*¡Hola!*" he called through the opening. It was only mid afternoon, but from inside the house there was an unnatural silence. Through the gap he saw on the opposite wall of the *sala* the lurid glowing heart of the Christ painting. The picture was askew.

Suddenly, the oldest son, *Jorge*, was at the door, frowning up at him over the chain. "You can't come here anymore!" he shouted in Spanish. Kit took a step back. Had he understood him right?

From behind him Kit heard the angry voice of *Señor* Martinez. Then the door slammed shut, the chain was brusquely removed and the door opened again. *Señor* Martinez stood in the doorway glaring at Kit through eyes swollen to slits. A bandage was wrapped around his hand and wrist, which rested in a sling improvised from a shawl. Behind him *Señora* Martinez made high-pitched imploring noises to her husband. "*¡Regresa por favor… regresa a la cama!*" —Come back to bed!—Jorge had a protective hand on his father's arm, which *Señor* Martinez shook off.

He shouted at Kit, "We know nothing about this girl! Why do you bring us trouble with the army?"

He muttered an order to his son, who withdrew into the interior and returned again almost immediately with Kit's large backpack. Jorge stepped around his father and pushed the pack through the door, shouting at Kit to go away and not come back. From the entry to the hall, the younger Martinez children peered, big-eyed and frightened. *Señora* Martinez shooed them away.

"*¿Qué ha pasado?*" Kit said. "*Yo no*—" But Jorge stepped outside and shoved Kit backward.

"Don't talk to us. We don't know anything. Go away. Now."

Standing behind her husband, *Señora* Martinez called tearfully, shrilly, "Go to the school, go to the school!"

Kit backed from the door and bent painfully to pick up the pack, which was three fourths of the way zipped up, revealing his belongings hastily shoved in. Then he turned and limped away. The *Candelaria* courtyard, where children were usually found on a Sunday afternoon kicking a half-inflated soccer ball or jumping rope or chasing the skinny neighborhood dogs, was completely empty. Inside a few of the concrete block houses, the shadowy silhouettes of people could be seen peering through flimsy lace curtains.

Kit retreated down the sidewalk, carrying the backpack in his arms until he came to a ruined church façade. There he dropped the heavy pack onto the crumbling stone steps, eased himself painfully to the ground and lay back. For the time being he couldn't go any farther.

Along the street came the crunch of tires, a vehicle slowing, coming to a stop, a door opening. Kit stiffened.

"*Amigo*." Rub slammed the door of the Peugeot and sauntered over. "You look like something a vulture hacked up." He slung Kit's backpack over a shoulder and took Kit by the arm. "Get in," he commanded. Kit hesitated, glancing down the avenue. No Cherokee. "Christ, don't get paranoid on me. I'm taking you to Phil's place."

Kit lowered his long frame into the seat, gasping at the pain in his ribs. Rub nodded. "They did a number on you, I see." Kit didn't reply.

Rub drove fast across town, brought the Peugeot up to a high, wooden gate and honked the horn. Phil himself opened it and Rub pulled into the driveway.

"Here he is!" called Rita from the entryway. "*Pobre muchacho*, come take a rest."

Phil led Kit to the central patio, where he sat him down on a lounge chair in the shade of the flame tree. The only sounds were water splashing into the fountain and a bird chirping overhead. He lay his head back on the cushion.

Rita reappeared with a pitcher and glass on a tray, the maid following behind with a platter of food. She set a glass of ice water in his hand and waved the maid over with the food. Fluttering around him, Rita frowned and tutted at his swollen, sunburned cheek and caressed it lightly, leaving the scent of her heavy perfume.

"I'm sorry I stink," muttered Kit.

"Don't worry." Rita patted his hand. "You will have a nice long bath and then you sleep. But now, you drink and eat somethings."

He drank all the water in the glass without taking a breath, and she poured him another. "This boy has thirsty!" she called to Phil. "Like a horse at the—how you call it!"

"Trough." Phil was standing with one foot on the fountain ledge. At the sideboard Rub was looking over the cluster of bottles with the purpose of helping himself.

"So," Phil said mildly. "You won't be returning to the Martinez's."

Kit looked up at him. "Yeah." How did he know?

"One of the sons came and reported it. It's unfortunate that they got dragged into this." He gazed across the patio at Rub and said, with an edge of irritation, "That family has been with us for years. It won't be easy to find another home stay as reliable as theirs." Then he shrugged. "Such things happen."

"The army beat him up?" Kit asked.

"The thing is," Phil continued, ignoring the question, "we're running a school. It's a business. We rely on decent relations with the powers that be, and they trust us to stay out of politics. Otherwise—" He held up his palms. "So I gather you got yourself in trouble over some girl who's a subversive?"

Kit set his glass down and sat forward. "I was arrested for no reason."

"I told them we'd never seen you with a girl. As far as we knew you had nothing to do with any girl here in Antigua, you are a devout evangelical who is entirely apolitical. That's true, I take it?"

Kit nodded, slowly.

"They know that we don't harbor leftists of any stripe at the school. So what's the story with this girl?"

"You were screwing some *guerrillera* chick on a beach?" said Rub.

Rita had joined her husband and was perched on the edge of the fountain.

"No," Kit said. "I just met her. In San José. She was a tourist." He looked away. "We were just ... fooling around."

"Oh, he is so *shy*, this boy!" exclaimed Rita. "Rub, do not ask rude questions! He is young, why not 'fool around'?" To Kit she said, "Eat. You feel better. Then you take a nice cool bath." She snapped her fingers at the maid and ordered her to take his things and go fill the bathtub. The little maid picked up Kit's large back pack and day pack where they lay by his chair, hefted them onto her small shoulders and took them away.

He did eat. Four tamales, two sandwiches, an avocado, and a peeled mango. He drank two more glasses of water. While he ate, he glanced at the three. Rita, one high-heeled sandal dangling from her swinging foot, smiled at him. Phil, examining the underside of a small stone figurine—a new one?—wore his usual bland, detached expression. Rub was turning bottles around to read their labels. Was there any possibility of getting help here for Colleen? How much influence did they have with the authorities?

Nothing more was said about Kit's ordeal, and afterwards Rita took him down a corridor into a bathroom open to a patio. Thick white towels and a terry robe and slippers were laid out next to a large, deep stone *pila* filled to the brim with clear warm water.

When Rita left, he stripped, and holding his breath against the knifing pains spasming his back, lowered himself slowly into the *pila*. He closed his eyes, lay back and, sinking up to his nose, floated. He thought of nothing, only the exquisite relief he felt and the sensation of rising weightlessly to the surface and sinking back as he filled and emptied his lungs.

He dozed in and out of sleep. When he finally climbed out, toweled off and put on the terry robe, the little round-faced maid appeared as if by magic to lead him to a bedroom. His backpacks sat side by side on a chest. The bed was turned down. The smooth white sheets smelled as if they had dried in the sun. In moments he was asleep.

He was walking along a street in Antigua. Ahead was a shop with a large plate glass window displaying many bright colored *huipiles* on hangers. He hurried forward, thinking if he bought four more *huipiles* all his gifts would be taken care of. But when he got closer, he saw that there were only two of them and they weren't *huipiles* at all but Lorie and Edie dangling upside down by their feet like dead chickens in the marketplace. Their faces were a bright purple. He rushed at the window and struck it, but his fists were soft and spongey and had no impact. Dean, lounging in the back of the store with his arms folded across his chest, mouthed the words, "Can I help you, *amigo*?"

He woke flailing and shrieking. When his eyes fluttered open, they stared into complete blackness. He held a hand up in front of his face, but it was as if he had gone blind in the night. *He'd been thrown into an underground cell.*

He almost knocked over a lamp on the bedside table, before recognizing it for what it was, and switching it on. He gazed around the room. Mayan masks and idols gazed back at him empty-eyed from niches and pedestals. He didn't know how many hours he had slept.

The night was cold, and he shivered, though his skin was still feverishly hot. Reaching tentatively for his clothes, he found his body still ached all over. A clean shirt, pants and underwear had been removed from his backpack and laid over a chair. Though it was still the middle of the night, he dressed. His dream lingered, with its sense of having to do urgent, though hopeless, battle.

Colleen. She should get out of the country right away. She should pick up her money from the *Pensión El Arco*, get herself to Guatemala City, and take a plane back to the U.S. today, before somebody saw through her disguise.

But suppose the army had made inquiries at Antigua hotels and *pensiones*, with a description of the long-haired *gringa* who had been seen on the bus. The landlady at *Pensión El Arco* might say yes, there is someone like that staying here. Colleen's room would be searched.

What would the landlady do later if she caught a teenage boy in a ragged crewcut sneaking into the room?

His bowels were becoming unsettled again and his bladder was full to bursting. He made his way quietly down the empty corridor to the bathroom. The sky was black and glittering with stars. It was late Sunday night or early Monday morning. Colleen was probably still crashing with the Australians, maybe unable to sleep too. She probably couldn't get on a bus, much less board a plane without getting her papers checked. And what would she do with the canister of film? Probably she couldn't mail it. He had noticed at the Antigua post office that packages going out of the country were routinely opened and searched. Maybe she had thrown it away. He couldn't imagine her taking the risk of their finding it on her if she got caught.

A faint ripple of laughter came from somewhere in the house—Rita's voice. They were still up. He felt a tug of yearning for those touches that she gave so freely, her cooing defense of him.

When he left the bathroom, he walked through the house and found Phil and Rita still sitting around the fountain and Rub pouring a drink at the sideboard, as if they had been left in suspended animation during the hours he slept. A shawl was wrapped around Rita's shoulders now. Phil was saying to Rub, "Shouldn't you be exercising a bit of restraint in the current situation? A certain level of alertness will be expected of you—"

He broke off on seeing Kit in the entryway. Rub looked up.

"Eh, *amigo*!" He took an unsteady step toward Kit. "This proper limey gentleman—" He gestured with his glass toward Phil and, slipping into a good imitation of Phil's accent, said, "—this gentleman thinks that I have had perhaps one too many, to the extent that I am impairing my mental and physical functioning." He took a swig from his glass, walked carefully over to Kit and laid a hand on his shoulder. "But here is how *I* look at it, old chap. I model myself after His Excellency, our illustrious U.S. Ambassador, whose capacity for drink is renowned throughout the Western Hemisphere." He drew away from Kit and, swaying a little, took up an oratorical stance. "I give you one of Mr. Ambassador's most famous quotes." Putting his hand over his heart, he switched to a vaguely

New York inflection. "I only regret that I have but one liver to give to my country!"

"Ah, *Señor* Nystrom—" said Phil, coming forward and shaking his head.

"That's *Rub* to you, you limey bastard!" He clasped Phil around the shoulder to support himself.

Rita took his other arm. "There is a bed *muy confortable* ready for you—"

"With you in it, darlin'?"

"Rub, no talk naughty to me. My husband is here."

Phil guided him from the patio, supporting him under his armpits. Rub called back, "They pour me into bed, the next day I'm up with the birds and fresh as a goddamn daisy." At the entryway he shook his finger at Kit, "Don't fornicate with any more enemy sympathizers while I'm sleeping it off."

When the two men had left, Rita led Kit by the hand to the cushioned lounge chair and folded herself into the chair next to it. Crossing one leg over the one tucked under her, she propped her elbow on the arm of Kit's chair to rest her cheek on her hand. Her whole body inclined toward him casually, intimately. Her shawl fell off one shoulder and she breathed a drawn-out sigh as if to say—Finally! Just us.

She reached out and stroked his swollen cheek lightly, her little finger grazing the corner of his mouth.

"Poor boy," she crooned. "What you have suffer only because you get some love." She sat back. "But even if you suffer I am jealous. You know why? I wish I am young like you." She sighed again. In a slow, dreamy voice, she said, "I love, of course, Felipe, my husband, but I never forget first love when I am young. That is the mos' *sincere* love, the *bes'* love." She touched his arm. "Your girl in San José—even she is in such a big trouble, I believe she is think about you, Kit. I do! She can't help it. This is the mind of women. I know. No matter what is happen, we dream about that boy."

Her talking about Colleen this way, in such a wistful, hungering voice—it was as if he had been injected with some fast-acting drug, and he was overcome once more by the image of that slender body, shoulders hunched inside his own shirt, her hair shorn in the ragged crewcut, the eyes dull with fear. If he could take her hand and make a run for it. Race to the border over those chains of volcanoes hemming them in …

"Is beautiful, this girl on the beach?"

He nodded.

"Mmm, of course she is. She is—" Rita kissed the tips of her fingers. "—the mos' beautiful one in the world!" She cocked her head to one side and smiled coyly. "And does she tell you she love you?" He hesitated, then shook his head. "But she *does*! By expression in her face, body language. Maybe she is shy like you."

"No, she isn't." For all these weeks, he hadn't said anything about her to anyone.

"No? She is *passionate* woman! She feel *everything*. I am right?" She took his chin between her fingers and turned his face to hers. He saw for the first time that she looked tired. There were circles under her eyes, her mascara had run and left spidery flecks on her cheekbones. Small pockets of flesh at the corners of her mouth seemed to pull her lips downward even as she smiled at him ruefully. "Sometime to be passionate makes problem. But … what can you do? If you feel, you feel." She let his chin go. "I am sorry for that girl. All these mens try to find her. For what? *Probablemente* she do nothing wrong. And now you suffer so much, you say to yourself, 'I am sorry I meet her, I wish it never happen.' That is sad."

"I'm *not* sorry." The words came out. He didn't want her to think of him as cowardly and faithless. And it was true—he *wasn't* sorry.

"Ahh!" She tilted back her head and gazed at him with admiration for a few moments. "So you are *true* lover. True man. Well, who knows, may-be you will see her again. Some day, in America. She is American?"

"Yes." He picked up and set down an empty shot glass left on the chair arm. "Or … Maybe Canadian. I'm not sure."

She shrugged. "Who can tell? They speak the same. But she travel alone in this country?"

Saying nothing would be some kind of admission, but what else could he do?

"Well, she is brave woman, maybe because she is young, *inocente*.

She maybe has no idea is so dangerous, Guatemala. This is why she take pictures of *soldados*. My opinion, she must *muy rápido* go back to her country."

She lowered her voice now and glanced toward the house. "But you know, it maybe is no so easy for these girl—what is her name—?"

How could he say he didn't know it?

"We ... didn't really have a chance to tell each other our names," he tried to look her in the eye.

"Well, is no easy for ... this *girl* to return to U.S. How can she do it, no friend to help her? My husband—always he is too careful. Felipe has not romantic feeling to take risk. And *Rub*! Oh, that one—his hands are dirty. But—" She leaned into him again, speaking quietly. "I know the ways and—what do you call it?—the *ways and the means*. Relation *es más importante* than the politic in Guatemala. If you have relationship, you pass by the rules. Do you think this girl is in Antigua?"

"I don't know where she is."

"Mm. Too bad. If she is in Antigua or maybe Guatemala City, I can call on the telephone, *ffft!* one, two days, she is out of the country. Safe. *No sería necesario* tell to Felipe. What my husband don't know don't hurt." She winked.

"I don't know her name. I wouldn't know where to find her."

"So. Maybe that is the end of the love story. But—" She spoke in a whisper. "If she find you and she need help, don't talk to—" she tossed her head in the direction of the house "—these guys. Come to me. I will help." She smiled. "You know that movie, the teacher in Siam, she help the young lovers escape the cruel king who separate them? She sing, 'Hello, young lovers, wherever you are ...' " Rita sang it in a soft, breathy voice. "I will do like *that*. Even to risk my life." She threw a hand in the air and her bracelets tinkled as they rolled down her arm. "See how passionate, stupid woman I am?"

She unfolded herself and got to her feet. "Okay—I go to bed now. It's too late. Soon comes up the sun." She took his hands and tried to pull him out of the chair. "You come to the bed, too."

"I think I'll just stay here for a while," Kit said. "I don't feel tired anymore." She let him go then and leaned to kiss his swollen cheek.

"Okay. *Mañana*—" she laughed. "No—*today*!—we will decide what you must do." She flung the end of her shawl over her shoulder and clicked across the stone tiles and into the house.

He got up from the lounge chair and went to sit on the edge of the fountain. In the dim light of the sconce lamps he could just make out the three shadowy carp. The fish was a symbol for Jesus. He couldn't remember exactly why. Something about a secret code the persecuted early Christians used to identify each other. He trailed a hand in the water. In a moment there came the startling nip of a fish mouth on his skin, like a blundering kiss. His hand jerked reflexively and the fish darted back.

He stood up. The dark courtyard with its tomb-robbed statuary made him long to leave. They weren't holding him captive. But where would he go? Out on the dark street, watching for vehicles with tinted windows?

Somewhere in some room only a few blocks away, Colleen must be feeling trapped as well, with nowhere to escape to. If only he could pray.

What would he do today, and tomorrow, and the next day? He remembered what was said at Aurelia's. *The German Embassy isn't like the American Embassy. It would actually do something.*

The idea of staying on and on here, going through the motions of learning Spanish from his indifferent teacher, it was inconceivable. Even if he wanted to go back to his storefront *iglesia*—for the comfort of the music and the hugs of welcoming strangers—what suspicions would the congregation come under for accepting him?

Might even the indigenous children in the *parque central* get picked up and questioned because he had been seen drawing their portraits?

Eventually, as the sky began to get light, he went to lie down and wait for the household to waken. On his way past the kitchen courtyard, he noticed what had been hidden in darkness earlier. In a corner of the patio, the little indigenous maid, María, slept on a thin pallet spread out on the cold flagstones. Her legs were tucked up inside her skirt, and she was covered only by her cotton shawl.

In the morning, Kit asked Phil whether it was possible he was being followed.

"Mm. I shouldn't be surprised," Phil replied. "I've told them you were an innocent bystander, but they're fond of their game of cloak and dagger."

María had laid a buffet breakfast in the dining room on the massive Spanish colonial sideboard. Rita was still asleep, but Phil, up since 8:00, was shaved and dressed in pressed corduroy pants and open-neck shirt. Rub, too, seemed none the worse for wear as he spread pepper sauce on each tortilla in a prodigious stack he was piling on his plate.

"They still think I'll lead them to—the woman?" Kit asked Phil.

"Possibly."

Rub said, "'Course, if things are getting too hot for you, you could just buy yourself a plane ticket and get out of Dodge." He looked up at Kit.

Without Colleen? Of course. If, as he claimed, he had no personal attachment to her, who wouldn't want to get out as fast as he could after what had happened? For a moment he didn't reply.

"But would the authorities let me leave?"

"Ah. That is a question." Phil sipped experimentally at his coffee. "Of course they'll let you leave eventually. You're an American citizen. They can't very well detain you ... well, not again, one would hope. But perhaps they'd delay your leaving until they found the girl or lost interest or some such thing."

Rub sat down at the long table and pulled out a chair for Kit. "Chow down, *amigo*. The school bell rings in half an hour."

"Only half days through Wednesday and no classes on Thursday or Good Friday," Phil reminded them. "It's *Semana Santa*."

So. He was to keep going to the school and celebrate Holy Week as if nothing had happened.

Kit said, "My pastor sacrificed to send me here. I should stay in Antigua. But I don't know what to do about a place to live. I can't afford a hotel."

"For the time being," said Phil, "I think it best for you to bunk down here with us. We've plenty of room—" Kit opened his mouth to speak but Phil interrupted, "—as our guest, of course, since we can't provide you with another home stay."

Kit said, "You don't think that would make them suspicious of you, too?"

"Oh," said Phil offhandedly. "I think they understand our position."

After breakfast, Rub and Kit walked to school. Kit didn't see the Cherokee Chief station wagon or the man who he supposed had driven it to Antigua. Or Colleen. What would he do if she suddenly came around a corner?

To be on his way to school as usual, made the whole thing seem unreal again.

"I know I'm being followed and watched," he said impulsively, "probably by you guys, too. I guess everybody thinks I'll lead them to ... that woman."

Rub ignored the accusation. "Tall, leggy girl with long, straight brown hair, around twenty-something?" he said. "I seem to remember a lady of that description hanging around Antigua the last few weeks taking zoom lens pictures. What she wanted with that pricey camera is an obvious question. I never saw a hippie *turista* carry around anything bigger than an instamatic. They prefer to keep their hands free for rolling joints. I suppose you didn't notice her in that gang of Yank-baiters at Aurelia's?"

Kit stopped breathing for a moment. He'd forgotten about that.

"She was the one who wasn't laughing." How had he remembered this detail? "Too skinny for my taste." Rub clicked his tongue disapprovingly. "Got the bod of a boy—no hips, not enough up top. Far be it from me to judge another man's taste, though." He winked at Kit.

So he remembered her. If she stepped around that corner, he would see right through the disguise.

"'Course you wouldn't have checked her out, would you?" Rub went on sardonically. "You'd keep your eyes straight ahead, hips or no hips. 'Pluck out the eye that offends you,' ain't that the deal?"

They had come to the school. Rub stopped in the doorway.

"Maybe it's just my Pollyanna nature," he said, "but I still don't see a nice born-again boy like you having an anonymous quickie with some horny chick he's never met before."

All of Kit's classmates seemed to be staring at his swollen, discolored cheek. Marlena Bontrager hurried over to ask if he was all right. Yes, he said, fine, just bumped into something. She took a tube of cream from her handbag and gave it to him. "Arnica," she said. "For bruising and swelling. It might soothe your sunburn, too."

He sat down at his table and applied the cream to his cheek. His teacher eyed him curiously. Kit tried to concentrate on the lesson, but his mind refused to register anything. He shifted in his seat, staring unseeing at the yellow bird in the bougainvillea as his teacher flipped through the textbook.

Kit, son, if the Lord's challenges feel too overwhelming to face alone...

People kept telling him he was a babe in the woods, and it was true. There was so much he didn't understand. Ezra seemed to speak of hell as if it were real, but the Bible was full of symbols—the Lamb, the Shepherd, the seven golden candlesticks in Revelation—maybe hell represented the desolation of unbelievers at having separated themselves from God.

He decided to leave school before the end of the morning session. It was time to make a phone call to Ezra.

❖ Eighteen ❖

As Kit crossed the patio, Rub looked up from a conversation with his teacher. Fine, let him follow me. Even so, Kit took a roundabout route to the public telephone office.

The phones were all in use. He gave the woman at the counter Ezra's name and number and wondered if his phone call would be listened in on—was it possible that, in a country where you couldn't flush the toilet paper, there could be a phone system sophisticated enough to be tapped into on a moment's notice? But he wouldn't tell Ezra anything more than he had told everyone else.

He was next in line now. His palms began to sweat. When his turn came, he sat down in the booth, wiping his hands on his pant legs. The phone rang. He picked up the receiver. On the other end a ringing tone started and went on for several seconds. He hadn't considered the likelihood that nobody would be home on a Monday morning. Ezra worked Tuesday through Saturday. But of course he could be on a hospital visit or—

"Aw Kit!" Ezra exclaimed. At the sound of that exuberant baritone Kit choked up. He was afraid his voice might be taken from him. "Jeannette's going to be hopping mad to have missed you."

"I don't have much time, Ezra," he said. "I'm at a public phone. There are people waiting—" Already he felt his voice starting to break.

Ezra's tone changed abruptly. "Okay, son. Take a breath. Bring the Lord into your heart."

"I have to ask you something."

"I'm here, son. Anything you want."

"Ezra," he paused. "Is hell a real, physical place, or is it only—" he was scared to say the word "—a symbol?"

228

The reply came unequivocally and without hesitation. "It's just as it's described in Scripture, Kit. It's a physical place of eternal bodily torment and spiritual separation from God. As it says in Revelation, it's a lake of fire." For a moment they were both silent. Kit gripped the phone against his ear and listened to his own breathing.

At last he said, "And who goes to hell?"

Ezra spoke with the sternness of a kind father. "You know who goes there, son. People who have refused to accept the sacrifice of our Lord Jesus Christ."

He found he was hunching over the phone, collapsed in on himself. He straightened as if Ezra could see him and said dully, "I can't believe in it."

"Kit," Ezra began, and there was a hint of condescension, almost humor, in his voice. "Have you sinned, son? Is that what's going on? And you're afraid of the Lord's judgment?"—Kit suddenly hated him— "Because remember that God loves the sinner even as he despises the sin. You're instantly forgiven the moment you sincerely repent."

"I haven't sinned!" A man in the next booth leaned out and glanced at him, and Kit lowered his voice. "I'm not afraid of God's anger." He felt tears threatening. "I don't think ... that hell exists."

"Wait a minute—"

"And if it doesn't, then what else isn't true?"

"Kit, son." Ezra's voice was earnest and serious again. "You aren't the only Christian who's ever worried about this. Hell is a tough idea to get your mind around. Most Bible-believing Christians at some time or other are brought up short by it because they start ... trying to second-guess God, and—"

"Ezra," Kit broke in. It was the lunch hour, and people were pressing in. He cupped his hand around his mouth. "Have you ever been tortured? Have you ever watched someone be tortured?"

"Kit you have to understand that even though our Lord is a God of love, he is also a God of wrath ... There are some things that God hates."

"Like someone refusing to believe in Him. Is refusing to believe in Him a worse crime than torturing someone for eternity?"

"What's going on, Kit?"

"*Is* it?"

"Son, have you prayed about this?"

"I can't."

"Kit," the voice was gentle again. It reminded Kit fleetingly of the tone Ezra had used with Karen when she had confessed her love to him. "I think you should come home, son."

"I can't come home yet."

"You probably think you'd be letting us down, or letting God down, but I think we've sent you out too soon. There are pressures on a young person all alone in a foreign country. Satan is clever at confusing young people in times of isolation."

"I'm not coming home—"

There was a click and the line went dead. For an instant he thought Ezra had hung up on him. Then he realized he had accidentally clutched the receiver hook and cut himself off.

He couldn't ask for another turn. He left the booth, and the next caller slid in.

Feeling hemmed in by the seven square blocks of Antigua but with no purpose in mind, Kit walked east along the *Calle Sucid* toward the *Iglesia de San Francisco*. At the church he found the ranks of souvenir vendors doubled or even tripled since the last time he had been there. People were busy with ladders, baskets, and wheel barrows of colored sawdust, preparing for Thursday's *velación* and *procesión Santos Viacrucis del Hermano Pedro*. Tourists were flowing in and out.

An elderly woman from the States said to Kit in a thick southern accent, "It's really something to see, isn't it?" Kit turned to her and made a polite sound. "This is our fifteenth time to come," she added, with a nod at her husband, a hunched, bald man haggling with a child vendor over the price of a miniature *Hermano Pedro* doll. *Hermano Pedro*, the woman told Kit, was a seventeenth-century monk revered for providing the poor with a great hospital, the ruin of which still stood on the church grounds. Kit escaped to a nearby plaza and sat under a eucalyptus.

Ezra would be praying for him right now. Lord, guide this lost young man back to the right and true path. But the God Ezra was praying to was a torturer. Not a lamb, not a shepherd.

Across the way, the people en route to the church reminded him of ants—moving past or clustering around each other, meandering back onto the street. Ants marched in processions, too. As a child he used to watch long lines of them on sidewalks carrying dead beetles three times their size. Maybe they, too, held vigils and processions honoring their all-powerful ant god, who crushed them underfoot if they didn't pay enough respect or worship him in the right way.

Everything was just ritual, the habitual motions people went through to avoid facing the fact that they were all really alone. Even the connection between his twin sisters could be snapped if Dean put his mind to destroying it.

A small group of *ladino* children had come into the park, apparently on holiday during Holy Week. They sat down and unwrapped lunches tied up in bright colored cloths. From where he sat he could only hear the high-pitched cadences of their speech, and although he had many times heard Spanish coming from the mouths of children, at the moment it seemed utterly fantastic that there could be children who spoke a language as remote to him now as the chattering of squirrels.

He spotted the Cherokee station wagon parked a block away, the darkened windshield facing him. He pictured the man in the sunglasses and Hawaiian shirt sitting in the front seat, one arm draped over the steering wheel. Maybe he, too, was eating lunch out of a bright colored cloth that his wife had sent him off to work with.

Kit stared back at the windshield and the anonymous face—or faces—behind it. Okay, so you're watching me. Guess what, *amigo*? I know *nada*.

A crack on the top of his skull jolted him up and out of his seat. He cried out at the shower of … blood? … raining down onto his chest. Only for an instant did he think the shrieking laughter was something demonic. A giggling child skipped away to her friends and Kit brushed the eggshell and red confetti from his hair and shirt. His heart pounded wildly. He looked toward the darkened windshield and wondered if the driver of the Cherokee was laughing, too.

Kit got up and headed toward the vehicle.

He was just close enough to make out the one shadowy figure in the driver's seat when the car pulled out and passed him in the opposite direction.

Kit turned the next corner and started jogging, feeling some sense of control seep back into his limbs. He ran down streets randomly, through the *parque central* and back across it, around its periphery and down along the street of *El Arco*, then backtracking again. Several times he caught sight of the Cherokee. He grunted aggressively at each back spasm as if the pains themselves were his opponents. When he needed to catch his breath, he turned onto the most congested streets, where the Cherokee was stymied by Holy Week traffic.

The traffic now was much denser than before his trip to the Coast. More and more shiny sedans packed with *ladino* families from the city clogged the streets. Indigenous men pulled sawdust-laden carts, and indigenous women swayed along the sidewalks under wide baskets of produce and flowers for the street carpets—the *alfombras*. The air reeked of auto and bus fumes, and wafting from the entrances to every church— was the smell of copal incense and melting candle wax.

It was mid-afternoon. He hadn't seen the Cherokee for the last fifteen minutes and he was suddenly very hungry. He dreaded going back to Phil's house of stolen loot and offhanded hints at a connection with torturers and murderers. But as he reached into his pocket for a few *quetzales*, it occurred to him Colleen would need cash. If most of her money was in traveler's checks, she wouldn't be able to cash them without showing her passport.

When he arrived back at *Casa Fuego*, María let him into the entry hall.

"*El señor y la señora no están en casa.*" She led him to the patio, where lunch for one was laid out under cheesecloth to keep off the flies. It was a relief to be eating alone.

María appeared at his side with a note in Rita's rounded handwriting. "*Do you need, you can to use the telefone. No charge!*" it said.

It was two-thirty now. Ezra might still be at home and they could finish the conversation. He hated for Ezra to think him capable of hanging up on him. If he could explain what was going on here, how hell on earth

was being inflicted by a Bible-believing born-again Christian dictator—.
He would tell him about the pregnant woman on the bus, the old man
and his son, what happened to Colleen's brother, to himself.

The armpits of his shirt were damp and clammy. Saliva pooled in his
mouth. He ran to the bathroom, but only retched and spit into the toilet.
After a few deep breaths, the nausea passed. Still, he went to his room
and lay down on top of the made-up bed.

There was no way he could talk to Ezra about that part of it. Certainly
not on the phone. He wondered if Rita was in the house after all. It would
be easy for her to listen on an extension or just eavesdrop behind a door.
He thought he smelled her perfume in the room. Had she been looking
through his things? But what could she hope to find? She must have been
told that his belongings had been thoroughly searched.

He got up and sniffed at his backpack. He couldn't tell, though, now
that her scent—or the illusion of it—was already in his nostrils. For the
first time since having his pack thrust at him through the Martinez's
front door, he began to look through its contents, pulling out one thing
at a time. His T-shirts and underwear were balled up and in a jumble. His
extra shoes were shoved in separately.

Mashed down and rumpled at the bottom was the beautiful red *huipil*.
He wished the thugs had taken it. But, presumably, it was worth nothing
to men who looked on Mayan peasants as devils and subversives. He left
it at the bottom of the pack.

When he had folded and repacked everything, there was too much
space left. It took him a minute to realize what was missing—Jeannette's
instamatic and his large drawing pad.

He tried to remember whose faces he'd caught on film. Not Colleen's,
thank God. She had dodged that bullet on the roof of *Capuchinas*. But had
he ever tried to sketch her? If he had, they would know he was lying.

Oh Lord. Who had he snapped or drawn a picture of? Not Colleen, but
the students and teachers at school, studying at tables under the cascading
bougainvillea; children in the park; shoppers and vendors at the *mercado*;
a family in their Sunday best on the steps of San José church.

He was sweating, his heart tripping. Calm down. It would be obvious
that they were just tourist pictures, nothing to damn anyone.

He left the house, and out on the street it hit him what today—*Lunes*

Santo—the beginning of Holy Week would mean: cover. With so many people and cars on the street, and even more as Easter got closer, Colleen might venture out with some possibility of blending into the crowd.

He was suddenly revved up. The goon in the station wagon should see him making the rounds of church vigils, watching processions, standing at the edges of crowds listening to the funeral bands, browsing the goods at the *mercado* and watching *alfombras* being made—doing what every other tourist was doing in Antigua. Colleen, if she was in those crowds, would see him and find some way to communicate.

He went directly to the bank to cash some traveler's checks. He wanted to have plenty of *quetzales* to slip to her if she needed them. Then he immersed himself in the stream of worshippers and tourists moving along the *Alameda Santa Rosa*. He turned with them onto *6ta Avenida Norte* until they came to the *Iglesia de La Merced*, where a vigil was in progress. Outside the church, the *velación* was announced by two men playing a flute and drum at the entrance. Vendors were selling *juguetes*—small, cheap children's toys. Inside, a crowd of kneeling, standing, and milling worshippers prayed before the spectacle at the back of the sanctuary—an enormous floor-to-ceiling colored backdrop depicting Jesus bearing the cross to Calvary, while a black-robed, praying Mary seemed to block His passage along the road.

On the floor in front of the backdrop lay an immense *alfombra* of colored sawdust, designed in bright red, green, purple, yellow and white geometrical and floral patterns. Plates piled with fresh melons, pineapples, cabbages, and loaves of bread surrounded it. Along the sides stood the gorgeously carved holy figures that would be carried in the Good Friday processions.

Prominent among these was the life-size *Jesús Nazareno* which had moved him to tears at the beginning of Lent. Now he avoided the ecstatic eyes, and moved slowly through the throng, pretending to take in the tableau.

Later, he made his way to the *mercado*, usually not so busy on a Monday especially late in the afternoon but this week doing a brisk business. Under canopies, Mayan women weighed out squash, tomatoes, beans and peppers. *Ladino* vendors held up hand-carved masks of grinning *conquistadores, jaguares* and *diablos*. Tourists were handing over fistfuls of bills. Kit felt in his pockets to be sure of his stash of *quetzales*.

He worked his way through the whole of the sprawling market without seeing her. What if she was sick? Too sick to get out for food and water, even if she dared to. Where were the Australian guys? He had expected them to be on the street during Holy Week, like everybody else.

In the evening he returned to *La Merced* church to stand in the crowd listening to the dirges—a brass band's off-key versions of classical funeral marches. He stayed until the *velación* ended at eleven p.m. and everyone went home, crossing themselves as they left the church.

After school on Tuesday and Wednesday afternoon the crowds increased. Each day, at intervals, he spotted the Cherokee, and occasionally Rub, seemingly at leisure under the awning of a *comedor* or idly chatting with a *jugueta* vendor. He never saw them both at the same time. Were they taking turns watching him?

At night he couldn't sleep, or when he did, his dreams were of lurking armed men, or of Colleen screaming behind a locked door, or of the old man forced by a boot in his ribs to pick weeds from between bricks unceasingly. He woke with a stiff back and a headache from grinding his teeth.

The pain in his ribs was intermittent now, and often took him by surprise. On Wednesday night, Rita heard his sharp intake of breath when he reached for the salt at dinner. She flitted around the table and sat beside him.

"Poor boy! You have pain! You must to relax." She turned to Phil. "I give him a little pill will make disappear the pain, help him to sleep?" Phil shrugged.

Kit shook his head. "I'm okay," he said.

Later, he lay fully clothed staring at the bedroom ceiling and trying to will his muscles to let go. There was a knock on his door, and Rita pushed it open. She held out a glass of water.

"It is for pain," she said. She took his hand and closed it over a gray and orange capsule. "For one night you have no pain and good sleeping."

He knew the pill. Claudia took it for migraines. Her face, white and drawn, would turn rosy again and she would float dreamily around the house, smiling with benign affection at everything and everybody.

His hesitation lasted only a moment. He took the pill. She kissed his cheek and left.

When she returned twenty minutes later, he was lying as limp as a dog on its back in the sun. If he had had a tail to wag, he would have wagged it. She wore a low-cut red dressing gown of some shimmering fabric, and he contemplated her lazily. She padded barefoot across the carpet to the bed.

"You feel better now?"

He nodded. "Thank you," he said. "Thank you very much." She sat down with a swish of fabric and put a hand on his chest.

"You look *suave*—soft—like a man who is in love," she said. "I can see in your face. *Eres un hombre feliz.* How it is to be in love?" She trailed her fingernails back and forth across his chest. "Do you think you will see ever again your love? If no, that would be so sad. *Es como Romeo y Julieta.* Everyone separate that boy and girl. But why? They should be together."

She took a lock of his hair in her fingers and tugged it teasingly.

"You smile!" She moved her fingers to his lips. The painted nails looked edible, like miniature oranges. He took her fingertip into his mouth, touching his tongue to the nail, but it had a surprisingly acrid taste, and he let it go.

Her casting herself in this movie role of temptress/spy to get information from him struck him as humorous, almost endearing. It would be unfeeling to disappoint her. Maybe there was some harmless information he could confess to keep her from feeling foolish.

His whirling thoughts had slowed down and begun to settle, snowflakes drifting onto white-covered ground while he watched from inside the warm house of his body. He wondered idly if Phil knew where Rita was. Phil and his relics. A guy who wanted people to pay attention to him. Who didn't?

Rita gently nudged him over and lay down beside him, tucking herself into his side, her head on his shoulder. "*¡Tengo frío!*" she said. —I'm cold!— He put an arm around her and she snuggled closer.

"It's not like Romeo and Juliet," he said, drowsily.

She lifted her head to look into his eyes. "*¿Por qué no?*"

"Because I like her more than she likes me."

"*Imposible,*" she said softly. She reached up and stroked his face. "Any girl will be infatuate with a boy like you—tall and so handsome, but so shy. He doesn't know how he is attractive." His eyes shut now, he smiled. "But why you think she does not like you?"

"Because …" His tongue was becoming thick, and it amused him how sleepy, in the arms of a seductive woman, he had become. "Because she doesn't like my thinking."

"But what is your thinking?"

He replied—though he knew now it was a lie— "My love of the Lord."

She asked another question, but her voice had grown fuzzy. He became lost in his dreamless sleep.

On *Jueves Santo*—Maundy Thursday—*Tres Américas'* full holiday had begun. His time was his own, and he had left *Casa Fuego* early in the day and begun to prowl. The Cherokee hadn't made an appearance since Wednesday morning. By now traffic was so thick on the narrow streets of Antigua that the station wagon would no longer be a practical mode of surveillance, and Kit would have to be tailed on foot. That gave him pause. If Colleen could blend into the crowd, so could the goon, or an unrecognizable replacement. Rub, at least, was easy to spot.

He saw her at the *mercado*.

He was browsing through bins of cheap men's shoes, when he heard her voice behind him.

"*¿Cuánto cuesta?*" she asked the vendor. She had deepened her voice to sound more like a teenage boy's, but the voice, with a slight catch in it, was still unmistakably hers.

He felt an electrifying brush of her shoulder against his back as she stepped forward and stood next to him, holding up a pair of shoes. She flicked him a sideways glance, which he returned before they both looked away. As he pawed through the bin, he heard her ask the vendor when the Chimaltenango bus was supposed to leave.

"The one on the end there." She was nodding toward the long row of idling buses at the western edge of *La Polvera*. Her voice was unnaturally loud and slow—for his benefit, he realized, so that he would understand her Spanish. The vendor shrugged and said he didn't know. Colleen thanked him, and, for an instant met Kit's eyes again before moving toward the bus ranks.

He scanned the crowd. No Rub. No sunglasses guy. Still, he would be conspicuous if he made his way directly to the buses. He would have to go by a round-about route, even if it meant losing sight of her.

He skirted the large, indoor produce area—where he would have towered over the *chapinas* shopping for their families' meals—and mingled instead with any available *gringos* wandering through the maze of souvenir stalls. He worked his way around toward the southern edge of the market until, momentarily camouflaged by a contingent of teenage Texans in cowboy hats, he slipped through a gap in the stalls and out onto the dusty unpaved ground of the bus ranks.

The air was thick with diesel fumes and the uneven throb of engines many times rebuilt. Buses were pulling in as others pulled out. The Chimaltenango bus was the last bus in the row. The drivers who weren't leaning tiredly on their steering wheels were outside with the fare takers, pulling bundles off roofs and handing them down to passengers, whose eyes were only on their belongings.

Standing hidden between two empty buses parked close together at the end of the row, she was putting her sandals into a ragged day pack. It was the first time he'd had a good look at her since he had watched her stomp up the beach six days before. Her cropped hair was a darker shade of brown now and had been evened out so that it was extremely short all over. She still had on his shirt, but over it she wore a nylon baseball jacket—a cheap knockoff that she probably found in a bin at the market. The too-short pants had been replaced by new ones that came down over her instep to hide her slender ankles. The shoes she had just bought were already on her feet.

At sight of him she seemed to cave, like an exhausted marathon runner after crossing the finish line. He rushed to her and pulled her into his arms, where she clenched the fabric of his shirt and trembled like a shivering animal. "Colleen, Colleen," he murmured, grazing his lips over her short hair. She shuddered, and he thought she must be crying, but then she pulled back to look at him, and her eyes were dry. She touched the place on his cheek where the bruise had blossomed. Inadvertently he recoiled. He had forgotten what his face looked like.

She gripped his arm. "What did they do? Did they—"

"Nothing." He shook his head, forcing a smile, but he felt suddenly cold inside. "I'm okay, I'm fine."

She ran her hands cautiously down his back and chest, his shoulders and arms.

"Tell me what they did to you."

"Nothing. They asked me questions, that's all. Then they let me go." She touched his bruised face again, frowning. "I bumped into something when I got in the truck. It looks worse because of the sunburn." He nudged her and said lightly, "You *warned* me about that." His teasing tone sounded bizarre even to himself.

"They only asked questions? That's all? They just let you go?" He wanted to shout, It's none of your business! Quit asking!

"That's all," he said, shrugging. "They took my passport for a while and left me alone—while they checked on my story, I guess. I just told them I didn't know your name, I was studying in Antigua, and I'd met you on the beach. I said I had no idea where you were staying, as far as I knew you were just a tourist. They wanted to know about the pictures you'd taken. I said I didn't know anything about them."

"And they were *satisfied* with that?"

"Yes. Don't worry about me," he said. Almost dutifully he bent to kiss her, reassuringly, protectively, trying to disguise his inexplicable anger. Then, in the aliveness of her lips on his, his anger left as fast as it had come, and it was as if the time on the beach were the only thing that had happened after all, and they were still in that free, ecstatic moment.

"Colleen," he whispered again.

She was the one to draw away first, looking around nervously. He followed her tense glances. Danger flooded back—the locked windowless room, men with unlimited power to do what they wanted. "I'm sorry," he said, shamefaced at how easily his lust had made him forget the reality of their situation.

"I've got to get out of the country," she said.

"I know."

"But I'm trapped."

The Australians had left for Belize on Monday. She hadn't told them she was in trouble. She only said it was easier to travel around Guatemala dressed as a boy.

"They just left you here? Couldn't you have gone with them?"

"They were hitchhiking. How would I get through all the check points?"

The boys had booked their room through Holy Week but by Tuesday, they had gotten tired of Antigua, so they handed their room on to her when they took off. She paid them for the five remaining days.

She had only a few *quetzales* and some change left. All the rest of her money was in travelers checks at the other *pensión*. She was afraid to go back for it. "You think I'm paranoid, don't you, after they treated you okay," she said, with some of her old defiance.

He closed his eyes and drew her to him again, overwhelmed by the fear of not being able to protect her. "No," he said quietly. "I know you're not paranoid."

And then she could tell. "What *really* happened?" she implored. "Tell me." For some seconds he didn't speak. He felt her draw in a breath, and he held her tighter, not resenting her for asking this time.

"I saw some things," he said, "and— ... there were things done ..."

Her body began to shake with sobs. He caressed her cheeks and stroked the nape of her neck. She looked so vulnerable with her hair cropped short. "Colleen," he said. "Listen. Forget about it. It could have been worse. I'm okay now. But they're still trying to find you. I'm sure that's why they let me go. We can't be here together." She nodded, wiping her eyes on her sleeve.

Suddenly the bus shuddered with the vibration of the engine turning over. They had been there too long. His disappearance would have been noticed.

She grabbed his arm and they edged quickly around the bus to stand close against the last bus in the row, but now they were exposed on the other side by an empty lot. He pulled out the folded bills and pushed them into the pocket of her jacket. "Take these for now, and I'll try to figure out some way to get you out of here. That guy from school—Rub—he's been watching me, and some guy I saw in San José followed me to Antigua." People were approaching the other bus now.

"I'm in *Pensión Flor*," she said into his ear, "two streets behind the cathedral. Room five. The family that owns the *pensión* will be out on the street making an *alfombra* for the afternoon procession tomorrow and then they'll be carrying floats. The streets along the route to the cathedral will be packed around one or two o'clock. I'll try to leave the gate unlocked. If you can get lost in the crowds and think you're not being followed, come to my room."

"Okay," he whispered back. "I'll come. We'll figure out something."

The other bus pulled out and they heard footsteps coming their way. He touched her hand and she slipped around the side of the bus. He moved into and along the narrow space between the bus ranks and the perimeter of the market. In the gaps between buses he caught glimpses of her, loping like a teen-age boy, her day pack slung over one shoulder and one hand in the pocket that held the *quetzales*. By the time they both came out into open space, they were immersed in separate crowds.

Just as she crossed the *Alameda Santa Lucía*, she glanced over her shoulder at him. He hated having to take his eyes off her. If he could keep watching, even for the brief time it would take her to disappear into the streets of the town, he would, at least for that minute, know where she was and that she was safe.

As he turned away, his gaze fell on a face some twenty yards distant, whose eyes were fastened on Colleen.

Leaning against the side of a bus, his arms folded across his barrel chest, Rub was watching Colleen's retreating figure. He turned an amused grin on Kit and wiggled his eyebrows in a Groucho Marx leer.

Kit stood there for a moment, frozen. Then Rub sauntered toward the street. Instantly Kit moved to go after him, but he had taken only a few steps when the Cherokee station wagon pulled up to the curb. He saw Rub hesitate, a slight frown crossing his face, before he jerked open the passenger door and got in. He rolled down the window, tossed away his cigarette and hung his elbow out. The goon, the *archivo*, whatever he was, sat partly visible at the wheel. Rub said something to him, and the man nodded.

Blood seemed to drain away from Kit's body, leaving him weak. People jostled him, as they streamed to and from the market and the buses, partly blocking his view of the two men. The car didn't move. The men didn't get out. Colleen had crossed the street by now and was out of sight. Rub gave the goon a cigarette. He lit it, and from the way he inhaled, Kit realized it was a joint. The goon passed it back to Rub, and the two sat in the car smoking. Why was he letting her get away? Kit quickly crossed the road and headed back into town.

He spent the rest of the day and early evening outdoors at the Holy Week festivities. From the sidelines watching the processions and listening to the somber funeral bands, he had been puzzling over what happened that afternoon. It made no sense. Could Rub have simply been drunk or high, and falling down on the job? Or was he making some kind of game out of the whole thing, to prolong the chase, now that he'd seen her disguise? Or maybe he hadn't seen her after all.

❖ Nineteen ❖

Rub showed up at *Casa Fuego* that night with his usual blend of presumptuousness and self mockery demanding drinks and companionship. "I've had it up to here with these Jesus parades," he said. "Somebody's gotta keep me inside so I don't get mobbed for stomping across an *alfombra*. It's too damn tempting."

Soon after, Phil and Rita left to meet friends for drinks and dinner. So, thought Kit, Rub is the babysitter.

In the patio, Rub stretched out on a chaise lounge, his blunt fingers hugging the bowl of a salt-edged margarita glass that rested on his chest. Kit stood by the trunk of the flame tree. They eyed each other without blinking.

"So I guess," Kit said finally, "that I'm still being followed."

"Could be," Rub replied. He dipped his chin for a slurp of his drink. Then, as if picking up a conversation they had already been having, he smiled blandly and said, "Some people might think the girlfriend was a boyfriend."

Kit held his breath and was silent.

"On the other hand, Colleen isn't a boy's name." The travelers checks in her room. "Colleen Tierney, begorra!" The exaggerated Irish brogue rolled off his tongue. "Catholic lassie is she then?"

Tierney. Hearing it for the first time, he wanted to punch Rub for knowing it before he did. For knowing it at all.

Rub sat up, setting his glass down on the paving stones. He contemplated the glower on Kit's face. "As I said before, *amigo*, I was having a hard time putting you in a wham-bam-thank-you-ma'am scenario with this peacenik chick or whatever she is. Anybody can be excused for getting it up over some hot stranger on a beach. But I couldn't see you 'engaging in intimacies' "—he said the phrase mincingly—"without doing that getting-to-know-you dance. You know the dance? Hi, what's your name, where are you from, you like reggae or are you into hard rock? Do you know Jesus? That kind of thing? What people with consciences think they have to do? I could buy your not being aware of the shenanigans she was up to with that camera, but you have all kinds of information about her that you're not telling, and the only reason I can see for that, *amigo*, is she is more to you than a casual lay on a beach."

"Yeah, well," Kit said stiffly, "you're free to think whatever you want."

Rub laughed. "Ah! True love. She's got you up to your asshole in trouble, laddie, and you're still protecting her." Kit couldn't control the color rising in his face and ears.

"You know what's in store for her if they find her?"

Kit looked away. "I have some idea."

Rub nodded. "Yeah. You have some idea."

Kit looked Rub straight in the eye. "I'd try to help her if I knew where she was."

There was silence between them. Faintly, over the burbling fountain, came the dull thud of bass drums, the clash of cymbals, and the dissonant blend of brass instruments. Rub scratched his chin and looked down at his glass on the floor.

"Your lady needs to get out of the country. No lollygagging. Sooner or later the *archivos* will find her." So that put the name to the man in the Hawaiian shirt, the Cherokee station wagon crawling along the street. "It'd all be unofficial, an 'unfortunate attack by unknown assailants.'"

"Couldn't she go to the Embassy?"

"Sonny boy, this ain't the Philippines or Vietnam. Or pre-revolutionary Cuba. In those sovereign nations you could stick a dollar-wrapped pole up the ass of any pissant dictator and steer him around with it. Not that Ríos Montt is indifferent to a dollar bill, but he ain't takin' it on a pole. It's that macho mentality—'No strings, *gringo*. Hand over them *Yanqui dólares*, but don't tell us whose heads we can or cannot bust.' "

"Then what's the point of the U.S. supporting him?"

Rub shrugged. "The point is, *we* don't have to be the ones to bust the heads."

"But doesn't the Embassy care about publicity if—"

"Yeah, they'll issue their little protest, set up a bogus inquiry and come out with the official statement: one more naïve young communist sympathizer who got more than she bargained for."

"You think … she has something to do with the insurgents."

"Subversives, *amigo*. Get your damn terminology straight or you'll sound like you're one of them." He considered the question. "*Amigo*, subversion seems to run in her family. Am I right?"

So. They knew everything.

"But didn't you tell me," Kit protested, "that Reagan just got Congress to allow weapons sales to Guatemala? Wouldn't the Embassy want to be sure nothing happened to an American here? It would make the human rights situation look bad." He felt foolish quoting the borrowed words, as if he knew anything about it.

"Bingo. Your little sweetie took pictures with that fancy camera that'd make Reagan look like a goddamn gullible rube. According to him, *El General* is 'a man of great personal integrity, totally committed to restoring democracy.' Them's his very words. No, laddie, you run to the Embassy and you'll be lucky to get a finger shaken in your face—*the* finger—with a ticket home and a lecture: 'Young man, do you want to take responsibility for disrupting the fragile balance of this *fledgling* democracy?' " Rub laughed and passed his hand over his chin. "Don't you love that expression? Can't you just see the old *General* and his cronies fluttering at the edge of their fragile little nest, all ready to take off and spread democracy on their downy wings and then—bam!— they're all splattered on the ground for the communist vultures to feed on. Heart-breaking, ain't it?"

"Why do you have anything to do with it then?"

"Did I say I did?"

"Don't you regret it?"

"Regret? *That* is a tunnel you don't want to crawl down, laddie. You don't know where it'll come out."

"You don't think there will be a judgment at the end?"

"This *life* is the judgment." He downed the last of his margarita, licked the salt off the rim and went over to the bar, but only stood there looking down at the array of bottles. "Jesus," he said, "I'm going Buddhist on you. There *is* no judgment. Or if there is—hell, *I* don't know. I have no idea."

Kit said tonelessly, "I don't know either."

Rub turned and studied him. "Hnh," he said. For a moment Kit noticed again the sadness he had seen as he drew his portrait on the balcony in Panajachel. "*Amigo*," Rub said, finally, "when you first came here you had that oh-boy-oh-boy, rubbing-your-hands-in-glee attitude—'*Wow, check this out, ain't this something!*'—like you were walking on water." He shook his head. "But they surely did a number on you."

"'They'?" Kit said.

Rub stared down at the bottles again. Then he raised his head to the night sky. Through the boughs of the flame tree, there was a sprinkling of stars. A sliver of moon showed. He sighed heavily. "Tell you what. If you can get me a photograph of your lady friend—excuse me, your little *brother*—I'll get her a passport made. It'd take a few days—everything and everybody is clamped down shut for Holy Week."

Kit kept his expression neutral. "Why would you do that? You don't even know her."

"Hey, I'm a fucking good Samaritan. Don't you know that by now?"

"Maybe she's already left Antigua."

"Maybe. If she'd had some kind of network to call on. Friends who knew how to get her into Belize, for example. That's a somewhat open border. But getting to Belize is not something a wanted woman could do by herself. There's usually at least eight checkpoints from here to there."

"Maybe she does have friends."

Rub came over and stood in front of him. He put his hands on both Kit's shoulders and said quietly, "Just in case you're thinking of our lovely, motherly Rita as a friend, let me tell you something about her. Her old man is the *patrón* of a ten thousand acre *finca* in *El Petén*, the heart of guerrilla country. Papa is very, very down on the *chingados subversivos* for riling up the *campesinos* and sabotaging the family logging and cattle operations. And ... *Señorita Rita* is about as motherly as I am." He gripped Kit's elbow and steered him toward the corridor. "Let's take a walk." Kit balked.

"Where?"

"My place."

Kit pulled his elbow out of Rub's grip. "Why?" Rub bent down to snatch up Kit's day pack where he had dropped it at the edge of the fountain. "Why?" Kit said again.

"'Cause I'm going to handcuff you to my bed and screw you, then call my *archivo* colleague to coerce Colleen Tierney's name out of you." Rub shook his head. "Don't be a *burro*. You'll need a camera."

"Why can't you give it to me here?"

"Because it's in my apartment."

"Why can't you get it?"

"What am I, your maid? I don't feel like trekking back here tonight and running into that limey asshole and his siren, so-called wife."

Kit stayed put. "What are they going to think when they come back and find you've left me on my own? Aren't you supposed to be babysitting me?"

Rub grinned. "Nah. This was a social call. Phil thinks my *chapín* colleague is on duty. My colleague thinks *I* am. So everybody gets a break. Free holiday. Ain't that convenient?"

When they stepped out onto the sidewalk, Kit instinctively looked up and down the dark street for the Cherokee. What motive could Rub possibly have for helping them?

Tourists, vendors, and worshippers crowded the streets. To reach Rub's *pensión* they had to walk an extra block to avoid crossing the *alfombra*-covered avenue. The Peugeot was parked just inside the gate. Rub passed a hand over its rusted fender as they walked by it to cross the courtyard.

The apartment consisted of two rooms divided by a curtained doorway. The front room was furnished with a full-size bed covered with an army green wool blanket tucked tightly in at the corners, military style. Next to it was a bedside table with a gooseneck reading lamp and an ashtray full of butts, and across the room was an upholstered chair with a hassock drawn up to it. On the hassock lay a neatly folded stack of *Prensa Libre* newspapers. A large two-sided metal wardrobe stood against one wall.

Rub waved Kit toward the chair, took a key from his pocket and opened one side of the wardrobe. From the top shelf he removed a cardboard box and disappeared with it through the curtained doorway.

The bedroom had no photos or pictures or decorations of any kind except a polished bullet attached to a silver chain like a locket, hanging from the handle of the wardrobe, and—lined up all along a narrow, dusty wooden shelf running the circumference of the room—a hundred or more empty liquor bottles.

In the open wardrobe hung a single gray suit and two blue shirts with ties looped around the collars. Shelves down the side held t-shirts, under-wear, and jeans, folded and stacked as neatly as if they were in a clothing shop. Behind the suit, from a hook, dangled a holstered hand gun.

His tidiness wasn't the result of maid service, Kit thought. He seemed to put up with dirt but didn't like mess. The opposite of himself—a slob squeamish about germs. Rub probably learned to keep things neat in the Army.

On the floor of the wardrobe a pair of dress shoes—toes aligned—sat beside a pile of neatly stacked skin magazines. The top cover displayed a severely pouting naked woman holding up gigantic balloon-shaped breasts as if trying to give them away. Kit couldn't avert his eyes fast enough to keep a mild state of arousal from flaring up.

There was a musical tinkling of the bottle collection when Rub stepped heavily through the curtain, carrying a camera. He handed it to Kit, slid the box it came in back onto the top shelf and shut the door to the wardrobe.

"I've loaded it with film," Rub said. He told Kit to shoot the whole roll to be sure of getting one good one. The camera had a flash, but he was to take the pictures in good light if possible to avoid red eye. "Head shots, like on your own passport—from here to here—" he indicated with his hands— "and have her write and sign on a piece of blank paper the name she wants to use. Keep the camera in your pack—"

"I don't know if I'll see her—"

"Oh Christ, let it go, will you? You know where she is, you *are* going to see her. The only question is when, and how to get the pictures back to me. There's no way I can get documents made before Monday at the earliest, maybe Tuesday. Even forgers take off for Holy Week. But the sooner you get them to me, the sooner I can get at it." He shook his head. "Too bad she couldn't take advantage of the exodus on Sunday afternoon. Every *turista* in town will be headed back to Guatemala City." He seemed to be thinking out loud. "But she wouldn't be able to get a plane reservation 'til Monday or Tuesday at the earliest. Still, it'd be safer for her to be in GC on Monday than sticking around after Antigua empties out. I don't know. I'll work on it."

Rub seemed energetic and focused, unlike the jaded middle-aged adolescent image that he usually projected. He was undoubtedly drunk—he was never *not* drunk—but even so, Kit's trust in him ratcheted up a notch and he sat down again, opened his backpack, and set the camera inside. It struck him that he would have no way to explain the situation to Colleen.

"For chrissake, don't tell her. I don't want my fucking name involved."

"She'll ask. She'll want to know the risk."

"She trusts *you*, I take it?"

"Yeah." Did she?

"Just say you can't tell her who's helping. Because if she gets caught and they start to squeeze it out of her—"

"Yeah, okay."

"She understands how things work here?" Kit didn't reply.

Rub sat down on the edge of the bed and shook his head with mock chagrin. "So she turned out to have subversive leanings, did she? I'd have thought that would have made her unfuckable in your eyes." Kit rose suddenly. "I didn't fuck her, Goddamn it!" Lurching toward Rub, he ran into the edge of the hassock and almost fell over it. The reflexive thrusting out of his arms to catch himself sent a spasm of pain through his back. "You fucking asshole! You think it's funny?" he said through gritted teeth, holding his ribs. "You don't give a shit about anybody. What are you messing with us for? Why am I here?"

Rub stood up, kicked the heavy hassock away and pushed Kit into the chair.

"Don't get so touchy, for chrissake. Nobody's messing with you. I'm jealous. I'm not getting any, so why should you be? You gotta expect to put up with a little razzing—" He grinned into Kit's furious face—"I know, I know. You're *not* getting any. Whatever. So, go take the pictures and get them to me—the sooner the better. But choose your moment— officially I'm supposed to be keeping a watch on you, not biting the hand that feeds me. Go on, get out of here." Kit got up and stood glaring at Rub for a moment, then without a word picked up the daypack with the camera inside. As Kit stalked to the door, Rub said, "And don't invite *Señorita Rita* into your room to show her your big camera."

Kit stood between the gate and Rub's Peugeot in the dark courtyard, trying to concentrate. The drums of the funeral band in the distance thudded in a slow cadence under the teardrop pattering of piccolos. The camera's additional weight in his backpack, though slight, drew attention to itself as if he had stuffed a live animal into it. He leaned against the Peugeot and thought of the caress Rub had given the car. Why was he trusting a man whose only tenderness seemed to be for a piece of machinery? He must be the world's most simpleminded fool to let himself be talked into a plan that could completely strip Colleen of her cover. But then … her cover was already stripped. So what could Rub be up to?

He saw himself and Colleen snatched off the street and shoved into the back of an *archivos'* van. Neither of them left behind to help the other.

That was it. The photos would prove that he was helping Colleen acquire a false passport for subversive purposes. Justification for relieving the U.S. Embassy of responsibility. '*We don't have to be the ones to bust the heads.*' He was sweating now even though the air was cold. There was going to be no passport. He was just helping spring his own and Colleen's trap.

But … he couldn't understand … if they wanted to discredit both of them, they could simply haul them in, take the pictures themselves and claim he had taken them. '*Complete impunity.*' They could do whatever they wanted.

Colleen would be holed up in that room waiting out the hours for him to come. If he told her about Rub's proposal, she would go berserk. She wouldn't agree to it in a million years. But what was the alternative?

He closed his eyes. Not long ago, he would have said a simple prayer for guidance. How far away that consolation was. Sadness welled up in him. There had been a day when he was slain by God with a joy and release almost too intense to bear. And from then on Ezra's voice was in his head, telling him he was in God's merciful hands every minute, every hour, every day and would never be alone again.

None of it was true. He was alone now.

Instead of leaving, he went back to Rub's door. It was still unlocked. When Kit entered, he heard the sound of a shower running somewhere beyond the kitchen. The wardrobe stood open again, the shelves inside set to accommodate the height of liquor bottles, neatly ordered—whiskey on one shelf, tequila and rum on another, gin and vodka on a third. The top shelf held a large plastic baggy of marijuana and rolling papers.

The curtain to the kitchen was drawn aside. In the middle stood a porcelain table with a single wooden chair and a topographical map spread out, and next to it the tablet Rub used for jotting down his Mayan teacher's instructions on the *Ixil* language. On top of this was an unheard of piece of equipment in an Antigua *pensión*—a shiny black desktop telephone. Kit moved quickly. He would simply set the camera on the bed and leave.

The sheet and blanket had been pulled diagonally back, hotel-style, and on the bedside table Rub had placed a bottle of scotch, a pack of cigarettes and lighter, and the skin magazine with balloon breasts on the cover.

Kit set the camera on the bed. As he backed away, glancing toward the kitchen, he caught sight of something out of the corner of his eye he hadn't been able to see from the doorway. Taped neatly to the inside of the wardrobe door where a mirror would be was the portrait he had drawn of Rub's face. The eyes, he noticed for the first time, seemed to be focused on some private internal view.

The shower turned off. Kit snatched the camera back and slipped out of the room.

Kit woke in darkness to the blast of trumpets and the pounding of drums. He got out of bed and unlatched the shutters. Through the barred windows he saw shadowy figures dressed as Roman soldiers, some on horseback, some marching alongside in the dark street and holding up banners or carrying trumpets and drums. They were illuminated by the candles of silent, black-clad onlookers. It was three-thirty in the morning.

Families of carpet makers were crouched on the cobbles in front of their houses, putting final touches on their *alfombras*. The riders kept a tight rein on their nervous horses to prevent them from rearing onto the carpets.

A red-caped man in a white toga stopped in the crossroad and held high a tasseled banner declaring, "*Yo Poncio Pilate.*" The deep, booming voice called out the sentence of death. Then the contingent of Romans moved slowly forward, leaving behind the echo of hoof beats striking the cobbles.

Kit backed away from the window with a sense of menace. The Roman soldiers' breast plates and helmets were probably made of molded tin sprayed gold, and their togas sewn from bed sheets, but the flickering candlelight casting shadows in the hollows under the men's cheekbones had given them a cruel look.

He remembered the face of the *Jesús Nazareno*, below the gilded thorns and sculpted brow the expression of anticipation and hope in the midst of agony.

But what if Jesus was just a man after all, who believed, with innocent certainty, in his own purpose. Then how could he have endured it when the instant came—maybe as the first nail was being hammered, or as the cross was hoisted into place and the shifting weight of his body tore at his hands and feet—when he cried out *Father, why hast thou forsaken me?* and got no answer. The crushing terror and loneliness of it.

What if, in fact, he didn't rise again, but after days of unimaginable agony was snuffed out like a candle?

Kit drew the shutters closed against the chilly night air and stood shivering in his T-shirt and undershorts. He felt that he should go outside and follow the procession, that he should keep witnessing it from street corner to street corner, as a kind of penance.

But penance for what?

He got back in bed and shut his eyes. In a few hours he would be with Colleen. Her body against his. His hands on her bare breasts under that shirt of his that she had taken ...

It turned out to be easy to slip unseen through the gate of Colleen's *pensión*.

There came a moment after a procession of Roman centurions and drum and flute players and the small *andas* displaying the events of Christ's betrayal and seizure, after Pontius Pilate and the thieves and the banners and before the children's procession and the great float with the sculpture of *Jesús Nazareno*, when everyone in the street was obscured by a blinding fog of *copal* smoke sent up from the swinging *incensarios*. Kit disappeared from the street in the cloud of smoke, ducking behind a mass of purple-robed *cucuchurros* ready to take their turn at holding up the three-ton float.

The gate was ajar, as she had promised. There was no one in the court-yard; the three doors were all closed. At number five he knocked once. "Me," he said quietly. Immediately there came the scrape of the metal latch as if she had been waiting just on the other side. The gladness in her face erased everything. He stepped into the room and pulled her to him. Nothing had changed since they lay together on the beach.

They stood for some time just holding each other without speaking. His arms felt her heart pounding against the ribs in her back. Finally, she released a deep sigh, warm on his neck. "I was so scared you wouldn't be able to come." Her lips formed the words against his throat. He tipped her chin up and kissed her.

"Your face looks better," she said, touching it. "Are you still having pain?"

He shook his head. "Pain's gone," he said. It was almost true.

She led him to the bed, where they sat side by side. There was no chair. Atop a battered dresser was a washing bowl and pitcher, a water bottle, oranges, open packages of cheese and store-bought tortillas moldy at the edges. A Spanish language paperback and newspapers littered the bed. The small army surplus backpack, frayed at the seams and packed full of whatever other belongings she had, sat close to the door.

"Kit,"—It still thrilled him to hear her say his name—"could we just lie on the bed together? I've got to calm down." There was something timid and self effacing in her voice, which both touched and disquieted him. He placed the books and papers on the floor, put his arm around her shoulders and drew her gently down onto the narrow bed. She lay curled with her back against his chest.

After awhile she said, "Do you want to tell me what they did? It's okay if you need to. I can stand to hear it."

He shuddered at the thought of telling her. The old father lunging without a moment's hesitation toward the window, the crack of the rifle on his skull, the bruised, naked son, dangling and twitching from the post. From himself no roar of protest. No outrage forceful enough to pull apart the rope tying his wrists.

As he talked, she clutched the forearm he had laid across her chest. She didn't gasp or cry or ask questions. When he had finished, she let go of his arm and turned to look directly into his eyes.

"Kit," she said, "you have to understand that in this country, no matter what you do or don't do, it's impossible not to end up betraying someone."

That was all she said, but from deep in his solar plexus there came a slow relaxing of muscles that had been held tense for days. He was suddenly, amazingly, able to take easy breaths in and out, and he stretched his legs and turned onto his back, pulling her with him.

"Thank you," he said.

They lay there drowsing to the steady thump of each other's hearts. The sweet piney scent of incense blew through the window, along with the muted sound of swaying, creaking *andas*, and marchers' shuffling feet. In the distance the brass instruments played a dirge to the beat of a bass drum and the occasional bang of firecrackers.

The afternoon sun cast a warm, slanting beam through a slit in the curtain. Kit felt it on his face, and he came back to himself with a start. The photographs had to be taken while the light was still decent.

"Colleen," he said, "I've found a way to get you out of the country." She sat up abruptly. He sat up, too, and took her hand. "I can get you a false passport."

She shook her head in disbelief. "How?"

"I can probably get it done in the next few days."

"But who's—?"

"I can't tell you."

She got up from the bed. "Is it someone from that school you go to?"

"Don't ask me." He got up, too, to close the slit in the curtain.

Her eyes narrowed. "Is it those *evangélicos*? That would be like—"

"Colleen, I can't say."

Now she was studying him. "I have to know if they can be trusted."

"They can."

"How do you know?"

"I just do."

"But you don't know anything about how things work here."

"I do now."

She was silent for a moment. "But why can't you tell me?"

"Why do you think?"

He held her gaze. She blinked. Then she stared off at the curtain lifting on the breeze.

"Can you at least tell me the reason *why* they're willing to do it?"

How to express the inexpressible. "It's ... gratitude," he said.

"Gratitude."

"Yes."

She leaned against the wall, arms across her chest clutching herself. "But you're absolutely sure you can trust whoever it is?"

He didn't allow himself a second's hesitation.

"Yes," he said. "I'm absolutely sure."

He used up all the film and put the camera in the bottom of his pack.

"Okay," he said, "it's done, so you have to stop worrying about it. By Monday or Tuesday you'll be on a plane out of here."

"What about you?"

"When you get home safely, I'll leave, too."

"What if they don't let you?"

"They will. Someone's looking out for me."

She grabbed his hand in alarm. "Not God! You're not relying on God, are you?"

"No. Someone with more inside information."

She raised her eyebrows. "That sounds sacreligious."

He wasn't going to go into it with her. Maybe eventually. If there *was* an eventually. He didn't know where she lived in the States. She might get on a plane and he'd never see her again.

"Kit, how will I know you're okay?"

They memorized each other's phone numbers. She told him that for the two and a half months she had been in Guatemala, her family believed she was in Costa Rica working on her Spanish. She had pre-written postcards, which were mailed regularly to her family by a friend who actually was studying in Costa Rica.

"If they knew I was here, after what happened to Tom, they'd be out of their minds. If *he* knew, it would kill him." She stood by the dresser and fidgeted with an empty water bottle. "I know it was stupid and selfish, but I just felt like I had to do something. And now I've got you in this horrible trouble. And even those guys—those Australian guys—if I'd been caught with them, think what would have happened to them."

"Like you said, though. It's impossible not to betray someone."

She smiled wanly. "Yeah." She sat down next to him, and he laced his fingers through hers. "Those guys had no idea I was carrying that film I wanted to get back to the States." —*Was* carrying it?— "I just don't know how far you have a responsibility to try to change things. And what it's okay to do to survive. I used those guys."

❖ Twenty ❖

She told him the story then—what happened from the time she left him on Saturday afternoon—was it only six days ago? After catching sight of the covered army truck idling in front of her *pensión*, she had run behind a block of buildings, away from town and toward the deserted part of the beach. She had had to swim across the canal first, fighting a current that pulled her back toward the bridge and people. She chucked her beach bag in the canal, ran to the shore, and plunged into the ocean. It was the only place she could think of to hide, but once in the water she could see how conspicuous she was—a single head bobbing in the waves. Up the beach she would be one among others. The Australians were swimming pretty far out. If she could keep low in the water, she could swim among and past them and maybe make it unnoticed to the pier.

Within seconds after she reached the pier, soldiers came running down the beach and ordered people to get out of the water and line up at the shore. The soldiers passed down the line, looking them over before letting them return to their activities. Most left the beach as soon as they could. Only the Australians stayed. Meanwhile, the soldiers took up their post.

She had clung to the pilings, far out toward the end of the pier, buffeted by the swells and waves, getting colder and more exhausted as the hours passed and the sun went down. In the darkness she watched the light of the Australians' bonfire and the soldiers' flashlight beams playing up and down the beach. She had grown numb with cold and fatigue; sooner or later, she knew she would have to leave the water, but she had no idea where to go. Then the flashlight beams moved away from the beach, up toward the canal and the town. And that was her chance.

257

At this point in her story, Kit wanted to leap up like a kid, thump his chest and say "*I* did that! I decoyed them away from you!" He let the moment pass.

The tide was coming in and she had swum furiously with it to shore. In the dark, she made straight for the shadowy projection of the thatched palapa. That's when she remembered his shirt. Scrabbling on her hands and knees in the sand, she found it under a bench, snatched it up, dove into the shed and collapsed inside. The shed door having been left hanging open, she figured they had already searched for her there. She pulled it partly shut behind her.

It was warm in the shed. She stripped off her wet beach dress and sat for some time recovering her strength and waiting for her shivering to stop. Then she set about creating the disguise. She ripped the skirt and bodice off her bathing suit, put on his shirt and buttoned it to the neck. Maybe she could pass for a boy if she could find a way to chop off her hair.

After unsuccessfully trying to break it off, first with her fingers, then with the key to her room, she felt around in the dark for something sharp—a tin can lid, anything, and that's when she came across the two things that saved her: the rusty handleless machete that the woman had split their coconuts with and a pile of rags which turned out to be a pair of men's pants with a broken zipper.

Her arms and shoulders ached and her scalp was on fire when she finished sawing off her hair. She buried it and the remnants of her clothes in the sand floor of the shed and rubbed black sand into her scalp and hair to darken them.

When she crept around the side of the shed, she saw the soldiers were back on guard. There was no way to get from the shed to the bridge and cross it without being noticed. For several hours she hid there, trying to figure out a plan. Then she heard voices. The Australians were leaving the beach.

She stood just inside the door and waited. As they came abreast of the shed, she emerged and inserted herself among them, greeting them casually and walking at the front of the group. Flashlight beams lit them from the back. She asked the boys if she could crash in their room, wherever they were staying, because she was low on money and it was too dangerous to sleep alone on the beach.

They were slaphappy, only just beginning to suffer the effects of too much sun and alcohol and were in the mood to help out a hippie kid from the States. They were staying in one room, sleeping on bedrolls. It was close to the canal, and they didn't have to parade through the streets of San José under the lights of the *comedores* and *cantinas*.

They shared their bottled water and saltine crackers with her and, when they realized she was female, made her take the only bed in the room. The boys slept until a half hour before the bus was due to leave. Colleen woke before dawn and lay there agonizing about how she would get past the soldiers who would inevitably be watching the bus, and whether her conscience could allow her to use the innocent Australian boys as a shield.

Initially she hung back behind them so that if necessary she could say they weren't together, but when she saw the waiting army truck and the soldier standing next to the bus, her nerve failed her and she got in among the boys and concentrated hard on looking *macho*.

"Then I saw you in line," she said, "all bruised. I thought, 'They've tortured him into giving me away.' And I just moved along, numbly. I was thinking, 'Well, this is it.'

"When we were at the door of the bus, that soldier was standing right there looking everyone over, and then—what did you say to him? All I saw was you holding up a piece of paper, and I couldn't hear because I got on so fast I almost fell on my face."

Kit told her about the drawing he had done while waiting to be questioned. "I saw you coming, and I thought, 'Oh man, if they've been paying any attention they're going to see that there are six beach boys now, not five. I didn't think. I just pulled out the drawing. It was kind of a Laurel and Hardy moment," he said. "The two stooges go, 'Wow, the Captain's dog! What do we do with this?' "

She grinned and he thought of the unguarded pleasure he had seen on her face when they had lain in the sand and talked about being not in love, yet in love. He grinned too. And now he really felt like thumping his chest.

He threw his arms around her, laughing and pulling her down on the bed, and she laughed too, and kissed his mouth, his chin, his ears, his mouth again. For the moment, the horror and guilt of San José were sucked away in the undertow of desire.

He reached under her shirt and, just as in all his fantasies since their afternoon on the beach, he slid his hands again over her bare breasts, heard her gasp and whimper with pleasure. She moved her hands on him, too, clutching and claiming him—I want this part of you, and that. All up and down his body, it felt as if she were throwing power switches open.

In a quiet frenzy, they fumbled each other's clothes off. He was scarcely aware of the fumbling, in his hurry to look at her and touch her and feel her. Where the bathing suit had covered her skin, she was pearly white against her tan. A deep inward belly button pierced her like a little cave in the taut stomach above the triangle of dark, dense hair. Below all that, were the long shapely legs.

She drew back to gaze down the length of him too, her eyelids half-closed and pupils wide with just the sliver of white showing underneath, that sultry look that had turned him on from the first time he had seen her.

He brought his mouth to her breast, and she shuddered. Her hand found the flat of his belly between his jutting hipbones and slid downward. He was going to come, he wouldn't be able to help it, and he pulled her to him by her tight, round little buttocks.

She said, hoarsely, "You know we can't do it. We're not protected."

"I know," he said.

They stopped and lay panting in each other's arms for a moment.

"Don't worry," he whispered. "We won't."

She kissed him then and pressed her hips into his, and they moved against each other, fondled and explored and rubbed and came—her cries and convulsions fusing with his—they gripped each other like two people on a roller coaster before the descent, and started over and came a second time, until there seemed no part of her that he didn't know or she didn't know of him.

As they lay entwined on the narrow cot, their heartbeats slowly returning to normal, she pushed his bangs off his forehead and rested a hand on his thigh. It made him feel as if he hadn't been real before, and now he was.

They almost forgot she had to make up an identity for herself. They cleaned themselves up with water from the pitcher and basin on the dresser then sat down on the bed again to figure it out. She decided on 'Tom' for a first name. "Not an Irish last name, though. I don't want to sound Catholic."

"How about 'Tinker'?" It was the first name that came to mind. He didn't tell her it belonged to his pastor.

"'Tom Tinker'?! Sounds like something out of Hans Christian Andersen."

She agreed to it, though, admitting it would be easy to remember. On a blank piece of paper, she scrawled the new signature: Thomas E. Tinker. Born in Scranton, Pennsylvania, March 25, 1965. Just turned eighteen last week.

He had brought avocadoes, fruit, peanuts in the shell, and bottled water. It wouldn't last long, but he had been afraid of buying too much and arousing suspicion. They sat side by side on the bed pensively cracking peanut shells. In the last hour it had grown dark. The *Merced* procession had passed by, and they could hear the shouts of the clean-up crew as they swept the street clear of *alfombra* debris.

At any time now, some member of the landlady's family might return for a rest before the next procession or *velación*. He would have to be careful when he let himself out.

He didn't want to leave, but by now whoever had been following him would be roused to action over his disappearance. The army headquarters was only two blocks away. He started to get nervous at the image of booted soldiers kicking in the door.

Colleen clasped his hand. "How am I going to stand it," she said "when I have to be here alone again?"

"Maybe it'll be okay tomorrow to go out a little in these crowds," he said. "And if I think it's safe, I'll come back tomorrow. In a day or two, I should be able to bring you the passport."

Rub had said nothing about how they would make the transfer. He couldn't just show up at Rub's door, and there was no school until Monday. Kit held Colleen tightly and kept his worry to himself.

On Saturday morning, the streets were empty, except for families crouching over the construction of new carpets to replace the ones trampled by the night's procession. Twice he noticed an idling vehicle—a white van this time—with smoked windows and no license plates. He watched for an opportunity to slip into Colleen's *pensión*, but the landlady and her family were on the street in front of the house all morning.

Rub was nowhere to be found. Kit was conscious all the time of the camera in his backpack.

In the late afternoon, a long *procesión* of women in black carried the weeping *Virgen de la Soledad* on her *anda* up and down the streets and avenues, hundreds of others walking before and behind. It was the day of grief after Christ's entombment, when His disciples, and even the virgin mother, all seemed to have forgotten His promised resurrection. Black crepe was draped over the doors and windows, and black robes replaced the purple, red and gold that had adorned the weighty *imágenes* the day before. All Antigua was dressed in mourning for the Savior.

Kit followed the *procesión* of the Virgin past Rub's *pensión*. The gate was closed and too high to see over. Was he there? He thought of Colleen alone in her room waiting. The *procesión* turned and continued along the street past Aurelia's. At tables under the awning, tourists stood and snapped pictures.

"*Amigo.*" Rub beckoned him over and pulled out a chair for him. From his vantage point in the corner against the wall, he could see anyone coming within earshot. There was a menu and a bottle of *Gallo* on the table. A waiter came up, but Rub waved him away. "*Regresa en un minuto.*"

"So," he said. "Been enjoying the festivities, have you? Taking a lot of pictures?" He took a pull on his beer.

Kit spoke in a low voice. "I have the camera with me."

"Okay. Shut up about it." Rub handed him the menu.

The waiter was at their side.

"*¿Qué desea, señor?*"

"Bring us an order of *ceviche* and *tortillas*," Rub said in Spanish, leaning forward familiarly. "This guy here—jerking a thumb toward Kit—"wants a *cerveza*." He tapped the bottle. "And one more for me, too."

Kit sat tense in his chair.

"Take it easy, laddie," Rub said after the *Gallo* arrived. Kit's hand, holding the bottle, was shaking.

The last time Kit had had a drop of alcohol was in high school when he had drunk stolen whiskey with a thug acquaintance. Kit took a long swig of the tepid beer.

Silently drinking, Kit and Rub watched the last of the women's procession go by. Kit began to relax, and a feeling of warmth seeped into his arms. His head felt pleasantly foggy.

The waiter set the food in front of Kit, and Rub said, "Eat." Kit felt instantly ravenous at the fresh, vinegary bite of tomato, sweet peppers, onions and shrimp in the *ceviche* and the cornmeal and lime aroma coming off the stack of warm tortillas.

Rub watched him wolf down his food. "Well, my laddie, you look like a satisfied man. In more ways than one." Kit blushed. Rub leaned toward him confidentially. "But you gotta stay away from her now except for when you make the delivery."

Kit put his fork down. "When is that going to be?"

Rub said he would run the film into Guatemala City some time on Sunday. If he could roust out the man with the equipment, maybe he would have the passport for Kit by as early as Monday noon. "Then *you*—not just your friend, but *you*—need to get your ass out of here."

"She doesn't have any money, and I want to buy her a ticket home, but I have to ask Phil to get my money from the safe at school. How will that look?"

"How do you think it'll look?" Rub picked up a tortilla, considered it and plopped it back onto the stack, taking another swallow of beer instead. He sat for a minute, scratching his neck. "Christ," he sighed, "you're a lot of trouble."

In the end, he offered to buy Colleen's plane ticket once he had the passport in hand. There were two flights out on Tuesday morning.

Why would Rub be that generous? "I'll pay you back when I can," Kit said.

Rub smiled complacently. "*No es necesario, amigo*. It'll come right out of the rich uncle's discretionary fund."

"What rich uncle?"

"Yours and mine." It took Kit a moment. "It's the least he can do for a good nephew in up to his ears on his account. When you grow up and become a tax paying wage slave, you can consider the debt paid in full." He rethought the tortilla, dragged it through the *ceviche*, and chewed on it reflectively. "Then, my son, you *gotta* say *adiós* to this hellhole— excuse me, this Land of Eternal Spring. Call your parents and tell them to tell the preacher, their senator, anyone with clout that you're coming home. Announce to Phil that all the home folks are expecting you very, very shortly, then have him fork over your dough and buy a ticket out of here."

"I want to fly out with her."

"Oh, yeah. Since they'll be triple checking every person down to fucking infants who's traveling on the same plane with you." Rub folded his arms across his chest.

"Before I leave," Kit said, after a silence, "I've got to see with my own eyes that she leaves, too."

"*Jesus!*" Rub grimaced as if his gut were giving him a pain. He shook his head. "All right, we'll do *this*: The flight to Houston leaves at 10:30. I'll book her on that. You book the New Orleans flight for yourself. You can catch the last bus into GC Monday night, stay overnight and get to the airport around 9:45 Tuesday morning. *Inconspicuously* watch her get on the plane. *Inconspicuously* watch it take off. Hang out for another hour and a half, and leave on the 12:15 to New Orleans. Does that make you happy?"

"That means she'll need to go in to the city on an earlier bus than I do, so we won't be on the same bus."

"She ain't taking the bus."

"What do you mean?"

"Sometimes they set up checkpoints between here and GC just to pat down backpackers for pot. They can score a baggie and extort a few *dólares* for not turning the kid in." He repeated, "They pat them down."

"God." Kit bit his lip. He felt exhausted.

"It'd be safer for me to run her in."

Rub take Colleen in the Peugeot? "Wouldn't that look strange? Wouldn't it be risky for you?"

Rub grunted. "Risk. It's all relative. I'll pick her up as a hitchhiker. She stands on *4ta Calle Oriente* and sticks her thumb out when she sees the car. I drop her off in GC, she gets a cheap room for the night. No checkpoints, no pat downs. Only airport immigration to get through." Rub seemed animated, as if the intrigue were starting to pump him up.

How would he ever persuade Colleen to get into the rusted-out Peugeot with Rub, the half-drunk G-Man? "I don't know if she'll trust you—"

"Hey, if the passport and the plane ticket aren't enough, then fuck her." Kit flinched. "In the figurative sense," Rub added, dryly.

"What if she gets caught before then, knowing you're involved?"

"Then you and I, *amigo*, will both be screwed. This is why you want to expedite the program. This *cherchez la femme* bullshit is getting very tedious for our *archivo* friends. It's not their style. They're asking themselves, why haul our asses all over town following some *chingado gringo* when we can just bring him in for another two- or three- hour chat? Or even if it takes two or three days and we find out the kid still doesn't know anything, at least we get piss breaks and a little fun while we're finding it out." He set down his bottle of *Gallo* emphatically.

"That chat you had in San José, *amigo*, that was an *actual* chat *only* because I vouched for your born-again credentials and Phil has customers in the *Policía Nacional*. He prefers there not be suspicions about students at his school. But if someone says, 'Fuck it—bring the kid in again,' I won't be able to stop it. I might not even know about it until it's too late."

Kit pushed his plate away.

"Not that the Embassy likes American citizens to be invited to these little chats. Once they get started, there's no telling how they'll come out, and it's hard to explain the appearance of a *gringo* in a body dump. But—and I can't emphasize this too much, *amigo*—the Embassy does not run the show.

"So," he continued. "Tomorrow is Easter Sunday. Be damn sure you go to church. And I don't mean some mumbo jumbo subversive Catholic mass at the cathedral. Get your butt out of bed and head straight for your Jesus shouters' *iglesia* down on *Calle de Hermano Pedro* and make sure you're shouting as loud as the rest of 'em. Do not try to see your little subversive friend again until we have something to give her."

"I can't leave her sitting there, not knowing what's happening for the next two days. She's already going crazy."

"You can, and you will. She's far better off where she is than where she could be. Best thing you can do for her is keep up your credibility, son. Nobody's seen you set foot in that church this week, and you'd think a guy in your position would be having a lot to pray about."

Kit was silent. How did Rub even know he went to that *iglesia*? "I'm staying away," he said, "because I don't want to get people there in trouble by being associated with me." It was only half the truth.

"That church is untouchable. Two senior army officers are members. Just don't go shouting anything too personal, like *'Forgive me, Lord, for I've hidden a communist!'*"

Kit confessed in an anxious undertone, "I told Colleen she might be safe to come out for a while today."

"You told her wrong. Everyone not wearing black and holding up an *anda* or a banner might as well have *'gringo'* printed across their chest. Furthermore, she doesn't look half as butch as she thinks she does."

Kit grimaced.

Rub said, almost kindly, "Christ, don't freak out. If she has a grain of sense, she'll know as soon as she puts a foot on the street it's not a good idea. But I'm telling you, stay away from her now and quit wandering all over town. Any time that church of yours has its doors open, get your ass inside and keep it there." He glanced up at a passing car and shifted in his chair. "Go to the men's room now, leave the camera behind the trash basket, and then get the hell out of here."

Kit rose to go, but sat back in a panic. "How am I going to get the passport to her without being seen?"

Rub said, "I don't know. I'll figure out something." He gazed reflectively into space for a moment, and then a bland, self-satisfied smile appeared on his face. "Your faithful *archivo* friends probably wouldn't mind taking an hour off from watching your ass to look over some choice under-the-counter items on sale one time only. I should be able to scare up a Barret M82, a couple of Ingram Mac 10s," he mused, "maybe a Glock 18 automatic at a discount in the city. Have a little Tupperware party, hopefully some time on Monday. I'll let you know when." He arched an eyebrow. "But that means when the time comes, no dawdling. You get in and out, so to speak." He waved Kit off.

When Kit came out of the *baño*, Rub had moved to an inside table and was offering a cigarette to a man in a black suit who was leaning over him.

All of Saturday night he was inside Colleen's mind, thinking her thoughts, feeling every terror or hope she would be having each time she heard the gate creak and wondered who it was, what it meant that he hadn't come. What if she fled the room and found some other place to hide without telling him where, or risked the bus to Guatemala City? He lay all night with his eyes open.

Eight days was the longest Kit had not been inside a church in five years. The jubilant music issuing from the little storefront church on Easter Sunday reached into the street and reeled him in. Shoulder-to-shoulder worshippers in one jumping, twirling, hand-waving, hand-clapping body swelled the room. Tears streamed from uptilted faces. At the front, the gold and red streamers of the tambourine swayed with the player's hips. The strumming fingers of the guitar players were blurred in their attack on the strings. To a bouncy accordion melody, people sang in full voice: *¡Gloria al Señor! ¡Jesús Cristo ha resucitado! ¡Alabanza al Señor! ¡Jesús Cristo Nuestro Salvador!*

He shut his eyes to keep unwanted tears from spilling over. It surprised him how he could be so instantly overcome, and his lack of control exasperated him. He seemed unable to push away the need to have it all back, everything. The righteous joy of surrender to a greater power. The profession of helplessness in the face of sin. The solace of prayer. Faith that God's unfathomable acts had meaning.

He was too choked with emotion to sing, and instead just let himself be rocked by the human cradle swaying around him. After three months immersed in Spanish, he understood much of the simple praise lyrics without having to translate, and he wondered if God had given him the gift of learning a foreign language for just this purpose and just this moment, in order, after testing him, to welcome him back into the fold.

As the music subsided and the preacher began speaking of the risen Lord and the sacrifice of His blood for the sins of humanity, Kit prayed silently to be forgiven his pride, his cowardice, and the lustful acts he had committed with Colleen. He prayed for forgiveness on her behalf, too, and for guidance in protecting her and bringing her home—to their country and to the Lord. He prayed for the trust to believe in a divine plan behind the cruelty they had witnessed and experienced. Finally, he prayed to understand and reconcile himself to the mystery of hell everlasting.

With this final plea he felt a subtle hardening just at the edge of his consciousness. The tears he had been restraining dried up. But he forced out a shout of praise and blended his voice with those around him.

The church service left him stirred up and restless. The enthusiastic Daniel called out a greeting in his eccentric English, and began to plow a determined path through the crowd. Kit pushed out the door, pretending not to see him, and made his way at a half running clip down the block and around the corner.

Rub had warned him to stick around *Casa Fuego* when he wasn't in church, but he had to keep steering himself away from the direction of Colleen's room. His brain was taken over by the question that had worried him all night—how, without actually seeing Colleen, could he get some kind of message to her? There had to be some way to let her know things were moving forward, that he was okay, and her ordeal would be over soon.

With the week's pageantry almost ended, the town was quiet, everyone either at church or sleeping in. As he walked along the curb, he kicked at the colored sawdust, flower petals, ground corozo seeds and cellophane *juguete* wrappers which drifted in the streets. Green, fan-like palm branches littered the cobbles. He picked one up and passed his fingers along its smooth flat fronds. He remembered holding a palm branch for the first time on Palm Sunday the year he gave himself to Jesus. The congregation paraded around and around inside the church waving their palm boughs high above their heads to the rhythm of a hypnotically repeated praise song—which song?

The green palm fronds lay smooth and cool in his hand. He gathered up several more, and waved them in a wide arc to feel and hear the swish. At once, and as clearly as if he had rationally thought it out, he saw how he could send her a message.

He almost ran back to the church, hoping Daniel wouldn't be loitering there and waylay him. Fortunately, only the pastor and a few of the congregation still lingered inside. He scattered perfunctory greetings as he went directly to the *baño*—a single small cubicle—hooked the door closed and put the toilet lid down.

He fished out the drawing pencil which had been in his money belt all week since doing its job on the captain's dog. Then he closed his eyes to think. It had to be something to attract her attention, something she would recognize as being addressed to her, but that wouldn't arouse suspicion. Something religious. He thought of her new name. Tom. Thomas. What saint was named Thomas? There was a St. Thomas More High School back home, but that wouldn't be a Spanish saint. Thomas. Thomas. The disciple Thomas. The *doubting* Thomas. Perfect. What was the word in Spanish for doubt: *Duder? Dudar?* "*¡No lo duden por un momento, comunistas!*" —Don't have a moment's doubt, communists— Ríos Montt had shouted it under his circus tent, shaking his finger at imaginary subversives.

He lay a palm branch on the toilet lid and wrote in block letters across the flat green fronds:

NO LO DUDES, SANTO TOMÁS

It could easily pass for a remnant of an *alfombra*. But she would see it and she would know the message was for her: Don't doubt! Don't be afraid! I'm still out here. I'm working on it.

He wrote the same message on a second palm and was about to do a third, when he had another inspiration. The memory of Colleen's soaring alto voice resounding off the stone walls in the cellar of *Las Capuchinas* gave him the idea. What were the Latin words she sang? In English, it meant "Give us peace," wasn't that what she said? In Spanish how would it translate? *Dános paz.* She had written the Latin words down for him on a pamphlet, which he had saved just to look at her writing. But it was somewhere in his backpack at *Casa Fuego*—no use to him now. He closed his eyes and let the round they had sung drift back into his head. In an undertone he hummed his part, hearing the harmonies of Colleen and that cheerful, anonymous tourist who had unwittingly brought them together. Suddenly the Latin words came to him: *Dona nobis pacem.*

He wrote the words on the other two branches and then turned their faces inward to hide the writing. Remembering in time to flush the toilet, he came out of the cubicle as a woman had her hand poised to rap on the door.

"*El estómago,*" —My stomach— he apologized, holding his gut. The woman patted his arm. "*Toma un té de manzanilla,*" she advised.

He passed out of the church and meandered with studied casualness toward the block of Colleen's *pensión.* Along the way, he bent to pick up two other discarded palm branches and swung them at his side. Before entering Colleen's block, he allowed these last branches, one then the other, to slip from his fingers as if he were losing interest in collecting palm branches. As he drew near to her gate, he perused the sidewalks and gutters for other procession souvenirs. Finding a wilted carnation, he held it to his nose and simultaneously let the message of peace drop face up on the sidewalk. Just in front of the gate he gathered a handful of colored sawdust from the gutter and sifted it through his fingers as he let the Doubting Thomas messages flutter to the ground side by side. One that had fallen face down he kicked over with his foot. The last palm branch he left lying where it fell as he stooped to pick up a *cucurrucho's* discarded sash.

❖ Twenty-One ❖

That night, he showed up for Sunday evening prayer service.

"¡Hermano Cristóbal!" It was too loud to ignore, even above the praise music that was a prelude to the service. Kit turned to acknowledge Daniel's grinning display of flashing silver teeth. His heart leaped. Beside Daniel stood Ezra.

Ezra's own grin stretched across both sides of the beloved face almost to his protruding ears, which looked like they might start flapping from sheer exuberance. He was taking a step toward Kit now, but Kit was already stumbling through the crowd and had crossed the room before Ezra had gone a yard. He threw his arms around his pastor with an incoherent shout of joy. He could easily have picked him up in his arms, Ezra was so much shorter and smaller, but somehow he found himself instead wrapped in Ezra's unaccountably encompassing embrace as if he were the small one. And now he was inhaling the Ezraness of Ezra, his nose buried in the gabardine-covered shoulder.

"Son," Ezra said softly in his ear. "Son." He held Kit for a long time before letting him go.

When they separated, Ezra stood back and took him in. "Say, Brother Kit, that's some tan you've got on you." He pinched his arm. "But you need to put some meat on those bones." He moved in for a closer look at Kit's face. "What'd you do, have a run-in with a door?"

Kit put his hand up to the yellow discoloration lingering on his cheek. "It's no big deal," he said, turning slightly away. "Why did you come? How did you get here?"

"The waters parted and I strolled on down." Ezra laughed. "Jeannette and God told me to bring you home. If it had only been God talking, I might have hesitated." He winked.

"Ezra—"

"That telephone conversation got us worried about you, son."

Kit looked away. "This cost you a lot of money."

"That's not important. The Lord always finds a way to chip in when the need arises."

The prayer service was starting. They sat down together, Kit too full of the idea that Ezra was sitting there beside him to concentrate on praying or anything else. Ezra didn't understand enough Spanish even to open to the texts referred to, but it didn't seem to matter. He closed his eyes, interlaced his fingers and rested them on his knees, slipping into what looked like a state of perfect contemplation.

Kit, on the other hand, couldn't keep still. His eyes shifted about in a nervous surveillance of the room. His foot jiggled nervously. He wondered which worshippers were the two senior army officers.

When the service was over and they were all milling toward the door, Daniel stuck close to them. Kit darted a glance at him. What did Daniel have to do with it? Ezra, though his hand was familiarly cupping Kit's elbow, seemed all at once several arm lengths away. Kit looked at him and for one bizarre moment saw him exactly as he had seen him the first time they met, in the parking lot of Light and Life—a self righteous, sanctimonious little man enjoying the opportunity to rub Kit's powerlessness in his face. The image so disturbed him that he stood there gaping, unable to speak.

Ezra turned to Daniel and shook his hand warmly. "Thank you, Brother Daniel. God bless you for your help. The Lord was looking out for us when he put you in my path today." He clapped him on the back. "And now we're going to leave you. I'm going to get this young man to show me around your beautiful town this evening and tell me all about what he's been up to these days."

Kit let himself be steered out onto the sidewalk. Ezra gazed up at the star-studded sky and caught sight of the floodlit cross which stood out against the blackness at the top of the *Cerro de la Cruz*. "How about if we take a walk up there, son? It looks like a place made for us to talk with each other and to the Lord."

They sat on the pedestal below the cross and looked down at the lights of Antigua. Kit picked up a bit of crumbling stone that had cracked off and turned it over and over in his hand. He wondered whether anyone had been following them. At least the large open space prevented whatever they had to say from being overheard. He asked Ezra how he knew Daniel.

After Ezra had flown into Guatemala City on Sunday noon and taken a bus into Antigua, God had sent him into the first hotel he encountered, which he knew would be beyond his means but where he might meet someone who spoke English and could help him find the house of the family Kit was staying with. Earlier in the week he had tried to call the school office, but it was closed—for Easter Week, he realized after inquiring about flights and finding them all booked until Sunday. So he had gone up to the front desk of the hotel and explained his mission to the man at the counter.

"Praise God," said Ezra, "it was your friend Daniel! He said, 'I know that American guy. He attends my church.' He'd seen you in church that morning and thought you'd probably be at the prayer service."

Daniel had given him half price on a room and a free dinner and sat down with him while he ate, singing the praises of Ríos Montt and telling him what the president was doing to turn Guatemala into a godly nation. "There are no coincidences, Kit," said Ezra, patting his knee. "The Lord walked me into that hotel today."

"He's wrong about Ríos Montt," Kit said harshly. "His government is murdering and torturing in the name of Jesus Christ." In the dark, he heard Ezra's intake of breath. There was a pause.

"Well, tell me about it, son."

It was what he expected from Ezra, and he felt relief and the pressure of tears behind his eyes. He waited for it to recede before speaking.

"I met a woman—"

Ezra expelled his breath with a chuckle. "Ah! A *woman*!"

It dismissed him. And he knew instinctively that if he talked about Colleen, everything else he had to say would be discounted.

He said, "She was just someone I spent a few hours with at the beach. I didn't know anything about her." Lying to Ezra made his palms sweat. "But the army thought she was someone who supported the guerrillas, and they picked me up because they'd seen me with her. She got away, I guess, but they brought me in for questioning."

"And they were rough with you, son?" Ezra put a gentle hand on his shoulder.

It was good that they were talking in semidarkness and he didn't have to fight the blood rising in his face or hide the tremor in his hands. He hated himself for it—nursing his little injuries and skulking around instead of denouncing the ones responsible. Today was Sunday—Easter Sunday—he should have been in Guatemala City, walking into that circus tent of a church, and telling the people what they had allowed their General to do. Grab the dictator's thick wrist, force his hand into the air and part the three fingers: *He lies*! *He murders*! *He tortures*!

"They were rough with you?"

"Yes."

Ezra reached up and caressed the place on Kit's cheek where he had seen the yellow bruise. Kit pulled away.

"It wasn't so bad. For *me*. But I saw a man being tortured." Now the agitation was rising in him again. "And an old man, completely innocent—they smashed his skull with a rifle butt and dragged him off." The tears burst through. Ezra brought his arm back to Kit's shoulders and held him close, rocked him as he talked through sobs.

"I didn't do anything. I *couldn't* do anything. They all had rifles. They'd tied my hands behind my back. I was helpless. And I saw them drag a pregnant woman by her hair onto a truck." His voice came out in gasping bursts.

Softly, Ezra murmured tender, commiserating words and touched his hair. "Ah, Kit, son." He was quiet for a while as Kit got his crying under control. "Kit," he said, "you're a young guy. You probably think I don't know about these kinds of things. Remember that Jeannette and I took in refugees from the Pol Pot regime —"

"Yeah! It's like that! But it's not a communist government. It's a government that we *support*—"

"In this sinful world, Kit, all governments are tainted by evil and corruption because they're run by men, and men are fallen, sin-filled. Even the best of men, like this president, Ríos Montt. The Lord has put him in charge of a deeply depraved country and he's trying to get it back on a moral course, from what I hear. But it won't happen overnight."

"It's *propaganda!*" Kit flung away the stone he had been clutching and got to his feet. He felt wild, almost as if he could kick Ezra. He stepped down off the pedestal. His hands were clammy and his heart beat erratically.

"Ríos Montt is the biggest hypocrite on the planet, or else he's totally deluded about what the army does. And how the hell can he be deluded? He's the commander in chief of the country. He knows what's going on—people are poor and starving, and he sends the army out to murder them and torture them and make them disappear to keep them quiet."

Ezra got slowly to his feet but remained on the pedestal and stood half a head above Kit. "It's distressing to see the suffering of the poor," he said, "but it's easy to be tricked into coming to the wrong solution. No government is as bad as one that forbids the spread of the Gospel. That government may seem to offer things to the poor—every opportunity for all the material things in this lifetime—but as long as it denies people the opportunity for life everlasting, it deprives them utterly."

"*Who* is denying people the opportunity for life everlasting? Who are you talking about?"

"You know what the threat is." His voice was level and calm. "You heard it from *Señor* Reina. I've just heard it again from our friend, Daniel. Communists are waging a war here to spread their atheistic philosophy. They're exploiting the poverty, they're—"

What do you think it means when people have to sleep on sidewalks and sell the clothes off their backs?

"What about the reason the poverty is here to exploit in the first place?" Hearing his own shrillness, he took a breath to calm himself.

Ezra sighed. "Son, that's exactly the rhetoric that leads young people down the wrong path. It sounds so simple, so easy. But trust in Scripture. Only when each individual finds his moral compass through faith in Jesus Christ will poverty and oppression be ended."

Kit's hands were clenched. He forced himself to relax them. "Ezra, there *is* no moral compass here. I talked to an evangelical missionary. His wife saw an Indian girl raped by soldiers. He whispered when he told me. He was scared somebody would hear him criticizing the army. And that Reina guy, that got us to send the fire truck, I went to the village where it's supposed to be. It isn't there."

"Come on, Kit. You probably went to the wrong place—"

"Santiago de Atitlán," Kit said furiously. "He sent us a letter from that village, thanking us. I asked soldiers there about the fire truck, and they laughed. They said—their exact words—'*Better to burn down the village than protect it from fire.*' "

"Now Kit, you're sure that's what you heard? In Spanish? Remember how easy it is to get things wrong when you're learning a language."

Kit controlled an urge to yank Ezra off the pedestal. "Listen to me, Ezra, even a guy who *works* with the army—an American guy at my school—he's CIA, Special Forces, something like that—even *he* admits that the government here is corrupt, and the U.S. takes its side."

"Kit, a CIA guy?" Ezra stepped down of his own accord and gave Kit's elbow a shake. "Come on. You've gotten tangled up with a bunch of people who are taking advantage of your innocence—"

Kit pulled his arm away. "I heard it from Ríos Montt himself when I went to Guatemala City and heard him preach in his church."

Ezra's voice rose a little in excitement. "What was he like?"

Should he say? It was just a gut feeling. "He was … a tyrant. Not like you. He was—"

Ezra chuckled. "You mean he was *tough*? Not a softie like Ezra Tinker?" He punched Kit's arm affectionately. "Don't you imagine he *has* to be tough?" Kit moved out of reach. "Kit, son, there are all kinds of preachers of the Gospel. God gives each one his own unique abilities for the task he has to do."

"That's not what I mean—" He couldn't express himself well in the best of situations, how could he describe the ruthlessness he had heard, the arrogance in the man's gestures. He stood helplessly looking out over the lights of the town.

Ezra took his arm. "Come on, sit down."

He felt childish, defeated. The one argument that might have driven home his point was the one he couldn't use—Colleen's brother's story. He lowered himself sullenly to the ground and lay back on the grass to stare up at the floodlight beam that cut the darkness. He imagined the towering cross tipping over on them.

"Son," Ezra said gently, "this experience you had being picked up by the army has, of course, shaken you."

"That's not the point," Kit said. He no longer wanted to have this conversation.

"You saw someone mistreated. You were mistreated yourself. At times like those we ask the hard questions of God, how He can let things like this happen—"

"That's not the question *I'm* asking. I'm asking how there can be a loving God who would torture people eternally for simply not believing in him." He sat up and looked Ezra in the eye. "How can you believe in God as a torturer, Ezra?"

Without a word, Ezra got up onto one knee—a little awkwardly—and stood up. Kit turned to watch him climb to the top of the pedestal, where he lay a hand on the stone sphere, like a globe, which formed the base of the cross. He bowed his head and said nothing for several minutes. Kit realized he was praying and turned from the sight.

Finally Ezra raised his head and called down to him. "Kit, you have to understand that Satan has a whole bag of tricks, and his favorite one is to turn to his own ends the very gifts God by his grace gives to young people. Nothing makes Satan happier than when he takes the gifts of compassion, of purity and innocence, trustfulness, the ability to reason— and uses them as the basis of a whispering campaign against the Lord." His back to him, Kit shook his head and made a dismissive sound.

Why should he feel betrayed or even disappointed? He had heard the sermon dozens of times. He could have given it himself. He knew the part that would come next: the rebellious nature of sinful man. He got up and faced Ezra.

"To you—" Ezra continued, and he left the cross to lower himself down on one of the steps again. The apparent stiffness in Ezra's joints stabbed Kit with guilt and unease, but he didn't put a hand out to help him. "—to you, your doubt seems justified because Satan is manipulating the defiant nature in you that we all inherited from Adam. Remember what Abraham told the wealthy man who appealed to him from hell. It's easy to insist that something you see physically in front of you or something your rational mind cooks up is true, but the real test is to take God's word on faith alone. That is how we glorify Him."

"So you do trust a torturer," Kit replied harshly.

"Don't blaspheme!" Ezra exclaimed. Kit shrank back a little. Ezra had never spoken to him angrily. "Don't think that Jesus sits up there on His throne laughing at the people who are lost. He doesn't want even one soul to fall. He sends His followers into the world to stop people, in their sinful and willful arrogance from condemning themselves. And when they choose their own downfall, Jesus weeps."

"He weeps?" Kit snatched up his Bible and scrambled to his feet. They had both brought their Bibles to the prayer service and placed them on the pedestal, where they lay like swords before a duel. He held his—the one Ezra had given him—and shook it in Ezra's face. "In Revelation it says, '*He shall be tormented with fire and brimstone in the presence of the holy angels and in the presence of the Lamb*—'" From that night of searching Scripture in his sweltering San José room, the passages came easily. "'—*and the smoke of their torment ascendeth up forever and ever and they have no rest day or night.*' In Matthew: "*They are thrown into the blazing furnace,*'—" Kit's voice cracked with anger. "'—*the place of wailing and grinding of teeth.*'" On *teeth*, he choked on his own saliva and swallowed the word down, feeling foolish and furious, but he kept on quoting. "'*The fire that never shall be quenched where their worm dieth not*—' That's *Jesus* talking, Ezra. He shouted it three times. It's in *capital fucking letters*. Doesn't it sound like he's getting off on the idea?" He slapped the cover of the book. "How can you believe this book and believe in God at the same time?"

He felt sick to his stomach. His voice wobbled and his hands shook. He dropped the book on the ground.

Quietly, Ezra said, "Kneel down and pray with me."

Kit shook his head. "No."

Ezra picked up the Bible. "Then let's leave it alone tonight." His voice was cold, and Kit was afraid.

Ezra put up a hand and Kit silently helped him up. They began to make their way in the dark across the clearing. Ezra said calmly, "Open your heart to Jesus and listen to what He has to say. Then tomorrow I'd like us to buy plane tickets back to the States."

Kit stopped walking. "I can't leave. I know I'm here on your money, but I'll pay you back."

"The money isn't important. Your soul is in danger here."

They heard footsteps ahead of them in the dark. Kit froze. He drew Ezra back with an instinct to run with him and crouch behind the pedestal, but he planted his feet and held himself straight. A flashlight beam suddenly shone in their faces, blinding them. Reflexively Kit pushed Ezra behind him. They were exposed, on top of a hill with nowhere to run. In the next instant, the lights were switched off and two armed, uniformed soldiers were loping in their direction. He recognized them as soldiers he had seen around town, one who often guarded the bank.

"¡Hola, señores!" called the bank guard as they drew up. They held their rifles loosely at their sides. "Señores, no es seguro por aquí en la noche," he said genially. "Váyanse." He nodded his head toward the road.

Ezra stepped to Kit's side. "What's he saying?"

"He says it's not safe here at night," Kit tried to keep the tremor out of his voice. "We have to leave."

The other soldier came forward and held out a hand. Ezra stepped up and shook it warmly.

"Gracias, gracias, señors," Ezra exclaimed. "God bless you."

The soldiers followed behind them, guiding their way with their flashlight beams as they walked along the road from the hill. When they got to the street, the soldiers left them, Ezra once again having shaken their hands. Walking Ezra back to his hotel in silence Kit thought about what it meant that they had pointed no weapons, asked for no papers, and he realized the scene was for Ezra's benefit. *They were told we were here.* While Colleen huddled on a cot in that cell of a room, hiding from rapists and torturers, he would now be walking under the protection of his born-again pastor.

At the hotel, they shook hands like strangers and parted without speaking.

In the morning, Kit told Phil and Rita that his pastor had arrived unexpectedly. Phil shot a glance at Rita. "Will you be going back to the States with this pastor?" he asked.

Kit mumbled a noncommittal reply and left for school. When he had parted from Ezra last night, nothing had been said by either of them about meeting for breakfast or what was to happen next.

By 10:30 he knew his teacher had blown off the morning, typical for Berto on a Monday.

The incessant splashing of the fountain and the drone of verb conjugations from the other tables was fraying Kit's nerves. Rub's absence could be a good sign or a bad sign. Would Rub have gotten sidetracked in some bar in Guatemala City? Maybe he had rolled the Peugeot down a mountainside trying to pass a chicken bus on a blind curve. Any number of things could have happened. Or, he might have had a change of heart.

At 10:45 he jerked his head up at the brisk slap of shoe leather crossing the flagstones, though he knew from the sound it was not Rub but Ezra. The sight of Ezra angered him. What if Rub came now?

Ezra came around the fountain and sat down at Kit's table. "This is just the way I pictured it from your letters and drawings," Ezra said, gesturing at the school courtyard. Then he put a hand on Kit's arm. "Well, son," he said buoyantly, "I prayed on it, and, praise the Lord, He showed me a path and took away the obstacles before they even presented themselves!"

Ezra had put in a call to *Señor* Reina in Guatemala City. Daniel had helped him track down the *Hermandad de Negocios Cristianos Guatemalteca*—the Brotherhood of Guatemalan Christian Businessmen—, Ezra said, and gotten Reina's office number from them.

"It took us a while, but God meant for us to get through to him because we caught him just as he was leaving his office. Fifteen seconds later he would have been gone."

Covertly Kit looked over his shoulder and at his watch. He shouldn't expect Rub earlier than noon, maybe even much later. Ezra was rambling on.

"The Lord spoke to me this morning and helped me see what you need to regain faith. You need to talk directly with the Christian man who seems to you to have betrayed your trust. If he sets things right with you, it will bring back your Biblical perspective."

"You talked to Reina?"

"I told him everything you told me—especially your concern about the fire truck, and he has an explanation for that. But I'll let him tell you himself."

Kit's mind came to attention. "You told him everything." What exactly had he told Ezra last night?

"Don't worry, son. He wasn't insulted at all. This is a man who truly walks with Jesus. The Lord stepped up as He always does and touched the man's heart. In the midst of his busy schedule—he's just gotten back from a speaking trip—Mr. Reina is going to get in his car and come to Antigua in person just to talk with you. How about that? He'll drive us into Guatemala City in the morning. Son, I've taken two days off work, and I need to get back, but I don't want to go back without you."

Kit sat in stunned silence.

Ezra had told Reina everything. Which amounted to what? Nothing more than what was already known. Except for his loss of faith. But that shouldn't matter now. He wasn't a suspected subversive. He was an innocent lamb who had strayed from the flock and only needed a gentle prod of the shepherd's crook. He thought of Colleen's 10:30 flight tomorrow morning. Where the hell was Rub?

"Maybe he could even drive us back tonight." Ezra beamed.

"Eh, *amigo*!" Rub was sauntering toward their table. Kit stood up abruptly. Rub was dressed in his usual minimalist fashion, with no place on his person to conceal a document. He hadn't gotten it. "Berto finally get the can?"

Rub squinted at Ezra. Kit introduced them. In his anxiety he couldn't remember Rub's real first name.

"Your pastor!" Rub said, amiably. To Ezra, he confided, "Your Mr. Lamb here has been trying to get my feet out of the fire since he got to town." He cuffed Kit on the shoulder. "What'd you do, *amigo*, call in reinforcements?"

Ezra laughed. "What are you doing in Antigua, Mr. Nystrom?" He pulled over an extra chair, but Rub stayed standing.

"A little of this, a little of that. I've been in the city finishing up some business. By, the way,"—He turned to Kit— "in case you're thinking about using the school's crapper, I just came from it, and that mouse strolled behind the tank." He winked at Ezra. "These *chapín* mice ain't like American mice. Too *macho* to scurry."

Ezra was getting a kick out of Rub. "Would you like to have lunch with us, brother?" he said.

"No thanks. Got a Tupperware party to go to. I'm the host. After that I'm gonna sleep off whatever it was I poured down my throat last night."

He turned and walked unsteadily toward the entry, pausing on the threshold to call over his shoulder—"Don't forget to watch out for that mouse. You don't want it running up your pant leg and taking a chunk out of your *cojones*."

Behind the single toilet tank in the small bathroom, an envelope was taped to the wall. Kit retrieved it and pulled out the contents. The slim navy blue passport fell out of his hands, and he picked it up off the floor.

The picture on the inside cover was so unlike Colleen, and at the same time so like her, that it might have been her younger brother. Opaque and barely discernible, the eagle graphic was repeated and superimposed across the photograph. It was the genuine article. The visas page inside was stamped with a *quetzal* bird in flight, the same pale entry stamp as on his own. March 28 was the entry date, two days *after* Colleen had been seen photographing the woman at the checkpoint. Rub had thought of everything.

There was a plane ticket in the envelope in the name of Thomas E. Tinker. One way to Scranton, Pennsylvania by way of Houston, leaving Guatemala City at 10:30 a.m. Tuesday, April 5. Clipped to the ticket was a note penciled in block letters: "Tupperware party noon to 1:15. No dawdling. Thumb should be out 5:30 at designated corner. *Adiós*." That lone *"adiós,"* separated from the rest by a space, and written in longhand, touched Kit and made him feel guilty somehow. He shoved the papers back in the envelope and put it into his money belt along with his own passport and cash.

He was ready to go back to the States, he told Ezra when he returned to the table. He would drop by the school office to have the rest of his traveler's checks withdrawn from the safe and then buy their plane tickets. They could catch the 12:15 flight tomorrow to New Orleans. At the news, Ezra visibly restrained a grin of satisfaction.

On the street, when Ezra began to walk along with him, Kit said he would get things done faster by himself. No part of this flimsy excuse made sense, but in giving it—guilty and shifty-eyed—he saw that Ezra believed he understood him, for he backed off with that tactful smile and nod he used with hard cases who were a little sheepish for finally having come around.

Rita was in the school office entering numbers in a ledger. She showed no surprise or regret that he was leaving, but watched impassively as, at her insistence, he counted his travelers checks and signed a receipt for them.

With a few minutes to spare after buying the plane tickets, he cashed some travelers checks at the bank and waited across the street in the *parque* for the remaining time. Just before noon, he made his way straight to Colleen's *pensión*.

The door to her room was padlocked from the outside.

For a moment, he couldn't take it in and knocked, then pointlessly pulled on the lock. He turned to look around at the empty courtyard, turned back and touched the lock as if to make sure he wasn't imagining it.

Of course he had known this could happen, but the ramifications had been so terrible that he had put it out of his mind. Now it seemed impossible to do anything but stand there like some stone figure guarding the entrance to a looted tomb.

It came on him forcefully that he couldn't leave the country now without knowing where she was, and he couldn't stay here either without cash. He had just used up almost all of it on two tickets home. Why hadn't he waited to buy them until *after* seeing Colleen? Had he done it backward on purpose, to force the easier choice, which was no choice but to leave?

He slumped against the door and bowed his head, catching sight as he did of a palm branch at his feet. He picked it up and turned it over. On the back was the "Doubting Thomas" message he had written. Turning it to the other side again, he saw in small letters along one frond: "Back in 15 minutes." He slid onto the pavement and sat against the door with his head on his knees. How much more of this could he stand?

The gate clicked open. He scrambled to his feet. She crossed the courtyard, her backpack swinging from one shoulder. She saw him and said, "Oh, thank god!" and jammed the key into the lock, snatched it off, and pulled him inside.

❖ Twenty-Two ❖

Having dropped her pack on the floor, she came close and leaned her head into the crook of his shoulder. Her hands hung limp at her sides. His did too, and an image flashed into his mind of a movie he had seen about marathon dancers whose feet no longer moved as they simply swayed and held each other up.

She snapped out of it before he did.

"Do you want some water?" she said. "I had to go out and get some." She stooped and started pulling water bottles from her pack, and he realized she was afraid to ask the question.

"It's here," he said. She straightened. He took the envelope out and handed it to her. Her hands trembled as she opened it.

She looked the passport over front and back and leafed through the blank pages.

"This is … the real thing," she said. She read aloud the details on the plane ticket. "Tuesday, 10:30. God! I can't believe it."

He kissed her on the top of her head. Then in as firm and matter-of-fact a tone as he could muster, he told her about Ezra's visit and broke the news about Rub and the Peugeot.

"The guy with the crew cut and the bad skin?" She remembered Rub from Aurelia's and from seeing him around Antigua. "He's the one?"

Kit went over the plan with her twice—where she should stand that night—what the Peugeot looked like.

"I'll pay you back for the plane ticket and the food and everything when I get home," she said earnestly, touching his arm. But he told her what Rub had said about Uncle Sam's footing the bill. With some of her old sarcasm, she said, "I guess, since it's blood money anyway, better to spend it on me escaping than on some CIA torture 'consultant's' bar tab."

He was getting nervous. It was 12:45.

"We'll call each other as soon as we get home, okay?" he said. They repeated their phone numbers.

"What if they catch me at the airport?" she said in a small voice.

"I'll be there watching. I won't take my flight if I see anything wrong."

"But *you*, they might detain *you*."

"Ezra will be with me. If I don't see you get on that plane, I won't leave. But the passport will get you through." He was scared to leave her now, in case there was some crucial detail he had forgotten to tell her or hadn't even thought of. His brain was hardly tracking anymore. He felt like he was just stumbling from one moment to the next.

They hugged. The hard, tube-shaped canister under her clothes pressed into his stomach. It hadn't been there the last time they were together. She had taken it with her when she went out today.

He took Ezra around to the convents and churches of Antigua, even to the cellar room in *Capuchinas*, where he sang a few scales to demonstrate the acoustics. Ezra broke into "I Need Thee Every Hour," and at the surprising amplification of his own voice, threw his hands into the air and let the spirit pour out.

Kit wondered how he could have let Ezra in on this experience, after sharing it with Colleen. He would never have back that first held-in passion bursting out through their voices. Ezra and "I Need Thee Every Hour" would always intrude. Even so, halfway through the first verse, he joined his voice with Ezra's, and when they came to the end stood with him silently, yielding to love and pain at the tears in Ezra's eyes.

At 5:30 that evening Kit sat, silent, in Ezra's hotel room watching him pack up his few belongings. There seemed to be nothing they could say to each other. Right now Colleen would be walking from her *pensión* to the corner of *Calle de Hermano Pedro* and *4ta Calle Oriente*, nervous, hurrying while trying to seem not to hurry.

Had there been an alarm clock on Rub's night stand? Would he have remembered to set it? Let him right now be heading out the door, maybe grabbing a pack of cigarettes to put in the glove box of the Peugeot. Let him be showered and shaved and wide awake.

Kit tapped nervously on the Bible Ezra had left out to pack last. Ezra took it from him, lay it in his battered old Travelaire suitcase, and snapped the latches shut. Having set the case on the floor, he lay down on one of the beds and heaved a sigh. "Boy," he said, "traveling sure takes it out of you." Kit stretched out on the other bed, guiltily. Ezra had seen more than enough exotic places. He had come all this way only for him. Ezra murmured, "You were Jeannette's last bird to fly the nest. She'll be glad to see you home, son."

They napped side by side for an hour. Ezra did, at least. Kit lay listening to his pastor's snuffling, fitful snores. Each small gasp and release of air went to his heart. Ezra would die someday. Would he see him again in heaven? Would there even be a heaven? He thought of Ezra's scrappy little body suffering and withering and finally becoming a not-Ezra—a shriveled, cold object like the corpse of a dog or a cat.

How did people cope without believing that their soul would live eternally? Could you tolerate life without it? Who had told him, *I can't believe nonsense just because it's reassuring nonsense?*

Kit wanted to curl up against him and tell him he was sorry. He reached across to the other bed and laid a hand softly on Ezra's sleeve. Ezra's snores stopped for a few minutes before starting up again.

Reina strode across the dining room, arms outstretched.

"Brother Ezra!" he called over the clink of glasses and murmur of diners. "Praise the Lord, He brings us together again."

Ezra jumped from his chair and bustled over to meet him halfway, walking into the man's embrace like a long-parted relative. Reina's black tailored suit was sharply cut at the shoulders, with a sliver of starched white handkerchief peeking from his breast pocket. He wore a pale gray silk shirt and patterned tie. The polish on his black Italian loafers reflected light from the chandeliers. Kit couldn't avoid shaking hands with him. It gratified him, though, to notice that the gold-ringed hands that clasped his were sweaty.

Daniel, in white shirt and black suit and tie, was suddenly at their table, pulling out a chair for Reina and bowing slightly. In colloquial Spanish, he barked an order over his shoulder to a dark-skinned waiter with high Mayan cheekbones, then greeted Reina effusively in English. "*Señor* Reina, how we have missed you!"

"Eh, Brother Daniel!" Reina did not, Kit noticed, use his double-handed handshake on Daniel. To Kit and Ezra, he commented, "Here I reserve a room every time I have business in Antigua. Our Lord has blessed this brother in Christ with fine skills in hotel management." Daniel bowed again with a modest smile. Reina flourished a hand at the room full of formally dressed diners—no backpackers here. "Look around you. Here is the true Guatemala!" he said. "Success and prosperity, by the grace of God. He helps us to become one country, not divided into *indio* and *ladino*, but *Guatemalidad*. All *chapines* and followers of our Lord and Savior."

He leaned back to glance at Daniel who was hovering by his shoulder. "Eh, Daniel? The sooner we erase those distinctions, the better for our country?"

"You are right, *Señor* Reina." Daniel gestured sharply to the waiter, who hurried over to place tall, gold-embossed menus before them. "Every day I thank the Lord Jesus for his blessings."

Señor Reina planted an elbow on the table and pointed into the air. "*'If thou hearken diligently to the voice of the Lord, He shall smite thine enemies and open to thee his treasure, make thee plenteous in goods, and bless all the work of thine hand.'*"

Ezra smiled broadly and Kit wondered for a moment if his pastor grasped the gist of the quotation. In fact he did. Also holding up a finger, Ezra said, "And Paul reminds us, *señor*, to '*charge them that are rich in this world that they be rich in good works.*' '*Let no man seek his own, but every man another's wealth.*'"

Reina nodded. "You are right, Brother Ezra. And to the Corinthians, Paul says, '*You are rich in everything and must be generous, but—*'" *Señor* Reina paused. "*'this does not mean that other men be blessed and ye burdened by your giving.*'"

Ezra finished the quote. "*'The aim is equality.'*"

"Yes, equality. Exactly. However, we are not communists. We pray we may all become equal in our love and commitment to Jesus Christ." Reina took a pair of glasses from an inside pocket, put them on, and picked up the menu.

Daniel continued to linger. The respectful inclination of his shoulders, coupled with a casual hand on one hip, seemed to express a hope of being invited to join the group as an equal but a willingness to carry out orders, whichever would be more obliging. His eyes on the menu, Reina said, "Tell us what the kitchen recommends tonight." Daniel snapped his fingers at the waiter, who came at once and ran down the specialties of the evening. "I would recommend the lobster," added Daniel. "It is fresh from the coast this morning."

Ezra smiled at him warmly. "Brother Daniel, do you have time to sit with us?"

"I'm sure our brother is too busy—with such a full house," said Reina. He closed his menu, put his glasses away, and ordered the lobster for the group. Daniel faded away toward another table. Reina folded his hands then and closed his eyes. "Thank you, our Master and Lord, for bringing us together—friends from different countries but united as brothers in Christ. For in Jesus Christ there is only one nation, one class, one race. The race of the children of God. Amen." Kit eyed Ezra during the prayer and saw him touch his pocket. How much for a lobster dinner in a place where prices were left off the menu?

They didn't get down to the reason Reina was there until after dessert. Coffee came. *Señor* Reina unbuttoned his jacket, swiped his napkin over his mustache and leaned back in his chair.

"So, Mr. Lamb, your pastor tells me that you have visited to the village where was sent the generous gift from your church. And you were disappointed to not see the fire truck that you sent to Santiago Atitlán. It is a beautiful place, Santiago, isn't it?" He turned to Ezra. "The villages are small jewels adorning the feet of those so green mountains whose toes dip into the lake. But it is sad that the *guerrilla* wish to steal that beauty and bring the people into servitude to the beast of communism—"

"Where *is* the fire truck?" Kit interrupted. Frowning, Ezra opened his mouth, then closed it again.

"Of course, after you took trouble to go there, you want to know."
Reina raised an eyebrow at the waiter and touched his coffee cup. "The
people of Santiago," he said, "asked the army to keep the fire truck for
them in case the subversives bomb their village. In such case the army
could quickly put out the fires."

There was a silence. Then Kit said, "I met some soldiers there and they
hadn't heard of any fire truck. Nobody had."

"Of course they would say so. Our soldiers are well-disciplined. How
could anyone know who you were and why you were asking?"

"I've heard," said Kit, looking him in the eye, "that the guerrillas don't
bomb villages, only things like highways and power stations and army
bases. It's the army that bombs villages and burns them to the ground."

Reina shook his head sadly. "Ah, you must not be fooled by all these
false reports, brother. Anyone who wants to discredit us has only to whisper in the ear of some atheistic, communistic organization and cry human
rights abuse. You have heard of the Amnesty International report which
accuses our president of genocide? These reports are discredited."

"Who discredits them?" Why don't I keep my mouth shut? A cold
anger was making him reckless.

"All who know the truth discredit them. Unfortunately, this doesn't
stop the communist sympathizing press to print the lies as if they are
the Gospel."

"The soldiers in Santiago told me it was better to burn villages than
to protect them from fire. They laughed when they said it."

Reina raised an eyebrow. "These were English-speaking soldiers?" Kit
didn't answer. Reina chuckled. "No? But you thought you understood
them." To Ezra he said, "When people have been told what they will
see and what they will hear, then that is what they will see and hear."
He leaned toward Kit and touched his arm. "Maybe you have been told
lies by misguided people. This girl you met at a beach—" he winked at
Ezra, who nodded, not at all guilty, apparently, for having betrayed the
confidence. "—Why was the army interested in her? They have more
important things to do than chase after innocent people." He leaned back
again. "Mr. Lamb, in the time of war, someone takes pictures of soldiers,
it is the duty of the military to find out why, of course. It is very serious.

THE DE-CONVERSION OF KIT LAMB

You thought she was a pretty girl? Someone to ... talk to maybe? You are young. It's understandable. We know you are a good Bible-believing Christian."

It hadn't occurred to him that confiding in Ezra could be dangerous. *Don't talk about politics in this country—not even with someone you trust.* She herself had said it, but hadn't she broken her own rule?

Reina held up a finger for the check, and Daniel came with it immediately. Ezra drew out his worn brown wallet, curved to the shape of his skinny buttock, but Reina insisted on picking up the tab. "Because you are in my country, brothers, you are my guests." He paid in cash, unfolding bill after bill from a money clip he pulled out of an inside pocket of his jacket.

A marimba band was starting up in the lounge adjoining the dining room. A few couples got up to dance. "Daniel!" Reina clapped the manager on the back. "*Por la gracia de Dios* some day soon you will have your own hotel, eh? You tell me when that day comes, and I will be the first to reserve rooms for my whole family."

Daniel shook hands with Ezra and Reina, then turned to Kit and hugged him.

"Together, praise God, we heard the blessed words of *Hermano Efraín Ríos Montt*. Is an experience I do not forget never. Come again to Guatemala, Brother Cristóbal. Our church is your church." When had Daniel found out he was leaving? Ezra must have told him that afternoon. Everyone knows everything about me.

At that moment, it struck him that he had never said anything to Ezra about Colleen's taking photographs of soldiers. Where had Reina learned that fact? Apparently, from the time Ezra had made the phone call to him in Guatemala City this morning until he left to come to Antigua this afternoon, he had managed to become informed of it.

Ezra took the back seat in Reina's BMW sedan. "More leg room up front for the tall guy," he said heartily, cuffing Kit on the shoulder. Kit was stuck in the passenger seat with nothing to say to Reina. Reina had plenty to say to him. Adeptly negotiating the mountain curves in the dark, he kept up a running testimonial to the achievements of Ríos Montt.

He talked about the grim days of the former dictator, Romeo Lucas García, who had pitted the old military hierarchy against young officers and pitted businessmen and political parties against the military and against each other. Corruption had ruled all business transactions and government appointments. In the streets of Guatemala City, even prominent citizens were found assassinated by the death squad hirelings of their political or business rivals. Leftist terrorists were winning the war, disrupting the business of the country and leaving it on the brink of economic ruin. Ríos Montt had changed all that with his three fingers of virtue. Now law-abiding citizens had nothing to fear, and the communists were on the run.

As Reina talked on, Kit stared silently out the window into the darkness. She would be safely out of Antigua by now. Already holed up in a cheap hotel, maybe the one she had found for him on his first night in the country. He remembered mistaking New Year's Eve fireworks for gunfire. In the darkness he blushed at the memory. 'When people have been told what they will see and hear, that's what they will see and hear.'

It was Reina himself who had primed him to expect warfare, with his luncheon slides of mutilated bodies and his talk of terrorists. It is true, he thought, that we see things the way we are taught to see them. One person saw an indigenous man carrying a hundred-pound load of firewood up a mountainside and said he was happy to continue in the ways of his ancestors. Another said he was oppressed and wanted justice and relief from his suffering.

But some things just were what they were.

Today was Monday. It was nine days since the man was left to hang from a pole in the sun. It must be over now. Either he had died there after so many hours or days, or they had taken him down and let him go, crippled for life, or they had kept him alive to do worse things to him, maybe starting by showing him his father's cracked skull. *Some things are what they are.*

He interrupted Reina's stream of conversation.

"I guess Ezra told you what happened when they arrested me?" Reina nodded. "But maybe he didn't tell you everything."

He described the hanging man. He told it coldly and in precise detail this time. When he had finished, he felt Ezra's hand on his shoulder. He pulled away.

Reina shook his head regretfully, and Kit expected another knowing reference to his naïvete, his innocence. "Ah," Reina said instead, "it is a very great pity that some soldiers—even some commanders in the field—exceed the limits of civilized behavior. It cannot be allowed, of course. Ríos Montt, if he knew about it, would demand an investigation and if necessary, a court martial for such men. He governs according to the highest moral standards. I am surprised—" he took his eyes off the road for a moment to look at Kit, "—that you yourself failed to report it." Then he gave a dismissive shrug. "It is understandable," he said, smiling compassionately. "You're young and you were probably too much afraid. We all make mistakes. So you must understand that these soldiers also do not always act honorably. They are only human, like you. They try to defend our beloved country, but every day they witness the heartbreaking treachery of terrorists—the torn and bloodied bodies of their *compadres* blown apart by Satan's subversive bombs. In this field of battle which is our country, soldiers sometimes succumb to anger. It is wrong. It is unprofessional and should be punished. But it is understandable."

Kit sat staring ahead. He held himself straight. Ezra apparently knew better than to touch him again. He said nothing all the way to the city, where they pulled up to a modern, high-rise hotel. Two porters opened their doors and took their baggage away. Reina guided them to the reservation desk and managed the details of registration. Once again, Ezra removed his brown wallet, and there was a polite altercation, which Reina won, saying, "It's nothing. It's covered. It's my pleasure."

On parting, Kit didn't put out his hand for Reina to shake, but Reina took it anyway, in his two moist ones, and said, "Let our Lord and Master speak to you, Mr. Lamb. He takes away all fears and unhappiness when you let him into your heart." He told Ezra he would meet them after breakfast to drive them to the airport.

Kit came to life then, protesting that they could take a bus or a cab to the airport, he wanted to get there early, well before the flight—9:30 or 10:00 at the latest.

"It is no problem," Reina replied. "I also must be early in my office. I will pick you up at 8:00. It is a very brief drive. Just a kilometer south. It will be no trouble."

They watched him go out to his waiting sedan. Hotel guests crossed the lobby in leather coats and furs. The click of high heels sounded on the parquet floor. A porter rattled a cart piled precariously with mono-grammed luggage into an elevator.

Their tenth-floor room looked down on the tree-lined *Avenida La Reforma*. Since leaving the Martinez house and moving into *Casa Fuego*, Kit had gotten used to luxury. He and Ezra took turns washing away the day's grime under hot water. In the shower, Kit wondered what it would be like to make love with Colleen in one of the double beds made up with clean white sheets. They would take a shower together afterwards, and they would soap each others' bodies with the fragrant soap he had unwrapped from its little package. After they rinsed off, he would lift her up, her legs would go around his hips and he would slip into her again, with the water streaming down their bodies. His arms and thighs would be so pumped up he would be able to move her against his thrust as if she were as weightless as a doll—

His release made him ashamed, with Ezra in the next room and prob-ably reading his Bible as he always did before turning in. But when Kit emerged from the bathroom, Ezra was asleep, with the Bible open on his chest. Kit closed it and put it on the bedside table. In the old days—nine days ago—he would have taken a look at the open pages and marveled at the aptness of the message God had chosen for his eyes to fall on.

They got up early on Tuesday morning, and Ezra suggested they pray together.

"There's no time," Kit objected. "We still have to eat, and Reina will be coming."

Ezra took Kit's arm and led him onto the balcony, where they stood for a moment looking out at the hazy volcano cones that ringed the city in the golden morning light.

"Master, we stand before Thee in confusion and ignorance—"

Kit couldn't bring himself to close his eyes. He turned his gaze from the mountains to the tiers of balconies that climbed thirteen stories up the face of the hotel's other wing. A couple was drinking coffee on the balcony across from theirs. On the table lay a basket covered with a white cloth. The woman, sitting with her legs crossed, was reading to the man from a newspaper. The man glanced toward the balconies on their right and on their left, before frowning and shaking his head. To the south, two military helicopters, one coming in, the other going out, droned above a mountain. Ezra's prayer fell on Kit's ears as gibberish.

He checked his watch and felt a tug of fear.

"We'd better go," he said, stepping back inside. Ezra stayed out on the balcony a few minutes more to finish praying silently. The silence seemed to project into the room as an accusation.

"I have thought about the experience that affected you so strongly," Reina said as he swung the car out into rush hour traffic on the *Avenida La Reforma*. Kit had started to roll down his window, but rolled it up again at the reek of diesel fumes. He braced himself for another veiled hint at his ignorance and cowardice. "I believe it is important that you should report these things so that justice is served." They had turned north instead of south on the palm-lined avenue. "I will take it as a duty and a matter of honor to accompany you to the *Palacio Nacional* this morning so that you can report to the authorities what you have seen." Kit looked at him sharply.

"We have a flight to catch," he said.

Kit glanced quickly back at Ezra. Was he in on this idea? But Ezra was frowning and leaning forward in his seat.

"No," Ezra said. "I think it's better that Kit gets back home to his church and friends. Maybe he could—"

"Of course. The flight is no problem." Reina stretched one arm familiarly along the back of Kit's seat. "There are three hours before you must be at the airport to check in."

Kit sat forward to avoid Reina's arm behind his neck.

"But we'll have to go through customs," he said, "and have our bags inspected and checked onto the flight—"

"No matter." Reina was weaving smoothly in and out of traffic. They passed a chicken bus and turned onto another main thoroughfare. "I will come with you to expedite the process. Your plane leaves at 12:15, you said, Brother Ezra? If we arrive at *La Aurora* by 11:00, 11:30, you will have sufficient time." Kit turned and shook his head discreetly at Ezra.

But Ezra nodded. "That's all right, then," he said, and sat back.

"Aren't you busy?" Kit tried to keep his voice casual. "You have to go to work early, you said."

"This is more important, I think."

Ezra said, "Bless you, brother. That's very good of you."

Kit looked helplessly at buses heading south, as if he might jump out at a stoplight and board one. How could he leave the country not knowing if she had gotten out? If she got to the airport and didn't see him there, would she think he had been taken and she was about to be taken, too? Would she run, not get on the plane? But what could he do? Continuing to insist on getting to the airport more than two hours early would sound suspicious.

They drove into *Zona 1*, the heart of the city. Reina pointed out new office and shopping buildings and the crush of cars and buses attesting to Guatemala's budding prosperity under Ríos Montt's firm hand. They came to the central plaza, dominated on two sides by the Metropolitan Cathedral and the National Palace, a turreted granite structure one block long, with broad steps leading to a pillared portico. Reina parked behind a tour bus in front of the building. The clock on the cathedral tower said 8:30.

Now, as he and Ezra emerged from the car and Reina came around to escort them into the building, Kit's chest tightened and his knees locked. He refused to let himself be herded into that stone fortress like a sheep to the slaughter. He grasped Ezra's arm to hold him back, too. Only now had it occurred to him that Ezra might be in danger. By association with him, Ezra could end up in a blood-smeared room facing sadistic, gun-toting boys, the least of whose antics would be to mock the sweet qualities that made Ezra Ezra—the small stature, the prominent ears, the shine of sweat on his bald scalp.

"No," Kit said. "I've decided to write a report after we get home and I have time to think better. Just tell me who to send it to."

Ezra looked back and forth between them uncertainly. Reina put an arm around Kit's shoulder and drew him forward. To resist would have meant digging in his heels like a child pulling a tantrum.

"A first-person account, *Señor* Lamb—face-to-face—that is the best way to get at facts. It allows for questions to be asked and answered. Also, the less time lost the better. You are concerned, I suppose, about the people whom you saw being mistreated."

Ezra said, "Would it make you feel better, Kit, if we prayed about it, and then decided—" Kit saw Reina suppress a small grimace of impatience.

"Some very busy people have kindly agreed to meet with our brother Kit. I have made some telephone calls this morning," he said to Ezra evenly. He looked at his watch. "I would not like to think I brought them here for nothing." He forced a smile then, and it seemed he meant Ezra to see that it was forced. Releasing Kit and holding out his hands palms up, Reina said, "Of course, it is entirely your decision."

"Don't you think he might be right, Kit?" said Ezra. "Better now than later, when you might have forgotten some of the details?"

As if he could forget.

He would look insane if he bolted. And he had no chance of getting away, even if he were willing to leave Ezra behind.

He allowed Reina to steer him up the steps and into the great hall, guarded by armed soldiers. Reina said a few words to a doorman sitting behind a reception desk, which bore a hand-written sign: *Jesús te ama.* —Jesus loves you—. Then he led them up a broad, curving staircase. The walls were lined with livid murals depicting Guatemala's history of conquest and violence: in lurid oranges, reds, and blues, a scene of mounted *conquistadores* skewering half-naked Mayan warriors on medieval pikes; a Mayan blood sacrifice in progress; between huge, uplifted hands, an armored *conquistador* and a young bare-breasted Mayan woman, her head bowed, standing close together in ambiguous intimacy; a robed monk and several young Mayans gathered around a large piece of paper.

At the top of the stairs they turned onto a wide corridor. There were posters on the walls displaying the three blue fingers of virtue against the white background, and others with slogans, which Reina paused to translate: "Guatemala Does Not Need Cowards or Opportunists in Its Path toward Strength and Victory." "Patriotism Is Not about Heroics. It

Is a Matter of Discipline." Their shoes echoed on the tiles as they passed the open doors of administrative offices. Inside one was a shelf stacked with Bibles. Ezra nudged Kit.

They turned into a large, attractive office with tall windows whose heavy drapes had been pulled aside to let in the morning sun. The room was furnished with upholstered chairs, a small sofa, and a desk of highly polished wood, bare except for a telephone, steno pads and a pen set. A young woman entered behind them and laid a coffee service with six cups on the desk. With a polite nod to Reina, she picked up the telephone from its console and punched a button. "They're here," she said in Spanish. Then she poured out coffee for each of them and left the room.

"Shall we make ourselves comfortable?" Reina sat down on the sofa and gestured for Kit to join him, but Kit drifted over to the windows, which looked down onto a leafy interior courtyard one story below. Several men in shirtsleeves sat in the sun, chatting and drinking coffee. The young woman who had left the office a few moments before clicked past them in her high heels and tight skirt, and the men reflexively turned to watch her before going back to their conversations. Kit looked at his watch again. Was it possible that this was what Reina said it was? He could just tell his story, and they would be on their way to the airport in time to see Colleen get on the 10:30 flight?

"I have spoken to a friend of mine, a brother in Christ and personal secretary to the president," Reina was saying to Ezra, who had taken a seat on one of the upholstered chairs. "He felt that a representative of the Ministry of Defense should be informed of the incidents that Brother Lamb described to us. He has also asked a political officer from the U.S. Embassy to join us." He consulted his watch. "It may take a little time to convene everyone at once." He leaned back and sipped his coffee. "We have all had to rearrange our morning. But we will undoubtedly be finished in time for your flight."

❖ Twenty-Three ❖

For the next half hour Kit remained at the window while Reina talked with Ezra about the generosity of U.S. evangelicals. "The Lord Jesus," he said, "has opened their hearts to those suffering Indians who had to flee their homes to escape *la violencia* of the subversives. With the help of our brothers and sisters in the U.S., the army can feed and shelter the refugees and uplift them with the good news of our Lord and Savior. At last these suffering people begin to have hope."

It was now 9:00. It might only take a half hour to drive to the airport, now that rush hour was over. But they would have to leave by 9:30 at the latest to get there in time. If they were later than that— What would he do? He would have to assume she had gotten on the flight. In the New Orleans airport he could go to the airline counter and find out for sure. And if she hadn't? Then he would call the number she gave him and raise the alarm. There was nothing else he could do.

A man in shirtsleeves came in. Reina introduced him, but Kit didn't catch his name. He was a personal advisor to Ríos Montt and a member of the president's church. The man looked to be in his forties—short hair parted at the side and combed flat across a high forehead. He had a dark mustache that drooped downward like the tailfins of a fish. He spoke some English, but Reina translated for him.

He was grateful, the man said, that God had moved Kit to come forth with information that would help the president in his efforts to bring about the transformation of Guatemala into a godly nation wholly dedicated to Christian principles of morality and integrity.

Despite this rather overblown and formal speech, Kit thought the man had a pleasant, open smile, what you could see of it behind the mustache. It seemed that every male evangelical he met here wore a mustache. Was it a Ríos Montt look-alike thing or just a Guatemalan thing?

The time was now 9:10.

Kit asked the man, "You're close to Ríos Montt, right?"

Reina translated.

"We are brothers in Christ."

"Then why don't I just tell *you* about San José and you can tell Ríos Montt himself?"

"Of course I will relay to the president what you tell us. He would want to be informed. But it is an army matter and military discipline may be involved. It is desirable that a representative of the army hear the facts in detail."

"Also, since you are a U.S. citizen," Reina added, "the Embassy wishes to be represented as well, to ensure—" He broke off to greet a prim man of medium build in a tweed suit and glasses, who was coming in the door, a TV version of a college professor. He was introduced as an Embassy political officer—Howard or Harold something; again, in his state of nervous distraction, Kit immediately forgot the name.

Reina poured coffee for the men. The Embassy man carried a thin attaché case, which he laid on the desk before taking a chair. He glanced at his watch, and, automatically, Kit did too. 9:30. "We're waiting for someone from Defense?" the Embassy man asked. Reina assured him that the *comandante* would be with them momentarily.

The window of time was now closed.

After pouring coffee, Reina sat down on the sofa next to Ríos Montt's man. The Embassy officer took the chair behind the desk. Reina and the evangelical, having run out of small talk, and the Embassy man maybe not having any to run out of, all began shifting nervously in their seats or fiddling with ties and hair. A little apart, Ezra sat calmly, his hands folded in his lap. From the frown of concentration furrowing his forehead, Kit knew he was in "eyes-open prayer." Always waiting for the Lord to tell him what to do, Kit thought, half angrily, half affectionately. At least Ezra wasn't fidgeting like a small boy in church as the others were.

The *comandante* arrived after fifteen minutes. He filled the doorway—tall, thick across the shoulders. In physique, he reminded Kit of Bill, the man at Light and Life that he had once called "The Hulk," but Bill wasn't usually clean-shaven and didn't reek of Brut. The colonel wore the camouflage field uniform that seemed to be worn by soldiers of all ranks, including the president, everywhere in Guatemala. The sight of the uniform set Kit's heart pounding. There were three stars on the man's epaulet, and the others addressed him as *coronel*.

When the colonel arrived, Reina breathed an audible sigh of relief, Ezra came up out of his meditation, and the Embassy man, picking up his attaché case, gave the colonel his seat at the desk. At Reina's insistence, Kit finally sat down.

"*Entonces*," —So— the colonel began, without introduction or pre-liminaries. He opened a steno pad and took up a pen. "You have a report to give about misconduct on a military base. What do you want to tell?" As Reina translated, the colonel sat relaxed but upright, resting one hand on the desk as he wrote. Whenever he looked up, his expression was neither threatening nor conciliatory.

Kit told the story—all of it, starting with the incident at the check-point and ending with his return to Antigua. Everything, including the soldiers' treatment of himself, he told factually with a minimum of words and emotional adjectives: I was struck in the back with a rifle and in the face with a fist. Thrown into a truck. Blood, urine, feces on the floor. My penis struck with a pencil. The same glove that searched my anus was used on the inside of my mouth.

Behind him, he felt the vibrations of Ezra's empathy. His pastor would be on the edge of his chair, preventing himself from rising and putting a hand on the back of Kit's neck. *The Lord loves you, Kit. Through it all, no matter how far away he seems, he loves you.* But Ezra stayed put.

He told what happened to the Martinez family and the constant pres-ence of the unmarked vans and station wagons in the days that followed. The only details he left out related to Colleen. "She was a tourist I met on the beach that day. I don't know her name," was all he said. The colonel wrote down everything, and when Kit glanced around, he saw that the Embassy man and Ríos Montt's man, too, were writing in notebooks.

Maybe—was it possible?—he should have done this right from the beginning. The day he got back from San José. He should have tracked down Reina then and made him listen. Why hadn't he? He had watched as soldiers hauled away the woman from the bus, killed an innocent old man. He had seen another man being tortured, probably to death, and he hadn't done anything about it, hadn't told anyone. It was hard to remember now, after so many sleepless nights and tense days, why he hadn't. This last week was full of holes, ragged at the edges. The only thing that stood out clearly since he had returned from San José was the afternoon in Colleen's bed.

"The officer who interrogated you—" the colonel was saying, "—what rank was he?"

"I'm not sure. He was like a captain or something. I don't know much about military ranks. He was in charge."

"You don't know his name?" The colonel's expression remained neutral.

"He had a dog. Like a terrier. It ate out of his hand."

This elicited an almost imperceptible pause.

"But you don't know what rank the man was? You haven't served in the military yourself?"

"He was middle-aged, kind of wide around the hips. He had a dog. That's all I know."

"This happened ten days ago? What took you so long to come forward? Why didn't you report it when you got back to Antigua?"

He had surprised himself that he could have told the whole story without trembling or getting red, but the flush rose up his neck and into his face now. "Who was I supposed to report it to?" he said.

"To the local authorities, of course. You had been living in Antigua how long—more than three months? Surely you knew by then that there was a military headquarters there."

"I'd have to have been suicidal to report it to the army."

"And yet you are reporting it now. Who has given you the idea that the whole army condones what three or four soldiers might have done in one small outpost?"

Ezra said, behind him. "The boy was traumatized. It's natural he would jump to the conclusion—"

Kit turned on him. "Don't talk for me. I can talk for myself."

Ezra bunched his lips together and nodded, putting up a hand in the rueful, apologetic gesture that said, Yes, the good father lets his son make his own mistakes.

This infuriated Kit more than the colonel's insinuations.

"I escape one bunch of torturers and was supposed to walk into the den of another bunch?"

The colonel said, "Your attitude is unfortunate. You know that leftist groups like your Amnesty International and Americas Watch condemn our government and our military for incidents of violence that may have been carried out by the *guerrilleros* themselves disguised as members of the army, or, possibly by isolated individuals within our army whom we would want to discipline. How are we supposed to know about it if people don't tell us that it happened?"

"The man in charge—the one with the dog—said that because Ríos Montt was a general, he understood why it was necessary to hang a guy from a post like that—as an example to others. That's what he said."

"Was this man in charge an English speaker, and if not, are you certain that you understood him correctly?"

"He pointed to the man and said, '*Necesitamos ejemplos.*' His translator said it in English: 'We need examples'."

The colonel shook his head. "But you don't know what rank this man in charge was? Can you be sure he wasn't some rogue enlisted man who took advantage of his commander's temporary absence to break the code of conduct which our president himself has put in place?"

Kit thrust his thumb and two fingers at the colonel. "This one?" *Kit what are you doing?* Ezra was sitting there in the room with him, just as vulnerable as himself.

The colonel smiled. He stood. The others stood, too.

"Now that you have finally come forward with your story, I will have the incidents investigated." To the Embassy man, he said, "I will call in the commander of *Departamento Escuintla* and talk with him. You may be there if you like. I will let you know when he arrives." To Kit, he said, "Mr. Lamb, we do not expect our soldiers to treat prisoners suspected of subversion as they would their own grandmothers," —He smiled, showing an array of even, white teeth— "we do, however, expect that they adhere to the basic code of conduct." He stood up, tore his written pages from the steno pad, folded them and tucked them into a flapped pocket on his field jacket, then set the pad and the pen neatly back on the desk. He nodded to Reina and the two officials, stared momentarily at Ezra, as if he hadn't noticed him before, and left the room.

The prim Embassy man—Howard or Harold—held up his own legal pad covered with writing. "Mr. Lamb," he said, "We'll send you a report of the investigation as soon as it's completed." After putting the pad into his attaché case, he shook Kit's and Ezra's hands firmly, thanking them for coming forward. "The State Department appreciates any information on the conduct of the Guatemalan military. With so many unfounded reports coming in, we do everything we can to separate fact from fiction. Eyewitness accounts like yours are invaluable." He started for the door then stopped and turned back. "You can leave it in our hands now," he said.

Kit said, "Don't you want my address? To send me the report?" The Embassy man blinked.

"My secretary looked it up when *Señor* Reina called this morning."

After he left, the three evangelicals—Ezra, Reina and the Ríos Montt assistant—all stood smiling at Kit reassuringly.

"That was a hard story to tell, son," said Ezra.

It was 10:50.

Coldly, Kit said, "We need to catch our plane."

Reina turned to the Ríos Montt man. "In case there is some difficulty at customs—some misunderstanding—could you perhaps provide a written assurance that these Christian brothers of ours will be allowed to—"

"Of course." The Ríos Montt man sat down at the desk and withdrew from a drawer a piece of official stationery franked with the insignia of the Republic of Guatemala—a *quetzal* bird and a flag inked in green. He asked for the spelling of Kit's and Ezra's names as they appeared on their passports. Then he wrote a few lines and handed the paper to Kit. Reina read it to them in English:

Mr. Christopher Lamb and Pastor Ezra Tinker, traveling on April 5, 1983, are on official business for the government of the Republic of

Guatemala. Allow them to pass through customs without delay. Do not detain either their persons or their baggage.

The Ríos Montt man had signed his initials over the stamped signature of General Efraín José Ríos Montt, *Jefe de Estado, Palacio Nacional, Ciudad de Guatemala, República de Guatemala, C.A.*

Ezra shook the hand of each, thanking them profusely. "We'll pray for you, brother, and for your president, who has such a hard task. Our whole congregation will be praying." There were smiles all around, except from Kit, who, standing close to the door, felt like a dog fixed on being let out.

They arrived at *La Aurora* airport at 11:45 with only half an hour to spare. Reina came in with them to help smooth their way through immigration.

By now she'll have landed in Houston. Kit looked longingly at the *Aviateca* ticket counter, where Reina was showing their tickets. Even if Reina and Ezra hadn't been nearby, it would be too risky to ask about the flight to Houston, and whether anyone named Thomas Tinker had been on it. At least, according to a departure sign, the 10:30 flight had gone out on schedule.

Passengers were standing in the customs line. Two young backpackers—a male and female—were looking indignant as the contents of their packs were dumped out on a table and sifted through. Another immigration officer was carefully examining their passports. The short, stocky female backpacker looked nothing like Colleen, but she and her partner were taken out of line and shown into a small lounge area, where a female immigration officer, followed in by a soldier, patted them down. Finally, the two were allowed to repack their belongings and board the plane.

Kit was sweating. What if these precautions had been instigated since Colleen had disappeared? What if all flights, not just his own, involved this kind of surveillance? She might already be in custody.

Everyone knows if someone doesn't get you out in the first hours, you'll probably be dead. And if you survive the first day ... you may not want to live anymore.

They would have made her remove the baggy jacket. The searching hands would be all over her, discovering breasts, crotch, and at her waist a hard cylindrical object—or, if it were hidden somewhere else, they would take her out of sight to find it. But maybe she hadn't been so reckless as to try to get out of the country with it. Without it, she might have a chance of bluffing her way through. Her Spanish was good enough.

Then he saw her. She had come out of the men's restroom and was making her way across the airport toward the customs line. She had on a cap, and was still wearing the jacket and the men's shoes and still carrying only the ragged little backpack. Their looks of recognition glanced off and past each other. His heart started to race.

Reina took Kit's and Ezra's arms to guide them around the roped area toward the front of the line. "We will expedite this procedure," Reina said. "Where is the pass?"

But Ezra said, "No, no. Thank you, but other people were here before us. You're in a hurry, brother, you go on to work now. Kit, you've got the paper?" Reina protested briefly, shrugged and shook hands with them both. Kit was afraid his icy hand would give him away.

"Go in Christ, brothers," Reina said, and left them.

As they stepped to the back of the line, Kit heard the tap of Colleen's leather-soled shoes coming up behind them. Why hadn't she taken the first plane?

"A good Samaritan, Kit. A truly godly man," Ezra was saying. He shook his head at the uncommon selflessness of it all. "Sometimes when you think the Lord has too many other things on His mind, he shows you that you're never out of His thoughts."

Why? Why was she taking this flight? She knew how risky it was. What if they pull her aside? The line moved forward quickly. No one else got searched—only a brief shuffling through suitcases, a matching of faces to passport pictures, exit visas stamped and "*¡El siguiente!*" —Next!— But they were all Guatemalans.

Ezra was saying, "I wouldn't want to be a subversive giving an accounting to that colonel. But, you know, that's what you have to have in the military. Tough men, but fair. Kit, it's going to help you put the ordeal behind you, knowing your story will be of use to the government."

"Get your passport out, Ezra."

They were next in line. The immigration officer held out his hand, and Kit put his own and Ezra's passports in it, along with the paper Ríos Montt's man had given him. The officer ignored the paper. He took a look at Kit, looked at his passport, then looked him up and down again. He turned to consult some stapled papers which he drew from a folder on the counter. He looked up at Kit again, then raised an eyebrow at the other officer—a uniformed woman about to search the luggage—and also beckoned the soldier over. The woman gestured for Kit to follow her, but Kit snatched the signed pass from the first officer's hand and said loudly, "*Éste es un pase especial, directamente del Presidente Ríos Montt, del Palacio Nacional.*" He pointed to the stamped signature.

Ezra said, "Maybe I should have let *Señor* Reina stay to help us out—"

"Read it!" Kit commanded in Spanish. The officer read it silently, frowning, then glanced again at the list on the table. It was a list of names, each with a physical description. Kit's own name was halfway down the page. The officer opened the two passports again and looked back and forth from the photos to Ezra's and Kit's faces. Then he shrugged, muttered a few words in Spanish to his partner and passed them through. The female officer pushed their unopened luggage back at them. Ezra picked his up and began to walk toward the door that led outside to the small waiting airplane.

Kit lagged behind. He took out a pen and knelt to go over the name and address on his baggage tags, darkening the letters. He pulled up his socks. He pretended to look for something in his bag, found a water bottle, opened it and took a drink, watching all the while what was happening at the customs line.

The immigration officer had Colleen's passport in one hand and his list in the other. He ran a finger down the first page. Colleen stood squarely, her arms hanging at her sides, like a clueless teenage boy with no particular thoughts—*just whenever we get this show on the road is fine with me.* The officer flipped the page over and scanned it slowly. He turned again to Colleen and looked her up and down. Then, glancing at his partner, he gestured to the soldier, who began to shamble over.

Colleen's eyes dulled. Her body began to cave. Kit's heart pounded wildly and for a moment he froze, as if the scene were in a movie and he could only watch it. Then he called out urgently and loudly, "Hey!" The officers looked over at him. He hurried back, fumbling in his pack as he came. The soldier raised his rifle.

Clutching the paper, he held it up, almost in the first officer's face. He pointed out Ezra Tinker's name on the pass and nodded toward Colleen "*¡Ella es el hijo del pastor Tinker!*" he said in a cracking voice. He snatched Colleen's passport off the table and pointed to the name: Thomas E. Tinker.

The officer gave a harsh laugh and shook his head mockingly. He turned to his partner and to the soldier, who was still holding his gun in two hands. Imitating Kit's drawling *gringo* accent, he said, "*Ella es el hijo del pastor*." Kit felt dizzy. He stared at Colleen in horror. She returned his gaze and he could read the dismay in it, though she was again trying to preserve a facade of clueless nonchalance.

The words had come out before he had taken time to think: *She* is the pastor's *son*. She, she. Ella instead of él. A fucking grammar mistake! *Two* mistakes. Because it wasn't necessary to use a pronoun at all. He could have just said, '*Es el hijo del pastor.*'

"I mean—" he said in English, stammering.

The female officer, suppressing a smile, corrected Kit, kindly, "*No se dice ella es el hijo, se dice él es el hijo del pastor.*" And Kit stood there with his mouth open for a moment before he caught on. They were simply laughing at the grammar mistake.

The male officer waved Colleen and her daypack on through, saying to her in a put-on falsetto, "*Pase, señorita.*"

At the gate, the flight attendant noticed the names on their tickets and said to Ezra in English, indicating Colleen, "This is your son, Mr. Tinker? You wish to have seats together? Now your seats are apart."

Ezra said, puzzled, "My son?" and before Kit could intervene, looked at the name on Colleen's ticket and glanced up at her. He looked at her hard for a moment. Then he said, genially, "Well, for goodness sake, that's quite a coincidence. I was going to sit next to this guy here—" He patted Kit's back. "—but I guess he won't mind trading. Maybe Thomas Tinker and I will find out how we're related," and he ushered Colleen ahead of him down the stairs and onto the tarmac.

Kit sat across the aisle. Ezra had offered Colleen the window seat, but she let him go in first. The plane lurched a little and now they were rolling down the runway, taxiing past a line of camouflage green and brown military helicopters. Then the plane stopped, took a wide turn and began its headlong rush. Kit closed his eyes and held his breath, waiting for the moment when the rubber wheels would lose contact with the ground and there would be space, free space, between themselves and Guatemala.

The moment came. The plane lifted then dipped, sinking him deep into his seat, before it settled into a steady climb. He let out a groan, which went unheard beneath the high-pitched drone of the engine.

Below them, the helicopters already looked like toys, and then the city appeared briefly as a cluster of lines and indistinct shapes beneath a layer of smog. The conical peaks of the encircling volcanoes loomed closer, revealing their hidden craters. A stream of volcanic smoke blew past the windows and was gone. Soon they were flying over the long, ragged seam that joined land and sea, then all that was visible was small flecks of white and bright bursts of sunlight glancing off the blue ocean. They were clear of Guatemalan airspace.

He turned to look at Colleen. Leaning against the head rest, she turned her face toward his. Her eyes were glazed with exhaustion. Though Ezra was for the moment engrossed in looking out the window, Kit didn't feel any urgency to speak. It was enough just to be sitting an arm's length apart. Colleen turned her head back and closed her eyes. Her long fingers drooped off the end of the arm rest. He would have liked to pick them up and hold them to his cheek. Her chest rose in a deep sigh like the one he had just exhaled. He imagined what he would be thinking now if she hadn't taken this flight. The bloody air of Guatemala would be ventilating the plane, while Ezra, sitting beside him, would have been perfectly oblivious.

He wondered why she had waited, switched her ticket, and taken the next flight even though it was so much riskier for her. Maybe she had been afraid she wouldn't see him again. She wanted to be with him on the way home after surviving the ordeal, wanted to be next to him, shoulders touching. He smiled. And she had ended up instead sitting next to Ezra. He glanced again at her hand on the armrest. She rested it there as if expecting—wishing?—he would put his own out across the aisle and take it.

But Ezra turned from the window just then and began to engage her in conversation, of which Kit, over the engine's roar, only caught her terse replies: "No." "The East." "Visiting for the holiday." Her artificially deepened voice made him think of an old rerun of the "I Love Lucy" show, when Lucy called someone on the phone and tried to impersonate her husband—a comical husky voice that couldn't fool anyone. The scenes of the last ten days seemed to pull back, slip out of focus, and career off the frame like some light, inconsequential experiment from a TV scriptwriter's imagination.

Then he heard Colleen say to Ezra more loudly—unconsciously slipping a little into her own voice, or at least into its fighting tone— "Really? And what is it you think the Lord had in mind with this non-coincidence?" Kit slid his gaze sideways. Ezra had turned to face her with that cheerful, engaging certainty of his. Kit watched her expression while she listened to his long reply. As he spoke, she stared into the back of the seat in front of her, and Kit wondered if she would lash back at Ezra for his inexcusable ignorance, the way she had with him so many times. He watched and waited, but she let Ezra talk on and continued to stare ahead without expression as his effervescent faith bubbled over. People at Light and Life used to joke that if Satan walked into church while Ezra was preaching, he would be in danger of losing his soul to Jesus.

Ezra thrust both his hands at his chest emphatically, smacked the heel of one hand to his forehead, shook his head ruefully, and from these particular gestures Kit recognized which story he was telling. It was his four-phase journey from Christian-in-Name-Only to Born Again, *Again.* The backsliding part he would tell with all the relish of someone reporting a fresh event: The Christian young man that he had been, who nevertheless took a fork in the road that led him away from the Lord and toward the worship of false values. Life in a college town, father often out of work, mother with an eighth grade education; himself a Christian young man at an age to envy what the college boys had—money, sexual license, freedom from family responsibilities; his disastrous experiments with alcohol and the pursuit of females who disdained him; then—then!—that never-to-be-forgotten chance encounter with the sunny, freckle-faced young woman who smiled at him with some inner source of joy—a server at the college cafeteria, all of two years older than he. "She must be a very sophisticated lady!" he had thought, lust in his heart. How she had shamed him and at the same time kindled new hope with her simple words: "All I'm looking for is a good Christian man." This angel, Jeannette, his wife for thirty-six, thirty-seven, thirty-eight ... now forty-one years—didn't care about money or appearance or ambition.

It was the stock sermon on every one of the Tinkers' wedding anniversaries since Kit had joined the church. God had sent Jeannette to open his heart once more so the Holy Spirit could pour back in. Jeannette always liked to say that Ezra had been born again, *again*. Ezra would pause after the first 'again' before exclaiming the second one, and every time he made this joke, the congregation chimed in with the second 'again'.

Kit couldn't read Colleen's expression. She wasn't smiling, she wasn't frowning. All he could tell was that she was listening. Suddenly he unhooked his seat belt and shifted over to the empty window seat. He stared down at the ocean through breaks in the clouds. The unease that had lifted from his chest with the plane's lifting off the tarmac was creeping back. He didn't want to analyze why.

The pilot came on the intercom to point out that the green expanse they were just starting to pass over was Cuba. Cuba again. All those desperate people he had been told about. But what did he really know about Cuba? Nothing.

None of them had anything to declare at customs, but customs officers pawed through their bags anyway, and Kit, just in time to prevent Colleen's seeing it, insinuated his body between her and the red *huipil*, which was held up before being shoved back into the pack. He pictured himself carrying the red garment through every move and life change ahead and cringing every time he packed or unpacked it but unable to think of a respectful way to get rid of it.

As soon as she was through customs, Colleen hurried on ahead of them and disappeared into the men's room. In a few minutes they would be heading toward their respective gates, and there would be no more chance to speak to her. Kit told Ezra he needed to use the restroom.

She was in a stall. He saw her black shoes from the Antigua *mercado* under the door. There was the rustle of pants being unzipped, then a silence. He waited, pretending to study the choices in the condom machine, rummaging through his pockets for coins, until two businessmen finished at the urinal, washed their hands at the sink, picked up their hand luggage and left. When they were finally gone, he called her name.

"Wait outside," she said, "I'll be out in a minute." He hesitated. There was more rustling and another silence.

He went outside and lingered by the doorway, heard a tap turn on then off, paper towels being jerked out of the dispenser. Suddenly, she was by his side, her hands plunged deep in her jacket pockets.

He wanted to take them out and hold them, with only a fleeting thought of how it would look—two males holding hands—but she backed up a step and glanced toward Ezra, who sat in the waiting area looking out the plate glass window at taxiing planes.

"We'd better say good-bye," she said. "I've got twenty minutes to make my connection."

"You're safe now."

"Almost." She looked away from him, impatient to get going, it seemed. He couldn't stand to let her go.

"Colleen, why didn't you take the first flight? This one was so dangerous." *Because I wanted to come back with you, Kit. I didn't want to leave you.*

"The guy never came."

"Who?"

"The guy. Rub."

She had waited for the Peugeot until she felt too conspicuous standing there, and by then the last bus to the city had already gone, so she had to go back and pay for another night in the room and take the 6:00 a.m. bus, risking a checkpoint. But some time before dawn, the guerrillas had blasted a chunk out of the highway in the mountains, and traffic was backed up for miles. Even after the army came and cleared the rubble, passengers had to get out and walk across while the vehicles crept along over that part of the road. The good thing was that it must have distracted them from setting up a routine checkpoint, but by the time she got to the city, the 10:30 plane had already left. Having to pay a penalty to change her ticket left her without enough money to stay another night, so she decided to get on the next plane and hoped she'd be lucky again.

He felt let down and foolish. He had set her up for this fiasco. Rub had been good for only so much.

She looked past him toward the bustle of travelers and porters moving down the corridor. Then she turned back to him. "Listen," she said, lowering her eyes. "I'm so sorry you had to get involved in this whole thing. It was horrible for you. It was my fault. And I couldn't have gotten out of the country without you. ... So ... I'm really grateful to you for that." Then she raised her eyes and looked directly into his. "But why are you still trying to convert me after what we've been through? It almost seems like you *planned* this escape to include your preacher friend." She held up her ticket envelope. "You gave me the same last name as his. Made it look like I'm his son. You wave some kind of free pass and get special treatment. He sits next to me and spends the trip telling me stories about being saved, finding a Christian mate. It's like I had to have some sort of born-again credentials to get out of there alive, and ... I don't know, it just makes me ... kind of sick." She bit her lip and looked away again. "Anyway," she said. "I've got to go."

"Colleen—" He glanced back to where Ezra was waiting. Where to begin?

But she was halfway down the corridor already.

"So," said Ezra, when Kit returned from the restroom. "She's on her way home?"

❖ Twenty-Four ❖

When they arrived late Tuesday, Kit told Ezra and Jeannette he would be moving his things back to his mother's and Dean's. They stood on the Tinkers' front porch. Spring had come early, the air smelled of fresh, damp earth mold after a rain.

Jeannette and Ezra exchanged a look. Ezra said, "Son, you know we're happy to have you living here with us. We want you here."

"I know. Thanks. But ... I guess it would be better if I didn't."

Jeannette touched his sleeve. "Oh, now Kit. Don't you think you should give it a few days? We're just so glad to see you, sweetie. We hate to lose you again so soon. You and Ezra have a lot to talk about."

Ezra stood a little apart, to let Jeannette do her work, Kit thought. And it was hard, seeing the worry in her face, all for him, all for his soul. She did love him for himself, he was sure. So did Ezra. His soul wasn't just any soul.

When he first went back to Claudia's and Dean's, he was glad the house was empty, nobody around to think anything about him. He walked through all the rooms. Everything seemed exceptionally clean and antiseptic, after Guatemala.

His own room had nothing in it of his. When he had moved out, they made it into a guestroom. That was all right. He would only be a guest, and not for long.

He put his things away in the empty drawers—his drawing and painting equipment, his boom box and Christian music tapes, the scrapbook and photo album put together by the Light and Life congregation for his twenty-first birthday, his few clothes, the red *huipil*. He had avoided

THE DE-CONVERSION OF KIT LAMB

looking at it closely after buying it. Now, before putting it out of sight again, he made himself spread it out on the bed.

It was made of four panels sewn together with openings for the arms and neck. For the first time he noticed that two of the panels were woven tightly and evenly, the others looser and more irregular with here and there a slight bulge in the weave or a pulled thread. The embroidered animals, too, and the geometric patterns, were not consistent—some finely stitched, others crudely sewn and trailing loose threads.

It occurred to him that half of the *huipil* had been made by an adult, the other half by a child, probably learning to weave from her mother.

That's straight off someone's back, someone who won't need it anymore.

He picked up the heavy garment and held it to his chest, tears swimming in his eyes. The alien, familiar smell of Guatemala overpowered him—wood smoke, bougainvillea, dust and incense. The guilt was unbearable. He wiped his eyes and laid the *huipil* back on the bed, folded it carefully, and put it away in the drawer.

Later, he went downstairs to the kitchen telephone.

An answer machine voice—not Colleen's—came on, asking him to leave his number at the beep. He hesitated before leaving a message: "Hi, Colleen Tierney—if this is Colleen's number. This is Kit. I hope you got back okay. I just wanted to tell you I've changed where I'm staying." He gave the new phone number and asked her to call him. After he hung up, he sat at the kitchen table for a long time, staring into space. Finally, he picked up the morning paper from the counter and started to scan the help wanted section.

He was lying down in his room when he heard the little girls come storming through the front door, calling his name. They scrambled up the stairs, and as he came out into the hall they threw themselves at him, flinging their arms around his neck when he bent to hug them. He hoisted them up and lugged them into their room, where he peeled them off and set them down on the rug.

He lay on the lower bunk and listened to a Gerald McBoingBoing record while the girls, with manic gestures and shrieks of laughter, mimicked the sound effects. When the record was finished, Lorie climbed the ladder to the top bunk and hung her face over the side, pressing her nose upside down to his. "You're going to live with *us* now, right?"

"For a while," he said.

"For *always*," said Edie, sitting beside him and pulling on his thumb.

Dean looked smaller when he entered the kitchen and set his *New York Times* on the table. "Hi," Kit said, giving him a nod.

"The prodigal son returns," said Dean. "No room at the preacher's inn?"

"Thanks for putting me up," Kit said. "As soon as I start working, I'll get an apartment."

"You checked out rents these days?"

Kit put down the paring knife. "Why?" he said, blandly. "You want me here for good?"

Dean seemed different to him now. What came out of his mouth was so predictable. Not *what* he said, but how he said it—the tone, the rhythm, the gist. Like a TV sitcom character—the grouchy guy at the bar who liked to bring everybody down. You looked forward to the character because you always knew what was coming.

Kit sat down at the table across from him. With a nod at the front section of the *Times*, which Dean had just laid down, he said, "I'll take a look at that if you're through with it."

After dinner he took a shower before heading out to meet Ezra at Light and Life. When he emerged from the bathroom bare-chested, Edie said, "You have a great big yellow spot on your back."

His heart fluttered a little as he turned to look at his back in the mirror. For a moment he felt the impact of the rifle butt crashing against his ribs, his hands thrusting forward to break his fall, the grit of sand on the road.

Kit parked Claudia's Chevy in the lot by the defunct auto supply shop and stood for a quarter of an hour in the shop doorway. Dusty auto parts lay jumbled in the window and yellowed newspapers littered the sidewalk. He watched, out of sight, as the doors of Light and Life opened and the cars pulled away from the church parking lot, all but Ezra's. Then he crossed the street.

The entryway of Light and Life smelled as it did year round, of damp cement covered by aged, all-weather carpeting, and, from the open door to the nursery, the smell of talcum powder. In the sanctuary, extra folding chairs were stacked against the back wall as always. There was the lingering perspiration odor of rapture and repentance.

Ezra was alone on the stage, unaware that Kit was standing at the back. He was running a vacuum cleaner over the carpet. Kit watched him stop to pick up and discard a used Kleenex crumpled at the foot of the wooden cross. He looked up when Kit came down the middle aisle, slowing his pace to hide the agitation that had risen up in him. Ezra turned off the machine. He came to the edge of the stage and stood as if to formally receive him. "Welcome back," he said.

Kit stopped a few feet away. He shrugged. "I don't know if I'm back."

Ezra's body seemed to unstiffen then and grow soft around the edges. He folded himself down onto the step and patted the carpet next to him. "Take a load off, Kit."

"That's all right." He remained standing and planted a foot on the spot Ezra had patted.

"Well," Ezra said, "as you can guess, I've been praying about you."

Kit glanced inadvertently at the wooden cross and it occurred to him that every elder of the church had probably, at Ezra's bidding, just spent the last hour crowded under it, focusing all their powers of concentration on his own obstinate heart opening back up to God.

"My prayers about you have been private," Ezra said, as if having read his mind. "Just between me and our Savior." Ezra had to tilt his head back rather severely to look up into Kit's eyes. Ashamed, Kit lowered himself onto the step. He sat with his elbows on his knees and stared at the back wall of the church. "As always, the Lord has been listening to my prayers and sharing His wisdom with me, Kit, and now I want to talk frankly about some hard truths He's helped me to see." Sweat was trickling down Kit's sides. He wanted to walk back down the aisle and out the door.

"Kit," Ezra said soberly, man-to-man. "I don't deny that your experience of brutality was traumatic. It may haunt you until the day our Savior takes you up in his arms to heaven. But I'm guessing that even before these things happened, you were already looking for an out that would allow you to have sex with that young woman without having to fear God's judgment." He paused. "Am I right?"

Kit felt his hands start to shake. He shoved them in his pockets. Ezra lay a hand on his arm.

"I've been there, son. I remember my own rationalizations when I was your age."

Now Ezra rose and looked down at Kit. "Here's the thing, son. If a born-again president is a murderer, if God is a torturer, then you're off the hook. You can satisfy your desires, like any hedonistic, humanistic, communistic worshipper of Satan. But remember, that the Lord sets us up with these experiences, and He does it for a reason."

Kit thought of himself galloping across town, praying, "Lord, I know you're going to make that bus late, and I know you've put Colleen on it."

If he hadn't caught that bus, what would have happened? His memory would never have been etched with the indelible sight of the hanging man, the woman dragged by her hair, the room with the dog, the temptation of Colleen pressed against him in the ocean waves. Had all of these experiences been given him for a reason personal only to him? But whether or not he had gotten on that bus, the six people would still have been hauled away, the old man struck down, his son tortured to death. And if he hadn't gotten on, the army would have caught Colleen.

"God can hammer us very hard to get our attention," Ezra was saying.

Kit shook his head. "Then why does someone else end up getting the hammer if it was meant for me?"

"Only God can answer that question."

Kit was drenched in sweat, but he was freezing. It was cold in the church. Ezra would have frugally turned the heat off after prayer service. He crossed his arms over his chest and tucked his hands in his armpits.

"God has given us the ability to come up with logical, plausible-sounding rationales for anything we want to do. Satan just provides the ideas."

"How do you know you aren't fooling *yourself* if we all have the ability to come up with rationales that sound logical and plausible?" Kit drew himself up straight, but the sullenness he couldn't keep out of his voice disgusted him. He wasn't, after all, a sixteen-year-old anymore.

"The difference is that I'm not telling you a bunch of stuff that Ezra Tinker has thought up. I'm passing on what's right there in Scripture, what God Himself has said." He seemed tired of standing then and walked over to a front row chair and sat down. There was a significant distance between them now.

"It's tempting to believe it just comes down to one person's logic vs. another's." Ezra sat back and crossed his ankle over his knee. "For example, you think the Guatemalan government is made up of vicious, deceitful men. But I saw concerned, upright men working for a government that's dedicated to ministering to its people through Biblical outreach. Criticizing the government or the military isn't going to make you friends anywhere in the world. Yet, *Señor* Reina stood up for you. He took a risk even though you did nothing to hide your contempt."

It was true. It had been a risk to be associated with him. *Señor* Martinez, a school principal with no involvement in politics, had taken a beating just for not knowing the answers to questions about him.

"Why did *Señor* Reina encourage you to report what you saw? Because he knew that as tough as that colonel was, he would want to know the truth and because you needed the burden of responsibility lifted off your heart."

"Reina knew all those hotshots personally. He could call up Ríos Montt's office, the U.S. Embassy, a high-ranking army officer. What does that tell you about him?" Kit said, the sullenness creeping back in spite of himself.

"It tells me he is a well-respected man." Kit looked away from Ezra, refusing to meet his eyes. "Come on, Kit. He helped you report a case of abuse by his own government. And no one said, 'Don't report it in the U.S.' They didn't prevent you from leaving. They helped you get home."

"Why not? If I do report it now, they'll have their stories straight."

"Wait for the outcome of their investigation before you judge." Kit gave a dismissive snort.

Ezra got up from the chair and came over to sit down next to Kit again. "You know, when I called *Señor* Reina, and he was so receptive and generous with his time, I told him that this was really the first you'd seen of the wider world, and it would be easy for you to be influenced not only by what you'd seen but how it got interpreted for you, maybe by this young woman you'd been with, along with some so-called CIA guy at your school—" Kit felt his face getting hot. "—acting like he had some inside story and badmouthing the president." *Don't talk about politics to anyone* ... "How would a naïve, impressionable young guy be able to distinguish these influences from the truth?"

Ezra's words came suddenly into sharper focus. "What?" Kit said. He gripped the edge of the step. The hairs rose on his arms. "*What* did you tell Reina?"

"Now, Kit, I didn't call you 'naïve' to put you down. It's part of being young, and in some respects it's—"

"You told him I was influenced by a CIA guy at my school who'd badmouthed the government? You said that? Those words?"

"Something like that. I don't remember the exact words—"

Kit stood up abruptly. "That was on Monday morning? Before you came to my school?"

Ezra stood, too. "What's concerning you, son?"

Kit swallowed hard. For several seconds he stood there, staring at the clock at the back of the church. It was 8:30 Wednesday night. *Everyone knows if someone doesn't get you out in the first hours, you'll probably be dead. And if you survive the first day ... you may not want to live anymore.*

He didn't know the phone number at *Casa Fuego*, and no one would be at the school office until morning. His teeth were chattering. He said, "I have to make some calls to Guatemala right now. I'll pay you back as soon as I have the money." He ran up the aisle into the church office. Ezra followed him in.

"Now, Kit, son—"

"How do I do it? Is there an area code? How do you get information—"

"Calm down there a minute, son. You want to take a breath."

Kit ran around the desk, drew open the side drawer where the phone book was kept and began shuffling through the pages. "Goddamn it—how do you make an international call?"

Ezra silently took the book and found the section for him. Kit, mis-dialing twice, followed the directions, cursing until he got the ring. An operator answered in Spanish and then in English. Kit asked for the phone number of Charles Nystrom in Antigua. There was a long wait. Had he been disconnected? Then the operator came back on and told him she couldn't find such a listing.

Kit gripped the phone tightly, almost shouting, "I know he has a telephone!"

"I'm sorry, there is no listing."

Phil and Rita's number at *Casa Fuego* was not listed either

"It's an emergency."

"I'm sorry."

He asked for the number of the school, and after some seconds she came back with it. He direct dialed it and let it ring and ring before he hung up.

Ezra said, "What's happening, son?"

Kit stared at his hand on the receiver. "I don't know who to call," he said to himself. "Who can I call?" He dialed the operator again and got a number for the *Hotel Los Conquistadores*.

Ezra said, "Kit, this could get pretty expensive. Maybe—"

"Por favor, yo quiero hablar con el encargado, el señor Daniel Mei-jia. Estoy llamando desde los Estados Unidos, me llamo Kit Lamb," he said. The operator said, *"Un momentito."* There was a long wait, then Daniel's voice.

"Es Daniel Meijia…"

"Daniel, it's Kit Lamb. I'm calling from the United States—"

"¡Hermano Cristóbal! ¿Como estás?"

"Daniel, do you know the people who own *Instituto de Español Tres Américas*—Phil and Rita?"

"Yes, sure! I know them. They came here last week with their friends."

"Do you know how I could get their telephone number? It's not listed."

"Mm. No. I don't know—"

"Or … do you know a guy from the States, his name is Chuck Nystrom? He's a student at the school. He calls himself 'Rub'?"

There was a silence on the other end. Then, "No, no. I don't know him. I don't know anything about him. I'm sorry, now I don't talk anymore. We are very busy here tonight. *Adiós.*" There was a click. He was gone. Kit replaced the receiver and sat down again. He looked up at Ezra bleakly.

"What's going on, son?"

Kit shook his head, got up again and made for the door. "I'll pay the church for the phone calls," he said.

At home Kit dialed Colleen's number and left another message.

"Colleen, if you get this," he said, "I need to talk to you. About the guy who didn't show up Monday night. Please call."

All night he dreamt of being unable to get to the phone. The phone was in the bathroom and Dean was taking a shower with the door locked. Or Rub was on the phone and Kit was yelling to him to get off, get off, I have to call you. Or next to the phone a room with a partly open door, a bleeding hand sticking out holding a dark blue passport, someone shouting, '*Amigo,* for Christ sake, take the goddamn passport! He doesn't need it anymore!'

He got up early and waited until everyone left the house. He took the number for *Tres Américas* out of his jeans pocket and dialed. No answer. He sat in the hall with the phone book on his lap and mindlessly blacked in the zeros in the 800 numbers. He tried again.

It was 8:25 when Rita finally answered.

"Hi," he said. His throat was dry and his tongue clicked off the top of his mouth. "It's Kit Lamb."

"Oh," she said. Then she repeated his name. She sounded distant, distracted.

"I wanted to know if—"

"Good morning, Kit." She had put Phil on. "What can we do for you?"

Kit took a breath. "I was wondering, about Rub, Chuck Nystrom."

Phil didn't answer, and the silence hung there.

Kit could hear his own heart beating. "I— Is he— I mean … Have you seen him?"

"Well," Phil sounded slightly embarrassed. "Unfortunately, I have."

"Where is he?"

"It's a very great shame, but if you remember his rather undisciplined 'lifestyle,' as you Americans call it, it won't seem surprising."

"What?"

"He died in his *pensión* sometime during the weekend. Overdosed."

"Overdosed?"

"He didn't show up for school on Monday, which wasn't particularly worrying—you know how he was. We assumed he was sleeping off a weekend bender or on some junket or other. But his landlord contacted the authorities—a smell coming from his room, that sort of unpleasantness—and they asked me to come 'round and identify him. It was what you'd expect—a junkie's pigsty—broken bottles, drug paraphernalia all over the floor—syringes, used needles and so forth." *No*, Kit thought. "He'd been dead since the weekend. Saturday or Sunday. Most probably an overdose of heroin combined with alcohol. Accidental. If you can call that kind of thing accidental. Underneath all that bravado, he was rather a morose sort of fellow." Kit heard Phil take a sip of coffee.

"Rub *was* at school on Monday," Kit said evenly.

"Pardon me?"

"I saw him there."

"You weren't at school on Monday. You left with your pastor friend."

"I went to school first. I saw him. I talked to him."

"Did you?" Phil paused. "That's odd. Well. I suppose these *chapín* police don't have a lot of—what do they call it—forensic experience? … Well, what a pity. If we'd checked on him on Monday afternoon, we might have been able to do something for him. At any rate, it's too late now." He cleared his throat. "Was there some reason you called to ask about him?"

"What happened to him—his body?" Kit said.

"I believe the Embassy's taken charge until they can contact a next of kin."

"Who is his next of kin?"

"No clue."

"I had to put an emergency contact number on my application to the school. Who did he put?"

"Oh Lord, he's been coming here off and on for so long, I don't think we even have an application form for him anymore. Do we, Rita? No, I didn't think so. To be honest, I doubt if he has relatives. Never heard him talk of any." There was another pause. Kit could think of nothing more to ask. "Sorry to have to break such grim news, but you didn't know him well, I take it?" There was the faintest hint of anxiety in Phil's voice.

"No."

"Right, then. Well, this call is costing you. I'll ring off." There was a click and the dial tone sounded in his ears with harsh finality. He hung up and sat there in the hallway staring ahead. He thought of the Peugeot, parked inside the gate of the *pensión* and Rub's passing his hand over it affectionately. Rub's next of kin.

It could be true. He said this aloud several times. Overdosed. Offed himself with drugs and alcohol and died quickly and quietly in a wasted stupor. But of course he hadn't. What had really happened was too horrible to think about.

He ran downstairs, grabbed the keys to the Chevy, and drove it out to the dirt roads above the water treatment plant, where he could work up a sweat running up and down the hills. He ran as hard as he could, but his muscles felt weak and he had no breath. Sickening images pursued him—Rub strapped down. Struggling. Screaming. Needles.

His breathing became short and his calves and thighs were burning. He stopped at the edge of the bluff looking out across the railroad tracks and the waterworks park below.

A junkie's pigsty. He was seeing Rub's tidy room, how he had set his skin magazine on the bed table just so, like a fussy spinster in a movie, the bed turned down as if he had maid service. He saw Rub on the balcony at Panajachel, how he had tipped back his head for the last drops in the bottle. *'Last time before I had to go up to El Petén, they tried to snag me for a yellow fever shot, I says, screw that. I don't do needles. I can't even watch someone else take a needle.'*

Was even one part of Phil's story true? Was Rub even dead?

They would have come for him as soon as he walked in his door—the Tupperware party guests—early, waiting for him. Helping themselves to the party favors and then dragging the host off to another venue where they could let him make all the noise he wanted. Dumping him back at his apartment in the middle of the night when it was all over. If this is how it went, then let it all be over.

Rub had to have held out at least until 12:30 the next day, Tuesday, when he and Colleen both were out of Guatemalan air space. Maybe just to be safe he'd held out until the second plane would have landed in New Orleans, because a plane could be made to turn around if someone higher up got on a telephone and gave a command.

Maybe Rub himself had been the consultant who taught them where on the body a needle could be put to most effective and discreet use.

A long freight train rattled slowly over the tracks below. Even high on the bluffs he could feel the vibration coming up through the ground. He wrapped his arms around his knees and rocked back and forth. Twenty-seven hours. For the sake of what? Gratitude. The gratitude of a homely, loveless guy who treasured a drawing that proved one person in the world actually saw him.

Oh Christ. If he knew that the babe-in-the-woods, his *amigo*, the artist, had given him up to a deluded Bible-believing preacher ... All at once it dawned on him, what had allowed Reina to take up the cause of a kid suspected of fraternizing with a subversive. Reina had traded him for Rub. Rub, the loose cannon that everyone was beginning to want out of the way.

Reina had known that getting Kit to report at the National Palace would discourage him from reporting the abuse back home to the press. And if he didn't stop army goons from yanking two U.S. evangelicals from the airport and murdering them in a room somewhere, there would be hell to pay among Reagan's Christian supporters. Oh yes. Reina was a well-respected man.

But what if Rub were alive and still being held somewhere, like Colleen's brother had been? Kit drove home as fast as he could.

He called the public library for the phone numbers of his senators and congressman. Having dialed the first number, he hung up on the second ring. He needed to get himself together. He needed to use the tone of an adult. He *was* an adult.

After twenty minutes of rehearsing—all the while feeling the urgency of getting on with it when even five minutes delay could be the last five minutes of a person's struggle to stay alive—he made the call. He remembered, as he listened to the ring, that Colleen told him the National Palace had been in direct contact by phone with the military outpost that had held her brother. One phone call—that's all it would take to stop whatever was being done to Rub, if it still was.

The congressman was out of Washington and would not be back until the end of the week. The senator was in committee meetings all day and would be on the floor tomorrow for an early morning vote. The other senator was gone from the office, too. But his aide was talkative and sympathetic. "Did you say this guy is a constituent? Where's he from?" Kit had no idea where Rub was from. "You might try your governor's office."

The governor's office told Kit to call his congressman.

It finally occurred to him to call the State Department. The same patient librarian looked it up for him.

He held the line as he was shuffled from one office to another, until at last he was connected with an assistant to the undersecretary for Inter American Affairs, who said she would contact the U.S. Embassy in Guatemala and make enquiries. If she could get hold of someone with information, she would call Kit back today.

The U.S. Embassy. Full circle. He pictured the prim man in the bow tie—Harold or Howard—taking the call: *Yes, we know of that young man. He's already made one false accusation.*

Kit waited. He opened the newspaper. He scanned the help wanted ads.

When the phone rang under his hand, he forgot the calls to the governor, the congressman, the senators. He thought—he was sure—it was going to be Colleen.

It was the woman from the State Department. "Mr. Lamb, the U.S. Embassy in Guatemala City has confirmed Mr. Nystrom's death. He died at his home of heart failure."

"When?"

"It says 'Sunday, April 3. There was no reason to suspect foul play. The Embassy has charge of his remains, and they'll be following the usual procedures for contacting next of kin. You aren't a relative of his, are you?"

"Yes," he said. "I'm his brother."

There was a moment's pause as she placed her hand over the phone and consulted someone. "In fact, Mr. Lamb," the woman came on again, "we know that Mr. Nystrom has no living immediate relations." She thanked him for his concern and hung up.

Not an overdose. Heart failure. They could at least have gotten their stories straight.

He got up and went into the girls' room. Taking Edie's mangled, grimy bear off her pillow, he lowered himself onto her small bunk and lay back, one knee up, one foot on the floor, the bear on his chest.

Whatever you do, you end up betraying someone.

It seemed that he would jump out of his skin if he couldn't talk to her. Of course he couldn't tell her what had become of Rub; that would be laying it right at her door, and that particular guilt was his own burden to carry.

Maybe what happened to Rub had been a kind of atonement for all the things Rub himself had done to other people—secret, evil things so bad he had to talk about them in euphemisms—was that the word? His job as a 'hands on Ann Landers,' giving his 'off the record advice' to the army in Vietnam on how to get someone 'mighty communicative.' There must be a lot of people who would have liked to be there to watch Rub get what was coming to him.

But how was one more cruel death an atonement? Had anyone atoned for whatever cruelty had sent Rub on his solitary, unprincipled journey? Maybe Rub himself, through his act of gratitude, had been trying to atone.

❖ Twenty-Five ❖

On Friday, he found a job clerking at a copy center, with the possibility of moving into graphic arts designing if the business expanded. The job would start in a week.

That day he called Colleen's message machine again, growing more convinced that he had memorized the number wrong. He checked the area code he had been dialing for Colleen and found it was for Boston. At the public library, he found thirteen Tierneys in the Boston phone book. None of the numbers matched the one she had given him.

Next morning, daylight seeped under the blinds, releasing him from a succession of exhausting flights from clutching, choking menace. Ezra had asked him to come over to the house on Sunday afternoon for another talk. They stood together at the picture window, watching Jeannette putter about in the yard with her trowel and basket.

"You were right to help that young woman," Ezra said. "Neither of you young people may realize it now, but it was a kind of ministering you did that's going to stay with her. It was a serious business. The authorities would have been tough on her."

"*Tough* on her!" Kit turned from the window. "Don't you have any idea what these god-fearing Christians would have done to her if they'd caught her? *What's* going to stay with her, Ezra—the sermon you gave her on the plane? That's what you think she got out of all this? Turn to Jesus through the love of a good Christian boy like Kit Lamb?"

"I forgive you for your anger toward me, son. I understand where it's coming from."

"No, you don't. You don't have any idea. If you did—" He stopped himself. What excuse was there for either one of them? He remembered now who told him he didn't believe in nonsense just because it was reassuring nonsense. It was Rub.

He put a hand on Ezra's shoulder. "Ezra. Our never being willing to question what we believe—it's caused terrible harm. To poor people in Guatemala. Maybe in other countries, too—I don't know, I'm ignorant." He walked over to the coffee table and picked up the Tinkers' big family Bible. "This Bible says that God is a torturer. There's no getting around that. You can rationalize it and excuse it every which way and say He gives people all the chances in the world to repent, and He laments and sighs when souls are lost, but the fact remains that this book—" he shook it "—tells us that God in his infinite mercy throws people into a lake of fire for eternity.

"I have no problem—" he opened the book and started flipping through pages of the New Testament "—with *'walk in love as Christ also hath loved us'*—where is that? I don't know—Ephesians somewhere. Or *'thou shalt love thy neighbor as thyself'* or *'do unto others as you would be done by'* or *'you who are without sin cast the first stone,'* even *'love your enemies.'* I believe all that. But—"

"But nothing!" Ezra stood up and took the Bible away from him. "You can not choose which of God's words to accept and which ones to throw out! 'I'll take these pages and these—' " He pantomimed ripping out leaves and flinging them into the air.

Kit shook his head. "No book can make me believe that a god who's capable of creating everything, every cell in our bodies, every star in the universe, is a being made in the image of a selfish, sadistic, tyrannical dictator who demands obedience just to show how powerful he is—"

"Without fear of God's wrath, people will do whatever they want, with no regard for anyone but themselves—"

"That's not true. Colleen's brother—" It startled him, made him feel even a little fearful to hear himself finally say her name to Ezra. He paused a moment and then said, more quietly, "Her brother was horribly tortured by the army in Guatemala for his work with poor *campesinos.* He always knew he was in danger, but he did it anyway. He was a Catholic priest. Colleen took up the work for his sake because he was so shattered.

And she didn't do it for fame or from ego. She did it from compassion. She was scared the whole time, but she did it anyway. She's an atheist. Where do you think *her* conscience comes from if—"

"I don't know what her motives were, Kit, and neither do you. What I saw on the plane was a cold, unyielding young woman with a chip on her shoulder exactly like the one *you* had before you let Jesus into your heart. Do you forget that you were throwing rocks through church windows, you'd thrown your conscience by the wayside, your heart was hardened against love?"

"You think I didn't have a conscience before that? You think I was hardened against love?" Kit glared at Ezra furiously. "I loved my little sisters more than myself. I loved them way before I loved God. I would have jumped off a cliff for them if I'd had to."

Ezra held out his hands, appealing. "But Kit, how are we able to love and feel compassion? How are we able to *have* a conscience?"

"I don't know."

Ezra smiled gently. "From God through Jesus Christ. Where else?"

"I don't know."

"You see? Conscience and compassion are proofs of God's love."

"No, Ezra. I'm saying I *don't know*. Not knowing isn't proof."

Ezra let his hands fall to his sides. "How do you think non-believers make sense out of all the tragedies and traumas in this life? How do they cope with them?"

"Probably they don't make sense of them. Maybe they just have the courage to accept that they don't know." He took a breath, held it a moment, then said it: "The man who helped Colleen get out of the country was murdered by a government death squad. Because you had too much faith in faith and I had too much faith in you."

"Oh, now Kit, come on." Ezra eased himself down onto his oversized recliner and sat there shaking his head, his hands resting in his lap.

Sad and close to tears, Kit sat down across from Ezra on the piano bench, where he had sat next to Jeannette so many evenings for the past five years singing old-time hymns together. Ezra would lie in the recliner with his eyes closed and sing along, one finger tapping out the rhythm on the padded chair arm, always that tap tap tap of the finger a little off the beat.

Kit sighed heavily. "I guess I won't be welcome at Light and Life anymore," he said.

Ezra leaned toward him. "Son, of course you'll be welcome at Light and Life. You should know that by now. Every single person who walks through that door, be he an atheist, a humanist, a fornicator, even a sodomite is welcomed. There's no one so deep in sin that we would deny him the chance to listen to the Master's Word." He frowned regretfully. "Right now, while you keep denying Scripture, we trust that you won't take communion with us or sing in the choir, but—"

"Yeah, I expected to be kicked out of the choir—"

"Because a choir is a special kind of ministry, not just for the enjoyment of singing." Kit gazed out the window again at Jeannette, who was kneeling now by her crocuses. Ezra said, "There will be a place for you the moment you welcome God back into your heart."

"Have I put God out of my heart?"

"When you deny one word of Scripture, you deny Him."

"I don't know if I'm denying God, but I think only human beings could have come up with an idea as sadistic as hell."

Ezra put his hands on his knees and stood up then, as if an interview had just been concluded. "Well, son," he said, "we hope we'll keep seeing you in church. You're always welcome there. We love you even as Christ loves the straying lamb. I hope you'll continue to pray." It was a dismissal.

When Kit walked down the sidewalk, Jeannette sat back on her haunches, shading her eyes against the sun, and gave him one of her heart-melting smiles. "Come back," she said.

He woke late on Sunday, wondering why Jeannette hadn't called down the basement stairs to get him up for church. Then he realized where he was. Was Jeannette missing that ritual, too? And their drinking coffee together while Ezra sat alone in the living room praying over his sermon before the three of them squeezed into Jeannette's Gremlin and headed for Light and Life?

On Monday, he was home alone when the envelope came by registered mail—"Official business of the U. S. State Department." It had come to

Ezra's address first and been redirected to Dean's because Kit himself had to sign for it. Inside was a letter with several attachments.

> *Dear Mr. Lamb,*
>
> *This is to inform you that an investigation was undertaken and has been completed regarding a report made by you to a representative of the U.S. Embassy in Guatemala City on April 5, 1983. In your report you complained of abuses by members of the Guatemalan army, which alleged abuses took place on March 26, 1983.*
>
> *Your complaints were as follows:*
>
> *1) That on March 26 at an army checkpoint between the towns of Escuintla and Puerto San José, members of the military removed several people from a bus; that one of those was a pregnant woman, who was dragged into a military vehicle by her hair.*
>
> *2) That on the same day, in Puerto San José, members of the military struck you in the back with a rifle butt and in the face with a fist, after which you were bound and taken to a nearby army base, where you were searched in a degrading and threatening manner.*
>
> *3) That while in custody, you witnessed a wounded man suspended by his wrists from a pole on the parade ground.*
>
> *4) That an officer who interrogated you remarked that the man had been hung there as an "example."*
>
> *5) That while in custody you saw an elderly man struck with a rifle butt on the head by a soldier and dragged away, unconscious.*
>
> *6) That although these events occurred on Saturday, March 26, you did not report them until Tuesday, April 5 because you feared retaliation by the authorities.*
>
> *The United States State Department takes any allegation of abuse of a U.S. citizen as a very serious matter and is also concerned that the Guatemalan government, as recipient of*

U.S. assistance, be held accountable for any instances of human rights abuses against its own citizens.

Attached please find copies of a detailed report and affidavits from an investigation carried out by the Military Commander of the Department of Escuintla. Taking your complaints one by one, the report, in summary, says the following:

1) At an authorized checkpoint on the Escuintla highway, six suspected terrorists were taken off a bus and arrested on March 26th. None of them was female. The bus driver, who witnessed the arrest, corroborated this fact and further stated that all the suspects were treated humanely. (See transcript of his statement, attached.)

2) The colonel of the San José army post verifies that you were detained there on the 26th because you had been seen with a woman suspected of having ties with the guerrilla army. A detention and interrogation are routine in such cases, given the State of Seige. The rough handling you reported was not routine. The soldiers who brought you in were young, inexperienced recent recruits, who may have gone beyond the behavioral restraints required by the army's military code of conduct. Such behavior by a soldier is considered unacceptable and dishonorable. The men involved will be reprimanded and made subject to military disciplinary measures.

3) and 4) What you took to be a hanging man on the parade ground was a dummy used for target exercises. The officer, in answer to your question, believes that you mistook the word "ejército," which means "army," for "ejemplo," which means "example."

5) A distraught man, demanding information about a missing relative, forced his way onto the military base, created a disturbance, and after a scuffle during which he fell, was escorted off the base.

6) The willingness of highly situated officials of the Guatemalan military and government to hear your complaints and investigate them promptly suggests that your fear of retaliation was unfounded.

The U.S. Embassy in Guatemala has stated that it is satis-fied with the results of the investigation and is confident that where army misconduct occurred, the perpetrators will be appropriately disciplined to prevent its happening again.

I direct you to the enclosed documents for more detailed ac-counts of the findings. Please do not hesitate to contact this office if you have further questions or concerns.

He had given his statement on Tuesday. The latest they could have sent the report for him to receive it today, Monday, was Saturday. So how thorough an investigation could have been made in four days? The documents must have been manufactured and dictated at the National Palace and handed on to the Embassy with no questions asked.

He saw immediately how Ezra would interpret it—that it was Kit who had lied, or had misperceived the situation. He wouldn't question the speed of the response, he would be impressed. "See, Kit, they got right on it!"

After everyone had left the house on Tuesday morning, he wandered into the living room and picked up Dean's paper, which lay face down on the floor. Turning it over, he felt disoriented seeing spread across the front page the photographs under the headline '*Rights Abuses Threaten Aid.*' The caption beneath the photo said, '*Mayan woman arrested by Guatemalan soldiers.*' He clutched the paper in both hands.

There it was, in a series of four full-color pictures, starting with the woman's hands being bound behind her and ending with the soldier dragging her up and across the tailgate of the truck. The details were clear and in focus—the furrow of pain drawing her brows together, the upper lip raised in a grimace of agony, her pregnant belly protruding beneath her sash, the indifference on the faces of the soldiers who were dragging her, the smirks on the faces of the others who stood by with automatic rifles pointed.

There it was: the event that, according to the U.S. State Department, had never happened.

A sob rose up in his throat. Colleen's zoom lens had captured even the incongruous spot of beauty in the scene—the brilliant red, blue and yellow of the woman's *huipil* and the red ribbon woven into her thick dark braid.

He sat on the edge of the couch with the page in his hand and began to shake. Now the woman seemed more real to him than she had even while he watched her through the bus window.

That morning she had gotten up and braided the ribbon into her hair. While she sat drowsing in the heat of the bus, she may have felt her baby kicking inside her.

He dropped the page onto his lap. He was crying now. As he closed his eyes, the pregnant woman became the woman hunched in the doorway holding up the red *huipil*— *Diez quetzales. Está bien*—she became Colleen at the *mercado* buying men's shoes, her hair shaved to her scalp, the catch in her voice—*¿Cuánto cuesta?*

He thought of her carrying around that perilous, precious cylinder of film on her body—*inside her body*—*knowing*, always knowing what would happen if they found it. She could have thrown away the film at any time.

He looked again at the photographs and tried to read the article, but couldn't see the words. He folded the paper, grabbed his jacket, and took the car from the garage.

Kids would have claimed the place by now. A few houses had gone up along the road since he had been there five years ago. He parked at the top of the slope, which didn't seem nearly as steep as it once had. The tracks were overgrown and neglected; the line must have been discontinued since that night when he wakened to a headlight beam and the rumbling of a train approaching his confused, messed up head.

His own graffiti had been painted over and new graffiti taken its place. 'Leo smokes weed.' 'Supertramp sucks.' Broken beer bottles, cigarette butts, and condoms littered the ground. A dirty blanket lay rumpled in the weeds.

He kicked away debris to clear a spot and sat down. Right away he noticed the silence. Before, there had always been the swooping wing beats of the cliff swallows, their single melodious notes, and the call of the baby birds from inside the crusted mud nests attached high up to the undersides of the overpass. He looked for them now and saw that the mud nests—what was left of them—lay shattered on the tracks. The concrete where the nests had been was pockmarked with holes. Scattered everywhere among remnants of nests were the remains of dead birds. He saw what had happened. Boys had been coming down here to shoot at the birds with BB guns—he could imagine their triumphal prancing and their profane shouts as their targets dropped from the air—and had finally driven the remainder of them away permanently.

He went down to the track to look at the dead birds. They were mostly skeletal—the shootings had happened a while ago—but a few of the bodies were still intact. On these the feathers retained that prismatic sheen that gave even the most common birds a surprising glory when you had a chance to see them up close. Here and there were soft tufts of deep red-orange and white and a shimmering blue among the subtler shades of brown in the long, fanned-out wing feathers.

He picked up one feather of each color and tucked them gently in the breast pocket of his jacket. Then, still standing on the tracks, he removed the folded newspaper and read the article.

Rights Abuses Threaten U.S. Aid

Citing continuing abuses by the Guatemalan army under the government of General Efraín Ríos Montt, human rights groups were calling on Congress and the Reagan administration to suspend military sales to Guatemala. The demand comes during a critical week as Congress challenges President Reagan's foreign and defense policies, particularly with respect to Central America ...

A member of the Latin American subcommittee of the House Foreign Affairs committee said it would recommend reinstating the embargo on military aid that President Reagan had convinced them to end. There was mention of the six men executed despite the Pope's request for clemency and of the recent killing of a U.S.A.I.D. worker by Guatemalan troops, which the Guatemalan government had failed to investigate.

> ...It was suggested that these incidents, coming close on the impending re-evaluation of U.S. Central American policies, have accounted for Ríos Montt's releasing an unusual public message last month considering his past denial of government-sponsored rights abuses: "We know we have sinned, that we have abused power, and we want to reconcile ourselves with the people." To this end, he announced an amnesty to leftist guerrillas and was replacing a 'State of Seige' with a 'State of Alert-A.' An earlier amnesty was seen by critics as a ruse for identifying insurgents and was not taken seriously by them.

On an inside page where the story continued, Kit found another photo. *Impoverished Mayans sleep on a sidewalk in Antigua, Guatemala.* It took him back four months to the night in the *parque central* when he imagined Colleen's face tilted to receive his kiss and was startled out of his fantasy by the flash of her camera. He cringed now, remembering how he had interpreted her secretiveness.

On the inside page the name Tierney caught his eye.

> Religious and human rights leaders testifying before the sub-committee yesterday gave accounts of torture, murders, and disappearances of thousands of indigenous Mayans and others by the Guatemalan military, who, according to eyewitness reports, commit atrocities with impunity despite Ríos Montt's claim to uphold high standards of military conduct. Father Thomas Tierney, a Catholic priest from Massachusetts, who had been working on literacy and land reform projects among impoverished Mayan campesinos in the Western Highlands, described his April, 1982 abduction along with four Guatemalan villagers he was escorting to a clinic.

It was the same story he had heard from Colleen.

> ... Tierney stated that an official complaint to the Guatemalan

government by the U.S. State Department was met with denials and contradictory statements, one suggesting that the group had been abducted by guerrillas dressed in army uniforms, despite Tierney's assertion that he knew his abductors by name and that his release had been obtained by a direct call from the National Palace.

The article went on to talk about the extreme poverty of the Mayan Indian population, the inequitable distribution of land, and the violence with which efforts to reform the system were met. The photos weren't credited.

He put the folded paper back into his jacket pocket. Outside of the deep shade of the overpass, blades of greening grass and weeds gleamed in the southern sun. He thought of the fourteen-year-old self who had scrawled obscene grafitti on the concrete wall and shouted unheard, ineffectual curses.

When had he started thinking of himself as a tall, reserved adult instead of a furious red-faced child, boxing like a cartoon character at an enemy who held him up by the scruff of his neck just out of reach? This old image of himself had never been accurate, he realized. The sanctuary was proof. Here, he had protected himself without having to blow off the heads of birds with a BB gun.

He had broken some windows, yes. But then before things got out of hand, he had had the sense to accept the first real love that was offered him. Of course they had wanted to save his soul, but Ezra and Jeannette were grieving for him just as if one of their own children were dying. He hated putting them through that grief.

On Wednesday he scanned the paper avidly for news about the committee hearings. By accident he spotted the one-paragraph notice on the *Times* obituary page.

Civilian Consultant Dies in Guatemala
The U.S. State Department reported the death on April 3 of Charles M. Nystrom, 46, from an apparent heart attack. His remains were cremated and will be buried at Antigua, Guate-

mala, where he had spent the last five years of his life as a civilian consultant on national security affairs for the Republic of Guatemala. A U.S. citizen and former member of the U.S. Army Special Forces, Mr. Nystrom had previously served his country in Vietnam. He leaves no family.

The use of the word 'civilian' twice in one brief paragraph struck him. They might as well have just come out and said, okay, so the guy was a CIA torture instructor, but officially there aren't any there.

Kit cut out the notice with the kitchen scissors. He walked out the back door with it and wandered down to the garden plot, already tilled into straight, tidy rows of fine dirt. What had they done with Rub's things, he wondered. The bullet necklace that hung from the handle of his wardrobe, the portrait inside the door. But it was really only Kit's drawing pencil that had seen Rub. The man—brutal and depraved, yet redeeming himself through this unexplainable sacrifice—was still a mystery.

Thursday afternoon Jeannette called to say there had been a message for him on their answering machine—a young woman's voice. She gave Kit the number to call. It was not the number he had been dialing. A machine answered, but as soon as he began to talk, she picked up.

"Kit!" Her voice made him short of breath.

"Colleen." He was shaking. He sat down and tried to think of anything he could say that would do justice to the occasion. "I read the news," he said. "Man!"

"I know. They listened." She sounded weepy. "Tom testified. Did you read that?"

"Yeah, I did. Wow." So much for eloquence.

"He went ahead and testified. He didn't think he could. And afterwards—he was kind of like his old self again." Her voice started to wobble, "Kit ..." then dissolved in sobs.

This cold hard telephone receiver. He shut his eyes. "I love you so much," he said.

When she could speak again, she said, "Kit, I'm sorry I didn't give you my real phone number. I was just never sure about you. But ... whatever you had in mind when you helped me get away, it doesn't matter. Without you—"

"Come on—"

"No, listen. All those men in suits—they sat around that table the whole morning just deadpan. Even when Tom told them what happened to him, even while they were reading his doctors' notes about his injuries, and throughout all the other testimonies, statistics—God! It was stuff that should have had them up on their feet, pissed off, howling—they just sat there with these pursed-up looks on their faces like *I don't want anyone to think I would cave in to emotional appeals.* But—you should have seen it!—when those pictures got passed around the table, one by one those poses dropped, they started frowning and their mouths got tense, and—it was like *their* daughter being dragged away. *We're letting this go on.* Oh, Kit, I saw it in their faces!

"There'd been thousands and thousands of words. But those pictures were what finally—" She paused. "I feel guilty for being so happy."

"Yeah, I know."

"We're here celebrating, while—"

Dean came on the line then. "Do you think you could relinquish my phone in my lifetime? I'm expecting a call," he said, and clicked off.

"Who was that, your pastor?"

"My evil stepfather."

He didn't want to let her go. "Oh man. It's ... your voice," he said. "Talk to me. Tell me something."

"What?"

"Anything."

She laughed. "I thought about something your preacher said on the plane. Before they were married, his wife told him all she wanted was a good Christian man."

His heart suddenly rapped out an extra couple of beats. He waited, scared.

"I thought about it a lot on the trip to Washington, and it hit me that all I wanted was a man who, right before he thought he was going to be tortured, would sit down and draw a picture of a little sleeping dog."

Could she sense the sudden lifting of the thing that had been sitting inside his chest and compressing his heart for so many days? The memory of himself that he fled from every time he caught sight of his own naked body in a mirror, every time he brushed his teeth or used the toilet or saw someone tapping a pencil or noticed a shirt or a robe hanging from a hook?

"Maybe I wasn't the one whose hand did the drawing." He couldn't stop himself from saying it. He waited for the inevitable hostility and withdrawal.

She just said, "All I know is your hand held the pencil. I don't care where the inspiration came from."

That evening he drove over to Light and Life with the *New York Times* clippings and the State Department report in hand. At 8:00, choir practice was almost over. He took a seat at the back of the church and let the song wash over him—a hymn he had sung so many times—'How Can I Keep From Singing?' In fact, he couldn't. Leaning his chair back against the wall, he shut his eyes and sang along quietly.

> *...through all the tumult and the strife*
> *I hear the music ringing;*
> *It finds an echo in my soul—*
> *How can I keep from singing ...*

When the hymn was over, he walked down the aisle and let himself be engulfed in hugs and *amens*. "Praise the Lord for bringing you back, Kit," "Praise Jesus." He returned the hugs and took the offered hands, still warm from the heat of singing and clapping.

"Hey, it's Mr. Lamb!" At the commotion, Ezra had emerged from his office, pulling off his reading glasses.

The choir members trickled away to their cars.

Kit said, "Sit down with me?" Ezra gave him a playfully solemn bow and they sat together on the edge of the stage. Kit laid the front page article with the full color photos across Ezra's knees. "You remember what I said happened on the bus to San José?" Ezra frowned and glanced down at the pictures. "Colleen was on the bus. She took these."

Ezra put his reading glasses back on, studied the photographs, nodded, then took the glasses off. "We already know that Satan tempts men in power to ignore the rules of civilized behavior," he said with cold formality. "Some do succumb."

Kit took Ezra's glasses from his hand and held them out. "Read the article," he said. Ezra put the glasses on again and read silently. Kit let his gaze wander around the church.

"News can be slanted." Finished with the article, Ezra took off his glasses once more. He handed the article back to Kit. "There are few enough of God-fearing leaders, and Satan doesn't want even one to be held up as a model of righteousness."

Ezra looked tired. The discussion seemed to depress him. It made Kit feel sad and guilty. The letter from the State Department was still in his hand, but he put it away with the newspaper clippings. Then he did something he had never done before. He leaned over and laid his cheek on Ezra's knees.

It felt different from what he had imagined. Through the worn fabric he felt the hard bones of Ezra's legs as if only a layer of skin were stretched taut over his skeleton. Suddenly he had the sharpest memory of himself as a boy, soon after he had learned to swim. The chilly water of the lake had sucked at him and numbed him as he struggled across the distance to a raft that turned out to be much farther away than he had expected.

Finally reaching it, with some effort he had heaved himself up and rolled onto the planks warm from the sun. The hardness of the planks under his own hard bones felt solid, holding him up and out of reach of the cold, deep water that slapped against the wooden posts. He lay there panting, and rested safe for awhile, knowing that eventually he would have to lower himself down into the deep water again.

It was hard to relinquish the bony, unyielding lap. Sooner than he wanted to, he raised his head and pulled himself upright to sit beside Ezra and grasp his right hand in his own as if they were about to shake hands at a temporary parting.

"Ezra. You, not God, are my real father," he said. Ezra's hand started to slide out of his, but he held on to it. "I'll always think of you like that. And … I forgive you for not seeing what I see. I wish you could, but I know you can't."

Ezra gave a sigh that seemed to deflate him. Kit released his hand. They sat without speaking for some moments, shoulders touching, heads bowed. Ezra took out his pocket handkerchief and wiped at a scuff mark on one of his creased old shoes. Then he pulled back to look at Kit. Kit gave himself a moment before turning his eyes to Ezra's gaze, knowing what his pastor wanted him to see in it: a vividly imagined future—tomorrow, a year, or a lifetime from now—and Kit Lamb, the still cherished, but unrepentant, son cast down and writhing for all eternity in that boiling, unfailing, and righteous lake of fire.

❖ Afterword ❖

General José Efraín Ríos Montt is not a fictional character. He was put in power by a military coup in March, 1982 and removed by the same means in August, 1983. His seventeen-month regime was later referred to by its victims as *la violencia*. In 1998 the results of two official human rights investigations were published—*Comisión para el Esclarecimiento Histórico* (CEH) and *Proyecto Interdiociano de Recuperación de la Memória Histórica* (REMHI)—examining the violence of the thirty-six year conflict between Guatemala's military governments and insurgencies. Between the two reports it was concluded that the military committed roughly 83% to 90% of the human rights violence, and of the approximately 200,000 people known to have died of it, some 43% died during Ríos Montt's regime. At least 80% of those were Mayans.

Ríos Montt has never accepted blame for the violence. He continues to project the image of a moral, honest, god-fearing leader, the same image that brought him accolades from the Reagan administration and many U.S. evangelicals even in the face of his government-sponsored reign of terror. Their enthusiasm for this born-again Pentecostal chief of state and his evangelical rhetoric blinded them to his brutal policies, which served the interests of the military, the state and the wealthy classes at the expense of the poor.

After such long-term political violence, Guatemala has, as Virginia Garrard-Burnett put it in her book *Terror in the Land of the Holy Spirit*, "given way to even more pervasive 'common' violence." Today in Guatemala, bonds of community are broken. There are generations who survived the destruction of their villages, the murder, torture and disappearances of their parents and grandparents, and forced conscription into

344

civil patrols which sometimes required them to kill their own neighbors. Many of these citizens are traumatized, rootless and alienated. The political and economic inequities that led to the insurgency remain. Human rights activists continue to be threatened and murdered.

Evangelical Christianity was only one force that legitimized Guatemala's violent repression of human rights, (the 1954 U.S. overthrow of a democratically elected reformist government was an initial catalyst). But Ríos Montt's demonizing of economic reform manipulated the Christian Right's fear of "godless communism," leading well-meaning Christians inadvertently to support a reign of terror. Guatemala's story should serve as an object lesson today for those who think theocracy leads to peace and justice.

Kate Kasten, October, 2010